THE MAKE

Jessie Keane is the bestselling author of *Dirty Game* and *Black Widow*. *Scarlet Women*, the third in the Annie Carter trilogy, shot straight into the Sunday Times bestseller list. Her most recent novel is *Jail Bird*. Jessie lives in Hampshire.

Also by Jessie Keane

Dirty Game
Black Widow
Scarlet Women
Jail Bird

JESSIE KEANE

The Make

HARPER

Harper
An imprint of HarperCollins*Publishers*
77–85 Fulham Palace Road,
Hammersmith, London W6 8JB

www.harpercollins.co.uk

This production 2012
1

Set in Sabon by Palimpsest Book Production Limited,
Falkirk, Stirlingshire

Printed and bound in Great Britain by
Clays Ltd, St Ives plc

MIX
Paper from
responsible sources
FSC® C007454

All my love, as always, to Cliff

Acknowledgments

A whole host of people helped me in many ways to complete this book – if I've missed you out, forgive me – you know what I'm like. Thanks to old friends and new – to Lynne and Steve for just being there; to Karen and Paul; and to Albert and Rosie for teaching me, for the first time, to love dogs. To Louise Marley for endless email encouragement, and Sue Kemish for the laugh-out-loud doorstep chats. To Sarah Ritherdon for her kindness, incisive editing and that lovely sunlit lunch at the River Cafe, and to Judith Murdoch for . . . oh, just about everything, really.

Gracie

DECEMBER

1

The instant the police were ushered into her office over the casino, Gracie Doyle knew there was trouble brewing. She was slouching in her chair, with her aching bare feet up on her desk after a long, long day. It was a cold, blustery Friday night, and in precisely a week's time – *seven days! Count 'em* – it would be Christmas Day.

She was already sick of all the jingle-bells and fake bonhomie, the endless Wizard and Slade tracks being pumped out of every shopping mall's sound system, the crazed crush of people wherever you went. Bad things happened at Christmas. For instance, her dad had died just before last Christmas Day. Fatal heart attack, right there in the middle of the casino boulevard. Boom! One minute there, the next – gone. Gracie *hated* Christmas.

Now she was just sitting, contemplating what she would actually do over the festive break – as usual, she'd made no real plans and *also* as usual she hadn't even put up a tree in

3

her flat – fuck *that* – when there was a knock on the door and two cops, one male, one female, were shown in by Brynn, the manager.

Gracie's feet slipped from the desk as she sat bolt upright in surprise.

Cops were rarely seen inside the casino, mostly because Gracie Doyle, thirty-year-old daughter of the late Paddy Doyle, ran a very tight ship here in the centre of Manchester. Since she'd been catapulted into the driving seat following her dad's death, she'd put lots of new security in place, even an ultra-sophisticated 'eye in the sky' video surveillance system that recorded every movement, every word, every bet placed, every chip handled. There had been scammers, of course; there always were. But no one had yet beaten Gracie's system.

So what were the cops doing here?

'Miss Doyle?' asked the male uniformed PC.

It was funny how, after all this time, she still half expected to hear her other name, but now she used just plain Gracie Doyle. Head of *Doyles*. She was proud of her achievements. She'd feared she would sink without her dad at the helm, but she'd swum. Hell, she'd *powered* through the waters of the casino world, glad now that Dad had insisted she work her way up the ranks; she'd kicked against it sometimes, but he'd been right.

She knew the business inside out. She'd started as a slots trainee, then a dealer; then she'd graduated to box man – or box *person*, to use the politically correct term. Then she was a floor person, then a pit boss, a shift boss, and finally she was shadowing the casino manager – Brynn. Today she was proprietor, sole owner. The buck stopped, very firmly, with her.

Now, when she walked through the vast sliding double-doors and into reception, moved with her easy, long-legged stride down the sumptuously thick gold carpet of the boulevard of slot machines and into the casino proper, she felt like a queen – and everyone treated her as such.

Gracie loved the late-night casino world; the ping and tinkle of the slots as players, 'comped' with free booze and soft drinks, chanced their luck; the intense concentration of the high-stakes punters as the gold-liveried croupiers scooped up their brightly coloured plastic chips and positioned them on this number or that, then spun the roulette wheel. Their howling yells of triumph when they won; their disappointment when they lost – and usually they did lose – but always, always, they came back and tried to beat the house again.

Someone *really* ought to tell them it was impossible.

This place was Gracie's *life*. She loved it all. Let the punters gamble, that was fine; but she played things straight down the line, paid her taxes, ran a good business.

So why the cops?

She quickly slid her feet back into her black high-heeled patent-leather shoes and stood up, rising to her full six feet. She smoothed down her navy narrow pinstriped skirt suit, straightened her open-necked cream shirt, ran a hand briefly over the long dark red plait of hair that hung, thick as knotted rope, down over her shoulder. Assembled herself. Took a breath.

'I'm Gracie Doyle,' she said, planting her hands on the desk. 'How can I help?'

'I'm afraid there's bad news, Miss Doyle.'

'Oh?' Gracie tensed, thinking. *Here we go. The Christmas curse of the Doyles strikes again.* 'This is a legitimate business, officers. Run strictly within legal boundaries.'

It was the truth. Her dad might have bent the rules a time or two – she particularly remembered his habit of only ever paying *red* bills – but Gracie liked sleeping nights, and if that meant being legit and paying her taxes, so be it.

'News of a personal nature,' added the female PC, glancing at her colleague.

Personal?

How could it be personal? All she'd had in the world was her dad, and he was gone.

'What is it?' she asked.

The male PC swallowed delicately. 'It's your brother, Miss Doyle.'

Brother?

She had to think about that. Her *brother?* Both her brothers were in London and she hadn't seen or communicated with them since they were teenagers – nearly fifteen years ago. 'Which one?' she asked.

The male PC consulted his notebook. 'Mr George Doyle. He's very ill in hospital, Miss.'

Gracie looked at Brynn. Fiftyish, skinny, with the leather skin and wrinkles of the dedicated chain-smoker, Brynn had been a close friend to her father and a great help to her when she'd still been a wet-behind-the-ears beginner in the casino game.

'What's wrong with him?' Brynn asked, seeing that Gracie was flummoxed by the news.

'He's been assaulted,' said the female PC, watching Gracie like she feared she was about to faint away or something. 'I'm sorry, Miss Doyle, it looks very serious. His mother – *your* mother – thought you should be contacted.'

What the fuck for? wondered Gracie. Her mother hadn't thought to get in touch for years. And when Gracie had dutifully notified her mother of her father's sudden death, she hadn't even received a reply. Neither her mother nor her brothers had come to the funeral, and they hadn't even sent a wreath. She would never forget that. Standing there alone, unsupported by her family, in the cold January graveyard.

George was in hospital.

She tried to take it in, but she couldn't get a handle on her own feelings about it. Was she sorry? Was she concerned? Did she – after all this time – really give a shit? She didn't know. The last time she'd seen George, she'd been sixteen and he was twelve; still a child. He was a stranger to her now, and really, after all this time, did she want it any other way? She had her life, George had his.

'Have they got who did it?' she asked.

'No,' said the policeman.

'And it's bad? Really bad?'

'I'm afraid so, Miss.'

Shit, thought Gracie. And it was at that precise moment when she felt, quite distinctly, her cosy, orderly, trouble-free world tilt on its axis. It felt to her like something had ended. Or maybe . . . maybe it had just begun.

2

19 December

When Gracie got home to her flat, it was just after midnight. The casino didn't close until six a.m., but Brynn was covering the graveyard shift this week. Pre-Christmas, the place was full of Eastern bloc playboys, footballers and high rollers, so, even in these recessionary times, they had to work late and hard, pampering their clients exhaustively with limousines from their luxury hotels to the door of the casino, complimentary gourmet food, Cristal champagne and Cohiba cigars – anything to keep them at the tables and happy while they handed over their cash.

And it didn't end there.

The day *after* play, you had to comp the punters even more, to show your appreciation by sending out the finest cognacs, big tins of caviar and bouquets of flowers – and while she had a team of people making sure that all this happened, still she had to oversee it all, she had to know that it was all *done*.

And now it was.

And now *she* was, too.

She kicked off her heels, locked the door behind her, and breathed out a deep sigh of relief. She loved being here at home in her duplex penthouse, with its private terrace and canal views. She'd *earned* it, and she relished it. She had it all now. The twenty-four-hour concierge, the twenty-metre rooftop pool, the huge open-plan living area, the cutting-edge kitchen, the palatial *en suites* to the two luxurious bedrooms, the on-site gymnasium, whirlpool bath and spa room.

Ignoring the post on the mat, she was padding barefoot into the bedroom when the phone started ringing.

'Shit,' said Gracie succinctly, startled. Who the hell could be calling now?

George, she thought. A tingle of misgiving hit her midsection. *Had he taken a turn for the worse?* After a moment's hesitation, she walked on, letting the answerphone pick it up.

'Oh damn, it's the machine again,' said a shaky girl's voice. Then: 'I don't even know if I've got the right number. I'm trying to reach Grace Doyle. About her brother.'

Gracie stopped walking. She stood there, staring at the phone like it might bite.

Pick it up, idiot.

But she didn't want to. She was tired, it was the middle of the damned night, and she was not in the mood to hear more bad news. She slipped off her coat, tossed it on to the couch. Kept staring at the phone.

'I knew *she* wouldn't phone you, so I thought I'd better. I'm Sandy. George is really bad. And it's only right that you know, in case . . .' The voice broke as the girl suppressed a sob. 'Anyway, I just thought you should know. If you want to phone me . . .' She rattled off the number.

Gracie walked over and picked up the phone. 'Hello,' she said.

'Oh! You're there. Is that Gracie? George's sister?'

'Yeah, that's me. How do you know George?'

'I'm his fiancée.'

'Oh.' She hadn't known that George had someone in his life. She knew *nothing* about the family she'd left down in London, her dingbat mother and her two brothers; and that had – until now – suited her just fine.

'Did the police contact you?' asked Sandy.

'They did, yeah,' said Gracie.

Silence hung between them. A *waiting* silence, in which the girl was obviously expecting Gracie to make sisterly noises, express concern. Gracie thought about it and realized that she *did* feel concerned. That annoyed her. She hated Christmas and she hated *this*; renewing contact with her family was not on her agenda. She was hoping for a quiet time over the festive season, then in early January she planned to take off – alone – for her annual two weeks in Barbados. She'd worked hard all year without a break, and she had been looking forward to a little downtime.

But now, *this*.

'Well,' said Sandy lamely, finally breaking the silence, 'I just thought you should know. That's all. And Harry's just vanished, taken off somewhere, no one knows where.'

Gracie's attention sharpened. 'What do you mean, Harry's vanished?'

'Well . . . he has. He's just *gone*.'

Gone where?

'Have you . . . have you got your mum's phone number . . .? Maybe you'd like to call her?' asked Sandy when Gracie didn't speak.

Yeah, and maybe not, thought Gracie. 'I've got it here somewhere.' She didn't think she had. She thought – *hoped* – that she'd lost it.

'I'll give it to you, just in case,' said Sandy. 'You got a pen . . .?'

'Sure,' said Gracie, and stared at the wall, not listening, as Sandy gave her the number.

'I think maybe you ought to call her,' said Sandy.

And I think maybe you should fuck off.

Too much dirty water had flowed under the bridge for her to even contemplate getting in touch with her mother again, however dire George's situation might be. Would George's condition really be helped by her turning up in London to sit by his bedside? Answer: no.

Her dad had been cool and controlled – like her – but her mother Suze had always been almost laughably hyper-emotional, big on pressing panic buttons and beefing up any bad situation. Gracie knew she could bust a gut, get down there, but then guess what? Everything would be fine. And why should she? They'd never given a *shit* about her.

No.

Fuck them.

But even as she *thought* that, she could hear her mother's final words to her. *You know your trouble, young Gracie? You've got a damned calculator where your heart should be.*

And what about Harry? Where the hell had he got to? She thought about that. He was probably upset about George and had taken himself off somewhere to brood. Harry and George had always been close to each other. Once, they had been close to her too.

'Well . . . I'd better go,' said Sandy.

'Yeah. Thanks for calling,' said Gracie. *And don't for God's sake call again.*

She hung up and stared at the phone for long moments. She felt annoyed and tainted, as if she'd been touched by something unpleasant. Then she dialled out. Brynn picked up straight away.

'Hello?'

'Did you give a girl called Sandy my number?' asked Gracie, breathing hard.

'She phoned just after you'd left. Said it was urgent family business. Normally, of course, I wouldn't give out your number, but after the cops called about your brother and—'

'Never give out my number. Not to anyone. Got that?'

'But she said she was his fiancée.'

'I don't care if she's Nefertiti, the last of the sodding pharaohs, I don't want my private number given out.'

'Okay, if you say so.' He sounded surprised and hurt. Brynn was her ally, her number one man; she never shot her mouth off at him.

'I *do* say so. Remember it.' Rattled, Gracie slammed the phone down.

Then she went into the bedroom, stripped off, pinned her hair up and headed for the *en suite* to shower the day away. She stood for a long time under the soothing heat of the needle spray, her mind blank; then she soaped up, rinsed and dried off, pausing before the big slab of mirror to brush out her hair.

Gracie stood there for a moment scrutinizing her reflection. She looked tired, but otherwise not bad. As always, she wished she was half a stone thinner and half a foot shorter, a little less *statuesque*, but there it was, shit happened. She was more Jessica Rabbit than Kate Moss, but so what? She had the luminous white skin that went with being a redhead, and a

12

thoughtful don't-fuck-with-me expression in her cool grey eyes. She had long since developed a style all of her own and she knew how to present herself to the world – mostly in neutral-toned crisply fitted shirts and sharply tailored suits. She had large breasts – all her own – a small waist, and richly curving hips. *Definitely* not Kate Moss.

'Ah, you'll do,' she told her reflection, and slipped on a cosy grey cashmere vest and pants before heading for the kitchen to stare in the fridge.

She hadn't eaten since early afternoon and now she was hungry. There was some pasta there, and a little tomato sauce. She'd heat it up, eat in front of the TV with a glass of wine, and she wouldn't think about her estranged family, not for an instant. She put the pasta and sauce in a pan and a plate in the oven to warm, then went over to the door and picked up the post. She took it back into the kitchen and put it on her tray with a knife and fork, a bottle of wine and a glass, salt and pepper.

When the pasta was done, she took the tray into the sitting room and aimed the remote at the TV, settling down with a sigh. She ate her meal watching the latest disasters in the world on the twenty-four-hour news channel, sipped the wine, and began to feel almost human again.

She reached for the post and started to sort through the junk mail and the bills. She spotted something that looked vaguely official – and then the name jumped out at her. Her stomach clenched, the pasta swirling in her guts, and for an uneasy moment she felt as if she might throw it all back up again. It was from a county court, and there was the name, the one she always half expected to see or hear but rarely did, these days. She had stopped using that name soon after the separation.

Connolly.

And there was *his* name too. Lorcan.

Shit. They were divorce papers.

Happy Christmas, Gracie, she thought, and she stared at the papers and fought down a most un-Gracie-like urge to cry.

George and Harry

OCTOBER

3

It had all started out so easily. Harry and George were chilling in their rented flat. They had ordered in pizza, they had beer, they were sorted. They'd watched the match and then a cheesy old Richard Gere film had come on. As the action unfolded they were paying it scant attention. They were busy moaning on about how they were always skint.

George was bored with working as a dealer at Lorcan's place, but what else could he do? And Harry was Job Seeking, only not really. They had few qualifications between them, and it was George's firm opinion that they were screwed from now until they fell off the twig at ninety. Well, sixty more likely. But it would *feel* like ninety years had crawled by, because the whole damned circus was going to be such a long dull pain in the arse. And there was Richard Gere, being a gigolo on the screen. Humping beautiful girls and – for God's sakes! – getting paid for the privilege. George liked the 'getting paid' bit. As for humping the girls, well, he could do it. He wasn't *crazy* for it like Harry was, but as Tina Turner so rightly said, *Keep your mind on the money.*

'We could go for that,' said George idly.

'For what?' Harry was yawning, nearly ready to turn in. He had to go and sign on again tomorrow – what a fucking treat.

'Being a thingy. You know. A gigolo. Boffing the birds for money.'

Harry burst out laughing. 'You what?'

'Look, the girls do it, don't they? Escort work? Guys do it too. And it's safer for guys. They make major money.'

'Oh sure.'

'Damn right I'm sure.' Now George was sitting up straight, and there was that mad light in his eyes that he always got when he had a bright idea. George's bright ideas had landed Harry in a lot of trouble over the years, involving him in gang fights, territorial disputes, all sorts of shit, so Harry was starting to feel a little nervous. He'd come *this* close to getting a knife shoved between his ribs once, and he wasn't eager to repeat the experience.

But still . . . escort work.

Maybe George did have something there.

'I could set up a website,' said George. 'We could get some cards printed.'

'Maybe,' said Harry.

'Oh come the fuck on, Harry, it'll be a laugh,' said George, grinning. 'You got anything else going on?'

Harry shook his head. 'No, but . . .'

'Well then.'

'I don't want any trouble, George.'

'Trouble?' George was wide-eyed and innocent. 'This'll be like taking candy from a baby. No trouble involved.'

'Oh yeah?'

'Yeah.'

'Well . . .'

'Oh come on. Let's do it. Okay?'

Harry started to smile.

'Okay,' said Harry, and they high-fived. Harry was confident that George would forget all about this conversation by the morning. He was drunk as a skunk. They both were.

But George didn't. Morning rolled around and George was still talking about his escorting idea. He was on a roll.

By the end of that week, their website was no longer a drunken dream in George's head: it was fact. And before long they had booked their first client, and then, in quick succession, came their second, their third, their fourth . . .

'Christ!' laughed George, his eyes dancing as he playfully waltzed his younger brother around the room. Their tenth client had just booked. 'Look at this, boy. We're going to be *minted!*'

4

'We got another bite. And she's a cougar,' said George. He was excitedly tapping keys and gazing at their brand-spanking-new website on the computer screen up in his bedroom.

'She's a what?' asked Harry.

George was very proud of this website. He'd drafted in one of their nerdier mates, Gaz, to do it, and it had cost them heavy, but it was done in double-quick time and it was good. Lots of red to excite the punters, but enough black and gold to convince them that this was a classy and efficient operation.

There were some good pics of George on there, but the best were of the wildly photogenic Harry. They'd purchased a dinner jacket and a dicky bow from one of the grunge shops, and in the first photo he wore that with a white shirt, à la James Bond, his thick, dark-red hair swept back, his soulful dark grey eyes smouldering into the camera lens.

'The chicks are gonna love you, boy,' promised George.

Harry had a relaxed, cat-like indolence about him, a

sweetness of nature that earned him many friends, and bucket-loads of lethal charm.

The second shot of Harry showed him, torso only, oiled, muscled and brooding; the third showed him dressed smart/casual in a tweedy jacket and open-necked shirt, giving it his best Sandhurst-officer-material swagger.

'So, explain. What the fuck *is* a cougar? Really?' asked Harry, sprawling back on the bed and watching his brother tap-tap-tapping on the keys. He felt just about shagged out, to be honest. All these women! And all of them so pitifully desperate to date men who were not old, boring, smelly or downright mean. Harry hadn't worked this hard in . . . well, actually, he had *never* worked this hard.

'You know so little,' sighed George, not looking round. 'Cougar's an older woman with a thing for younger men.'

'Ew,' said Harry.

'Not "ew" at all. Some of these older ladies are hot.'

'How old we talking here?'

'Forty,' said George promptly. Jackie Sullivan, their prospective client, was an interior designer in her fifties, but he didn't want Harry to completely freak out.

'That's fifteen years older than me. That's gross.'

'Keep your eye on the ball, grasshopper,' said George, pressing send. 'It's a hundred quid, that's fifty each, and all you've got to do is escort her to a black-tie do and home again.'

'Listen, *sensei*, you keep *your* eye on the frigging ball. I'm going to be beating off an old lady stoked up on HRT and looking for sexy extras. And why me? You looked good in the pics too.'

George sighed and swivelled his chair to look at his younger brother.

'You know the deal. It's your trembling young body she wants. You got the beauty, boy, I got the brains.'

'No, you got the gob.'

George considered this. 'All right, that much is true.' It was their sister Gracie who had all the brains, but George could blag with the best of them; that was his talent. That and working in his ex-brother-in-law's casino flipping cards for over-eager punters; and he was bored to death with that.

'And I got some looks too, I think you'll agree,' said George.

Harry didn't agree. George was chunky as a barn door and brutish-looking with a squashed-in nose, and his dark red hair was shorn into an unflattering crew cut, but he did have laughing dark-brown eyes and the roguish mouthy charm of a market trader, and some women responded to that. Harry was the quiet, gentle-mannered one. Looking as he did, he didn't have to say a word to get the girls to fall at his feet.

But . . . oh shit . . . a forty-year-old?

'What if . . . I mean, look, what if I have a – a problem?' asked Harry.

'Problem?' George looked at him blankly. 'You got the gear, we got the etiquette book.' The etiquette book was another one of their grunge-shop purchases; they had already learned a lot from that: don't drink from the finger-bowls, don't hold your knife like a pencil, twist the bottle – not the cork – when you open champagne. They studied the thing, quizzed each other over it like the *Highway Code*. They had it all off perfect. 'What problem can you possibly have?'

'Oh come on, George. I mean what if she wants . . . extras?'

'What, you mean bedroom-type extras?'

'What the hell else would I mean? And what if I can't – you know – perform?'

'Ah, you'll be fine. And think of it, boy. One hundred big ones,' said George with a grin. He gave Harry's foot a hopeful kick. 'What ya say?'

Harry lay back with a groan. 'Oh, all right then. I'm in.'

Jackie Sullivan didn't actually look much of a cougar. More of a mouse, Harry thought when she opened the door to him at her place in Notting Hill. A pretty, nervous mouse wearing a halter-necked floor-length black jersey dress that she looked distinctly uncomfortable in. Her hair was thin, but expensively styled in a blonde bob. Her eyes were huge and a washed-out denim-blue, and there were blotches of bright colour on her cheeks. She wasn't sure about this, not at all. He could see it writ large in every jittery movement her skinny body made.

Well, neither was he. He'd been bricking it all day, dreading tonight. But her twittering, anxious demeanour made him relax. This was no man-eater. This was a nice little lady who needed reassurance.

'Hi,' he said with a smile. 'I'm Harry.'

She stuck out a pale, narrow hand. 'Jackie,' she said.

They shook hands. Hers was icy cold.

'Cab's waiting,' he said. 'Hope you've got a coat, it's freezing out there.'

'Yes . . . well, you'd better come in for a moment . . .'

She went off upstairs, leaving him standing in the hall. Harry looked around him. *Some* place. The whole of his and George's messy little rented flat could fit into this hallway. Expensive-looking antique pieces were everywhere – side tables, chairs, blue and white vases – all lined up along the canary-yellow walls. Harry went over to one of the tables and looked at the array of pictures, all set out in silver frames.

Jackie looking younger, with dark hair. Jackie older, with a laughing grey-haired man by her side.

He heard her coming back down the stairs, and turned to look at her with a smile. She was pulling on a big fake-fur wrap, and clutching a black sequinned evening bag. 'Who's this?' he asked, gesturing at the photo.

Her face tightened. 'That's my husband,' she said.

Then why isn't he escorting you? wondered Harry.

'He died,' said Jackie, as if reading his thoughts. Suddenly the blue eyes were swimming with tears. 'Two years ago. This is the first time I've been to a social occasion on my own since then.'

Poor little mare, thought Harry. 'Well,' he said after a moment's hesitation. 'You're not on your own. Are you?'

'No,' she said, but the tears were slipping down her cheeks now, making tracks through the hectic splodges of blusher she'd applied. 'Sorry,' she gasped.

'Don't be sorry,' said Harry, and pulled out a clean white hankie and dabbed gently at her face.

At which point Jackie Sullivan – the cougar! What a joke – put her head against the front of his dinner jacket and sobbed her heart out. As she cried she made a high-pitched whining sound, like a beaten puppy. It pulled at his heart to hear it.

They never got to go to her black-tie do. Harry paid off the taxi and they spent the evening in her drawing room, talking about her late husband, her daughter who worked out in Hong Kong, and her lonely, lonely life. And later, when she asked if he would go up to bed with her, just to hold her, that was all, Harry said yes, of course.

And later still, just as dawn was breaking, Harry felt her hand sneaking over to delve inside his Calvins – he'd kept them on last night, not wishing to embarrass her by flaunting his nude body when she had been so careful to keep on her bra and pants. He lay still, surprised and extremely turned on, as she clutched and stroked at his tumescent cock; he had his usual waking-up erection; it felt enormous and her hand on it felt very good indeed.

'Goodness,' she murmured. 'So big. Would you . . .?' she asked, guiding his hands to her neat little breasts beneath her lacy bra. He could feel that her nipples were hard.

Oh yes. Harry found that he certainly would. He unclipped her bra with practised ease, pulling it off. Rolled her nipples around between thumb and forefinger, kissed and fondled them. He pulled off her pants and stroked her bush, then rolled over on to her, eased her thighs open. He found the ready opening and pushed gently in. She gasped. He could barely see her in the cool dawn light, they were just shadows heaving beneath the covers, and that was fine; this was just anonymous sex. He pumped hard at her, enjoying the usual hot sensations, and she clung to him without a whimper.

Then Harry remembered that he wasn't wearing a condom – could a forty-year-old woman get pregnant? He thought it was possible, so when he felt his climax coming he slipped out of her, groaning with pleasure as he spilled his seed out over her belly.

Sex with an older woman wasn't a problem after all. He gave her a long, shuddering orgasm and she cried again, but afterwards she seemed more relaxed. They lay in each other's arms until it was time for him to go.

5

'So what was she like? The Cougar?' George was hunched over the computer in his bedroom, bashing keys and staring at the screen the afternoon after Harry's 'date' with Jackie Sullivan.

Harry put down fifty pounds beside George's keyboard and threw himself back on George's bed, thinking about Jackie, how sweet she'd been, how small and shivery with nerves. And then, when he'd left, how embarrassed – avoiding his gaze, paying him and ushering him out into the dawn like a guilty secret. Which he knew he was. Of *course* he was. He'd escorted her nowhere. She'd literally just paid him for a chat and for sex. Still . . . Jackie Sullivan had brought out something protective in Harry, something he'd never before suspected was in his personality.

Of course he'd had women before. Plenty of them. He had the height and film-star looks. He was a snappy dresser and he knew exactly what suited him best. He favoured tight black slim-fit jeans, boots, black or white shirts – all of which flattered his pale skin, emphasized his grey eyes and made the best of his upright bearing and the auburn hair that fell in thick glossy waves on to his broad shoulders. Harry had a unique style, and it drew in the women like a magnet.

'She was okay.' He shrugged.

George stopped typing, pocketed the fifty and turned his bulky form in the swivel chair to smirk at Harry. 'What do you mean, okay? You didn't . . .?' He made a gesture with his arm.

'No. I didn't,' lied Harry. He was surprised to find that he didn't want to even suggest to George, let alone talk about, the fact that he had bedded Jackie. Usually they gave each other blow-by-blow accounts of their conquests, but this . . . this was different. The poor little bitch was vulnerable, still in a state of mourning over her dead husband. He suspected she'd acted totally out of character last night, and it had mortified her. Harry didn't want to turn her pain into sordid entertainment.

'Well, why the hell not?' demanded George with a grin. 'Look at you, boy. Mega babe-attractor. Thought she'd eat you and spit out the bits.'

'Look, we went out, she paid me, end of.'

George gave Harry a long, thoughtful look. 'Ohhhh . . . kay,' he said finally. 'Anyway, we got mail. Two new ladies, one for you, one for me. Not cougars.'

Thank God, thought Harry. He couldn't take another night like the last one. George had promised him that escorting girls would be straightforward fun with the occasional fuck thrown in: that was the deal and he was happy with it. He didn't actually want to start *liking* any of them.

'You got one too?' Glad of this new diversion, Harry adopted a teasing tone. 'Likes a bit of rough, does she?'

'Listen, I scrub up,' said George. 'Mine's a banker. Hasn't

got time for boyfriends and so needs an escort to her firm's pre-Christmas bash.'

'Bet she hasn't had it in *years*, poor cow. And you're just the man to put that right . . .' Harry squinted at George. 'Have you been entirely straight with me, bro? Is this job in fact less about eating out at five-star establishments, and more about jumping around between the sheets with desperate women? Is this job in fact going to be more about fucking than finger buffets?'

'Yep,' said George. All right, he didn't relish the job like Harry seemed to. In fact, it worried him. Did he have a low sex drive or something? He was never, ever going to discuss it with anyone, that was for sure. *Especially* not Harry.

'That's what I like to hear. So who's mine?'

George pressed 'Print'. The machine whirred and a sheet of paper emerged. He handed it to Harry.

'Laura Dixon,' Harry read aloud. 'Fashion designer, twenty-eight years old. Oh, and a pic.'

He looked at the photo. Long, straight-brown hair, a tanned, high-cheekboned face and serious dark eyes. Brunettes, blondes, whatever – he was game for anything.

'Hey, this could turn out to be fun, *sensei*,' said Harry.

'Grasshopper, you're learning,' said George with a wink.

6

'D'you know, you've been great,' slurred Jemma Houghton, staggering slightly and having to cling to the front of George's jacket as they left her office party.

Yeah, I have. Above and beyond the call of duty, thought George.

Fuck me, could this woman drink. She was pretty – blonde and rake-thin and very sexily turned out in a white mini-dress and little else. She'd told him the drill when they'd been heading over in the cab in which he'd collected her from her posh waterside apartment near Southwark Bridge. He was her new boyfriend, Michael. She'd been pretending she had been dating Michael for months and she wasn't going to turn up to a works do without him and have to admit that she was a saddo who'd been telling porkies all this time. So he was Michael for this evening, right?

'Right,' said George.

'And you're in property. Developing and stuff,' she'd told him.

'There still money in that?' he asked, curious. He thought

the bottom had dropped out of the property market and buy-to-let was dead. Not that he would ever be troubled by it one way or the other; he doubted he would ever have cash enough to speculate.

'There's money in anything,' said Jemma, slipping him a bundle of crisp tenners. She gave him an arch smile and lowered her voice so the driver wouldn't hear. 'Even escorting, apparently.'

And there still was in banking, too; George saw that from the minute they entered the building in Canary Wharf. It was a steel-and-glass cathedral, a soaring, holy tribute to the great god Money. In the office where she worked there were already expensive silver and white Christmas decorations up. It was surreal, it was not yet November, but Jemma said the markets were hectic and they'd had to schedule this party into the nearest available free slot – which was now. Everyone was crowded in, sweating in tropical heat, jiggling along to Christmas songs, necking a lot of booze and loudly congratulating each other on the anticipated size of their forthcoming bonuses.

George could see he was going to have his hands full with Jemma. She was throwing the drinks back with abandon while he hovered around at the buffet table trying to get some decent food down him – not easy, because it was all poncy bits and pieces: blinis with little piles of red caviar, wraps of Parma ham and melon, goat's cheese tartlets, one lonely little prawn stuck bog-eyed into a shot glass of spicy sauce. Not his taste at all, but he made the best of it, tucked in and tried not to drink too much, because this was work. It certainly wasn't pleasure.

As the evening wore on and the revelry became wilder, he found himself policing Jemma's behaviour like a maiden aunt. Pretending to be a developer, that was a piece of piss. He knew – vaguely – about RSJs, wet rot and dry lining. He could front it out with the best of them. But Jemma was going to be rat-arsed soon if he didn't get her to put the brakes on.

'Don't you think you've had enough?' he asked above the roar of the crowd and the noise of the sound system, when she returned to the drinks table for about the hundredth time. She was already slurring her words and staggering a little. Her white-blonde hair was falling into her eyes and her make-up was caking in the heat.

'Not until I'm wasted,' she grinned, and slung back another mojito.

They fell out of the building at just after twelve, along with a load of others who were all shouting and cheering like loonies.

I'm surrounded by bloody idiots, thought George.

He hailed a cab. 'Southwark Bridge, mate,' he said, and it was at precisely that moment that Jemma threw up all the drinks she'd spent the evening shoving down her throat. Vomit splattered the open back door of the cab and the driver rounded in fury.

'Fuck off, I'm not having her in my cab,' he said, and he reached back, slammed the door shut, and drove off.

'Fuck *that*,' said George.

'Oh Michael you've been so good . . .' Jemma was now telling George, turning a sick-streaked chin up towards him as if inviting a kiss.

George flinched back, disgusted.

'Show's over,' he said angrily. 'It's gone twelve and I'm about to turn back into a ruddy pumpkin. I'm *George*, okay?' He looked for an orange light in the gloom and was relieved to see one coming near. He hailed the cab and it swerved in to the kerb.

'Southwark Bridge please, pal,' he said, and hoped that this time Jemma didn't throw up. He shoved her into the back, and closed the door.

Jemma started clawing at the window. 'Aren't you coming too?' she mouthed at him.

'No luv. Need a walk,' he said, and the cab pulled away. *Thank Christ for that*, he thought.

If there was one thing he hated, it was the sight of a woman falling-down drunk. His stomach was complaining loudly after an evening of prissy little tartlet jobbies and mineral water. He longed to get some proper food down him, but it was too late to find a chippy. The crowds had departed, and he was alone in the crisp, chilly night air, a heaven full of stars above him and the open road in front. He breathed in deeply, relieved *that* was over.

His conscience niggled at him a bit. Maybe he should have seen her home to her door, but he thought bailing out when he did was the safer option. Next thing you knew, she'd be inviting him in for coffee, and he couldn't have got it up for the skanky mare if his life had depended on it.

Then he saw *another* one – a girl in jeans and a pale top, crouched just around the corner of a building in an alley, obviously drunk out of her skull, her arms over her head. He walked on. He'd had a gutful of Jemma and her type for one night. But . . . his footsteps slowed. He could hear the girl crying. She was all alone.

He stopped walking.

Stood there, thinking about it.

Ah, fuck it.

He started to walk back to ask if she was okay as it was pretty obvious that she wasn't. And it was then that he wished he'd just kept on walking, because now he saw there was someone else in the alley with her: a tall, stick-thin darkish man in a floor-length black leather coat.

Shit.

In the yellow light of the streetlamp he saw the glint of a long blade in the man's hand. A thrill of fear shot all the way up George's neck to the top of his skull. Suddenly all his senses were on high alert. The man was shrieking at the girl, looming over her threateningly.

George looked around. There wasn't a soul about. No cops when you needed them, no fucking cavalry pounding down the street; just him – and he wished he was a thousand miles away.

'You no-good *bitch*, you think you got the right to say yes or no when I've *told* you the way it's gonna go? You don't *ever* run out on him. You keep him sweet, okay? You keep him sweet or I'll cut you, cunt, I'll cut you bad. Give you a spell in the correction room, how'd you like *that*? You listenin' to me?'

The girl was crying, shielding her head with her upraised arms. George caught a glint of thick pale hair. With no intention whatsoever of doing so, he stepped forward and said: 'Hey!'

The man standing over the girl looked round but the girl didn't move. She seemed paralysed with fear.

'Hey,' repeated George more quietly, wondering what the fuck he was doing.

There was a flash of teeth in the gloom of the alley. The man was *smiling*, like he couldn't believe George had been so foolish as to intervene. Well, that was fair. George couldn't believe it himself.

'Walk on, bro,' said the man, the smile dropping in an instant. 'You just keep on walkin'. We got a bit of business here and you don't want to get involved in it, I'm telling you.'

But George stood there, wanting his feet to move but somehow unable to make them. 'What's going on?' he asked.

Now the man turned to fully face George. He was holding a knife in his left hand. It glinted in the cold sodium glare of the light.

Fuck it, this is crazy.

'Hey! *Move on.* I won't tell you again.'

He's right. Do the sensible thing.

George started to walk on. Whatever was going on back there, it was not his business. Best to keep out of it. He quickened his pace. Yeah, he was going to get home, have a shower, bung something in the microwave, then go to bed and forget this whole frigging disaster movie of an evening. He passed a building swathed in scaffolding, like the ecto-skeleton of some huge insect. A few sticks and stuff were piled up just around the corner – insulation material, some discarded scraps of polythene billowing like ghosts in the faint, chilly breeze.

Sticks.

George paused and looked at the sticks. And . . . there were scaffolding poles too, just left there. He picked up a stick. Picked up a scaffolding pole, and turned on his heel.

Oh shit this is so stupid, Georgie boy, what are you thinking?

He went back along the street. The bastard was still there, flapping his arms, waving the knife at the terrified girl, shouting and bellowing. George felt as if his bowels were about to let go as he broke into a run and headed like a bullet straight for the man.

But the man heard him coming. George was heavy and wasn't known for his lightness of tread. When he hit top gear, he made a lot of noise. He saw the man turn, and a panicky *oh shit gonna die* shot like wildfire through George's brain. He let out a jittery roar that was half fear, half anger as his pace picked up and he collided with the man like half a ton of frozen meat. The man flew back and down and hit the cobbles like a sack of shit.

'*You motherfucker!*' he shrieked.

George piled in. His eyes were almost entirely focused on the knife. He felt a vicious kick land on his thigh, and he knew that later it would hurt, but right now he couldn't feel a thing.

'Arsehole!' he yelled, and struck the man a hard blow on the knife hand with the stick.

The man was wriggling like an eel, cursing, throwing out a string of expletives.

'Yeah?' ranted George, so hyped on adrenaline he didn't know *what* he was saying. 'How'd you like *this,* you cunt?'

He wanted to get that knife away from him. That was all he was focused on, but the man was like rubber, bouncing around while George felt like dead weight. He felt the cold hiss of the thing go past his cheek and thought: *My God he nearly got me then. I could have bled to death right here in this alley, and for what? For a stranger. For something that ain't even my business.*

George dropped the stick and clamped down on the hand holding the knife. He squeezed, pummelled the man's fingers on the cobbles. The man was shouting, squirming and cursing and telling him that he was *dead,* dead and buried.

'Yeah, well, I'll see you in hell then, fucker,' roared George, not even sure what was coming out of his mouth.

He was so hyped up.

He was terrified.

How did I get into this?

The man got his hand free and was halfway up, struggling under George's superior weight but coming back with all guns blazing. He swished the cold night air, slicing through it with the blade, forcing George to flinch back. The man was grinning again; he knew he was getting the upper hand. George could feel his resolve weakening, could feel the malevolence rising off this fucker like mist off a bog.

This bastard was going to kill him, and he wasn't even going to care. The man came up on to his knees. *Fuck this,* thought George as the knife whooshed down, slitting open the sleeve of his jacket. It was sharp. He had time to think that. The knife was *extremely* sharp. Lucky it hadn't slashed deeper, caught the skin.

He'd ruined his best jacket.

That realization, the silly thought that the man had ruined his best jacket with that *fucking* knife, galvanized George. He swung the scaffolding pole round in an arc. It hit his opponent's head with a solid *clunk*.

The man seemed to freeze there on his knees. Then a slow dark line bloomed along his hairline and cascaded down over his face. His eyes turned up in his head. The hand holding the knife released the blade, which clattered on to the cobbles. His mouth remained open until blackish blood poured into it, staining his pearly-whites a dingy scarlet in the cold light of the streetlamp. Almost in slow motion, like a dynamited building, he lurched sideways and collapsed.

Suddenly, there was silence.

George knelt there, gasping for breath. He stared at the man. Not a movement. Nothing. George sank back and threw the scaffolding pole aside. It hit the wall at the side of the alley with a metallic *thonk*, then clattered down on to the cobbles.

Maybe he was going to be sick. He *felt* sick. He was built

like a brick shithouse but he was not a violent man. Tonight, he had surprised himself.

Then the man on the ground groaned.

All George's senses sprang to their feet and started dancing a panicky fandango.

The fucker wasn't *dead*, anyway. And George didn't want to be here when he came round. No way.

George stumbled to his feet. The alley spun around him. He had to sit down again quickly. He slumped against the wall of the building beside the alley. The girl was three feet away, and still crying.

'S'all right,' panted George. 'S'all right.'

He scrambled to his feet again. This time, he managed to stay up.

'Hey,' he said to the girl, trying to keep his voice gentle because she was huddled there, arms over her head, scared out of her skin. Poor little bitch. 'Hey, come on, let's get out of here.'

He reached down, touched one thin arm.

She flinched. Looked up. George saw a curiously androgynous face, tear-streaked, staring up at him; big wide eyes beneath thick, strongly defined brows, a neat nose with flaring nostrils, a pouting sweet mouth, a well-defined jawline.

'Come on,' he said again. 'Let's move, right?'

He clasped the arm, feeling the silken skin, the long stretch of muscles underneath, and he thought, *wait a minute,* and then the girl got to her feet, and he saw the shoulders, the hips, the . . . *well fuck me,* thought George.

He hadn't rescued a girl at all.

It was a boy.

*   *   *

The boy sat in the back of the taxi that George had flagged down, hugging himself, his teeth clattering together like castanets. George kept glancing at him, wondering what the hell he was going to do now. The words 'where can I drop you?' had been met with silence. So George had given the driver his own address.

The boy was in shock. That much was obvious. He couldn't just leave the kid out on the streets at this hour of the night. Look at what had been happening in that alley.

Yeah, look at that, George.

George thought about it. Something was off here, something was *wrong*.

He glanced again at the boy. Big, blond, overlong thatch of hair. Elfin face. The boy was tall and long and thin. Not like him. He'd been heavy, solid, *robust*, just about forever. The boy had only been wearing a white t-shirt and jeans, no coat. It was perishing out there, bitterly cold.

'What's your name?' George asked, and he saw the cab driver's eyes flick to the rear-view mirror, saw the judgement in them. He obviously thought that this was a pick-up, a meeting of two strangers heading home for some hot and impersonal sex.

The boy didn't answer. He was shuddering, although it was warm enough in the cab. George took his jacket off and thrust it towards him. He flinched back. How old was he? wondered George. Fourteen, fifteen, around there?

'Go on. Put it on, mate. You're cold.'

After a moment's hesitation, the boy grasped the jacket and slipped it on. It was miles too big for him. He looked lost in it.

Poor little sod, thought George.

'You can stay the night at mine,' said George. 'If you want. It's not a problem.'

The boy looked at him with limpid blue eyes. Slowly, he nodded.

What is he, deaf and dumb? Or just demented? Hell, what am I inviting in here?

He caught the look from the taxi driver again.

Pair of queers, said the look.

But it wasn't like that. Not at all.

7

Harry's booking was a divorce party in a pub. There was a three-tier cake set up on the buffet table, red and white balloons suspended on either side of it. On top of the cake was a prone, headless, bloodstained groom, and an upright, rather pleased-looking bride, all in white, holding a shotgun to her shoulder. There was an inscription, too. *Happy Divorce, Laura!* The minute Harry saw the cake, he thought *oh shit*, because he knew what he was in for.

Laura Dixon, fashion designer, may have looked demure, dark-haired and solemn in her photo, but in the flesh she was nothing like that. She was wearing a skin-tight sheath of pink satin and four-inch-high gladiator sandals. Her skinny arms and legs and her over-made-up face were all dyed orange. Above her dress, the top halves of two over-inflated pale fake boobs were exposed. As Harry arrived at her front door in Lambeth, neatly suited and booted, and announced himself, a chorus of shrieks went up and a bevy of semi-clad women descended upon him like he was a prize boar in a pig sale or some fucking thing.

'Ain't he *gorgeous*?' said one.

'Fuck me, just look at the arse on that,' said another, circling him.

He was pinched, prodded, and then the limo arrived and he was somehow swept along on a bevvied wave of oestrogen. In the car, they drank champagne, leered at him and squeezed his thighs. He kept smiling but he was glad when they arrived at the venue, until he saw the cake and understood that he was the token male at this shindig, and all men were bastards, up to and including him.

Oh happy days, he thought glumly.

They'd started the evening drunk, and as it progressed the twenty-strong group of women grew rowdier still. After the cake had been cut and the food consumed, an oiled and muscled male stripper came on to hoots and catcalls, and Harry – *so* glad that he'd been paid up front; that was always the deal and thank god for it – grabbed his chance to slip away to the Gents. From there, he was planning to slip away home, but when he turned from the urinal to wash his hands, Laura was standing there, watching him with a predatory glint in her eye. The thump and grind of the stripper's music – it was *Relax*, Frankie Goes to Hollywood – was a distant, heavy, background beat.

'Hi,' he said, smiling brightly because that was what he was paid to do, after all.

'Hi yourself,' she said, and without another word she popped both enormous white tits out of the top of her dress, and launched herself at him.

Harry got back late to the flat. He let himself in, worn out, *shagged* out, quite literally, wanting only a shower and then bed, to find George sitting in the lounge with a good-looking blond teenager.

'Oh!' he said in surprise.

George looked up and said: 'Hiya Harry. We've had a spot of bother.'

Harry would remember that later. George, master of the huge understatement. *A spot of bother.*

'Who's this?' asked Harry.

'This is Alfie,' said George.

'Right. Hi, Alfie.' Harry was bewildered. The boy was too young to be one of George's stable of loud, fun-filled mates. And . . . 'Holy *shit*, what happened to that?' he demanded, alarmed.

Alfie was still wrapped up in George's jacket, and Harry could see that the arm had been slashed right through.

'It's nothing, we're both fine,' said George.

'That's not nothing. That's your best jacket, you paid a *lot* for that jacket,' said Harry. 'What is that – a tear, or did someone swipe you with a razor?'

'A knife,' sighed George. 'It was a knife.'

'Fuck *me*, George, what happened?'

While Alfie sat silent, staring at the floor, George outlined the events of the evening.

'You hit him with a scaffolding pole? Was he all right?' asked Harry, flopping down on the sofa beside Alfie, who flinched.

George gave Harry a look that said *are you kidding me?* 'I *told* you. The bastard was waving a knife around, threatening this poor kid. I didn't . . . I couldn't just walk away and leave them to it, could I? So I, yes, I admit it, I did hit the guy with the pole, and what I *didn't* do, Harry, was hang around and wait for him to come round. He was okay when I left him, that's all I can say. I didn't stick around to enquire after his health and give him the chance to have *another* go, all right?'

'So why'd you bring him back here?' asked Harry, getting irritable. He was tired. He'd had a stressful evening. The last thing he wanted was to hear about George's troubles.

'What else could I do?' asked George, glancing at the boy. Poor little sod. 'He's told me his name, but that's all. He was shit-scared, Harry, I'm telling you. He's in shock maybe. I couldn't just let it go. You wouldn't have. Would you?'

'I think I would.' Someone waving a knife around? Oh yes, he'd have let it go all right. He didn't fancy being a dead hero.

'No you wouldn't. Look, Alfie can stay the night on the sofa bed, I'll sort him out with a pillow and we've got a spare quilt, it's no biggie.'

Harry looked at Alfie. He was almost effeminate in his beauty. He certainly didn't look like any sort of threat. They weren't going to get shot or shagged in their beds by this little squirt, that was for sure.

'Okay,' he sighed, and stood up. 'I'm turning in.'

'Good evening?' asked George, belatedly remembering that Harry had been out with a client tonight too. He felt like an age had passed since he had last seen Harry, but it was just a few hours ago.

'Oh, mega. Lucky I wasn't gang-raped by a pack of rampant females. Then our girl attacked me in the Gents.'

'Classy.'

'I thought the same. I'll square you up with the cash tomorrow, okay? Night, Alfie. Night, George,' said Harry, and went yawning off to his bed.

8

Deano Drax was furious. All his boys knew it, and that made them nervous. You never wanted Deano to be that way, because then he was likely to kick your bollocks out from under you, just for the fun of it.

Lefty Umbabwe wished he had some of the other boys here with him, but he didn't. It was Tuesday – three days after the night-time fight in the alley – and he was alone with Deano in Deano's country house, in the big sitting room with the inglenook fireplace and the blackened oak beams overhead. There was an Aga in the kitchen and a swimming pool out the back. It was a choice house, expensive; but then it would be. Deano owned Shakers in Soho, and he also controlled a huge proportion of the drug action on the streets. He wasn't about to live like a pauper with all that loot passing through his hands on a regular basis.

Lefty stood on the rug in front of the roaring log fire. His head still hurt. It had throbbed like a bastard ever since that *fucker* had whacked him with the scaffolding pole on Saturday night. The cut was stapled now, and he'd been checked over in A & E. They'd kept him in overnight, fearing concussion, but he'd checked himself out early next morning – didn't want no questions being asked. He'd live. Although . . . not for long, by the looks of it. Not with Deano sitting there staring at him like he was nothing but a useless pile of shit. Not with Deano's favourite bitch on the missing list.

'So what's the story, Lefty? Hm? What's the tale?' asked Deano.

Deano had a small, fast-paced voice, husky and low, but then he didn't have to shout because his very presence was bloody terrifying. He was sitting there, his huge bulk jammed into an ornately carved chair that looked like a throne. And Lefty thought that was fitting, sort of, because Deano was king of all he surveyed. The last thing anyone in their right mind would want to do was upset him.

And Lefty had upset him.

It wasn't a very cheering thought, but he knew he had screwed up badly. He'd been supposedly keeping an eye on the boy – a service he'd often performed for Deano, with other less well-favoured boys – but *this* boy, who had been Deano's big pash for *months*, had given him the slip.

Alfie was a stunning kid, Lefty had to admit that; and if *he* was a bender maybe he'd even like to get stuck in there too. Lefty had been pleased as punch with himself for sourcing such a peach for Deano's delectation. Maybe at seventeen Alfie was a little – okay, a lot – older than Deano's usual prey, but the beauty of it was that Alfie looked *so* much younger than his actual years. He could pass for fourteen, easy. Alfie had been everywhere with Deano over the past months, cosied up to him, sitting in a drug-induced haze on his lap – frankly, it had turned everyone's stomach, but what could you do? This was *Deano*.

Lefty, for a brief, shining time, had been flavour of the month, the golden one. Now he was the *crap* one, the one who'd let Deano down, and he was in the shit up to his neck. For Deano, Alfie was *it* – the big obsession; and his anger at Alfie's loss was making him ultra-pissed off with everyone in general and Lefty in particular. It was strange to realize that even a bastard nonce like Deano – a monster, really – had feelings, too.

Anyway, Alfie had nicked Lefty's Oyster card and legged it. Maybe he hadn't liked the idea of being shafted by this fat fuck, but that was beside the point. Whether the kid liked it or lumped it was not Lefty's business. He had to keep the boy *there*, at Deano's disposal.

He'd never forget chasing Alfie all through the tube system, catching teasing glimpses of him, then losing sight of him again, then spotting him once more. Then he'd lost him for real, and he thought, *That's it, I'm screwed*. But no. He'd caught sight of the blond head weaving and bobbing along, half running, half stumbling through the concourse and up the escalator of Canary Wharf station, under its big, curved-glass canopy.

Alfie had staggered out of the station and run away to hide in an alley. He'd already spotted Lefty hot on his heels; he *knew* he shouldn't have run off like that. Lefty was hopping mad with the boy, a madness further fuelled by his fear of Deano. When he cornered Alfie at last, Lefty was out of breath and wheezing like a bastard – Jesus, he *had* to try and cut down on the cans – and he'd whipped out the knife to show the little runt who was boss around here. But he'd found him. And at that point Lefty felt the situation was not beyond rescuing. He gave the boy a little glimpse of the blade, made him quiver, threw a great big scare into the youngster, which was good, stop him doing the same *fucking* thing all over again.

Deano wanted him.

Deano would *have* him.

What the hell did he care? And then that *bastard* had whacked him with the pole, and it had been goodnight nurse. When he'd come round, both boy and bastard had fled the scene and he'd limped off to the nearest hospital to get stitched up.

'You're not sayin' much, Lefty old son.'

Now Deano stood up. Lefty took a step back. Deano was so big that he seemed to fill up the entire low-ceilinged room with his bulk. Deano could intimidate without even trying. He was solid as a brick wall and his eyes showed about the same level of feeling. He had a shaven head as big and round as a bowling-ball and a ridiculously neat little goatee beard. Deano was a vicious bender, everyone knew that; he'd been worked over good and proper by his father at an early age, everyone knew *that* too. Everyone also knew that Deano had offed his own father as soon as he'd had the size and strength to do it. Whether or not being shafted by his own dear old dad had turned him, no one knew – and no one was going to *ask* either, that was for sure. Certainly not Lefty, anyway. Live and let live, that was Lefty's motto. Just so long as the big creep wasn't trying to stuff it up *his* arse, he didn't give a shit.

'I told you what happened, Deano. It's the God's honest truth,' said Lefty. He could hear the pathetic whine in his own voice, but he couldn't help it.

'But you were meant to be keeping an eye on my boy,' said Deano mildly, drawing closer.

Jesus, thought Lefty in a spasm of terror. His guts were going up and down like Tower Bridge.

'I know that.' Lefty held his hands out, palms down, in a gesture of suppression, saying, *Hey let's calm this down, shall we?* And Deano looked calm, but then, he always did. Even when he was getting ready to rip someone's throat out. 'Listen, Deano. It's not a big deal because I'll find him, okay? I got the boys out looking already, and he can't have gone far. We'll get your boy back. No sweat.'

'Oh, you'd *better* sweat, my friend,' said Deano, looming ever closer. Now he was standing right in front of Lefty.

Lefty *was* sweating, he was sweating buckets. He could feel nervous perspiration popping out all over his body. Could feel his face wreathed in a shit-eating sort of grin, like a junior ape trying to placate a silverback. His heart was beating very fast. His wounded head was throbbing with every single beat.

'Tell me again, Lefty.'

'Nothing to tell, Deano. This bastard hit me with a pole. When I came round, Alfie was gone.'

'This *bastard*, what was he like then?'

Lefty shrugged hopelessly. 'Big. Thickset. Darkish hair. I don't know.'

'Only, you know those Bond films, the bit where Blofeld sits there stroking his cat?' asked Deano.

'I . . .'

'And you know what he says, that bald, ugly, scar-faced bastard, you know what he's telling his troops?'

'I don't . . .'

'You don't? Well I'll tell you. It's a gas, Lefty. One of the boys has fucked up some vital thing, and what Blofeld is saying is, *This organisation does not tolerate failure*,' Deano grinned, displaying perfect white veneers. 'Well, guess what, Lefty? This one don't either.'

Deano reached out a casual hand, grasped Lefty's testicles, and squeezed.

Lefty shrieked and went up on tiptoe. 'Holy *shit*, Deano,' he cried out.

'That hurt?' asked Deano, close in to Lefty and inflicting terrible, sick-making pain.

Lefty could only nod, his face twisted in anguish now.

'Try this.' Deano squeezed tighter. Lefty thought he was going to pass out from the agony of it. 'Hurt?' enquired Deano.

Lefty nodded.

'Good.' Deano released his grip and Lefty collapsed in a blubbering heap to his knees. Deano stared at the crumpled man for a long moment and then he casually drew back an elegantly shod foot and kicked him hard in the stomach.

Lefty sprawled back, gibbering *no Deano, don't, please don't, no more* and curling himself into a tight ball.

Deano shoved him hard with his toe. 'Now you listen up, *cunt*. I want my boy Alfie back, you got that?'

Lefty was nodding frantically.

'Or else I'm going to cut your freakin' balls right off, you got me?' Deano said. 'And then I'm gonna stuff 'em down your stupid *throat*.'

Alfie was *his*, and some *fucker* had dared to snatch him away. When Deano caught up with this arsehole – and he would – he promised himself that this *cunt* and anyone associated with him was going to suffer. His family, his friends, *anyone*.

'Now get your useless arse outta my house, you tosser,' he told Lefty.

Lefty crawled to his feet and, limping, left the room. Everything hurt. And what hurt even worse was the panicky knowledge that he didn't have a clue where to start looking for the boy. Not a fucking *clue*.

9

'Shall I tell you what I'd do, Lefty?'

Gordon was built like a tank and he was sitting, over-spilling his cheap plastic seat, in a café in the Mile End Road with his colleague Lefty Umbabwe. Lefty looked like death; his dark skin was greyish with strain, his head stapled up like Frankenstein's monster. He'd come in limping, and Gordon had said, hey, wassup? Trying not to laugh, and failing. He'd never seen such a mess as Lefty in his entire life.

'What would you do?' asked Lefty, drinking tea and wishing it was whisky. His bollocks ached. His head ached. His mind whirled with desperation. He needed another whiff from his butane can, but he couldn't do that here in the café; he'd get them both chucked out. 'Come on man. Really. I'd like some help here.'

Lefty had poured out the whole tale of woe to Gordon. How he'd lost track of Deano's boy, during the honeymoon period. Deano wasn't sick of the sight of the kid yet, which was what always happened in the end with Deano and his grand amours.

What *always* happened was this: Deano's people picked the kids off the streets, because the streets of London were paved with gold, everyone knew that, and they all headed here. The stupid kids thought they were going to make their fortune, join a band, become a star; it was all going to happen for them in London town.

Sadly, it didn't work like that. It worked like *this*: the kids found themselves cold and hungry on the streets and, if they were lucky, they went back home with their tails between their legs. If they were *unlucky*, they fell prey to loitering paedos like Deano, who drugged them up and used them for their own amusement for a few weeks; then, when the nonces grew weary of their charms, they farmed the kids out at a handsome profit to their fancy bender friends.

'I'll tell you what I'd do. I'd throw myself in the bleeding river,' said Gordon, and burst into peals of laughter.

Lefty stared at Gordon. 'Hey, you think this is *funny*?' He jumped to his feet. It hurt. He winced. Gordon caught the wince and that made him laugh even more.

'Sorry, sorry,' said Gordon, wiping tears of mirth from his eyes. 'But Christ, Lefty, what a fucking to-do. What the hell happened? You've played babysitter lots of times before, why'd you balls it up now?'

Lefty slumped back into his seat. 'I got the dose wrong. Thought the boy was well under, but he gave me the slip. Ran out of the club, legged it. It was night-time, black as your frigging hat too. I had a bad time tracking the little cunt down, then this *bastard* butts in – and before I knew it he whacks me and then Alfie's gone.'

'Well, my friend, now it's official: you're in the shit.' Gordon worked for Deano too, as a bouncer on the door of

Deano's fetish club Shakers. He knew Deano from way back. Knew what a twisted git he was, and he knew Deano would make Lefty pay hard for this.

'I *know* that.' Lefty stared at Gordon, who was tucking into a big fry-up.

'You should have used your loaf in the first place, checked the dose, and you wouldn't be *in* this bind.'

'Yeah. I know.'

'Fact is, Lefty, you're lucky you can find your dick to take a piss these days, the amount of stuff you keep sniffing. Something like this was just *bound* to happen.'

Gordon was right and Lefty knew it. Lefty couldn't face food. He still felt dizzy and a bit nauseous from that blow to the head. And he needed his fix. Deano had given him this week to find the boy, or else his arse was well and truly cooked and he didn't have a clue where to even start.

'Yeah, so come on. Where would *you* start looking?' he pleaded.

Gordon speared a sausage, bit off a hunk and chewed thoughtfully, his eyes resting all the while on Lefty.

'Right,' he said at last, swigging down a mouthful of tea, 'here's what I'd do. Go back to where you found him at around the same time of day. Start asking the cabbies, the night-bus drivers. Nearest tube station, talk to station staff, any buskers, anyone. You got a picture of this boy Alfie?'

Lefty shook his head.

'No matter. Just describe him. Take one of the girls with you, though: don't do it alone.'

'Why?'

'People see a big black bastard asking around about a cute white boy, they might get antsy. Take Mona, she's got a sweet face. You know?'

Mona was one of the fetish-club dancers. It was true, Mona had a kind face. And a *gorgeous* arse.

Gordon was mopping up skeins of sticky yolk with his bread and Lefty had to look away.

'Get her to tell everyone she's the kid's mother, shed a few tears, my lost boy, my tragic life, blah, blah, blah. You know the drill.'

'Yeah.' Lefty felt slightly better now. It was good advice, and he was going to take it.

'Another idea,' said Gordon, talking fast now, waving the dripping bread about in Lefty's direction. 'Am I on fire or what? The ideas are comin' thick and fast. Go to the nearest YMCA, get Mona to do the business: her little boy Alfie ran away from home, is he there? And the tears, don't forget the tears, man. They pay dividends.'

Lefty was nodding. 'My man, you are a scholar and a gentleman,' he congratulated Gordon.

'Hope it helps.' Gordon shrugged modestly. 'Besides all that, I'll pass the word around, get all the mates to keep 'em peeled. I really hope you find him, Lefty, because if you *don't*, seriously, I would take my first piece of advice if I were you. Just throw your arse in the river. Because Deano's going to do that – and much worse – to you, and then you know what? He's gonna post you home to your mama in a plastic bag.'

Gracie

DECEMBER

10

Gracie didn't sleep well the night after the police visit. She had blackout blinds at her bedroom windows and an eye mask to keep out any hint of residual light because working so late she often slept in until gone noon. She was usually an eight-hour girl – anything less and she woke up grouchy and stayed that way for the better part of the day – but things were playing on her mind, despite her best efforts to ignore them. Like her family, for instance. The family she had distanced herself from long ago, and barely gave a thought to any more.

When her parents split, she'd been sixteen years old. George and Harry had been twelve and eleven respectively. As kids they had endured years of furious rows and recriminations, their father cold and withdrawn, their mother shouting and screaming. There was talk of affairs, and it became obvious who'd done the cheating – their mother.

How the hell could she have done that to Dad. To all of them?

Dad had been managing a casino in the West End at the time, working all hours, and Mum had cited that as the reason she had strayed. Gracie had been numb at first, and then coldly enraged at her mother. Of all the trampy, despicable things to do. Dad had worked hard to give them a comfortable home, a decent life, and this was how she repaid him.

Gracie remembered the pain of it all, even now, and how judgemental she had been, as only a teenage girl with her hormones in turmoil could be. Her relationship with her mother had never been an easy one. Gracie was cool, and Suze was a bundle of out-of-control emotions. She made no secret of the fact that she preferred 'her boys', and found logical, strong-willed Gracie hard to manage or understand – but after the affair thing blew up in all their faces, Gracie had detested her.

So when Dad decided to go and work in Manchester, Gracie had winged the last school term and abandoned her exams. She knew she wanted to work in the casino business, so what was the *point* of more school? She'd been blessed with a prodigious natural talent for maths, so she could weigh up odds in an instant, and add up a row of figures at lightning speed. She knew exactly what she wanted in life; she didn't need any careers adviser to tell her. Coldly, dispassionately, she had announced to her mother that she intended to go with him.

George and Harry had of course sided with Mum, and had been angry, hurt and resentful that Dad and Gracie were choosing to leave them. And although Dad tried to keep in touch with his boys, asked if he could visit them, Suze had said a flat, spiteful no. Gracie knew that he'd sent them presents and cards and letters, but he never heard a thing back from them, not a word. She knew how much it had hurt Dad. She knew too that he could have tried for proper controlled access through the courts, but the split had been so devastating that he had quickly lost heart.

So, time passed.

Contact was lost.

Ancient messes – ones she preferred not to think about now.

But the phone call from the girl – what was her name, Sandy? – had brought it all back, unnerved her, made her go on the defensive. She'd shut down on her emotions, snapped at Brynn. She felt bad that she had lashed out at the one person who had always been solidly supportive of her, helping her through the hideous time after Dad's death. Brynn had always schooled her in the business, never running out of patience when she was slow to pick up anything. She promised herself that she would apologize to him as soon as she got in to work.

Gracie showered and dressed and ate breakfast in the bright, well-fitted kitchen with its view out over the Manchester ship canal. Yet even the view failed to charm her today. Her flat was in a converted corn mill, its old antecedents clearly visible in its bare, minimalistic brick walls and high ceilings. She'd bought it with a huge mortgage, and had loved it from day one.

Yesterday's post mocked her from the kitchen table, where she'd left the letters in the small hours of this morning. *Divorce papers.* So, finally, it had come down to this. Lorcan wanted rid of her, wanted to make it all legal and above board.

Probably – and she felt another little stab of unease, a little niggle of something suspiciously like genuine pain – *probably* he had found someone else. After all, he was a good-looking man. And there he was, in her mind. Lorcan Connolly. Black, close-cropped hair, bright blue eyes that skewered you where you stood, a mouth like a gin trap. Six feet four inches of Alpha male who looked like he could get physical – in the bedroom or out of it – without any trouble at all.

Stop it, she told herself. *You made your choice. You walked away.*

Ancient messes.

She wasn't going to think about them now. She pushed them to the back of her mind and took the lift down to the secure underground car park.

Gracie loved her car. It was a smooth, powerful beast, the silver Mercedes SLK-Class roadster, and she steered it effortlessly through the traffic, watching out for manic cyclists and distracted Christmas-shopping pedestrians with iPods stuck in their ears, meandering across roads strewn with multicoloured Christmas light displays with barely a glance at the traffic. She cut all thoughts of trouble out of her brain and hummed along with 'Addicted to Love' on her bass-heavy sound system, safe in her luxurious cocoon. Warm, too. Heated seats. Outside it was frosty-cold, with a pink-tinted sky up ahead. They were forecasting snow and Gracie thought that for once they'd got it right. The sky looked odd.

Red sky at night, shepherd's delight, she thought. *Red sky in the morning, shepherd's warning.*

A white Christmas. How romantic.

Oh yeah? This from a woman who just got divorce papers?

Shit. Why did she have to keep thinking about that?

She heard a siren long before she saw the fire engine in the rear-view mirror; cars behind her were edging in to the kerb to let it pass. She did the same, nosing the Mercedes in as far as she could. The huge red Dennis, lights flashing, siren blaring, eased past the long line of cars, then whipped through the red light up ahead.

Going the same way as Gracie.

The lights changed, traffic started moving again. The sun was a golden ball hanging low in the crystal-blue sky to her left.

Gracie's gut tightened.

Hold on. Ahead was where the sky was lit up so peculiarly. *Not* to the left. That wasn't the sun that was . . . a pretty big fire. There was a plume of black smoke spiralling up, and now another fire engine was coming through, everyone easing out of the way, Gracie too; and that ominous pink light was still there in the sky. Someone had a real mother-fucker of a fire going on somewhere.

Gracie got closer and closer to her destination, and now she could see the front of Doyles casino. Her heart leapt into her throat and her hands clenched on the steering wheel. She stared in disbelief. The engines were there, firemen were unravelling hoses, shouting at each other. People were running, yelling; others just stood and stared. And the frontage . . . *my God, the frontage was on fire.*

Later on, Gracie had no memory of actually stopping the car. All she knew was that she was unsnapping her seat belt and throwing herself out of her seat, then running hell-for-leather across the road to where the firemen were milling around, and the only thought in her head was *oh my God, where's Brynn?*

Brynn lived in the flat over the casino, alone. She half staggered up the middle of the road, cars honking as they swerved and came to a halt, a policeman there, waving cars back. Gracie just stood there; she could feel the heat from here, could hear the hungry crackling of the flames. The glitzy 'Doyles' sign was gone. A gust of wintery air blew a choking veil of spark-spattered smoke back into the road and her breath caught on a wheezing cough.

The policeman turned and looked at her. 'Move back, miss, will you? Right back.'

'I own the place,' she gasped out. 'Where's Brynn? The manager? Is he still in there?'

Jesus, not Brynn, she thought in anguish.

'I don't know. Just move back, it's not safe.'

But Gracie charged forward, hearing the policeman let out a shout behind her.

'Brynn?' she yelled at the top of her voice. 'Brynn, for God's sake! Are you out here?'

He *had* to be out here.

The heat was blistering, scorching her skin where she stood, even though she was yards away from it. It was terrifying, the height and spread of the flames. The gouts of water from the hoses seemed to be having no effect at all. She looked at the firemen, and called over to the nearest one.

'Is the manager out?' She had to shout to make herself heard above the noise of the flames.

The fireman glanced at her absently, then carried on with what he was doing.

The policeman had followed her. He tapped her shoulder. 'Miss! Come on now! Out of here!'

'Fuck off!' said Gracie, her eyes everywhere, frantic. She could see the front of the upper floor – Brynn's flat – was well and truly alight. She looked around, her eyes crazy with fear for Brynn, spotted the fireman with the white helmet – the chief, wasn't that right? She ran over to him, ignoring the policeman who was dogging her footsteps, and, just as she was going to grab the man, roar at him to get Brynn out, for the love of God, he was going to die in there . . . *just* at that moment she saw him.

Brynn was sitting, slumped over, wrapped in one of those ridiculous silver space-type blankets, at the back of one of the fire engines. There was an oxygen mask clamped over his nose and mouth. His thin face was grimy with soot, and he looked rough, but he was there.

'Brynn!' Gracie hollered, and he looked up at her.

The white-helmeted fire officer was standing close by. 'We've got an ambulance coming,' he told her as she dashed up. 'Best get him to hospital. Check him over.'

Gracie knelt down beside Brynn and put a hand on his knee. She stared up at him anxiously. 'You all right?' she asked.

Brynn nodded. He looked exhausted, hunched there in grubby pyjamas. There was madness all around them, men bellowing orders, the flames roaring, people – for fuck's sake! – taking pictures of the blaze on their mobiles. The policeman had abandoned Gracie and gone to harangue them instead.

'What the hell happened?' she asked Brynn.

Brynn moved the mask away from his face.

'I came down . . .' He paused, and coughed hard. '. . . I heard something at the front of the building about an hour ago. Woke me up. I came down, and got the shock of my life. The outer door was well alight. It didn't set off the sprinklers straight away, it wasn't close enough to the lobby for that.' He stopped speaking again, coughed, drew in a whooping breath. 'I got the fire extinguisher out and sprayed it from inside, but it was too fierce, I had . . . had to leave it. Came out the back way.' He stuck the mask back over his face, shaking his head.

'Don't worry,' said Gracie, patting his knee. His pj's smelled smoky. Running chillingly through her brain was the thought that if he had *not* heard that noise at the front door, he would now be upstairs in his flat, asleep and drifting into death as rolling black smoke stole the air from his lungs.

The casino alarms were bellowing, and through the smoke-haze and the orange glow of the flames Gracie could see that the sprinklers were working now inside the building, drenching the lobby, the slots, the tables, *everything*. She stood up and looked at the wrecked building and felt a spasm of real pain. There was going to be a lot of damage. It was going to take a long time before they could resume business. Thank *Christ* for insurance.

'What could have set it off?' she wondered aloud. 'Any idea?'

'Not the bloody foggiest,' said Brynn. 'Electrical fault's my best guess. Something blew. They'll look into it.' He coughed again, long and hard.

There was an ambulance nudging its way towards them now down the packed street, siren wailing.

Gracie stood up and tapped him on the shoulder. 'Think that's our lift,' she said.

'You don't have to come too,' said Brynn, getting to his feet and standing there swaying like someone caught out in a gale. 'They'll want to talk to you here.'

'Of course I'll come too,' said Gracie. 'I'll leave my details with the chief fire officer, and he can pass it to anyone else who wants it. And . . . Brynn . . .?'

He swayed and Gracie found herself putting an arm around

his thin shoulders, half supporting his slight weight against her.

'Feel a bit shaky,' he said, half laughing. He looked very pale.

The ambulance men were opening the back doors of the ambulance, sliding out a stretcher.

'You've got every right to feel shaky – you've had one hell of a fright,' said Gracie. 'Brynn . . . look, I'm sorry I snapped at you last night on the phone.'

'Ah, forget it.' He waved a limp hand, dismissing it.

'When I drove up I thought you'd got fried in your bed,' said Gracie with a trembly laugh. She felt pretty damned shaken herself. She'd lost Dad, and for a horror-filled few minutes she seriously believed she had lost Brynn too.

'Can't keep a good man down,' said Brynn. His eyes turned up in his head. His legs folded just as the ambulance guys reached them. If they hadn't grabbed him right then, he would have collapsed on to the road, unconscious.

11

20 December

Gracie stood looking at the wrecked frontage of Doyles the next day. She felt drained to the point of exhaustion by all that had happened in the last twenty-four hours. Going to the hospital with Brynn, making sure he was all right, phoning his sister because he had no wife – Brynn had never been married. The job was his life. Angie was anxious, asking, 'Is he all right? How did it happen?'

Good question, thought Gracie grimly.

They released Brynn later in the day, not even keeping him in overnight. His swift exit from the building had saved his lungs from the worst of it. Angie pitched up at the hospital in double-quick time and said he was coming back to stay with her, and she wasn't going to take no for an answer.

To Gracie's surprise, Brynn was so shaken by the whole thing that he didn't even raise a murmur in protest. Sometimes, she guessed, all a person wanted was a safe haven, a friendly hug.

She wasn't about to get one of *those*, she knew that. She rang round all the staff, told them what had happened and that she or Brynn would be in touch when Doyles was operational again. By the time the fire officer had finished questioning her at the scene next day, asking her if she had any money worries, any enemies (she answered no to both), and she had contacted the insurance people and the building had been secured, she was worn out.

She drove home, looking at all the twinkling Christmas lights, the shoppers in search of that perfect last-minute present. A giant inflated blow-up Santa bobbed past on the back of a flatbed truck. It was three thirty in the afternoon and already beginning to get dark. There'd been more talk of snow on the forecasts, but she thought it was too cold for that. She parked up underneath her building, and with relief took the lift up to her flat.

There was more post on the mat. She picked it up and took it through to the kitchen, with that *other* thing niggling at her again – the divorce papers. Talk about 'it never rained but it bloody well poured'! She leaned on the kitchen counter, weary to the bone, and thought about her short-lived marriage to Lorcan Connolly.

There had been something wild, almost indecent, about the passion that had flared up between them. Gracie liked to be in control. But with him . . . she had lost that. Found her inhibitions being thrown to the wind, and it had made her feel too vulnerable. Like she couldn't steer the good ship Gracie any more; as if she was being buffeted by some force stronger than herself. She was cool and logical, whereas Lorcan was fiery and impulsive. They attracted and repelled each other, like powerful magnets.

Lorcan had worked for Gracie's father when he had

managed a casino in London's West End. Then, when Paddy had taken off for Manchester with Gracie after his divorce, he had head-hunted Lorcan and installed him as manager of his new casino up there. Inevitably, Lorcan and Gracie had met. She'd been learning the business, working her way up the greasy pole as Dad insisted she should. She and Lorcan had fallen in love, then married on Gracie's twentieth birthday.

It should have been happy-ever-after. But Lorcan hadn't been content in Manchester. He was a Londoner, and he wanted to return there, to open and run his own place. Gracie, however, was settled in Manchester. Her dad was there, she loved Doyles and was thrusting ahead with her own career. So Lorcan went off down to London to get started up, expecting her to join him – but by then she had his old job, managing the entire casino, and she was happy.

There had followed weekends together, arguments, endless wearying debates. And all it boiled down to was this: he was settled in London. She was settled in Manchester.

Gracie heaved a sigh that shuddered through her frame. She'd *loved* him. But she had loved her career too, her burgeoning, swiftly growing career up here in Manchester with Dad.

Never one to mince his words, Lorcan had told her flat out that something was going to have to give, but it seemed he was sure it wouldn't be his career to go, it would be hers. Then he had said he wanted children, but Gracie had been so busy forging a career that she didn't want children, not yet anyway. Why couldn't he understand that?

He didn't.

During one bitter, final phone call he'd laid down an ultimatum: either she moved back down to London, or it was over.

'Okay then!' Gracie had screamed down the phone at him. 'Okay, you bastard! Enough! It's over!'

She had slammed the phone down. After five years of trying – and failing – to reconcile their differences, they gave up. They never spoke again.

She poked the papers with one finger. *Divorce.* Horrible word. An admission of failure. She looked down at her long, pale hands, bare of ornamentation. She hadn't worn her wedding or her cabochon-cut, *beautiful* emerald engagement ring in years. Why the hell did he have to choose *now*, when she felt so stressed, when bad memories of her father's death and new disasters were besetting her, to start proceedings?

Irritably she turned away, shrugging off her coat and throwing it aside. Time for the other post. Bank letters, those blank credit-card cheques that she never used and were a bugger to dispose of. A jiffy bag. She tore open the fastenings and tipped the contents out on the table. A bundle of mid-length dark red hair fell out, and a note.

She literally leapt back, away from it, her hands flying to her mouth.

It was a dead animal.

What the fuck?

Her heart started stampeding around in her chest as she stared wildly at it. She felt a hot sour surge of sickness building in the back of her throat. Oh Jesus. Had some sick *bastard* posted a dead thing to her? Then she noticed that the hair was exactly the same colour as her own.

Gulping hard, she reached out and tentatively touched it. There was no substance, no form, no small dead body. It was just hair, a lot of it – and it was just like hers. She looked at the folded note. Her hand shook with shock and fear as she picked it up, unfolded it, and read the typed words.

Smoke getting in your eyes?
Blame your scumbag brother.
I'm watching you, Red.
Call the filth on this and you're all dead.

Gracie sat down hard on one of her bar stools. Her brain felt hot-wired suddenly, the blood singing in her ears. She couldn't get her breath. She wondered for a moment if she was actually going to pass out. *Smoke getting in your eyes.* The fire at Doyles. *Blame your scumbag brother.* George in hospital. The tearful call from the girl, Sandy. Harry . . . Harry was missing.

George had always been trouble, and Harry had always followed his lead. What had they been getting into this time? And even more frightening than any of *that*, which was terrifying enough, the final line. *I'm watching you, Red.*

Gracie snatched up the jiffy bag. The label was neatly typed, like the note, and postmarked London. Whoever had sent this, they knew where she lived. They knew where she worked. They could be watching her right now.

Gracie glanced at the window. Outside, night had fallen, and there were stars starting to twinkle in the sky. There was no wind; the air was still, clear and cold. There would be frost tonight. Lights were winking cheerily down there on the narrow boats moored all along this stretch of the canal. There were buildings right opposite this one, with windows that faced right on to her kitchen. She got up, crossed quickly to the kitchen window and slammed shut the blinds with a shaking hand.

She looked again at the hair. It was the same texture and colour as her father's had been before it became peppered with grey; the same colour as her own. Was that George's?

Harry's? It wasn't her mother's; mum had been bottle-blonde just about forever.

Suddenly she didn't want to be here alone in this big, echoing apartment with its lovely views. She went through to the sitting room and shut the blinds in there too, then went to the front door. She checked it was locked, and put the chain on.

After that she began to unwind, just a bit. Aware that she had been holding her breath, she told herself *breathe, you idiot. No wonder you thought you were going to faint, you have to breathe.*

She wished someone was here with her, someone who was a bit of a bruiser, an action-man type. *Oh, you mean like Lorcan Connolly?* shot into her brain. *The one who caused you tears and heartache, and turned out to be the rottenest, most chauvinistic bastard you'd ever met?*

Come on, she told herself. *Get a grip, okay?*

She went back into the kitchen. The hair still lay there on her table. Gracie stared at it and shuddered. Then she hurried back into the sitting room and went to the answering machine. She hadn't wiped the messages. She replayed them, five altogether, two about business, and three from the girl called Sandy, each one more distraught than the last.

She listened to Sandy's messages again, tuning in this time, paying close attention. George was in hospital, Harry was fuck-knew-where. Sandy gave her phone number – a mobile, not a landline. Gracie wrote it down on the pad, cleared the messages, and dialled.

No answer.

Gracie went and took a shower, slipped on her slouchy indoor-wear, and made herself a warming cup of tea. She kept glancing through the open doorway at the hair on the kitchen table. She didn't think she could keep down any food, so she didn't bother trying. Instead she turned on the evening news, listening but hardly hearing any of it, the note constantly replaying in her mind. *Call the filth on this and you're all dead.* She phoned Sandy's mobile again at seven, then at eight. It went straight to voicemail. She left a message, said please call.

At nine, Sandy did.

'Hi. Sandy?' asked Gracie, quickly muting the TV with the remote.

'Yeah. Hi. How are you?' The girl sounded exhausted.

'Fine. How's George?'

'I've been at the hospital all evening with him. He's about the same. Still in intensive care.' She sounded tearful again. 'It's horrible in there.'

'I can imagine,' said Gracie, although truthfully she couldn't. 'Did Mum go in with you?'

'She's going tomorrow. We're taking turns, makes it a bit easier.'

'Can you give me her number again? I mislaid it after you left it yesterday.'

'Sure.' Sandy repeated the number. 'Pity you're not closer, you could come and see him.'

'Yeah I could.' Gracie glanced through to the kitchen, looked at the dark red hair there – one of her brothers' hair. It belonged either to handsome, gentle, idle Harry, or loud, chunky Jack-the-lad George. Probably it was Harry's. She wasn't going to tell this poor, wretched-sounding girl about the hair. She wondered if she should tell the police about it, show them the note, but it had stipulated no cops . . . and Harry was missing. *And* they'd said they were watching her.

'Listen, I'm coming down to London,' she said, the words coming out almost of their own volition.

'Really? When?'

Gracie thought about that. She looked again at the hair. 'Tomorrow,' she said.

12

21 December

Gracie called in on Brynn next day at his sister's place and told him to take over, that she was going down South for a bit.

'How long's a bit?' asked Brynn, still coughing and spluttering after yesterday's fire.

'I don't know. You can keep in touch with me on the mobile, and I'll be back soonest, okay?'

'Not much is going to be happening for a while,' said Brynn, wheezing then letting out a hacking cough. 'If the insurance people come back with anything, I'll let you know.'

'You look after him,' said Gracie to Angie.

'Will do,' said Angie.

She dropped an awkward kiss on to Brynn's leathery cheek, registering his surprise at this small show of affection. *Gracie Doyle*, she thought, unable to help herself. *The girl with a calculator where her heart should be.* Wasn't that what Brynn, what the whole world, thought? That she was cold? And maybe he was right; maybe she *was*. But perhaps right now, when everything was hitting the fan, that was a *good* thing to be.

She'd already thrown a few bits and pieces into a suitcase and a bag this morning, put them in the back of the car. Now, with Brynn primed, she drove off into the cold, leaden-skied morning down the M6. She picked up the M1 east of Birmingham, stopping briefly in the services to refuel. Four hours later, she was in London.

It was starting to snow. Maybe it would be a white Christmas after all. She snagged a parking space a long way from her mother's door in the familiar Hackney street, bought a parking ticket, and went and knocked at the door of the plain Victorian house she'd grown up in. There was a small, red-berried wreath hanging on it. Mum had kept the house after the divorce, and Dad hadn't objected. Gracie guessed he'd just been glad to be free, to start anew.

'Who is it?' asked a shaky female voice from the other side of the door, after she'd knocked on the damned thing for what felt like an age.

'It's Gracie,' she called out.

'*Gracie?*' echoed the voice. 'What the hell . . .?'

There was a noise of chains being unfastened, bolts being thrown back.

'What, you had a crime explosion round here?' asked Gracie as her mother swung the door open. 'What's with the—'

Gracie stopped speaking. Her mum was standing there. Her mother had always been a youthful dresser. She was pushing sixty now, but still she wore skinny jeans and a fashionable turquoise top. Her hair was cut close to her head and skilfully dyed a flattering ashy blonde, but her face looked pale and puffy. Her bloodshot brown eyes were darting and nervous.

Her lips trembled. She looked like she'd had the stuffing kicked out of her.

'Oh fuck,' said Suze wearily. 'Not you.'

'Nice to see you too, Mummy dear,' said Gracie, and pushed inside the hall with her case and bag.

'I suppose Sandy phoned you.'

'She did, that's right. And the police called too. Said you'd notified them. Why didn't *you* call me?'

Suze shrugged, as if it wasn't worth dignifying Gracie's comment with a reply. 'I'm just surprised you actually bothered to turn up.'

Gracie turned a gimlet eye on her mother. 'Yeah, well, I actually did,' she said, refusing to rise to the challenge of a fight so soon. She was tired from the trip. She didn't want arguments, she wanted tea, biscuits and answers – in that order. She went on through to the kitchen. So familiar, but all different – the units were new beech-effect, the worktops a shiny black granite.

Suze was busy refastening the defences at the front door. By the time she joined Gracie in the kitchen, Gracie had taken out the jiffy bag and decanted the hair inside it out on to the worktop.

'Someone sent me this,' she said, as her mother stopped dead in the doorway and let out a small cry.

'Oh *shit*,' Suze moaned, putting her hands to her mouth.

'George is in hospital,' said Gracie. 'So Sandy told me.'

Her mother nodded. 'Yeah. He is.'

'Did someone cut his hair? Does this look like George's hair to you?'

Her mother was shaking her head. She went over to the worktop and lightly touched the hair, her hand shaking violently. 'No. I mean yes. They cut his hair, they had to, but George never wears his hair this long anyway. And look.' Suze

pulled a jiffy bag out of a drawer and tipped out the contents.
More hair. And it was the same.

'Was there a note with this?' asked Gracie, feeling sick.

'Yeah. Here.'

Gracie took the note Suze handed her. It said '*Doyle scum.
No cops.*'

Gracie stiffened. 'You haven't. Have you? Told the police?'

Suze shook her head. 'I was too frightened to.'

'I guess this is Harry's then,' said Gracie.

'He wears it long, like that,' said Suze.

Gracie stared dumbly at the hair. George had been a mouthy
little pain in the arse through most of his childhood, but Harry
had never been any trouble. Gracie didn't like to think of
someone hacking Harry's hair off like this. She didn't like it
at all. It spoke of a spiteful need to inflict visible damage.

Her mother was still fingering the hair. Gracie set her bag
down on the floor, looking around her. The same old place.
She hadn't been happy here. Mum and Dad ranting and raving
at each other, Harry and George sitting on the stairs in a state
of terror and tears, her trying to reassure them . . .

Bad, old memories that she didn't want to look at all over
again. She didn't even want to *be* here. But she was.

'They still living here, with you?' she asked.

Her mother looked up. 'What?'

'George and Harry? They live here?'

'Nah, they moved out when Claude moved in. About a year
ago.'

'Who's Claude?' asked Gracie.

'I am,' said a masculine voice.

A man had just appeared in the kitchen doorway. He was
tall with a beer gut, a receding hairline and blue eyes magnified
by hugely thick rimless glasses. He looked in his fifties, and he

had a smarmy smile on his face that put Gracie's hackles up straight away.

'This . . .' Her mother looked at her with less than friendly eyes. '. . . This is my daughter Gracie, Claude.'

'The famous missing daughter!' Claude came forward, holding out a hand in greeting. 'Well, I never.'

'Hi,' said Gracie, pulling back when he tried to kiss her cheek.

Claude noted it straight away. He turned a smile on her mother. 'She's a bit frosty, Suze,' he said jokily.

'You don't know the half of it,' said her mother sourly. Gracie saw her mother's eyes snap to his hand, which was still holding hers. His grip felt soft and damp and Gracie pulled her hand away.

'Bad business about your brother being in hospital,' he said, twisting his face into an appropriate expression of sympathy.

Gracie could see why George and Harry had moved out. She'd taken against Claude on sight and she was willing to bet he'd driven them away.

'Yeah, it's bad all right.' Gracie turned her attention to her mother. 'What's the latest on that? Is George any better?'

Suze shook her head. 'Just the same.'

'And what's this?' Claude was crossing the kitchen and was now prodding at the hair. 'What on earth . . .? Is this *another* lot of hair?'

'Yeah. Some was posted to me, too,' said Gracie, not really wanting to discuss any of this with him. 'It's got to be Harry's.'

'Well, it's got to be some sort of *joke*, don't you think?' asked Claude.

'A *joke*?' shot back Suze. 'Well it ain't very funny, is it?'

'Yeah, but you know what these youngsters are like. One of their mates larking about, and maybe him and Harry thought it'd be a laugh.'

Gracie looked coldly at Claude. The man was an idiot. And clearly he didn't know Harry at all. *She* could only dredge her memory, but what she did remember told her that Harry would never go in for a sick, demented prank like this.

Gracie wondered for a moment about showing her mother the note *she'd* got, but decided against it. Her mother could wail and shout for England, and Suze throwing a fit all over the bloody kitchen wasn't going to get Harry out of bother.

Gracie reviewed the facts. Harry was in trouble, George was taking nil by mouth, her casino had damned near burned down and *would* have burned down if not for Brynn's quick thinking. She was only surprised that something hadn't yet happened to Suze or her live-in lover Claude.

'You got a room I can stay in for the night?' she asked wearily. She scooped the hair she'd been sent back into the bag and stuffed it into her holdall. 'My old room will do.'

Her mother opened her mouth to speak – probably to say a flat no, but Claude, the oily bastard, chipped in.

'Of *course* she has.' He was beaming with bonhomie. Gracie bent to pick up her coat and she didn't miss how the creep's eyes lingered on her arse.

Gracie wondered what on earth her mother saw in him, but then Suze's judgement had never been entirely sound. Her mother was the perennial good-time girl, preferring to dance on tables all hours of the night, play bingo and get bladdered rather than take proper care of her house and kids. Suze thrived on flattery, and seemed unable to distinguish between fake and genuine. Gracie had always thought her dad did the right thing in leaving her; she still did.

'I'll take my things on up,' she said, grabbing her bag just as Claude reached down to get it. 'Thanks,' she said with a tight smile at him. 'And Mum – can you dig out their addresses?'

'Address,' said Suze, looking at her daughter with a cold eye. 'They got a flat together, it ain't much.'

But better than staying here with you and this arsehole, thought Gracie.

'Jot it down for me, will you?'

'Jesus, what did your last slave die of?' asked Suze with a sniff.

'Insolence,' flung back Gracie, dismayed to find that when dealing with her mother she still felt like a snippy teenager. 'You going to see George tonight at the hospital?'

'No.' Her mother's eyes filled with easy tears. 'Not tonight. Tomorrow. My poor boy.'

'I'll tag along then. If you don't mind?'

'Mind? Why should I mind? I'm only surprised that you care enough to bother.'

Gracie gave her mother a long hard stare. But what was the use? They'd never got on; they never would. She turned her back and pounded off up the stairs to her room. Her mother hadn't hugged her, and she hadn't hugged Suze, either.

Two hours later, she was awakened by grunts and bangs from the room next door to her own.

Oh, terrific.

As if she didn't have enough to contend with, now she had to listen to creep features and her own damned mother doing the nasty through the thin partition wall. A perfect end to a perfect day. How the hell could Suze *do* that, in these circumstances? She thought of George, lying in a hospital bed. And Harry. Where the hell was Harry? She thought of the note with the hair. *No police.* Then she thought of gentle, easy-going Harry out there somewhere, in trouble, alone, and it pulled at her heart. Finally she turned over and pulled the pillows over her head. It was hours before she could get to sleep.

George and Harry

NOVEMBER

13

Some time after Laura Dixon had shagged him shitless in the Gents at her divorce party, Harry was crossing Covent Garden when he spotted his former client, the cougar – Jackie Sullivan – browsing among the blooms outside a florist. He stopped walking and stared. He was getting to be an old hand at the escorting business now; he had plenty of dosh; he was happy.

It was cold today. Freezing. His breath plumed like smoke with every exhalation. The cougar was wrapped up in a white fake-fur hat and matching gloves. She wore black boots and was carrying a Kelly bag. Her coat looked expensive, patterned in a large black-and-white dog's-tooth design. Harry thought she looked adorable; he started to smile, and approached her as she halted to stare in the window at a display of red hothouse roses.

'Hey,' he said, touching her shoulder.

She turned. Her face was the same; small, sharply formed, anxious of expression. Her pale denim-blue eyes stared at him with something like panic.

'Hey, it's me,' said Harry, beaming.

'Um . . . hello,' she said uncertainly, 'How are you?'

Another woman came up beside her. This one was large, hard-faced, dark-haired and wearing a Burberry trench. Harry had thought the cougar was alone.

'Jack darling, I don't like the red,' she said in a hectoring tone of voice. 'I much prefer the cream – so much softer, don't you think?' The brunette's eyes, full of curiosity, were now resting on Harry. There was a predatory half-smile on her crimson-painted mouth. 'And who's this?'

The cougar's cheeks flushed the same hectic red that Harry had found so charming on the night they'd spent together.

'Oh, this is . . .' she hesitated.

'Harry,' he supplied for her, shaking the woman's hand.

'He's a friend of my daughter's,' said Jackie quickly. Harry glanced at her. The blue eyes looked back at him without expression. 'They were at uni together.'

Harry felt a stab of hurt at that. Like he was a dirty secret. Then he remembered her pushing him out through the door into the dawn, and realized that was precisely how she saw him – as something shameful and disgusting, to be concealed.

He shouldn't have touched her shoulder. Shouldn't have smiled at her. Shouldn't have breezed over here like she'd be pleased to see him. It was patently obvious that she wasn't.

Of *course* she wasn't. Why would she be?

'This is Camilla,' said Jackie formally. 'A client of mine.'

He understood that Jackie was marking out her territory, drawing boundaries. Jackie was an interior designer. She was posh. She spoke *like thet*. Like one of the nobs. She was *way* above him in the social scale of things; he was nothing but a good-looking chancer, living on benefits and selling his nubile young bod for undeclared amounts of money. He felt he'd made a major error, made a complete bloody fool of himself. He should have been more careful, more discreet.

'Well, it was nice seeing you again, Mrs Sullivan,' he said.

'You too, Harry,' she said, very polite.

Harry looked into her eyes again. Saw nothing there, no small spark of the connection that had been there on the night he'd stayed. He nodded once, then turned and walked away.

'Emma's a very lucky girl,' said Camilla, her eyes following Harry as he walked off. 'What, darling?' asked Jackie vaguely, looking with intense concentration at the cream-coloured blooms that Camilla favoured.

'What an exquisite young man.' Camilla was still watching Harry, admiring the luscious fall of his shoulder-length auburn hair, his wide shoulders beneath the black leather bomber jacket, the tight fit of the stonewashed jeans on his long, long legs. Finally he was lost in the crowds. Camilla gave Jackie a louche look. 'Imagine waking up to something as wonderful as *that* in the morning.'

'Yes,' said Jackie with a cool smile. 'Imagine. A mixture of the gerbera and the roses, do you think? Yes?'

14

'Lefty in?' Stew asked Gordon, who was policing the door of Deano Drax's fetish club in Soho. Stew had nipped over from the strip joint over the road. They were both doormen, and they had become pals, so they often stood out in the alley beside the industrial-sized wheelie bins and had a smoke and a chat.

The immaculately attired Gordon ushered in a few more punters, stopping a couple, giving them a quick frisk. Perversions were all very well, but weapons were a no-no inside Shakers. Satisfied, he motioned the punters through into the dark, pulsing body of the club.

Gordon gestured for another of the bouncers to take over the door. He moved to one side, taking Stew Baker with him. Stew was a solid man, in build and in character, one of the best, a good mate to Gordon – and to the hapless Lefty, too.

'You mean you ain't *heard* about Lefty?' asked Gordon over the roar of the club's huge sound system.

'Heard what?'

Gordon shook his head. 'Man, you missed out on a treat.'

He explained about Lefty's miscalculation with Deano's latest young squeeze. 'He is *deep* in the manure, I'm telling you. Deano is *very* taken with that boy and he's spitting blood over this. You know Deano – he just *loves* to terrorize anybody smaller than he is. And, let's face it, nearly everybody *is* smaller than Deano – including these boys he likes, *and* Lefty.'

Stew said nothing. He felt pity for Lefty's predicament, but then if you mixed with shit one thing was certain – sooner or later, it was going to stick to your skin. He had no time for nonces, and Deano Drax was a bad one. He looked back into the club's dark, gaping maw. Sometimes he thought it was like the mouth of hell in there. He'd looked inside it once, and there were dingy back rooms for orgies; dungeons too. He was glad he worked over the road in a nice straight-forward strip club and not here. A few tits and bums never hurt anyone. He didn't mind that, or the lap-dancing places – hell, live and let live. But people crawling around on dog chains, being pissed on or beaten and tied up for entertainment? Nah, he drew the line right there. He thought that Shakers told you everything you wanted to know about its owner's mind-set.

'Go through to the bar, see Chippy, he'll sort you out with a drink,' offered Gordon. Things were getting busy on the door and Gordon had to get back to work. People were queuing up now, weirdos wearing skin-tight plastic and fetish boots with heels so amazingly high they could barely stagger along. Which was the whole point, of course. If you couldn't walk, you could be caught. You were easy meat.

'Nah, that's okay,' said Stew hastily. 'Got to get back. Catch ya later, Gord.'

Stew left the club and was halfway over the road when

he saw Deano Drax's big motor with its black-tinted windows pull into the alley at the side of the fetish club. He kept walking, tried not to stare but, despite himself, he couldn't resist a look. Deano, massive and bear-like, was getting out of the back of the car. Huge bald head; neat goatee beard. Stew's face wrinkled with disgust. That fat smarmy-faced nonce made you feel sick just to see him, swaggering about the place like he owned the whole damned world. In the shadows of the alley it was hard to make out much, but Stew was sure there were others with him, two smaller figures. Maybe kids, maybe not.

Stew shuddered and averted his eyes. He thought of Lefty, who was out looking right now for Deano's *grand amour*. He didn't think Lefty was a bad bloke at heart. Actually, he'd been fine until he started on the hash and the E and – worse – on the butane, and after that . . . well, now his brains were screwed, his lungs were black lace and he was Deano's own personal lapdog, bought and paid for. Deano said jump, Lefty said how high? That being the case, Stew hoped, no he *prayed,* that the golden-haired boy he'd seen hanging round Drax a month or so ago, sometimes staggering a little like a crippled foal, sometimes staring around with drugged and bewildered eyes, Stew *prayed* that the boy was long gone, back home where he'd be safe, or that someone kind and good was helping him right now.

Kid needs a guardian angel, he thought. *I just hope to fuck he's got one.*

15

George sat in his local café, across the table from Alfie, the morning after their run-in with Lefty Umbabwe. George had a big smile pasted across his face. He couldn't help it. The kid had devoured a plate of Full English in record time, knocked back two teas and two rounds of toast, and clearly wasn't about to throw in the towel yet.

'More toast?' offered George.

Alfie nodded. He still hadn't spoken much, apart from to give his name. That bothered George. He looked even younger in daylight, and that bothered George too. To think of a kid like this wandering about on the streets. And what had been going on between Alfie and that bastard waving the knife around?

George lifted a finger to Bert the café owner. 'Can we get some more toast over here, when you're ready. And two more teas?' He had no trouble making himself heard over the hubbub of noise in here. George had a voice like a foghorn – and a laugh like a bronze gong.

While Bert got busy with the toaster, George thought back

and tried to recall what the man in the long black leather coat had been yelling at Alfie before George had decided he was crazy enough to intervene. Something about 'the man'. That was what the man wanted . . .? It was driving George nuts. He'd drunk hardly a thing that night, but still he couldn't remember fuck-all. Mostly because he'd been scared right out of his brains.

'Alfie?' he said.

There were other patrons in the café; it was a good place, one George and Harry often frequented. It was busy, bustling with life. Outside it was cold, but in here it was hot, everyone talking and laughing and eating, the windows steamed up, the coffee machine hissing and frothing; it felt cosy.

Alfie looked up at George's face.

'How old are you, Alfie?'

This was a point that really bothered George. The boy looked very young. He must be a minor. He shouldn't be out on his own like this. Shit, *anyone* could have picked him up, and what George really ought to do was take him to the nearest cop shop, see about getting him home. He had said as much to Alfie earlier this morning, and had been alarmed to find Alfie halfway down the stairs half an hour later. George had caught up with him. 'No police!' Alfie had shouted. 'No police!' Five minutes more, and the kid would have been out on the streets again, prey for any loitering monster. It made George's blood run to ice, the thought of that.

So – no police. Not *yet*, anyway. That was cool with George. He didn't want involvement with the filth if he could avoid it, anyway; he'd done dodgy deals around town a few times, fly-pitching and ripping off a few tourists, minor stuff, but it was best to keep a low profile. Alfie was just staring back at George with those big baby-blues that seemed to hold so many secrets. He said nothing.

'Come on, Alf. Straight up, how old are you?' George persisted.

'Fourteen,' said Alfie with a quick grin.

'Holy *shit*.'

'*Kidding*,' said Alfie with a roll of his eyes at George's gullibility.

George tipped his head to one side and looked Alfie in the eye. George played a mean hand of cards. The Doyle poker gene had not passed him by. He was ace at reading people's reactions, but angel-faced young Alfie flummoxed him. He could read his accent, no problem. Well-bred. Nicely rounded vowels. From a good background, that much was obvious. So what had he been doing, wandering around the dangerous night streets with someone waving a knife in his face?

'Which is it then?' he asked. 'Fourteen? Fifteen? Sixteen? What?'

'Seventeen. That's the God's honest, George.'

George stared across at Alfie. 'You going to tell me what happened with that guy, Alf? The one in the alley?'

Alfie's smile dropped away. The shutters went down. He said nothing.

'Alf?' prompted George gently.

Alfie exhaled sharply and sat back in his chair. He looked into George's eyes. 'Please let me stay, George,' he said. 'Please.'

George pushed back his chair and leaned back too, puffing out his cheeks with exasperation. Bert came and put more toast and tea in front of them. George nodded his thanks and looked at Alfie.

'Seventeen?' he asked. Alfie could easily pass for younger, with that puckish, elfin, Peter Pan quality, the big eyes, the golden mop of hair; he'd look twenty when he was thirty-five. He'd look fifty when he was ninety.

Alfie nodded and dived into the toast.

George felt a smile forming on his face again. 'Seventeen, with a tapeworm.'

He watched the boy eat. There was something about the boy eating that just made George feel happy. Maybe he was a compulsive feeder – certainly he fed *himself* with a vengeance. But it was more than that. George knew the state Alfie had been in last night. Shaking. Shot away. His eyes huge from the after-effects of some drug or other. And then, during the night, the boy'd had nightmares. George had heard him crying out, rambling on about dungeons and shit. He had tried to ignore it, but it had gone on, and on, and he'd thought, fuck it, he's going to wake Harry up in a minute; Harry is not going to be a happy bunny.

So he'd gone through to the lounge, and there had been Alfie, curled up in a corner of the sofa bed, sobbing. George had sat down in his vest and boxers and said *hey kid, what's the matter? You okay?*

And then, because Alfie had seemed so distraught, he had put his arm around him and hugged him. Saying over and over, *it's okay, hush, it's all right, what was it, a bad dream? It's okay, you're safe.*

After about an hour, Alfie had lain down again, and finally drifted back into sleep. George had felt tears prick his own eyes, he was so affected by Alfie's distress. George had sat there, watching him for a long time. Watching *over* him, sort of.

Like he was doing now. Caring for him, feeding him, and

feeling glad that the haunted expression in his eyes was starting to go.

'Say I can stay. Please,' said Alfie again, past a mouthful of toast.

George stared at Alfie. 'It's a small flat,' he said.

'*Please.*'

Harry wouldn't be happy. Said the place was too small to swing a cat anyway, but with *three* of them in there . . . and fuck it, what if Cuthill found out? He'd stick the rent up at the very least, or – worst-case scenario – boot their arses out the door. And then where would they be? He'd be damned if he'd go back home again and watch that creepo Claude pawing his mum day and night. *Yuck.*

'Okay, you can stay,' George heard himself saying, frightened that if he said no Alfie was just going to leg it, vanish into the warren of streets and never be seen again.

He'd have to square it with Harry, that was all. It would work out. It would have to.

16

'You *are* joking,' said Harry.

'Nope. Deadly serious, my man,' said George, handing Harry a sheet of A4 paper that had just been coughed out by the printer beside his small computer station in his shambolic bedroom. 'Your assignment – should you choose to accept it,' said George, sending a collusive grin to Alfie, who was sprawled out on the bed watching all this going on, 'is to escort Ms Melissa Whitehead to a family wedding. She's a bit of a dog, I grant you, but she needs an escort for this do, if she ain't going to look like a total lost cause to her nearest and dearest.'

'Oh my God,' said Harry, staring at the photo. It wasn't pretty. 'If she wants a shag, I'm *definitely* not going to be up to it.'

'Unkind, unkind,' tutted George. 'And speaking of such delicate matters, you know that cougar, the one you *also* worried you wouldn't be able to do the deed for . . .?'

Harry looked up. 'Who, Jackie?'

'See, you're on first-name terms. And, my boy, your face lit up at the very mention of her. I think it's *lurve*.'

'Don't be a prick,' said Harry. 'What she say?'

'Needs you – and no one else, I might add – *you* specifically, to escort her to another do.'

'Oh.' After the Covent Garden incident, Harry thought she'd never want to see him again. He felt cheered, all of a sudden, and Melissa Whitehead didn't seem quite so daunting after all.

'I'm hard at work this Friday night too.' George glanced at Alfie. 'You'll be okay here on your own, won't you Alf?'

'Yeah. Sure.'

Harry looked at Alfie. He didn't understand all this with George and Alfie at all. Alfie was a posh kid and he ought to be at home, not roughing it here with him and George. But he was George's friend, and Harry had had plenty of *his* friends bunking over in the past, so he couldn't complain.

And why should he bother? Life was treating them pretty good right now. The escorting business was paying like a bastard; they were busy and there was cash rolling in wholesale, tax-free. George was ducking out of his job with Lorcan on a pretty regular basis, taking sickies as often as he could, then going off instead to escort and sexually service the lonely and sometimes downright desperate women of London town. Harry had even stopped signing on. They could *stick* their dole money. He had plenty. Yeah, life was pretty damned good. And he was – a little to his surprise – really looking forward to seeing Jackie Sullivan again.

'So who's yours?' he asked George.

George whipped off another print-out. Looked at the paper. 'Oh, she looks okay. Pretty little blonde. Sandy Cole.'

17

Lefty Umbabwe hauled back and belted Mona a hard one right across the cheek. What else could he do? She was a loud-mouthed cow, always complaining. Lefty was beginning to regret his decision to take Gordon's advice and draft in the club dancer to help him track down Alfie.

'Ow! You *fucker!*' yelled Mona.

'Mona by name and *moaner* by nature, that's you,' shrieked Lefty, right in her face.

'Listen, I'm shagged out here. My legs are worn to stumps, these bleedin' heels ain't meant for walking in. How much longer you planning to drag me around town, Lefty, uh?' Mona grumbled, cupping her sore face with one hand. It was a bitterly cold night. Her breath was like fog in front of her face. Her toes were numb. All she wanted was to be home, indoors, in her own bed, nice and cosy.

'What, you want me to tell Deano you didn't want to help with this?' demanded Lefty, playing his Ace card.

Mona frowned. How had she got into this? Her ma was babysitting her little girl Josie at Mona's place, and that was where she wanted to be, too. Josie was only five; she needed her mama. Josie's dad had taken off just as soon as he'd put Mona up the duff, but that was okay: she had her ma to help, she had her baby girl, she was happy enough.

But now Lefty had railroaded her into this. Okay, he was offering some bucks and she needed the dosh, but she didn't even *like* Lefty. She certainly didn't like Deano; she was shit-scared of *that* creep. But it was work, it was money, what could you do?

'No, but . . . for fuck's sake, Lefty, I'm done. I really am.' She didn't want it getting back to Deano that she was a reluctant helper, no way. Deano Drax was a horrible, pervy bastard, she didn't want to go crossing him.

Lefty drew back. Rummaged in his big leather coat, found the can, took a pull. Mona was watching him with distaste. Bloody junkies. If Deano Drax was so damned keen on the boy, he shouldn't have left this butane-sniffing fool in charge of him. And look at the *state* of him. Stapled head, greyish, sweat-smeared skin. He looked like death warmed over and served up as fresh. And they'd looked for the boy, oh *God* how they'd looked, searching for any trace of him and the man who'd snatched him away. They'd questioned cabbies, late bus drivers, tried down the tube, they'd even done the nearest trimmed and tinselled YMCA, but Lefty didn't seem to be finished, even now.

'This is hopeless,' Mona told him, trying to keep her tone light and reasonable. She didn't want another smack in the chops. 'Come on, Lefty honey, can't you see it's no good?'

Lefty said nothing.

'Look,' said Mona, pushing forward her advantage. Personally she shuddered over what had become of the boy. Probably he had been picked up by another stinking nonce, and if he was ever found at all it would be on waste ground, stone-cold dead. She didn't like to think about the boy too much, it made her feel bad. 'Come on, Lefty. You've done your best.'

'No, you don't understand,' said Lefty. 'Best? That ain't good enough. Not by a *mile*. The only thing that's gonna work in this situation, babe, is a *result*. And that result is to find the boy. Find Alfie. That's *all* that's gonna work here.'

'Oh come on . . .' Mona wheedled.

'No!' Lefty grabbed her arm, his fingers digging in viciously. Mona cried out as her upper body was hauled in horribly close to his. He smelled sour, disgusting. Junkies didn't wash. His eyes looked demented and bloodshot as they glared into hers. His teeth were clenched in a grimace of utter determination. Suddenly she realized that Lefty Umbabwe frightened her.

'Lefty . . .' she protested faintly.

'No. You listen up, girl. You think a cheap whore like you's going to lay down the law to Lefty Umbabwe? We go on looking. If we don't find him tonight then we come back and try *tomorrow* night, and the night after that, and the night after *that*, you got me? We find him. That's all there is to it, girl. No other option. None at all.'

Mona nodded her head slowly. She was really in the shit here, being linked up to this lunatic.

'Sure, Lefty,' she said. 'Let's do that, okay? Let's do that.'

Lefty released her arm. Mona rubbed at it gingerly. It would be all colours of the rainbow tomorrow, she knew it, and her cheek still stung painfully from the blow he'd inflicted. *Bastard*. But she had to keep on his good side. He was still looking at her face. She raised an unsteady smile with an effort. She didn't want to cross him. Most especially, she didn't *ever* want to show up on Deano Drax's radar.

'We'll keep looking,' she smiled.

Lefty nodded sharply, satisfied that he'd put his point across.

He took another long toke from the can, and together they walked on.

Gracie

DECEMBER

18

Gracie had never visited anyone in intensive care before, so she didn't know what to expect. Claude offered to drive them to the hospital, but Gracie said that she'd drive; and she was relieved when he said he was off down the pub to meet his mates, leaving them to visit George alone.

She found a stranger lying there, his head shaven and heavily bandaged, attached to a multitude of machines. There was a tube in his mouth, another in his throat, a thing pumping air into his chest. There was a steady beep going up from one of the monitors and there was a blood-filled tube going into his wrist, with a dial endlessly turning.

They had to tap in a code on a keypad to enter the ward, where there were just six beds in a big, overheated room, each one occupied by pale, corpse-like figures hovering in the nether world between life and death.

Gracie could *smell* death in here.

Suze sat down on one side of George's bed; she sat on

103

the other. There was a small, dark-haired nurse checking read-outs, and she gave them a cheery smile.

'They have one nurse to every patient in here,' said Suze to Gracie.

Gracie nodded, not trusting herself to speak. She stared at George's closed eyes, his bruised and pallid face. He was still bulky – he always had been; as square and squat as a barn door, that was George – but now his bulk seemed soft, spongy, and his fingers looked swollen.

Gracie swallowed hard and remarked on this.

'His kidneys packed up,' said Suze, blinking back tears. 'That's why they've got him on dialysis.' She was stroking the back of George's hand. There was a little sensor clipped on one chubby finger, monitoring vital signs.

And he's not even breathing for himself, thought Gracie, feeling sick.

'What . . . what happened to him?' she asked Suze.

'Someone done him over. We found him at the gate. There's a crack in his skull. They had to drain off some fluid that was pressing on his brain.' Her voice caught and she clapped her hands over her mouth to stifle a sob. 'He's been like this ever since we found him.'

'He's going to be all right,' said Gracie, surprising herself with the need to give comfort to this woman who had never thought to comfort *her*.

Suze glared at her. 'Yeah? You got that in writing, have you? That's *bullshit*. They told me to expect the worst when they brought him in here. Have you any idea what that's like, to have someone say that to you about your boy?'

'He's getting the best possible care,' insisted Gracie. What was Suze attacking *her* for? She was here to help, that was all.

'There could be *brain damage*, for God's sake. Someone knocked the *crap* out of him. He could be a *vegetable* for the rest of his life, and you're telling me he's going to be fine. How do you *know* that he's going to be fine?'

Gracie said nothing. It was clear that Suze needed someone to kick off at. She didn't seem willing to do that with Claude, but – as always – she was quite happy to let her ire rain down upon Gracie's head.

'I don't even know what you're doing here,' said Suze venomously, still glaring across at her.

Neither do I.

Gracie looked at George lying there. She had this *other* image fixed in her brain. Chunky little George at five on the beach at Westward Ho, wearing black bathers and a vast grin. Way back before Mum and Dad had parted company and split the family in half.

'Has George been dating Sandy long?'

'Not long, no.' Suze sniffed and fished out a hankie from her bag. She honked loudly.

It felt so strange to Gracie, to be sitting here. This was *George* lying here in bits. And there, across the bed from her, was her mother, Suze. It was surreal. But she'd had to come. She *had* to be here.

'Months, days, years?' she coaxed. 'What?'

'Couple of months, she says, although George has never mentioned it. She's keen.'

'She must be, she's calling herself his fiancée.'

Suze's eyes opened wide with surprise. 'Is she? Well, that's a turn-up. Fiancée? Well, then she must be. You'd have thought he would have told me though. But then – you know what George is like.' Suze's mouth twisted in bitterness. 'But no, you don't, do you? You didn't bother to keep in touch.'

Gracie stared across at Suze. 'Excuse me, but it was *you* who didn't keep in touch. I wrote to you. A lot, as I remember. That first year after you and Dad split.'

'No you didn't.'

'I *did*.'

'Well I never got a bloody thing.'

'Oh come on.' Gracie sighed. Her mother had always been a fantasist, embellishing dull reality with drama and excitement. They were so unalike, it was as if she'd been dropped to earth from another planet.

'I didn't.' Suze was glaring a challenge at Gracie now. 'You never cared about me after you and your dad left. You never gave a *shit*.'

'I did. I still do. Or else why would I be here?'

'Pass,' sniffed Suze.

'And while we're on the subject of not caring, what about when Dad died? What about his *funeral*? You didn't come to that. Neither did George or Harry.'

'Look, I'm not a hypocrite. I couldn't stand there lamenting the loss of your dad while I still hated him. And, as for Harry and George, I thought it would upset them.' Suddenly Suze's eyes were shifty. 'So I didn't tell them.'

'You didn't . . .' Gracie's jaw hit the floor. Her voice raised a notch. 'You didn't *tell* them their father had died?'

'Can you keep it down?' said the nurse, hurrying past. 'They can hear you, you know. Every word, sometimes. So no arguing.'

'Sorry,' said Gracie.

She looked at George. Shot a glare at Suze and hissed: 'So you're telling me this poor sod's lying here at death's door, and he don't even know his father's gone?'

'I couldn't tell them,' said Suze, lowering her voice. Her

eyes were desperate. 'They blamed me when he went and took you with him. If I'd told them he'd died . . .'

'It all comes back to you, don't it?' said Gracie, shaking her head. 'Everything's about you. As usual.'

Suze made an agitated move with her shoulders. 'Look, can we skip this now?'

'Yeah. For now.'

'You don't know how hard it's been,' whined Suze.

'Spare me.'

'Christ, Gracie Doyle. Cold as fucking *ice*, that's you. You haven't changed a bit. You're just like your dad; all you know is bets and odds and tells. Real life don't matter.'

That stung.

Gracie drew breath to answer, to snap back a scathing retort, but at that moment one of George's steadily beeping monitors started emitting a high-pitched whine instead. The nurse was there instantly, pressing a button.

'Go and wait outside, will you?' she said quickly.

'What's—?' started Suze.

'Outside,' said the nurse, shoving her away.

And suddenly there were other people rushing in, and Gracie and Suze were swept out into the corridor. The people flocking around George's bed were wheeling machines, attaching paddles to his chest, and finally Gracie and Suze understood what was going on here. George's heart had stopped beating.

19

21 December

'Oh my Christ! I never want to have to go through anything like that ever again,' said Suze, collapsing into a chair at the kitchen table when she and Gracie arrived home.

'Do you think that was our fault?' asked Gracie, sitting down opposite her mother and exhaling sharply.

Suze looked up. 'What?'

'That nurse told us they hear things. People in . . .' *Comas.* '. . . People out of it. Did he hear us arguing, you think? And it upset him?'

'No.' Suze frowned. 'Jesus. I hope not.' She sank her head into her hands. 'Thank God they got him stabilized.'

Gracie nodded. She felt shaky with the aftermath of fear. George's heart had stopped. George had *died.* But, somehow, they'd brought him back online again. Saved him. She and her mother had left the hospital an hour after it had happened, both shaken to the core. They could have lost him, right then and there. George – big jovial confident George, so full of life – could have been gone forever.

Gracie raised a trembling hand to her mouth and felt like she might cry again, which she rarely did. Oh, she'd shed tears at her father's death, shed tears at his graveside, but tears never came easily to her.

Yeah, she was cold.

No, not cold, she corrected herself. Just logical, reasonable. Always looking for answers, weighing up odds.

So what are the odds on George coming out of this, Gracie?

The odds were bad. She didn't even want to start thinking about it.

'Jesus,' she groaned, 'I need a drink.'

'That,' said Suze, levering herself upright with her hands flat on the table – looking like an old, old woman all of a sudden, 'I can do. Got sherry here, or brandy . . .?'

'Brandy,' said Gracie, and watched while her mother went to the cupboard, got out two glasses and a bottle, and came back and threw herself back down into her chair.

Suze slopped the brandy into the glasses. Looked at Gracie. Then she picked up her glass.

'To George,' she said. 'To my darling Georgie.' Then her eyes filled and she put the glass back down, starting to sob.

'He's going to pull through this,' said Gracie. She looked at her mother, half exasperated, half feeling like joining in and wailing like a banshee too.

'You don't *know* that,' blubbed Suze.

'I know George is tough,' said Gracie.

She looked at her mother's hand, there on the table. A few wrinkles were on that hand now, a couple of age spots. She hadn't seen or known her mother in a long time, but those hands were as familiar to her as her own. Families might splinter apart and loyalties might be tested to the limit, but blood ties remained forever strong, and that surprised her.

Tentatively Gracie reached out and put her hand over her mother's.

'It's going to be all right,' she told Suze firmly.

'No!' Now Suze was shaking, crying, shouting. 'It *ain't* going to be all right. George could have *died* tonight. Someone did this to him, put him in fucking *hospital*. He might never recover. *Never.* And Harry. God knows what's happening to Harry. Where is he, Gracie? What the hell's happening to our lives?'

Gracie stared at Suze, unable to give her comfort. She was almost relieved when she heard the key in the front door, glad of someone else's presence, *anyone's*, because she didn't know what to say to ease Suze's pain.

It was Claude, coming in red-nosed from the pub, bringing in a waft of icy winter air with him. He came into the kitchen and looked at Suze, sitting there in floods.

'What's going on?' he asked.

'Oh Claude, it was horrible,' said Suze, and sprang up and flung herself into Claude's arms.

Claude looked a question at Gracie. 'George's heart stopped,' she explained. 'They restarted it. He's okay.'

For now, anyway.

Gracie threw back the brandy. It warmed her all the way down to her toes. She stood up. Hated this feeling of being powerless, swept along like a reed on a current of water. She was used to being in charge, in control. Owning her surroundings. But all this was so strange to her. She didn't like it. Not at all. It didn't suit her, and she wasn't about to accept it.

'I think I'll go on up,' she said, easing her way past her mother and her boyfriend.

She went wearily up the stairs to her room, feeling exhausted. She went to the window and looked out at the dark street. There were little wisps of snow drifting down, but it was too thin and it was still too warm for snow to settle.

Christmas was coming and here was a perfect winter's scene to go with it. But George was lying half dead in intensive care. And Harry . . . well, where the fuck was Harry? She thought of the matching bags of hair and felt her guts twist with anxiety. And the notes. The bloody *notes*. Maybe they *should* get the police involved. But Harry. She had to think of Harry. If somebody saw them talking to the police, where would that leave him? Up shit creek.

There was a cough behind her.

She turned.

'Settling in?' asked Claude, smiling at her from the open doorway. She hadn't heard him coming up the stairs.

'Yeah. Fine,' said Gracie.

'If there's anything you need, anything at all,' he said, addressing his comments to the front of her shirt.

'There ain't,' she said coldly, and walked over and shut the door in his face.

Creep, she thought, then dismissed him from her mind. She had come down here to find answers. And she was going to bloody well do that, starting first thing tomorrow.

20

22 December

By ten next morning, Gracie was slipping one of Suze's spare keys into the outer door of the building where George and Harry rented their flat. The building was a soulless, Thirties block of ten flats, set on a busy main road. Outside there was no greenery, no ornamentation, nothing to suggest homeliness. Stepping inside, Gracie looked round at a bare concrete hall, a utilitarian staircase. The grey-painted doors to flat 1 and 1A were on her left. The air in here smelled of cooked cabbage and curry.

'George and Harry live on the first floor,' Suze had told her at breakfast. 'Flat number two. I don't know what you think you'll gain from going there, but here's the keys if you really want them. And you can fetch a clean pair of George's pyjamas and a dressing gown for him if you don't mind.'

Suze had handed over a bunch of four keys – two for the outer door to the block, two for the flat door. Gracie didn't know what she was going to gain, either. She just knew she had to start somewhere, and their flat seemed like the best place to begin. She went up the stairs. There was no one about. Flats 2 and 2A were to her left. The same, putty-coloured paint on the door. Spyholes on both, just like on the flats downstairs. She brandished another key and slipped it into the keyhole.

The door swung open. It was dark inside the flat, the curtains drawn. She sniffed and wrinkled her nose. It smelled stale, too. She stepped inside and closed the door behind her, then smoothed her hand down the wall beside the door and found the light switch, knocking a phone off its hook, and swearing. She flicked the light on and pocketed the keys.

George and Harry's flat was revealed to her. The phone on the floor was an entry phone, attached by its flexible wire to a small intercom. She replaced it, then looked around her. It wasn't exactly the Ritz. There was a dirty-looking beige carpet on the floor, and the curtains were dark blue. It was warm in here, the boiler obviously set by a timer to automatically switch on. She picked up a few envelopes from the doormat and went over to the curtains and yanked them back. Dust plumed.

Two young men living on their own. Well, did I expect it to be neat and tidy?

There was an old-looking telly with a digibox. Several dusty-looking, blue-shaded lamps. An open bed-settee, with a rumpled quilt and pillows laid out on it. Lots of clutter. Some dead roses in a vase of stinking water. Guitars and bongo drums and clothes all over the place. She remembered George and his clutter. George was a magpie. Hated to throw anything away. Harry was tidier, she remembered that, but he wasn't going to win any domestic prizes.

There was a small kitchen to one side of the living room, and that was in disarray too. Unwashed cups in the sink.

Pans left to dry out on the sink top. There were garments behind the glass door of the washing machine. Gracie walked along the small hallway where there was a bathroom – tiny – and two bedrooms, both beds unmade. A computer desk and chair were in the corner of the larger one, with an empty, scummy mug with GEORGE on the side, a PC, monitor and printer set up on the desk.

She went over to the dressing table and opened a couple of drawers. In the bottom one she found a pair of what looked like unused pyjamas and she stuffed them into her bag. She grabbed the dressing gown hung on the back of the door, rolled it up and stuffed that in there too.

Gracie moved back into the living room and flicked off the light. The weak yellowish sun shone in the dirty windows and highlighted all the dust and disorder in here.

Well, what now, Gracie Doyle?

If . . . no, *when* George came out of hospital, he wouldn't want to come back to a tip like this. She was going to have to have a word with Suze; they were going to have to get this place shipshape. That much, she could do. Organize a cleaner or something.

So what else are you hoping to find here?

'I don't know,' she said aloud, and she wandered over to the telly, looking at the pads of paper and pens and scrawled notes set out on a low table beside it.

She unbuttoned her coat, sat down and started picking up bits of paper.

Get milk and bread, said one.

Phone Tone!, said another.

Mr Cuthill, followed by a phone number.

Gracie picked up the phone and dialled. It was answered straight away.

'Hello? Mr Cuthill?' asked Gracie.

'Who's this?' He didn't sound particularly friendly.

'I'm Gracie Doyle, George and Harry's sister. I'm just tidying up their flat,' she lied smoothly. 'And I came across your number, and—'

'They missed last month's rent. I *told* them. Payment on the dot, I told them that when they moved in or they'd be out the door. I *warned* them.'

Ah. Mr Cuthill is the landlord. And what a charmer, too.

'They ain't been answering the fucking phone,' he said, sounding aggrieved.

'George has been in hospital, and Harry's away.'

'That ain't my problem. When do I get my rent?'

Gracie took up a pen. 'Tell me what's due and give me your address, I'll sort that out for you straight away.'

'This month's due soon too. Fat chance I'll get *that*, I reckon. If they're late on that, they'll be out.'

'I'll pay both months, okay? I'm sure missing last month's was just an oversight.'

'It'd better be,' he sniffed ungratefully, and gave her the details.

Gracie put the phone down and put the slip of paper in her bag.

She sifted through the other notes there. Nothing helpful. She looked at the post. Should she open it? That would feel like snooping, but what else was she doing here, if not to snoop around, look for some sort of answer to what had been going on? She put the post into her bag, undecided.

I'm watching you, Red.

Stifling a shudder, she stood up, took off her coat, then went and put the kettle on. Then she wandered through to the bedroom where the computer station was. She was standing there staring at the blank dead screen when a buzzer sounded loudly.

Gracie jumped. What the hell . . .?

It was coming from the lounge. She walked back through. The kettle was starting to boil. The buzzer sounded again. It was the entry phone. Someone was at the door downstairs, wanting to get in.

Harry? She felt a wild surge of hope. But then Harry wouldn't be ringing his own damned doorbell . . . would he? Well, maybe if he'd forgotten his key and thought George was in here to let him in. She lifted the receiver and said, 'Hello?'

A moment's silence. Then: 'Who's that?' asked a male voice. It was tinged with a faint Irish brogue.

'Who's *that*?' returned Gracie, although a strong feeling of recognition had shot through her as he spoke.

'*Gracie?*' asked the voice, sounding incredulous.

She did know that voice. She knew it very well.

'You'd better come up,' she said, and pressed the release tab.

It didn't take him long to get up the stairs. He rapped on the door a few seconds later, and Gracie opened it, her heart in her mouth. It *was* him.

'Fuck *me*,' she said faintly. 'What the hell are you doing here?'

Lorcan Connolly stuck his hands in his coat pockets and looked her dead in the eye.

'Hi to you too,' he said with a wry half-smile. 'Is that *really* any way to greet your husband?'

21

Gracie drew back and Lorcan stepped inside the flat. Her heart skipped several beats as she closed the door. *Not a good sign.* She didn't want to react to him at all. They'd been apart for five years; all those feelings should have been dead and gone by now.

But . . . she sneaked a peek at him as he moved from the hall into the lounge . . . he was still so damned good-looking. Dark, neatly trimmed hair, strong face, sharp suit. That black coat was cashmere, she could tell, and snowflakes were melting on his shoulders in the fuggy warmth of the flat. She caught a whiff of his aftershave as he passed by, something new – sharp and lemony with an undertone of sandalwood.

Lorcan Connolly.

Her husband.

Who – incidentally – had just petitioned to divorce her.

That thought made Gracie snap back to attention. That, and Lorcan's next words as he turned and looked at her with

117

unfriendly eyes. 'So. Come on, Gracie, tell me now. Where the fuck is he?'

'What?' Gracie was half afraid that her tongue had been hanging out, but now she straightened, focused. All right, the shock of seeing him after five long years of silence and distance was considerable; but she had to get over it, compose herself. After all, *he* certainly didn't look fazed by seeing *her*.

Lorcan Connolly wanted rid of her. Fine. If that was how he wanted it, then that was how it would be. And she wasn't going to relive the past by behaving like a star-struck teenager around him. She had more dignity than that.

She reminded herself sternly that she was a good game player, she could bluff for England. She could be cool. In poker – and she was an expert at poker – you didn't play the hand of cards you'd been dealt, you played your opponent. You read his reactions, his 'tells' – the movements or gestures he unconsciously made that gave away his thoughts. She had a *great* poker face. She could do this.

'George,' said Lorcan impatiently. 'He hasn't turned in for work yet again, so where is he? Jesus.' He was looking disgustedly around at the unmade-up sofa bed with its crumpled sheets, the dusty surfaces, the clutter. 'It's a tip in here.'

Gracie tried to get her head around what he'd just said. 'George has been working for you?'

'Yeah, as a dealer. Didn't your mother tell you?'

'She hasn't mentioned it, no.'

He swung round and looked at her. 'And what are you doing down here? I thought your time was fully occupied in Manchester. How *is* the business, by the way?'

'Fine,' snapped Gracie, and went into the kitchen before she forgot about playing it cool and lamped him.

What the hell was he talking to her like that for?

She rummaged in the cupboards and found a packet of cheap-brand tea bags amid the jumble and spills and out-of-date goods. 'I'm having tea, you want one?' she called through.

And I hope it chokes you.

'Yeah, go on.'

She looked in the fridge. There was milk there, but she took a quick sniff, pulled a face and dumped the glutinous white mass into the sink. She looked in the cupboard again. A tub of instant milk powder, which would have to do.

'You haven't answered,' said Lorcan, coming into the kitchen.

It was too small in here. There wasn't room for a six-foot-four-inch man *and* a six-foot woman. They manoeuvred around each other with inches to spare. Or at least *Gracie* manoeuvred. Lorcan just leaned against the worktop like a wall of stone and watched while she made the tea. She could feel herself getting hot, could feel her face flushing with embarrassment.

'I didn't realize answering was compulsory,' she said, stirring with a vengeance. 'And while we're on the subject of questions, I've got one for you.'

She dumped the tea bags on the sink top – the bin was overflowing – and thrust a mug towards him.

'Thanks,' he said, taking it. 'All right, shoot. What's the question?'

Gracie swept past him, clutching her mug of tea, and went into the lounge. She turned and stared at him as he followed her. *Fuck* it. He was still seriously gorgeous.

'Why now with the divorce papers?' she asked flatly.

'Why now?' He put his mug down on the dusty coffee table. 'You really want to know the answer to that? Okay,

I'll tell you. George has been letting me down for weeks, throwing sickies, rolling in late. Some of the boys have said he has something else going, some little sideline that pays better. You know George, he never could keep his mouth shut. But I gave him a job because he was your brother, Gracie. You ran out on me, but I believe in loyalty so I thought, hey, he's her brother, I'll keep him on. And now *he's* playing silly buggers too.'

Gracie opened her mouth to say something cutting, she didn't know what.

She ran out on *him?* The bastard, how could he say that? She was getting angry, forgetting she had to be cool. But then – this had been the pattern of their lives together, hadn't it. She remembered it oh so well. Tearing lumps out of each other during screaming rows. Ripping each other's clothes off during frantic making-up sessions. And in the end it had all come to nothing. Nothing at all.

'So I came here today to tell him to fuck off,' Lorcan went on, glaring at her. 'The whole Doyle family's a nightmare, so I thought, sod it, I'm firing George's arse. And then I started thinking, why not make the whole thing neat and tidy? It's been five years since we last communicated, and *that* was just you shouting down the phone at me that you'd had enough and our marriage was over. I'm cutting ties with your brother, and I guess it seems like a good time to cut ties with you, too.'

Gracie shut her mouth like a clamp. Then she opened it again, and said: 'George is in hospital.'

'He's . . . you *what?*'

'In hospital. In intensive care.'

Lorcan paused for a beat, staring at her face. 'What happened?'

'Someone did him over. Mum found him unconscious outside her place.'

'What's the damage?'

'What, you mean you care?'

'Hey, don't start getting all antsy with me,' said Lorcan sharply. 'I like George. I always have. All the staff like him, too. What I don't like is him taking the piss.'

Gracie sipped her tea. She knew he had a point; George had always been a lovable rascal, pushing his luck in every possible direction. Now, it looked like maybe he'd pushed his luck too far.

'Which hospital?' asked Lorcan.

Gracie told him.

'You have any idea what happened?' he asked.

'How would I? The first I knew of any of this was when the police pitched up at work and broke the news.'

'I didn't think you had anything to do with your family down here.'

'I didn't. But Christ, Lorcan. I'm not made of wood.'

Lorcan looked at her. 'Really?'

She wasn't going to rise to it. She gritted her teeth, forcing herself not to. She was cool, controlled Gracie Doyle, wasn't she? She held on to that. Lorcan was fiery, passionate, impatient, given to grand gestures and not afraid of angry scenes. He came from a huge extended family in Donegal, a family who hugged and kissed and enveloped each other in a comforting blanket of warmth. Consequently he was expansive, confident, chatty and charming. Her upbringing had been completely different; she'd realized early on that her mother wished she'd been a boy, not a girl, and she had retreated into wary coldness to protect herself from further hurt.

'Lorcan – this is George we're talking about.' Gracie blinked hard, feeling that choking edge of tears. 'They're saying it could go either way. We were there last night, and his heart stopped. They got him stabilized, but . . .' She shrugged.

'As bad as that?'

'Yeah.' Gracie took another sip at her tea. It was too hot, almost scalding her lips, but she barely noticed. She wasn't going to cry in front of Lorcan Connolly, and she was having to concentrate hard to stop herself from doing that.

'So why come here, to the flat? Thought you'd be staying at your mother's.' He turned away to stare out of the dirty window at the busy main road.

Gracie looked at his broad back and almost, *almost* poured it all out then. The fire at the casino. Harry missing. The bags of hair. Those horrible notes. Instead she said: 'It's okay, Lorcan. I can manage perfectly well. I don't want your help or anything. I'm used to managing alone, I've had a lot of practice.'

Lorcan turned, and instead of the sharp retort she expected he said: 'Your car's not a silver Merc, is it?'

'What?'

'Sports job?'

'Yeah. It is.' Gracie quickly joined him at the window.

'Only I think someone's down there doing something to it . . .'

They got down the stairs, out the front door and raced over to the Merc. They looked up and down the road, but there was no one about. Whoever had done it had gone. Moving around her lovely car, Gracie stooped and gawped in horror at the damage. All four tyres had been slashed through and the beautiful sleek Mercedes was lying there in the gutter like a diva with her legs cut off.

'Oh *shit*,' she wailed out loud.

I'm watching you, Red.

Gracie looked up and down the road again. Someone *was* watching her; that much was obvious. The very idea gave her the creeps. And her car, her beautiful car . . .

Lorcan was stooping down too, looking at the tyres and then up at Gracie. He frowned.

'What?' she snapped.

'Someone doesn't like you,' he said.

'Talk about stating the bleeding obvious.'

Lorcan was staring at her face, his expression thoughtful. He walked around to the front of the car. 'Is this to do with George?' he asked her.

Gracie sighed and said nothing. She didn't want to talk to him. She didn't *trust* herself around him. She could manage alone, hadn't she just told him that? And she could. She would lock up the flat, take the tube back to Suze's place, arrange for a garage to collect the Mercedes, then think about what she would do next.

'Gracie?' prompted Lorcan when she didn't speak.

'I don't know, okay?' she said angrily.

He was staring at the windscreen. 'Come and look at this.'

All Gracie wanted to do was get away from him. Impatiently she joined him at the front of the car and looked where he was looking. Her mouth dropped open.

YORE DEAD

Someone had sprayed the message on to her windscreen with black paint.

'Well,' said Lorcan after a beat. 'They can't spell, but even so it's not exactly a message of friendly intent, is it?'

Gracie could only stare, feeling sick and afraid.

Whoever had tormented her with fire and bags of hair in Manchester now knew she was here, in London. She felt, amid the fear, a spasm of anger. The bunch of long-estranged fuck-ups she called family had royally pissed off someone – so badly that this 'someone' had deemed it appropriate to travel north and inflict harm on her there before following her south and wrecking her car.

Lorcan got out a key. There was a chirp and a flash of tail-lights from the black BMW across the road. He looked at Gracie, frowning. 'Drop you somewhere?' he offered.

'No thanks,' said Gracie, and walked away from him, back into the flat to lock up.

22

22 December

When Gracie got back to her mum's place, there was a slight, pale-skinned girl with long, glossy, ash-blonde hair sitting at the kitchen table with Suze, drinking tea. Both looked up as Gracie came in but neither smiled.

'Hi,' said Gracie, sore of foot and heavy of heart. She'd phoned the garage to get her precious, beautiful car towed and the tyres replaced, and they 'couldn't say' how long all this was going to take; they would phone her to let her know when she could collect it.

'But I need my car,' she'd protested.

'Lady,' said the mechanic at the end of the phone, 'have a heart, will you? We're up to our arses here, and it's Christmas. Lighten up.'

Then she'd schlepped from George and Harry's flat over to where Cuthill, the private landlord, lived. Paid the miserable bastard, got a receipt for her money. By the time that was accomplished, it was mid-afternoon, and getting dark.

She'd caught the tube, passing a Santa strumming a banjo down there in the depths, his small black dog wearing reindeer horns; then she'd walked until her feet throbbed, and pitched up back at home.

Home.

Well, once it had been that. Years ago. Now it was a strange place, filled with strange people.

'This is Sandy Cole,' said Suze.

'We spoke on the phone,' said the girl, in that same high, almost childlike voice. She got to her feet and held out a hand. 'You're Gracie, right?'

Gracie shook hands briefly and sat down. She was tired. Worried about her brothers and her business. Unsure of her feelings after seeing Lorcan again after such a long time. She wanted to grab a hot shower in her own beautiful flat, to sit on her own big couch and eat supper in front of the telly. She wanted everything back the way it was, normal. What she *didn't* want was to be here, feeling her mother's hostile gaze upon her, having to make conversation with a stranger.

'I told Sandy about what happened with George last night,' said Suze.

The smile dropped from Sandy's face. 'It's awful.' Her eyes filled up with tears. 'My poor George.'

'So you and he are quite an item,' said Gracie, thinking that it would have been better if her mother had spared Sandy the grim details. What would it gain, distressing the poor cow even more than she already was?

Sandy nodded and sat down when Gracie did. 'George proposed to me,' she sniffed. 'We're in love. Look.'

She extended her bony little left hand and showed Gracie the ring on the index finger; it was a clear stone the size of a pinhead, possibly a diamond, set on a thin band of what looked like white gold.

'He didn't say a word about it,' complained Suze. 'You'd think he would, now wouldn't you? But then, I don't suppose I matter, do I? I'm just his mother, after all.'

'Oh, I'm sure George would have told you soon,' said Sandy, clearly anxious not to offend. 'It was a whirlwind romance. We'd have been having an engagement party very soon. George promised. And then this happened, and now he's in hospital . . .' Her voice tailed off. She looked down at the table.

'He's tough. He'll be fine,' said Gracie, feeling sorry for the girl.

Suze gave Gracie a sour look. 'Easy to say, when you don't care.'

Gracie had to grit her teeth to keep back the angry words that threatened to come out at that. 'I wouldn't have driven down from Manchester if I didn't care,' she said instead.

'It's so awful,' said Sandy, filling up all over again.

'You going in to see him tonight?' asked Gracie.

'Yeah.' Sandy had the tissues out, mopping at her eyes.

'I might tag along. If you don't mind?'

'God no. I don't mind. I'd like the company.'

'Right.' Gracie stood up. 'I'm going up to get showered and changed.'

'How'd you get on over at the flat?' asked Suze. 'You fetch George's things? Bet it's a mess.'

'Yeah, I got his things. And it is a mess,' said Gracie. 'We'll get a cleaner in, get it smartened up for when George gets out.'

'*If* he does,' said Suze darkly.

'Unless you fancy getting your hands dirty?' Gracie couldn't resist that. She knew she should have, but she just couldn't. Suze had never been a housework fiend. Her nails were French manicured even now. She just glared at Gracie. And was that *really* going to help poor bloody Sandy, hearing Suze say *if he does*?

She left them to it, went on upstairs and into her old room. It was strange, being back in here. It seemed smaller. The decor had changed, and the bed linen was floral lavender – not her sort of colour choice, but it was clean, and neat. She kicked off her shoes, took off her blouse and was rummaging in her open suitcase for clean underclothes when someone tapped at the door and opened it immediately. Expecting Suze to start in on round two, Gracie was startled to see Claude standing there in the open doorway, with his eyes fastened to her front as usual. And to her intense irritation she realized that her bra was skimpy; there was a lot of her front to see.

'Oh – sorry,' he said, and gave a sheepish grin.

Gracie had had enough. The damage to her casino and then her car. The anxiety about George and Harry. Seeing Lorcan again. She felt suddenly as if her brain was about to implode with the stress of it all. And now, *this*. She stood there as if carved from stone and said: 'You will be if you come in that fucking door unannounced again, arsehole. You got that?'

He looked startled. 'Suze asked me to come up and see if you wanted something to eat, that's all,' he said, the grin vanishing, guilty colour rising on his florid cheeks.

'No. I bloody well don't.' She'd grab something at the hospital, fuck this place. She took three swift strides across the room, fury sending the blood buzzing in her ears, and shoved Claude out on to the landing. His face was an almost comical mixture of shock, arousal and awkwardness. 'Mother!' Gracie yelled full volume down the stairs.

Claude was edging away from her now and making *don't do that* gestures. But Gracie was only just getting up a full head of steam.

Suze poked her head out around the kitchen door. She gawped up at Gracie standing there on the top landing in her bra and skirt, and at Claude there beside her.

'Hey, Mum – tell your *fucking* boyfriend to keep out of my room. He comes in here again without an invitation, I'm going to cut his nads off and stuff them down his bloody *throat*, okay?'

Gracie went back into her room and slammed the door shut. She faintly heard Claude saying *I don't know what she's talking about*, and Suze shouting something from the bottom of the stairs. Gracie took a chair and jammed it under the door handle. Then she started, once again, to get washed and changed.

This time she was interrupted by her mobile. She picked up. Down in the hall, the shouting was escalating. *Well good*, she thought. *Better she knows what he's like*.

'Hi Gracie, it's me. Brynn.'

Gracie sat down on the bed. 'Hey, Brynn. How you feeling now?'

'Better.'

'That's good to hear.'

'Yeah, but Gracie, there's other stuff, I thought I'd better give you a call, let you know what's been going on.'

'How're the staff? You've been in touch with them?'

'Sure, sure. They're on full pay, for now. Hope that's okay.'

'For now, yes. Of course we don't know how long the repairs are going to take.'

'The police and insurance people weren't too keen on you shooting off so soon after the fire,' said Brynn.

'Yeah, but the police *knew* I had family trouble.'

'Even so, they weren't happy.'

Gracie was getting a horrible sinking feeling about this call. She thought of the bag of hair, *smoke getting in your eyes . . .?*

'I'm not sure the insurance will pay up,' said Brynn. 'I'm sorry to piss on your parade, Gracie, but they're talking about arson.'

Gracie stood there, feeling her orderly, safe little world crashing around her. *Smoke getting in your eyes?* 'They got any proof of that?'

'They said there're traces of an accelerant having been used to start the fire. You know I thought it might be electrical? The electrics were fine.' Brynn's sigh was audible down the line. 'Look, they've told me it'll be another couple of days for the police forensics team to finish combing the site for evidence, then four *more* days before the insurers get anywhere near being satisfied, and personally I don't see much hope of that . . . then the clearing-up can begin. It's going to be *weeks*. And Gracie, our own inside security system showed someone hanging about outside the building. Which ties in with the CCTV footage out in the road. Sorry, Gracie. It looks like the fire was started deliberately.'

Gracie was silent.

'And there's more,' said Brynn. 'The police were quizzing me about your finances; they were thinking maybe you'd started it.'

'Me?' Gracie blurted.

'They were asking if you had money troubles.'

'They asked me the same thing. Fuck *me*,' said Gracie angrily.

'Gracie – you haven't, have you?'

'I don't know how you can even ask me that,' said Gracie in exasperation. 'You've seen the books. You know we're well in the black.'

'Yeah, but personal stuff,' said Brynn, sounding uncomfortable. 'You know, personal debts . . .?'

Gracie stared hard at the phone. Brynn was asking about her expensive apartment, her car, her high-end holidays.

'For fuck's sake, Brynn, you know the wage I draw from the business. You know I have a budget. You know I'm not careless with money. I take money *off* the punters. I don't gamble myself.'

'I know that . . .'

'Look, I'm not in financial trouble, Brynn. I pay all my bills on time; I clear my credit cards at the end of every month.'

'Hey, don't shoot the messenger, Gracie. I'm trying to prepare you, that's all. For sure they'll want to speak to you in the New Year, and these are the things they'll be asking you about.'

Oh terrific.

This was just getting better and better.

George and Harry

NOVEMBER

23

It was another black-tie do. Harry arrived slightly early at Jackie Sullivan – aka 'the cougar's' – gaff in Notting Hill. She opened the door to him, wearing a different halter-necked maxi-length dress – white this time, not the old funereal black – and she still looked endearingly awkward and over-dressed. Her pale eyes were nervous as she smiled up at him.

'Goodness, don't you look gorgeous,' she said.

'So do you,' said Harry.

'And you're such a marvellous liar,' she smiled.

'I'm not lying,' said Harry, and he wasn't. She had the sweetest face and he was pleased to be here with her again. 'Do you think we'll make it this time?' he asked, stepping into the big lemon-yellow hallway with its myriad prints and antiques.

'Oh, to the . . .' Jackie paused, blushing – remembering, Harry knew, what had happened on their last date. The tears, the outpouring of grief over her husband; and then the night, the hugs and kisses and the surprisingly satisfactory sex.

'Sorry,' said Harry, seeing that he'd embarrassed her.

Jackie bit her lip. 'No, *I'm* sorry,' she said quickly. 'I'm so sorry that I as good as ignored you when we bumped into each other in Covent Garden. I felt awful about that afterwards, but I was with a client, and I was just so surprised to see you – all I could think to say was that you were a friend of Emma's.'

'Well, I'm a friend of *yours*, so I think I can stretch to Emma too – even if I didn't meet her at uni.' Harry hadn't been to university. He hadn't been *anywhere*. He'd left a pretty useless school at 16 without any qualifications, got a couple of dead-end jobs and wound up on the dole. Being an escort and actually earning well was the pinnacle of his achievements so far.

'My mind just went blank,' said Jackie.

'It's okay. Not a problem. You ready to go?'

Jackie paused. Checked she had her wrap, her tiny sequinned evening bag. Glanced back at the photos on the console table. Her husband; her daughter. Harry wondered if she was going to start crying again. But Jackie turned to him with a smile.

'Yes, I'm ready,' she said.

24

'So how's it going, Lefty?' asked Deano.

Lefty was in the back room behind the fetish club, summoned there by Deano Drax. This room was all business – desk, filing cabinets, cold steel and big mirrors – in complete contrast to the hot reds and golds and dim lighting out in the club itself. The pounding beat of the club's sound system was thrumming through the walls and into the body of the office, keeping pace with Lefty's rapidly accelerating heartbeat.

There was a boy who looked about fourteen years old sitting on Deano's desk. Deano's hand was resting on the boy's denim-clad thigh, smoothing over it caressingly. The boy was slim, dark-haired and blank-eyed. There was a dusting of white powder under his nose. He was sipping from a bottle of Bud.

Underage drinking popped into Lefty's addled brain. And that sure wasn't *talcum* powder on the kid's upper lip, now was it? But Lefty thought that both those things were the least of this kid's worries, if he was in Deano's hands. Lefty had the horrible queasy feeling that Deano's dick had been out of his trousers just a second before he came in the room.

Lefty's mouth seemed to have dried of all spit. He swallowed hard, came up empty.

'Only,' Deano went on, 'you been days looking for my boy Alfie now, and I said I'd give you some time. But there's a limit. You do *remember* I said that, don't you?'

'I remember, Deano,' said Lefty, gulping hard. 'And I'll find him. Don't you worry about that.'

'Oh, I ain't worried, Lefty. I got every faith in you. But time's moving on.'

Lefty saw Deano's hand wandering ever further up the boy's thigh. Oh *shit*. He had to look away. One thing turned his stomach, it was noncing.

'Only so far you ain't been doing too good, Lefty,' went on Deano. 'You been letting me down. Way you've been going on, if I asked you to post me a pair of bollocks, I'd end up with a set of tits, that's my feeling.'

The boy smiled vaguely at Deano's piercing wit. Lefty raised a wilted, trembling smile.

'I'm gonna find him, Deano. I swear to you on my mother's life.'

'Yeah?' Deano smiled too. The boy leaned over and tenderly held the bottle to Deano's lips. Deano sipped the ice-cold beer and the boy smiled. Then Deano looked straight at Lefty. 'I'm gonna hold you to that, Lefty. Your mother's life. Or yours. I don't care which. Okay?'

Lefty nodded. He couldn't speak; he was so frightened he was afraid he was going to piss himself. His mother, his sweet dear mother, lived over in Brixton, and he wondered if Deano knew that. He thought that Deano probably did. Deano knew *everything*.

'Now fuck off,' said Deano.

Lefty hurried from the room.

The boy leaned in close to Deano, who looked at him assessingly. He was a pretty thing, but he wasn't little-blond-angel Alfie. It was Alfie Deano craved – for now, anyway. It was Alfie he wanted, Alfie he loved, Alfie he was completely obsessed with. He missed him so much; he *had* to get him back again.

'Who's this you got him out lookin' for?' whined the dark-haired boy.

Deano smoothed a hand over the youngster's hair. Suddenly he grabbed a handful. The boy let out a yelp of surprise. Deano yanked him off the desk by his hair and threw him to the floor. The bottle went flying, spraying beer and the scent of hops. The boy lay there, clutching his head, the brown liquid seeping in and staining his t-shirt. He stared up with eyes full of tears and fear at Deano, who hadn't even moved out of his chair.

'Now don't you go getting jealous on me, babycakes,' said Deano. He wagged a finger at the boy. 'Papa don't like that. And you don't ever ask me about my business, you understand?'

The boy nodded, crying and gulping with shock and pain.

'Now don't cry, sweetness. Papa loves you,' crooned Deano. 'Come up here and sit on Papa's lap . . .'

Outside in the club, Lefty picked his way between the rubber-encased women and crawling, chain-locked muscle men. He went over to the bar and asked Chippy for a whisky, then spotted Mona, gyrating on her podium in her thong, with her heavily augmented naked tits swinging about like twin pendulums. He grabbed his drink and went on over there.

'Hi sweetie, is that make-up?' asked a stoned-looking blonde wearing nothing but a transparent blue gauze, lurching up to him and fingering his head wound.

Lefty pushed her roughly aside. Pervs. He hated fucking pervs. Worst of all, he hated the perv who ran this place. He pushed his way through the aimlessly milling people, the music crashing in on his ears and roaring around his pounding head; it was deafening. He reached Mona's podium and grabbed her leg.

'If you can't afford the goods, don't handle 'em,' she shouted. Then she looked down and saw who it was and her movements faltered to a halt. 'Oh for fuck's *sake* . . .'

'What time you get off tonight, girl?' Lefty demanded, swigging back the whisky, thinking that he was in hell here, deep in the bowels of hell, and he needed his next fix so bad, and what about his mum, his poor old mum over in Brixton? Had Deano meant that, could Deano target his mum if this didn't work out?

Lefty thought that Deano probably could. And *would*. Lefty knew he was well and truly in the shit, and he couldn't even warn his mum because if he told her what was going on in his life she would go mad, she would swipe him upside the head with her meaty fist and say, *You no-good little asshole, you are* exactly *like your waster of a father,* and he didn't want to hear that from her. He loved his mum; it hurt when she was angry with him. He cringed at the thought, because maybe she was right, maybe he really was just as bad as dear old dad, who'd done a bunk way back when Lefty was ten. His dad had smoked ganja and never worked. Now . . . now Lefty sniffed butane and, although he worked, what he did wasn't something to be proud of. He knew it. But it was his life; it was all he had. He didn't want to have to go south of the river and tell his mum he'd brought trouble to her door, no way. Desperation gripped him now. He needed to get a result. And for that, he needed Mona.

'I get off at twelve,' hollered Mona.

Lefty rummaged in his pocket and came up with a twenty. He stuffed it roughly into Mona's G-string. 'We got work to do,' said Lefty.

'*Fuck* it,' said Mona. 'No, Lefty—'

'You give me any more lip and I'll fuck *you*,' said Lefty. 'Take you down the dungeon room and give you what-for.'

Mona stiffened and missed her step. She'd *seen* the dungeon room under the club. She hated going in there – although she had entertained a couple of punters down there in a dark corner, just cash-in-hand quickies, she was always in a rush to get straight out of there, as fast as she could. And Lefty meant it. She looked into his half-crazed eyes and she just *knew* he did.

'Okay, okay,' sighed Mona, and danced on.

25

'Pick a card,' said George. 'Any card.'

Alfie smiled and rolled his eyes. He was sprawled out on George's bed while George sat at the computer, ostensibly taking escort bookings but in fact getting a little bored with that and shuffling a deck of cards instead.

George and his tricks.

But Alfie obediently selected a card.

'Seven of hearts, right?' said George.

'How do you *do* that?' It was the seven of hearts.

'Years of practice, my boy,' said George, flicking through the cards with eye-watering speed. 'We'll go down the caff in a sec, okay? I'll tidy this little lot away and then we'll get a fry-up down us. Yes?'

Alfie nodded happily. This was their ritual. Harry went out about his business in the mornings, while George caught up with the escort biz; then George and Alfie went off down the caff. Sometimes Harry joined them there, sometimes not. Alfie loved being here with George and Harry. 'You going in to work tonight?' he asked.

George nodded. Yeah, he'd better show willing, he supposed. 'You be okay here on your own?'

He still didn't like leaving Alfie in the flat alone. He was sort of afraid that one night he was going to come back and find that Alfie had fled back to wherever he had come from. Cleared out his stash and maybe Harry's too – even though Alfie had never shown himself to be light-fingered, he would need money, of course he would – and gone. And if that happened, George would be very worried. Alfie needed support, needed his friends around him. At nights . . . oh and it broke George's heart . . . sometimes at night Alfie had terrible nightmares, and he would wake crying and George would have to hug him, reassure him. If he wasn't there to do that for Alfie, who would? Poor little bastard.

If Alfie went . . . well, George admitted to himself that he would in fact be *more* than worried. He would be very sad, too. He was getting used to having cheery, sweet little Alfie around the place, and he would miss him if he was gone.

'Won't Harry be here tonight?' asked Alfie, cutting through his thoughts.

'Nope. Harry's got a job on.'

'Escorting?'

'You got it.'

'Not the cougar again?'

'I'm going to have to watch you,' said George with a wink and a grin. 'You're getting good.'

'What's going *on* with those two?'

George shrugged. Jackie Sullivan had called on Harry's services four times in the last two weeks. He had jokily asked Harry about it, said what was she, insatiable or something? But Harry was close-mouthed about it. Just said she needed an escort, she was a nice lady, she felt safe with him, was that okay? Did George have a *problem* with that? George said he had no problem at all, he just hoped that Harry wasn't falling in love with the daft old mare.

'Don't call her that,' snapped Harry, and blushed.

George took the hint and dropped it. Harry was all grown up, after all. And anyway, George had his own clients to contend with, *plus* he was trying to keep Lorcan sweet by pitching in to work on the odd occasion: no sense taking the piss *too* much.

George put the pack of cards in his pocket, answered a couple of emails, and switched off the computer.

'Okay, boy, let's get some meat down us,' he said, and Alfie jumped off the bed like an excited pet poodle when its owner says 'walkies'.

He *loved* being with George.

Harry was across town, having breakfast with Jackie Sullivan in her kitchen; croissants and good fresh strong black coffee. Several times a week now he popped in to see Jackie. It wasn't work, and for God's sake of course he wasn't going to charge her for it, that wasn't even mentioned. He just came to see her because . . . oh fuck it, he just liked to see her.

They were friends.

They sat at the table and chatted and ate. She told him what projects she was working on, showed him stuff from her daughter Emma who worked in PR in Hong Kong, asked him what he was doing with himself . . . hours passed, they just flew.

They *had* been lovers, but that was never mentioned or even hinted at any more. Harry knew that she was embarrassed by what had happened between them on the first night they met, and he was diplomatic enough never to bring it up in the course of conversation.

Harry was a little puzzled over exactly why he so enjoyed this woman's company. Was she some sort of mother substitute? Suze wasn't anyone's idea of 'parent of the year', so maybe it was that? But he doubted it. He had just clicked with Jackie; he *liked* her. There was no sexual spark there, not really, although there was a definite connection. Their sleeping together had been a one-off, an aberration, not to be repeated. Neither of them wanted that.

'Can you come over for dinner on Friday night?' asked Jackie, pouring him more coffee.

'What's the occasion?' asked Harry. He'd escorted her to various parties now, and he was getting used to it all. But by now they'd developed a code. When she said, 'Can I book you', that meant work. When she said, 'Come over', she meant as a friend.

Jackie beamed at him, her pale eyes lighting up. 'It's so exciting,' she said, almost hugging herself with glee.

Harry looked at her and remembered the woman he had first seen weeks ago, shivering with nerves and wrecked with grief. Jackie'd come a long way since they'd first met, and he thought that maybe he'd been instrumental in helping her get over the intensity of her loss. He hoped so. He liked to see this big smile on her face; he loved to see her so animated, so happy.

'Well come on,' he said, grinning himself now. Her joy was infectious. 'Spill the beans.'

'It's Emma. She's coming home, and I want you to meet her.'

Harry felt the smile freeze on his face.

'Oh,' he said flatly.

'What do you mean, "oh"?' asked Jackie, half laughing, delighted with her news and wondering why he wasn't instantly delighted too. 'Isn't it marvellous? She's only back for a fortnight, of course, but isn't it wonderful?'

'Yeah,' said Harry. He put down his coffee cup. 'Yeah, it is wonderful, but . . . Jackie, I can't meet her.'

Jackie stared at him. 'Why not?' she asked.

'Why *not*?' Harry gave a short bark of laughter. 'Jackie. I'm an escort. I've been squiring you around town for money. Do you honestly think your daughter is going to understand that? Much less actually *like* it?'

'Well . . .' Jackie shrugged her shoulders. 'All right, we won't tell her that's what you do.'

'Then what *will* we tell her? The same lies you've been telling all your friends and colleagues? That I'm an architect or some damned thing? What about that woman in Covent Garden? She thinks I'm a friend of Emma's from uni. Jackie . . . this is all going to get too tangled. Too bloody *messy.*'

Jackie's smile had faded while he spoke. 'But . . . I'd love you to meet her.'

'I know, sweetheart, I know.' Harry looked awkward. 'But think about it. It won't work. The escorting . . . well, that's business. But meeting Emma, that makes it something else. I'm very fond of you, but I don't want to get into this, lying all the time, I really hate it.'

Jackie looked stricken now. 'I didn't know you felt like that.'

'I just don't want to blur the lines, that's all,' said Harry.

'But haven't we already done that? You come and eat breakfast with me. Would you feel better about that if you charged me for your time . . .?'

'No. Of course not.'

'I'd just like you to meet Emma, that's all.'

Harry stood up. 'Jackie, no. It's not going to happen.'

Jackie stood up too, her eyes hurt, her mouth trembling. 'You'll still escort me tonight?' she asked, not looking at his face.

'Yes.'

'Because that's business. Because you're being *paid*.' Now her eyes flicked up to his face. She was looking at him with dislike. 'Okay. So what if I pay you for next Friday? Book your services?'

'Then I'd have to turn down the booking,' said Harry. 'I'm sorry.'

Jackie snatched up the cups and turned away, crashing them into the sink.

'I'd better go,' said Harry unhappily.

She didn't answer. Didn't even turn around.

Harry left.

26

'We're wasting our fucking time here. Don't you think, Lefty?'

Mona was still living up to her name, going on and on again about she was tired, she was usually in bed by this hour, her mum would complain because she was babysitting and she would want to get on home. They were looking for the proverbial needle in a haystack, why wouldn't he see sense?

'Will you shut the fuck *up*,' snapped Lefty, taking a long, sweet hit from his can of butane and instantly feeling slightly calmer; better.

Mona was watching him with distaste. 'You are gonna *kill* yourself with that crap,' she warned.

'This rate, I'm gonna kill you first,' he muttered, wondering if Gordy really was as smart as all that; he'd told Lefty to bring along Mona with the sweet face, but Mona didn't have a sweet mouth to match.

They were standing outside Canary Wharf tube station. They'd been down there, talking to staff, buskers, to anyone they could lay hands on – but no good. They came up on to the street and it was as dark as your armpit now, sleety rain in the air, a little slush underfoot. Traffic zipping past. Christmas lights twinkling. It was bitingly, toe-numbingly cold.

Lefty was flagging down cabs, saying, *You seen a big dark-haired geezer with a little blond boy a few nights back?* He was spelling it out for them. The time, the *exact* location, asking one after another, and he was getting so bloody desperate now. He'd tried so many of the London cabbies. They'd swerve hopefully into the kerb, thinking he was a fare, and then he'd start in with the questions.

You see a big chunky guy, dark-haired, with a slim blond boy the other night?

He must have pulled over a *dozen*, thought Mona, before *it* happened.

It was something that later she couldn't even bear to think about. The night was crawling on, and the traffic was thin now; it was gone two in the morning.

'Let's pack it in, Lefty,' she told him. Her ma was going to give her a lot of grief over this, she knew it. She'd phoned earlier, said she'd be late.

'*How* late?' Ma had demanded to know.

It was a question Mona couldn't answer. Ma had every right to be upset about it; this wasn't the first time it had happened, after all.

'We're not going to find a damned thing tonight,' whined Mona.

But one more cab was approaching, its orange light glowing through the frost-misted air. Lefty flapped his hands and it pulled over. The driver looked young, pale – maybe Polish – and he didn't seem to understand what Lefty was saying to him.

'You see this guy, big guy, dark hair, and a boy, blond, the other night?'

The driver shrugged, bewildered. He'd expected a fare, not questions.

'You speaka de English?' snapped Lefty. He was nearly dancing from foot to foot, so extreme was his impatience and anxiety now.

Another shrug.

'You understand what I'm *sayin'* to you?'

The driver shrugged again. 'You want get in?' he asked, thinking that this was a fare, a normal fare, Mona would always remember that.

'No, you listen boy, I don't want to get in. I want you to think hard. You see a big man, dark hair, and a boy, a slim blond boy? You *think*, you understand me?'

'He doesn't understand what you're saying,' said Mona.

'Yeah he does.'

'No he *don't.*'

'I'm tellin' you he *does.*' Lefty's grin was vast and manic now with determination. He turned again to the driver.

Mona caught his arm.

His head whipped round.

Mona almost fell back. He looked *demented.*

She swallowed hard. 'Look, Lefty, this is no good,' she said, trying to sound reasonable, when what she *felt* was just plain desperate. She couldn't go on with this. Neither could he, why couldn't he see that? 'Give it up, for God's sake.'

Lefty grabbed her restraining hand. 'Fuck *off*, girly,' he snapped, and now he was trembling, jittering around on the pavement.

The driver started revving the engine, getting ready to go.

He didn't need trouble, and Lefty was starting to look very much like it.

'Boy,' said Lefty to him, 'what you doin' . . .?'

The cab started to roll slowly forward.

Lefty grabbed at it, swearing.

And then there was a knife in his hand and he was leaning in, furious, lunging at the cab driver's throat with it.

'You understand *this*, you motherfucker? Do you?'

Mona staggered back, found herself up against the wall of a building. Her eyes opened wide with horror.

The cab driver started screaming as Lefty lunged and lunged and lunged at him.

Blood spurted.

Mona couldn't believe what was happening. She could see blood pouring out down the side of the cab, blood that looked black in the hard glare of the streetlights. The cab driver went on screaming, shouting, and it seemed to Mona that it went on forever, that it would never stop . . . and then suddenly, shockingly, it did.

Oh shit.

She cowered back against the building, wanting to run away, wishing she could move, but she couldn't. All her strength had gone. If not for the wall of the building behind her, she would have collapsed on to the pavement.

Lefty was just standing there now, panting; he'd stopped plunging the knife into the man's throat, but Mona couldn't look away. She wanted to, but she couldn't. Lefty was standing there with the knife dripping blood on to the ground, the driver silent behind the wheel, his head thrown back, his neck a mess of gaping wounds.

Suddenly Mona leaned over and was sick. She heaved her guts up while Lefty looked back at her dispassionately. Then he opened the driver's door, stopped the engine, yanked on the handbrake, slammed the door shut. He came back to where she was and said, quite calmly: 'We gotta clean this up.'

Clean it up? What was he talking about, washing the fucking dishes?

A wild surge of hysteria welled up in Mona. He'd hacked a man to death, and now he was standing there calmly saying they had to *clean this up?* He was crazy. He really was.

Mona shivered and retched again. Nothing came up but bile. Oh shit, how had she got into this? She was walking the streets with a crazy man and now she had witnessed a murder.

'Come on, Mona. You gotta help me out with this here. We got to clear this mess away.'

Like the dead man – Mona was sure he was dead – was nothing at all; a piece of rubbish to be disposed of.

Now Lefty was opening the driver's door again.

'What the hell you *doing*?' Mona demanded, gasping, half sobbing with shock.

The light was on inside the cab now and, oh fuck, it was horrible in there. She couldn't tear her eyes away from it.

Lefty didn't answer. He was pushing the body over, out of his way. Then he straightened and looked at her. There was the black, slick sheen of blood on his hands. He paused, took a long pull on the butane, and Mona thought she was about to be sick again, just looking at him. She hated him, but now she was mortally afraid of him too. She had never seen anyone lose it as suddenly as that.

'Come on, get in the back. We gotta clear this away.'

Mona pushed herself away from the wall. 'No. I don't, I can't . . .' she said shakily.

'You get the fuck in here!' hissed Lefty.

Mona actually jumped. She staggered across to the cab and with a groan of despair she got into the back. There was blood everywhere in the front of the cab, she couldn't look. She shuddered and whimpered and crouched there, hugging herself, trying not even to glance at the dark, slumped form of the dead man.

Lefty started the engine, and drove.

He drove to the river; an abandoned cement works or something. There was no one about down there and it was dark and damned scary. Mona wished she was somewhere, anywhere else. This was any sane person's worst nightmare. She'd been party to a murder. Didn't that make her an accessory? She'd had one or two brushes with the law before, just a little soliciting, a little recreational drug use – but nothing like this. This was *heavy* shit. The worst.

Lefty parked up near the edge of the dock and got out of the car. Terrified at the thought of being left alone in here with a corpse, Mona flung open the door and scrambled out too. She stood there, looking at Lefty, with no idea what he was going to do. She'd seen him kill this poor bastard; maybe he was now going to do her too? There was no way she could stop him, that was for sure. But he was leaning back into the car, taking off the handbrake. Then he cranked the window open a notch and slammed the door shut.

'Come on, push,' he said.

Mona stood there, frozen with fear.

Lefty came right up to her so that Mona was confronted by his grey-black face, sheened with sweat, that big, stapled wound across his forehead. He looked like a monster. He *was* a monster.

'Come *on*,' he shouted in her face.

153

Mona followed him round to the back of the car on legs that felt like rubber. Lefty put his shoulder to the back of the car, and Mona leaned into it and gave a shove too. The car started to roll forward, crunching over gravel. They pushed. The car rolled, gaining speed . . . and then suddenly it dropped away from them, fell over the edge of the dock and into the inky waters below with a huge splash.

Mona looked around, but there was no one to hear, no one to see.

Lefty stared over the edge of the dock and watched the car bob there for long minutes, slowly filling with water. It turned lazily, like a turtle bathing in the surf, and tipped sideways. Then slowly, inch by inch, it sank. Great bubbles came up and exploded on to the surface as it went down. A mini-whirlpool sucked the bubbles down, and then suddenly the waters were still, closing over the car as if it had never existed.

Lefty turned to Mona. She could see his teeth flash in a grin.

She shuddered.

'Job done,' he said, and took another pull on the can.

Gracie

DECEMBER

27

Sandy and Gracie sat on either side of George's bed in intensive care. George's nurse had taken the pyjamas and dressing gown from Gracie, said thanks, and was now scooting around them, smiling briskly, checking monitors, reattaching tubes. To Gracie, George looked just the same as he had last night – seriously ill. Maybe terminally. But Sandy was nattering on to him, spouting any old crap, telling him about the weather, how much she was looking forward to having him back with her for Christmas, her day at work.

'You're in admin? What line of business?' asked Gracie, butting in because now she wished she hadn't come, she hated this place, the stink of the antiseptic, the sheer heat and confinement of it, seeing George laid out there like a living corpse. She was desperate for distraction.

'Dental supplies,' said Sandy brightly. 'Anything you want to know about amalgam, drill bits or sterilizing units, I'm

157

your girl. I know all the terminology. Medial, occlusal, distal. All that stuff.'

Gracie nodded. She thought that Sandy seemed very 'up' tonight, which she supposed was fair enough. These places took different people in all sorts of different ways: who was she to judge? If it helped Sandy to witter on while clutching George's hand like a lifeline, what could it hurt?

'I'm going to nip outside, get some coffee. You want some?' asked Gracie.

'No thanks.' Sandy barely took her eyes off George's face.

Gracie turned away gratefully and was out of the door with indecent haste. She went out into the corridor and walked smack into Lorcan Connolly.

'What are you doing here?' she asked as he grabbed her arms to prevent a violent mid-corridor collision.

Gracie irritably shrugged herself free. Looked at him. God, still so good-looking, so imposing, so . . . *stop it, Gracie. Forget it. It didn't work then and it won't work now.*

'I came to see George,' said Lorcan.

'He's just the same,' said Gracie, fumbling in her bag for change. 'Jesus, it's red-hot in here.'

She went over to the vending machine and got a coffee, then came back to where he was now sitting. She sat down as well, not too close, sipping at the coffee, which was vile.

'They probably won't let you in anyway,' said Gracie. 'Near-relatives only.'

'I am a near-relative,' said Lorcan calmly. 'I'm his brother-in-law.'

Gracie gave him a scathing look. 'For now,' she said.

Lorcan sat back and folded his arms, his eyes on her face.

'Yeah, when *are* you going to get those papers signed and back to the courts?'

'As soon as I can,' said Gracie coldly. 'But they're in Manchester, and I'm in London, so no can do. Not yet, anyway. As you can see, I have *slightly* more important things on my mind. Why, you got some other poor cow lined up?'

Now he was smiling. 'Charming as ever,' he said.

'Hey – *you* sent the divorce papers.'

'So you think I must have someone standing in the wings, ready to hop into the marital bed the minute you vacate it?'

Gracie blew on the coffee and sipped it. It was displacement activity, but she needed it right at that moment, because what had just sprung into her mind was a vision of her and Lorcan in bed together. And *why* had she said the papers were in Manchester? She had them right here, in her bag. She'd stuffed them in there with the Jiffy bag of hair and the rest of the post, meaning to sort it all out later.

'Actually,' said Gracie. 'Just a small point, but an important one I think you'll agree – I vacated that damned bed five years ago. You could have filed after two, you know. Irreconcilable differences. Which pretty much fits the bill, wouldn't you say?'

'Yeah, I would. So why didn't *you* file?' returned Lorcan sweetly.

It was a good question. And Gracie knew the answer; she hadn't filed because the whole thing had been too painful even to think about. She'd loved him so much; but life – well, work – had intruded, pulled them apart. They'd been unable to find a compromise, and it had destroyed their marriage.

She shrugged. Kept her face blank. 'Too busy, I suppose.'

'Oh yeah. Gracie the dedicated career woman.'

'That's what I am,' said Gracie.

'Yeah,' said Lorcan. 'Hope it keeps you warm at night.'

'Listen, I am *plenty* warm at night,' said Gracie.

'Gracie, you love your casino, that's just bricks and mortar. And you were nearly in tears yesterday over a fucking car. That's not natural.'

The git. It hadn't *just* been the car. It had been everything. The threat on the windscreen. George and Harry. Her mother. The fire. The scare over Brynn's safety. The notes. Those bags of hair. *Everything*. Oh yeah – and seeing Lorcan again. That had upset her too. It was still upsetting her, even now.

But his words had hit home like a hammer-blow. Maybe she *did* love her job and all the sweeteners that went with it too much. For a year now she'd had no close family, no friends except work colleagues, not even a lover. She had no *time* for any of that. Work claimed every waking minute of her day, and by the time she got home she was too bloody *tired* to even notice the gaps in her life, far less actually care about them.

'Don't you think this is a bit harsh?' she demanded, going instantly on the defensive. 'Pitching up at George's hospital bed to tell him he's fired?'

Lorcan stared at her. 'I *was* going to fire him, but now I'm just hoping he'll recover. What sort of a shit do you think I am?'

She gave a cynical half-smile. 'Oh, you don't want an answer to that.'

'Yeah, I do. Come on. Let's have it.'

Gracie stood up abruptly. She dumped the plastic cup and most of its contents in the rubbish bin and glared down at him. 'You know what? I can't be arsed with all this. Tell Sandy I've gone home, will you? And in future, let's just do this through the courts, okay? I have *nothing* left to say to you, Lorcan. Nothing at all.'

When she got home, Suze was sitting at the kitchen table having a smoke, and from behind the closed lounge door came the sounds of gunfire. Claude was clearly in there, watching Bruce Willis – or someone like him – wreaking havoc.

Suze looked up as Gracie came in, and her face hardened into grimmer than usual lines.

Gracie took one look at her mother's face and thought: *No. I've had enough.* She turned in the kitchen doorway and made as if to go on up the stairs.

'How's George?' asked Suze quickly.

Gracie paused. 'The same,' she said.

Suze nodded, her face tight with dislike as she stared at her daughter. 'I know what you did,' she said.

Gracie looked at her mother's face. Suze's eyes were hostile.

'What?' asked Gracie, bewildered.

'You heard me. I know what you did. Claude explained everything to me.'

Gracie opened her mouth to speak, to ask *what the . . .?*

'No, you listen to me,' snapped Suze, stubbing out her cigarette with vicious movements. 'Claude told me *exactly* what went on with you last night.'

Gracie leaned against the doorframe and folded her arms. 'Oh really? This I've got to hear,' she said.

'Now don't come that acid tone with me,' said Suze, coming in close to her daughter. 'It all happened just as Claude said. He came up to your room and knocked on the door to ask if you wanted anything to eat. He was being *polite*. And you opened the door in your underwear and gave him the come-on; you invited him in.'

Gracie's mouth had dropped open as Suze spoke. 'Oh, that's priceless,' she said at last.

'Oh, it's not priceless,' said Suze, shaking her head, her eyes bitter as they glared at Gracie. She waved a finger in her face. 'It's just *typical* of you, Gracie Doyle. Seeing your own mother as competition, trying to score points.'

For God's sake, thought Gracie. *With that sorry son of a bitch? Is she serious?*

Gracie knew that this 'competition' thing was Suze's hang-up, not hers. While overindulging 'her boys', Suze had always seen the rapidly developing Gracie as a threat – not a daughter to be treasured and taken on shopping trips. As competition. And *younger* competition, at that.

Is that why I grew up cold? Gracie wondered again, thinking of Lorcan's derisive words about her attachment to material things. And her own mother's words too, once heard and never forgotten: *Gracie, the girl with a calculator where her heart should be.*

Maybe they were both right. But she was back here, wasn't she? She wasn't cold like they all said she was. She'd come to help. She was *determined* to help.

'I want you to leave,' said Suze, turning back to the table and shaking another fag out of the packet. She stuck the cigarette between her lips and snapped the lighter on, lighting the cigarette and inhaling deeply. Gracie wondered aloud when her mother had started smoking.

'After the divorce,' said Suze, seeing Gracie's stare. She gave a taut smile and folded her arms. 'I started on the fags then. It broke me, that bloody divorce. I loved your father.'

But you cheated on him. Gracie didn't say it. No good stoking up the animosity yet another notch.

Suze's face hardened again. 'I want you to pack your bags

and go, Gracie. I won't have you coming between me and Claude. He's a good man, he don't deserve it. There's the B & B just down the road – you can stop there if you want. Or there are hotels enough, God knows you can afford it.'

Her mother was taking the word of her lover against that of her daughter.

Why am I surprised? wondered Gracie. *Whatever I had to say, she never listened.*

'Well, ain't you got nothing to say about it?' prompted Suze irritably.

Gracie stared at her mother's face. Hostile. Closed off. Wreathed in skeins of smoke.

'Smoking's very bad for your health,' she said, and turned away. 'I'll go and get packed.'

Gracie started off up the stairs.

'Yeah, that's you, Gracie,' Suze bellowed after her. 'Don't react, will you? Cold as fucking ice and twice as hard, ain't you?'

28

23 December

It was past midnight when Gracie let herself into George and Harry's flat. She'd tried the B & B her mother had suggested, but it was full of people visiting their relatives for Christmas. She tried a couple of hotels, too, and found a similar story. In the end, she thought – *oh rats to it*. She still had the key to the flat, she'd just paid the damned rent and all it was doing right now was standing empty. And if Harry did by some chance show up, he'd come back to the flat, wouldn't he, right?

Right.

She switched on the harsh overhead light, then flung her bag aside and sat down on the open sofa bed among all the mess and disorder. How the hell could anyone live in this shit? She put her head in her hands. She felt dispossessed, exhausted, bewildered and – yes – hurt. She'd been at her mother's house for barely two days and already she'd been kicked out.

God, she was so tired. In a minute she'd make herself a drink, change the sheets – Jesus, they needed it! – and wash her face, clean her teeth. She kicked off her shoes and put her legs up on the sofa bed, thinking, okay, yeah, in a few minutes I'll move, I'll get cleaned up. And she fell instantly asleep.

When she woke up, there was sunlight filtering through the murky windows and beaming straight into her eyes. She'd fallen asleep fully dressed, half under the duvet and half out of it. For a few blissful moments she thought she was at home in Manchester, then it all came back to her. She was at George and Harry's place, in London.

Shit.

She grabbed her toilet bag and stumbled through to the bathroom, yawning. She took a quick shower, cleaned her teeth, put on a little make-up and brushed out her hair. Then she went back to where she had dumped her suitcase and bag in the lounge, dug out clean underwear, jeans and a black polo-neck sweater, slipped on cosy moccasins and warm socks, and began to feel a little better.

She went into the little kitchen, filled the kettle, and found bread in the freezer to make toast. Then the flat's landline rang. She went through to the lounge, plonked herself down on the sofa bed, and picked up.

'Hello,' she said cautiously.

'Hi,' said Lorcan.

'Oh. Hi.' She felt instantly tense; instantly hot.

'I called round at your mother's; she said you'd left after coming on to her boyfriend.'

'Did she.'

'I saw her boyfriend.'

'Hm.'

'He came on to *you*, right?'

Gracie sighed. 'It's academic, wouldn't you say?'

'She said you'd gone to a B & B, and I checked a couple but you weren't there. Everywhere's bombed out pre-Christmas, and then I remembered you'd been at George and Harry's flat and thought you must still have a key.'

'Well done, Sherlock.'

'Shrewd deduction, yes?'

'Lorcan, what exactly do you want?' asked Gracie irritably.

'Oh, I just wondered if there's anything you'd like to share with me?'

'Like . . . what?' She thought about the note with the hair. *No filth or you're all dead.* If she told Lorcan, would he insist on the police getting involved? She thought of Harry, out there somewhere, unaccounted for. Someone had hacked off his hair, someone had him; she was afraid for him, the fear sitting in her stomach like a constant, low-lying ache. Was he dead or alive? They had no way of knowing.

'Well, when I was at the hospital last night, one of the nurses told me and Sandy that George's brother had been in.'

Gracie clutched hard at the phone. 'You *what?*' Her heart picked up pace as hope surged through her.

'That's what she said.'

'*Harry*'s been at the hospital? My God, you mean he's okay? Well, what the fuck's he playing at? We're all worried sick about him. He ought to go and see Mum, set her mind at rest. It's bad enough she's got all this worry with George, without having to fret about him too.'

'Yeah, yeah. All correct. But the nurse described him, and

you know what was really strange? He didn't have red hair like yours, Gracie.'

She felt her spirits deflate like a pricked balloon. 'But who . . . what the hell's going on here?'

'I don't know. But this "brother" is young, slim – and blond. Whoever it is, it isn't Harry.'

29

Suze and Claude were in the lounge at the front of the house, watching *Dickinson's Real Deal*, when they heard the noise begin. It was instant and shattering. It sounded like a high-powered motorbike had just revved up outside the front door.

But it wasn't a motorbike that was revving . . . was it? They both shot up from their seats, alarmed, and were halfway out into the hall when whoever was out there started attacking the front door with a chainsaw. The noise picked up a gear, becoming deafening. Splinters of wood started coming off the inside of the solid wood door and dropping on to the welcome mat.

'*Jesus!*' screamed Suze.

'*What the f . . .?*'

Within a couple of minutes they could see the damned thing, chopping the door into firewood. In not many *more* minutes, whoever was out there would be in here, with a working chainsaw in his hand.

Suze retreated halfway up the stairs, milk-white with terror. Claude struggled to get past her, out of the hall, knocking her flat in the process. They were both screaming incoherently, both stricken with fear.

Then . . . silence.

Silence broken by loud, vicious swearing from outside the door, which was still bolted, still shut fast. Splintered, yes; wrecked, oh yes, certainly. But still in one piece.

'*Fucking cunting thing,*' they heard loud and clear. '*Bastard fucking thing, what the . . .*'

Suze sat quivering on the stairs. It was going to start up again. She knew it. And once whoever was out there was in *here*, they were going to be sliced salami.

'Oh Jesus,' sobbed Suze, noticing even through her fright and distress that Claude had already legged it upstairs.

Now she could hear other voices outside. Neighbours' voices . . .?

'What d'you think you're doing?' Frightened voices, but brave too; trying to help.

'*Fuck off.*'

Silence.

'*For fuck's sake, out of* petrol? *You tosser!*'

Suze sat there and listened. Her door was a wreck. They'd break it down now, come and get her. For now, something had saved them. The chainsaw was out of petrol. Some guardian angel; some fluke stroke of luck. But that sort of luck couldn't last.

She shivered and cried, huddled on the stairs, her hands clapped over her mouth because she was so afraid, so afraid that if she made a noise now, just the slightest squeak, they'd get that door down and, fuck the neighbours, they wouldn't care, nobody really cared, and before she knew it she was going to be dead meat.

Now there was no sound from outside the door. None

at all. She sat there for a full five minutes, too scared to move, while Claude cowered upstairs. When he ventured down at last and touched her shoulder, she was so jumpy that she shrieked.

'It's all right,' he said. He was sheet-white and sweating, his glasses slipping down his nose, his usual aura of perky arrogance a thing of the past. 'S'me, Suze. What the fuck?'

But she just shook her head and stared at her ruined front door. She knew with a sick certainty that he would have *stayed* upstairs, would not have defended her, if those bastards had got through the door with that thing.

30

23 December

With nothing else to occupy her time after Lorcan's call, Gracie got on with tidying up the flat. For one moment there she'd almost thought Harry was okay and had just been off on a bender or something. She'd thought, for one blissful moment, that there was going to be some good news among all the bad.

But no.

Now it turned out that this 'young slim blond boy' must have been a friend of George's, nothing more, who had realized the hospital wouldn't give out details, or allow a visit from anyone except relatives, and had simply claimed to be his brother.

Bugger it.

Gracie worked all morning tidying, cleaning – and by lunchtime she was hot, dusty and tired. She stopped for a shower and a bite of lunch straight from freezer to microwave, then wondered what to do next. She turned on the radio in the lounge – she'd refolded the sofa bed; all was neatness and order.

Yeah, you're anal, Gracie, and you know it had been one of Lorcan's angry jibes at her. And he was right. She was buttoned-up, neat, tidy, with a brain that whirred constantly, looking for solutions, answers – she couldn't help that.

Christmas carols boomed out of the radio. She disapprovingly tweaked down the volume on 'Hark the Herald Angels Sing'.

She wandered into Harry's bedroom, stood in the doorway, angelic voices trailing her. It was all immaculate now; he wouldn't even recognize the place – and would pretty quickly turn it back into a tip, given the chance. Right now, she would *welcome* Harry coming in here with his gentle grin and his charming good looks, and turning his room back into a pile of shit. He'd always been such a sweet boy . . . and she'd missed him. Now, she just longed for him to be safe and to come home.

She went on to George's room.

George wasn't sweet. The George she had grown up with was irritatingly overconfident and endearing in equal measures. She stood there and looked at the computer set up in the corner. She'd dusted around it this morning, carefully. She used computers a lot in the course of a day, and it would be something to pass the time, anyway, if she could get on line. She could email Brynn, catch up. And maybe there might even be some clues to Harry's whereabouts on there?

She went over and sat down at the computer. Found the plug, switched on. She supposed that George might carry his password around in his brain, like she did, but George was scattier than her and he *might* have written it down somewhere. She started opening drawers. Lots of crap in there: rubber bands, staplers, old batteries, discarded pizza receipts.

She opened the next, looking for a scrap of paper with the password on, a diary, something like that . . . and instead she found a drawer full of money.

At first she just stared, gobsmacked. The drawer was *stuffed* with money, overflowing with it. Fifties and tens and fivers, all bundled in there. There had to be thousands, just stuffed into a drawer. Why not in a bank?

Gracie sat back, frowning.

Well, why not? Why wouldn't *she* put money in a bank? She always did. But if she didn't . . . then it would be because it was hooky money. Ill-gotten gains. Something she didn't want the taxman to get wind of. But George worked for Lorcan, that all went through the books. Lorcan was straight-down-the-line legitimate in his business dealings, she knew that. He wouldn't pay George cash in hand and, anyway, George's earnings from Lorcan's business wouldn't amount to this in half a *year*. Keeping your cash in a drawer suggested eccentricity or simple guilt. Knowing George, Gracie was willing to bet on the latter.

She closed the drawer, leaned forward, focused again on the computer screen.

As she expected, the Omnipass box had come up, but she ignored it, closed the box down. A fighter plane logo flicked up, with *George* beside it. She clicked on *George*, expecting to get no further without the login password. But the system continued to open up. A full-page screensaver popped up next, a pic of George, Harry and a mate all gurning at the camera. Then she clicked on 'Start' and 'Internet Explorer', and within a minute she was on the World Wide Web.

He really ought to use a password, she thought. *That's careless.*

But she was glad he hadn't. A woman's voice with a posh accent was saying 'Welcome. You have email.' Gracie clicked on 'Read'. There were thirty-two emails waiting there. She sighed and went to the kitchen, made a cup of tea and came back with it. Then, methodically, feeling like a sneak thief, she started reading through her brother's mail. It was a revelation.

There was junk among the mail, of course; there always was. Spam and offers to 'expand your member' – yeah, even *she* got those. But there were other things, lots of other things, all intriguing, all bewildering. She glanced over at the window. The light was starting to go. It was nearly three fifteen and already the winter's night was closing in, and with it were coming great, yellow-grey clouds. There was a dusting of snow coming down out there again. She clicked on the Anglepoise lamp beside the computer, and read on.

What puzzled her most were the emails from all these women. Saying things like 'fabulous service, can't thank you enough' and 'will use you again, very pleased'.

Use him again for *what?*

And Harry wasn't exempt from this roll call either. The women mentioned both Harry and George by name. Fascinating. And these obviously weren't girlfriends. These were people who had clearly paid for a service.

She drank her tea, sitting back, staring at the screen, her mind whirling. Then she got up, went to the window. The snow was coming down harder and it was starting to settle. She could see bigger flakes in the car headlights passing on the road, could see a pristine carpet of white on the feeble stretch of lawn at the front of the block. Shivering a little, although it was warm in here, she flicked the blinds down and went back to the computer. Stared at the screen.

They'd been providing a service.

To *women*.

Gracie was drawing the only, the obvious, conclusion. On impulse she Googled *George Doyle*. Google came up with a maths professor; a chain of gents' outfitters; an estate agency in Pembrokeshire . . . and George Doyle who ran the 'hottest male escort agency in the whole of London'.

George, she thought. *You little bastard. What you been up to this time?*

She left George's room and went through to Harry's. Started throwing open cupboards, yanking out drawers. It didn't take her long to find Harry's stash, which looked to her highly trained, casino-boss's eye to be at least equal in amount to George's.

She went back into George's room, looked at the screen-saver of her happy, healthy-looking brothers, mucking about with their little blond pal. *What's been going on here?* she wondered. She clicked on and the screensaver vanished; there were the emails again. She selected the gushing-with-praise ones from the women. Then she looked in 'Recently deleted emails' and found a whole stack of them in there, too. There were so many. She picked a few at random. Jackie Sullivan. Laura Dixon. Jemma Houghton. Melissa Whitehead. Oh . . . and this was interesting. Sandy Cole was here. Gracie sat and thought about that. Sandy had been a client . . . and now she was engaged to George.

She printed them all, and turned off the computer. Her mobile started to ring. She picked up.

'Hello?'

'Gracie, can you come over?' said her mother's voice.

Gracie looked at the phone. Then she said: 'What the hell for? So you can have another go about me coming on to your boyfriend? I don't think so.'

'Shut up, Gracie, this is serious. Get over here, will you?' said Suze, sounding fraught.

Gracie heard the tension in Suze's voice. 'What's wrong?'

'Just get over here, for the love of God. Just for once in your life, will you do what I ask you to?'

'It's snowing,' said Gracie.

'Please!' howled Suze, and then she started to cry.

Despite herself, Gracie felt alarm shoot up her spine. She stood up. 'What's going on? Is Claude there with you? You're not on your own, are you?'

'Please just come over,' sobbed Suze.

'I'm coming, all right? I'm coming. Don't worry. I'll be there as soon as I can.'

31

Gracie got a taxi over to her mum's place. It was a long, hard journey and the driver moaned copiously throughout the trip. The traffic was a nightmare and the wheels spun and slipped on the blanket of snow.

'This lot's gonna freeze overnight,' he told her. 'You seen a gritter out here? I ain't. It'll be a bastard tomorrow.'

Inching through the traffic, he told her all about how mass immigration was ruining the country, how the Labour Party hadn't turned out to be New Labour at all, just old Labour repackaged. And look at the fucking mess they were in now.

Gracie kept her opinions to herself. She was worried about Suze. She phoned Suze's number on the way over there, but now Suze wasn't picking up. Anxiety ate at her. All right, she and her mother had never been the best of pals, but she hadn't liked the frantic edge to Suze's voice. Something bad had happened. Suze was scared. And, much to her surprise, Gracie found that she wanted to be there, quickly, if only to reassure.

She thought of seeing Claude again. Well, fuck him. He gave her the dry heaves, but she had met a great many creeps in her life and she hadn't backed away from any of them, not yet. Let *them* back away. She was fucking-well coming through.

At last she was there. She paid off the driver and crunched through the snow along the pavement and up the little front path leading to Suze's door. Once there she stopped and stared at it in disbelief.

Suze's front door looked like some gigantic cat had attacked it. Huge gullies had been cut into the wood, as if a tiger had scraped its massive claws down it. The wood was scored so deeply that in places she could see right through to the hall. Suze's pathetically cheerful little red-berried Christmas wreath was on the ground, and looked like it had been trampled underfoot by an invading army.

Gracie drew a startled breath, lunged forward and hammered at the door.

'*Mum!*' she yelled. '*Mum, it's me. Open up.*'

She heard movement from the other side of the door, saw shapes shifting through the vicious score-marks.

'Who is it?' came Suze's tremulous voice.

'It's me, it's Gracie. Come on. Let me in.'

She heard the chain come off, the bolts go back. The door swung open. Suze was standing there, her mascara streaked all to hell, her face sheet-white, her mouth trembling.

'Oh my God, what's happened?' asked Gracie, hurrying forward, taking Suze in her arms.

She hadn't intended to, but if someone looked this shot away, what else could a person do?

She pushed in, hugging her mother, looking back at the door.

'What happened to the damned door?' she asked.

'Ch-ch-chainsaw,' said Suze, shuddering.

Gracie's jaw dropped. *Chainsaw?*

A hideous chill stole over her. Someone wanted the whole Doyle family to suffer, it was clear. But for what? That was what she couldn't figure out. All she could think of was George in intensive care, and Harry fuck-knew-where.

'The damned thing ran out of petrol,' said Suze, and she gave a semi-hysterical laugh against Gracie's shoulder. 'I heard them talking. I was sitting on the stairs. It ran out of petrol, and if it hadn't . . . if it hadn't . . .'

Suze was crying again.

Jesus, thought Gracie, horrified.

'Where's Claude?' she asked, thinking that Suze needed him now, creep or not.

Suze pulled back a bit as Gracie closed the door. 'Oh,' she sniffed, 'he's gone.'

'Gone where?' asked Gracie. She hurriedly turned and put the chain and the bolts on.

Fuck me, and what good's that gonna do against a chainsaw if they go for petrol and come back again?

'Gone as in fucked off,' said Suze, and now she looked angry as well as scared. 'Half an hour after this happened, he just packed his bags and went. Didn't even say goodbye.' Suze's eyes filled with fresh tears and she flopped down on the bottom stair. 'I was going to *marry* that gutless wonder, can you believe that? When *this* happened, he pissed off upstairs. Left me to it.'

Tosser, thought Gracie. But maybe with a chainsaw about to burst through the door, any one of them would lose their nerve. And she didn't think Claude, for all his smiles and posturing, had that much nerve to start with.

'I'm supposed to be going in to see George tonight,' sobbed Suze. 'And now this . . . oh God, Gracie, what's happening to our lives? Why are these people doing all this to us? I've never hurt anyone. Neither's George, I'd bet my life on that. And Harry!' Suze was sobbing even harder now. 'My poor Harry. They've cut off his beautiful *hair*. What else might they be doing to him, Gracie? *What else?*'

Gracie pulled her mother into her arms and patted her back as she would pat a child's. Suze cried hard for a minute or two, and Gracie felt like joining in. But there were things to do. They didn't have the luxury of time right now.

'Come on through to the kitchen,' said Gracie as Suze's tears subsided a little. 'I'm going to pour us out a drink and you . . . just get some stuff together, Mum.'

Suze looked at her with reddened eyes. 'Stuff? What . . .?'

'Do it, Mum. Chuck a few things into an overnight bag, and hurry up.' Gracie looked back at the ravaged front door. 'We're going to get you the fuck out of here.'

32

Gracie suggested that Suze move in with her sister for a while.

Predictably, Suze didn't like it. 'Vera won't want me there. She'll be rushed off her feet getting ready for Christmas; she's got all the kids coming.'

'You'll have to tell her it's an emergency,' said Gracie. 'Boiler's bust, it's Christmas, you're freezing, no plumbers to be had, Claude's walked out, it's Christmas, yada, yada.'

'Christ,' said Suze wearily. 'That's going to make her day. You know how she is. I love her to bits but she's so fucking smug and superior. *She* never got divorced. Her kids go to uni and they're going to be doctors, solicitors . . . and what are mine? One deals out cards to sad sacks who haven't got a home to go to, one's on the dole and the other one runs a gambling den.'

So that's how she sees me, thought Gracie, feeling hurt.

But Suze phoned Vera and secured a bed for a few days.

181

'Well, that's good,' said Gracie, and while Suze was packing up a few things she stood there looking at the front door, willing the ones with the chainsaw not to come back before Suze got her act together. One of the neighbours had apparently phoned the police, and had even knocked on the door shortly after Claude's hasty departure. The police, with their hands full with Christmas revellers no doubt, hadn't yet shown up, and Gracie wasn't about to sit around waiting for them.

'Hurry the fuck up, will you?' she scolded, as Suze dithered around the place.

'All *right*.'

Once Suze was packed, they got a taxi over to the hospital to visit George. He was exactly the same – no change at all. Gracie wondered if there ever would be. She felt impossibly weary now, under siege, endangered by something, she didn't know what. So George and Harry had been squiring a few women about the town, so what? Surely *that* couldn't lead on to *this* . . . could it?

She stared at George, lying there, out of it. If only he could come round. If only he could speak. But he was so still it was like he was dead already. She thought of the emails, in her bag. Thought of Harry. And wondered – *worried* – about where he was.

'He's not going to pull out of this, is he?' said Suze, sitting there on the opposite side of George's bed, looking old and almost shrivelled; not herself at all.

'Yeah,' said Gracie firmly. 'He is.'

'Bullshit,' said Suze with a tired, tremulous smile.

They sat there for a full hour, listening to the beeps of the monitors, while the nurse hurried around them, sending them fake cheery smiles. George was going to be all right, he was going to pull through. Wasn't he?

Gracie doubted it. She really did.

From the hospital they went over to her aunt Vera's. Vera lived in some style and was justly proud of her faultless, clever family. Gracie could understand that Suze felt bitter when Vera kept – gently, but very firmly – ramming her own family's perfections down Suze's throat. But better to be safe and bitter than at home and at risk.

Gracie didn't go in.

'You ought to say hello, at least,' said Suze as they sat in the cab with the engine still running.

Gracie shook her head. 'No, I've got enough to think about without having to field Vera's questions about what I'm doing here. Don't tell her anything about what's happened, Mum. The less anyone knows, the better.'

'All right,' Suze relented unhappily.

Gracie looked at her mother. Usually dippy Suze would argue black was white, but now all the fight seemed to have drained out of her.

Suze returned Gracie's gaze and said: 'I'm glad you're here.'

Gracie stared at Suze in surprise. Then she swallowed hard past a sudden lump in her throat and was about to speak when Suze opened the cab door, and was gone. As the taxi pulled away to take her back to George and Harry's flat, Gracie glanced out of the back window and saw Vera opening the door, embracing Suze. Her mother went inside the house and the door closed behind her. Then Gracie saw the lines of dazzling headlights behind them. *Was* there anyone following her? *I'm watching you, Red.*

She was exhausted, confused, overcome. She sat in silence all the way back to the flat, and was grateful when the cab pulled in and she could pay the driver off and let him go.

She wanted to be alone, to think. The snow was several centimetres deep now, and it was still falling. A white Christmas. She started walking towards the block, fishing out George and Harry's keys as she went. She heard a movement behind her and half turned. She felt the stunning impact of the blow to her head, and saw the snow rushing up to meet her. That was all she knew before blackness and silence descended.

33

23 December

Gracie came back to consciousness because someone or something was tugging at her legs. She was aware of a dim sense of irritation, a befuddled awareness that she must be in bed and dreaming, but *someone was definitely tugging at her legs*. And her whole front section was achingly, bitingly cold. While the rest of her felt strangely warm and peaceful.

Very odd.

She tried to speak, to tell whoever was hurting her ankles and seemingly dragging her backwards through something very cold and wet and unpleasant, to *stop doing it*. But she couldn't get the words out. She frowned. *Definitely* a dream.

Ow. But her head hurt.

Ah, she'd just go back to sleep. She was aware of voices, angry shouting just a little way above her head, but she was out of it, nice and warm, and now she couldn't really even *feel* all that cold unpleasant stuff on her front, she was just really warm, really comfortable, really . . .

185

'Gracie!'

Hmm? Ah, shaddup. Wanna sleep . . .

'Gracie! Come on! Gracie!'

It was a familiar voice. She ignored it. Hoped they'd just go away, drift away out of her dreams, because she was so comfy, she wanted to sleep now, just to sleep . . .

'Fuck it, Gracie, will you bloody well *wake up*?'

She knew that voice. Her eyes flickered open, now he was *seriously* getting on her tits, what the hell was he doing here in her dream?

'That's it! Come on! Wakey-wakey!' said Lorcan, and she felt herself being not so much lifted as *hauled* – pretty bloody painfully – to her feet.

'Oh *shit*,' she moaned, feeling the world start to spin, feeling – in fact – extremely strange.

Gracie felt a biting wind on her face, on her sore forehead. What was she doing out here, outside in the cold and the wind and the . . . the front of her clothes were wet, icy.

It was just a nightmare. *He* was a bloody nightmare, always had been, that was for sure.

'You're a bloody nightmare,' she slurred out. 'Leave me 'lone.'

'Come on, Gracie. One foot in front of the other, that's the way.' She was being propelled somewhere, and now someone was yanking at her bag, and what was she doing with a bag if this was a dream? 'Jesus, you couldn't be a dainty little woman, could you?' he was complaining loudly right by her ear. 'Six feet of flaming trouble, that's you. Where the fuck's the key . . .?'

Gracie could hear him pillaging her bag, finding . . . oh yes, now they were half walking, half falling through the outer door into the hall. No wind now. All gone. She closed her eyes, started to crumple again.

'Hold up, Gracie. Come on.' And something hard was hitting her mid-section. She groaned, thought for a moment she was going to throw up, but it was a dream, you didn't hurl in dreams. And then – and this was horrible – she could still feel that hideous pressure on her guts and she could see the stairs swaying beneath her.

Gracie closed her eyes. Oh she *was* going to be sick, no doubt about it.

What the hell was going on?

Somehow they were on the top landing. She could hear the key scraping against the lock, could hear Lorcan swearing his head off as he tried to get the thing in there. He got it in. He was carrying her somehow. Fireman's lift? And now they fell forward into the hallway, both of them, just tumbled on to the hall floor, Gracie feeling like rubber, like soft floating swansdown, and maybe *now* he would just let her go back to sleep . . .

'Let's have a look at you,' he was saying.

What the hell for?

Something touched her forehead. She yelped. Opened her eyes and saw Lorcan leaning over her. 'You *prick*,' she said with feeling.

'Sore, uh?' He held up a finger and Gracie thought that if she'd had the strength she'd have bitten it right off. 'Can you see this? How many fingers am I holding up?'

'Ten,' groaned Gracie, wishing he'd fuck off.

'Gracie . . .'

'One.'

Now he was moving his finger back and forth. 'Just follow it with your eyes, how does that feel, do you feel okay?'

Gracie traced the finger's progress with her eyes. 'Oh, I feel just *great*,' she moaned.

187

'You're freezing cold. Gotta get you warmed up,' he said, and there he went again, pulling her to her feet like she was a sack of spuds.

'No, no! Just let me lie here, I'll be fine,' complained Gracie.

'You heard about hypothermia, Gracie? You lie down in the snow and you go to sleep, and then you *die*. You are terribly, terribly cold. Now come on.'

He was pushing her through into the bathroom, turning on the walk-in shower. Holding his hand under it. Tweaking up the heat. Oh. No. He wasn't going to. Was he? No. Not even he would be *that* crazy. She was fully dressed. She felt her eyes closing again, in the steamy heat of the room. She just wanted to *sleep*, couldn't he get that through his thick head?

And then she felt him pushing her, pulling her.

'Jesus, Gracie, I've felt blocks of *concrete* more movable than you,' he gasped out, and then *she* gasped, because she was getting soaked, the shower, she was in the shower, she was getting wet through, what the fuck was he playing at now?

'Argh!' she shouted. 'Oh you *fucker.*'

She'd been so comfy. So warm, just drifting . . . and now she was getting wet. Soaking wet. Her eyes flicked open and there he was. *Fucking* Lorcan Connolly.

And now . . . now she was aware that her skin was cold. Very, very cold. The hot water was hitting her face, but she could only feel the moisture, not the heat. And now . . . now he was unbuttoning her coat, pulling the sleeves down her arms, throwing it on to the bathroom floor.

'Ohhh,' moaned Gracie. What was he torturing her for? All right, she might be a hyper-ambitious cow, but that didn't warrant this sort of treatment, did it?

He was pulling her polo-neck jumper over her head now, *that* was going to be ruined – then he was kneeling, the water raining down on his head and slicking his hair into a sheen of black. He was pulling at her ankle boots, then he got busy at her waist, unbuttoning and unzipping her jeans, holding her upright with one hand while yanking them off with the other. Her socks followed.

'*Ow*,' yelled Gracie, because she was starting to feel the heat of the water. She looked down. Her skin – oh fuck – it was turning bright lobster-red, and the circulation that had been so deadened by the icy cold outside was coming back to life and it was *agony*.

'Feeling that, huh? That's good,' he said. He straightened up and started *rubbing* his hands over the cringing skin of her arms.

'Ow! Don't do that!'

'How's your head?'

'Absolutely. Bloody. Great. You *arse*.'

'Think you need to go to A & E?'

'No I fucking-well don't. But trust me, you keep doing that, *you* will.'

'Not feeling sleepy now?'

Sleepy? How the hell could anyone sleep under these conditions? Pins and needles were crawling all over her body, like an army of ants was under there, their little legs dancing around. It was *horrible*.

'Uh. Hurts,' she groaned.

'That's good. It's meant to. If it *didn't*, you might be losing fingers or toes to frostbite . . . How *are* your fingers and toes?' he said, and now he was rubbing her fingers – oh, the pain.

'You sadistic bastard, will you stop that?'

She was gritting her teeth but they were still chattering. She could hardly get the words out. But . . . the pins and needles were a little less painful now. She was starting to feel . . . warm.

Her head was throbbing horribly but, apart from that, she felt pretty much okay.

'Gracie?' he asked as she leaned back against the tiles, eyes closed.

'Hm?'

'Better?'

'Yeah. Better.' Her eyes flickered open. He was there, right there in the shower with her, and his coat was soaked through and she was standing there in her underwear. 'Your clothes are wet,' she pointed out.

Lorcan looked into her eyes and slowly he started to smile.

'What?' she asked.

'Gracie, if I take *my* clothes off too, this could lead somewhere neither of us wants it to go.'

Who says I don't? wondered Gracie.

But he was right. They were on the threshold of divorce; that was the sensible option. Being together had only ever made them miserable. He was *completely* right.

'I'd better get dried off,' said Gracie.

Lorcan switched off the shower. He pulled a bath sheet off the heated towel rail and swaddled her up in it like a baby. 'Can you walk okay now?'

'Of course I can walk okay now.'

'Only just now you could hardly stand up.'

'That was because . . .' *That was because someone hit me over the head.* She shivered again, not with cold this time. She stepped out of the shower cubicle, swathed in the bath sheet, and walked gingerly into George's bedroom.

She sat down on the bed, pulled up the towel and started to dry her sopping-wet hair. Instantly she flinched and paused. Her forehead was sore and she could feel a small lump coming up there. Her bra was sticking clammily to her skin, ditto her pants. Shuddering with distaste, she pulled both off and tossed them on to the floor.

'You okay there?' Lorcan appeared at the open door, peeling off his shirt. Lovely brown skin. Hard, sculptured pecs. How had she forgotten those?

'I'm fine, will you please *knock?*'

'The door was open.'

Gracie got up, staggered, righted herself and crossed the room. 'Well now it's not. Okay?' She slammed the door shut in his face.

She picked up her undies and draped them over the radiator. Then she went to her overnight bag and with trembling hands pulled out clean underwear, a fresh cream jumper, jeans and socks. She got out her hairdryer and a brush and started to dry and unknot the tangled mess that was her hair. Then she slowly got dressed, put the towel over her undies on the radiator, and went out into the hall. Lorcan's coat, shirt, trousers, socks and shoes were all lined up on the lounge radiator, moisture rising from the wet clothes and fogging up the window. Lorcan himself was in the kitchen making tea, wearing a too-small towel around his waist.

Gracie went on into Harry's room, snatched up his velour bath robe, and stalked back into the lounge with it. She tossed it through the hatch into the kitchenette.

'You can put this on,' she said pointedly.

'Thanks,' said Lorcan, and took off the towel.

Gracie primly averted her eyes while he got the robe on. When she thought it was safe to look, he was wearing it.

'Tea,' he said, bringing two steaming mugs out into the lounge.

Gracie sat down and he put the mugs on the coffee table. Lorcan sat down too, tucking the robe in so as not to offend.

But then, she thought, *nothing I haven't seen before, right?*
Which didn't mean she wanted to see it all over again. Did it?

'You could borrow some of Harry's clothes,' she said.

'In a minute.' Lorcan had been half smiling, but now his face was serious. 'I want to know what's going on here, Gracie.'

'What do you mean?'

'Don't give me that shit. I *mean* what the fuck's going on? I came over here tonight to discuss the divorce with you, and you know what I found?'

Gracie shook her head dumbly.

'You, face-down in the snow, unconscious. And some bloke trying to drag you back towards a car.'

The tugging on her legs.

Holy shit.

'Gracie, it's just as well you're *not* a dainty little woman. Or he wouldn't have had such a struggle shifting you, and I wouldn't have got here in time.'

'Did you see his face?'

'No. It was dark. He was tall, wearing a long leather coat. When I turned up and shouted and ran at him, he took off for the car and drove away.'

Gracie said nothing.

'Is this all connected? George in hospital, Harry missing . . . and what about the tyres being slashed on your car? And this fucker tonight, he was trying to *abduct* you, Gracie. Thank God I showed up when I did.'

Gracie sat there feeling sick and shattered. He was right. There was horrible trouble here, and somehow it was all linked to Harry missing and George at death's door.

'Are you going to tell me what's been going on? Have George and Harry been up to something they shouldn't?'

'You should know what George has been up to. He works

for you,' shrugged Gracie, unwilling even at this point to land George in it.

'When he can be arsed to show up, which is not very often,' said Lorcan. He stared at her speculatively. 'What is it Gracie? Drugs?'

'*No*,' said Gracie firmly.

'Only it looks like they've upset someone, wouldn't you say? Someone who knows how to hold a grudge.'

'Oh shit,' said Gracie, and picked up her mug and drank the tea. It was hot, reviving. 'You're right,' she said. 'It's a mess. Someone's got it in for all the Doyles. Including me.'

'Go on.'

Gracie took a breath. 'Someone torched the front of my casino.'

Lorcan was staring at her. 'You *what?*'

She nodded and swallowed hard. 'And they delivered me a bag full of Harry's hair. They sent a bag of it to Mum, too. And tonight . . . I'd just come back from Mum's place, and someone's hacked at her door with a chainsaw. They ran out of petrol, couldn't break through. But she's a nervous wreck. I took her over to Aunt Vera's to stay.'

'Holy *shit*,' said Lorcan. 'And you don't know why any of this has kicked off? Seriously?'

'No,' said Gracie, thinking about George and Harry's escort business. All those women. But . . . they could have husbands, boyfriends, people who wouldn't take kindly to their women being squired around town by a couple of young studs. Wasn't that feasible?

'What?' asked Lorcan, watching her face. 'Come on, Gracie. For the love of God, tell me.'

Gracie gave in. 'George and Harry have been on the make,' she sighed.

34

Christmas Eve

'I found loads of emails on George's computer, from all these women. And I found his website,' said Gracie to Lorcan over breakfast next day.

He'd stayed overnight at George's place, taking Harry's bed while she took George's. It felt odd, lying in bed knowing that Lorcan was just down the hall. Odd – but reassuring, too. She couldn't believe how close she had come to getting snatched yesterday, and her brain kept dishing up freak-show images to her as she sank into a light, troubled sleep. What would have happened to her? You heard reports all the time. Women raped, hurt, murdered.

But eventually she slept – and she only managed that because she knew Lorcan was there with her. She kept waking up and finding herself listening for his tread coming down the hall. But he didn't come near her all night. Which was exactly what she wanted, but it irritated the hell out of her at the same time. Next morning she phoned Mum at Vera's.

'Oh, the cow's loving all this,' moaned Suze. 'She's got the whole place decorated like Disneyland, all colour coordinated in silver and pink. Now she's out in the kitchen in her Cath Kidston apron making mince pies and doing some Delia Smith thing with the bloody turkey. All her perfect kids and their perfect partners are coming over to stay later today, and I'm here like the poor relation. I'm having *loads* of laughs, thanks for asking.'

'At least you're safe.'

'Yeah, but at what price? If I have to listen to one more tale about how great Col's qualifications are, or how well Kirsty's doing at that upper-crust uni she's attending, I tell you, I'm gonna blow. If I try to help out she just tells me I'm doing it all wrong. And I *still* can't believe that shit Claude's scarpered – do you know how much that hurts, that he just *abandoned* me like that? And I don't understand what's going on. Why would anyone want to hurt George? And where the hell is my poor Harry? And *why* in God's name would anyone want to take a chainsaw to my front door?'

'It'll all work out,' said Gracie. She knew it sounded lame.

'My life's in the toilet, Gracie. In the *toilet*.'

'Going to see George tonight?'

'Of course I am.'

'No change still.'

'No. No change,' said Suze, and hung up.

Gracie's head was throbbing from the blow to her skull last night; she wasn't in the mood for all this aggro. She caught up with Lorcan in the lounge. He was dressed in his own dried-off clothes, drinking tea and eating toast.

'How's the head?' he asked.

'It has been better,' said Gracie, going through to the

kitchen and raiding the cupboards until she found para-cetamol and a cup. She came back into the lounge, poured some tea out of the pot, filched a piece of Lorcan's toast, and sat down.

'These emails from these women,' said Lorcan. 'You're sure that's what's going on? George and Harry have set themselves up as escorts?'

'There's no doubt about it.'

'And they've upset someone.'

'Looks like it.'

Gracie sipped her tea and wondered where the hell this was all going to end. She felt more frightened than she had ever been in her life. Someone wanted all the Doyles roasted, that much was obvious. George was in hospital. Harry was missing. Her mother had been terrorized. *She* had been attacked and if Lorcan hadn't intervened she would have been dragged away, maybe never to be seen again.

'It's like a scorched-earth policy, you heard of that?' asked Lorcan.

Gracie nodded. 'Yeah. An army withdraws and they make sure everything left behind is ruined. They burn the land, poison the wells.'

'That's what this person's doing – total obliteration – don't you think?'

She didn't want to think that. If she *allowed* herself to think that, then she would have to acknowledge that they were probably all doomed, every last one of the Doyles. Because you couldn't fight an enemy you couldn't see. And this one was invisible.

'Scary, uh?' said Lorcan, watching her face.

Gracie's eyes locked with his. 'I'm worried about George lying there helpless in hospital. I've been thinking about this.

Someone – God knows who – has already passed themselves off as his brother and strolled in there. What if someone wants to finish him off, Lorcan? Nothing could be easier, could it?'

'Then we'd better get George some security.'

'Can you do that?'

'I run a casino, Gracie. You know security plays a big part in gaming.' He sat back, considering. Then he said: 'Actually I can't spare workers, not right now. But I could draft in the fellas who take the skim.'

'You what?' asked Gracie.

'The skim. You know.'

Gracie sat up straight. 'Lorcan. Are you telling me you're paying *protection* money to someone?'

Lorcan gazed at her. 'It's just like talking to the Babes in the Wood,' he sighed. 'Come on, Gracie. Surely someone up in Manchester's approached you to take a skim off the profits?'

'No. They haven't.'

'Oh come on.'

'Really. No.' Gracie was staring at him. 'Who takes this "skim", then?'

He shrugged. 'In London? The American boys.'

'Are you telling me the *Mafia* are hitting on you for money?'

'They always have. And they always will. They're into a lot of places in the West End. Grow up, Gracie.'

'I don't believe this.'

'Believe it. The good news is, the boys are generous in return. They look after their own. Which is me. And anyone connected to me.'

Gracie stared at him, feeling shocked, dispossessed and

unsure. She couldn't take in what he was telling her. This wasn't her usual stamping ground. She was in a strange environment, facing an unreadable enemy – and Jesus, her head ached. Added to all *that*, here was Lorcan, right here, telling her the Mafia were in his pocket. Or he was in theirs. And she was *still* finding him disturbingly attractive. And she didn't, she really *didn't*, want to go down that road again.

'Who's going to be keeping an eye on you while you find out more about all these women George and Harry have been escorting around town?' he asked her.

'I didn't say I was going to do that,' said Gracie.

'But that *is* what you're intending to do, ain't that right?'

He could read her mind. She remembered that now. The way he could snatch her thoughts out of thin air, could know exactly what was happening in her head.

'It's better than just waiting for the axe to fall. And I can't think of anything else to do,' she shrugged. 'Can you?'

'No. I can't. So while you're doing that, Gracie, I'll watch your back, okay?'

'No.' Gracie stood up. '*Not* okay.'

She'd been through all this before with him. She knew how easily he could take over her life, her mind, her body. He was a strong man and he didn't have a shut-off point. He'd push and push at something until it crumbled, which was fine in business, but not when it was *her* he was looking to take over. She was an independent woman. She was used to doing her own thing, thinking for herself, having complete autonomy. She didn't want to change that, and she just *knew* that Lorcan could change it overnight, given half a chance. She knew how forceful he could be. And she knew that beneath all her go-fuck-yourself-I'm-a-liberated-woman front, she was weak at the core where Lorcan was concerned.

'Come on, Gracie.'

'No!' she snapped. 'I don't want your dodgy heavies, and I don't want you. Clear?'

She spent the morning replying to as many of the emails from George's clients as she could manage, telling them that George was in hospital after an assault and that if they had any ideas about how George had ended up that way, or if they knew the whereabouts of Harry, would they please let her (his sister) know? She put her mobile number on the emails.

Lorcan came into George's bedroom after about an hour and stood behind her, looking at the screen.

'They won't reply,' he said. 'They've used an escort service. It's a dodgy sort of business. They might feel ashamed, worried their families will find out. You won't get a damned thing out of them.'

Gracie turned in her chair and stared at him. 'You got a better idea?' she asked.

Lorcan shrugged and went back into the lounge.

She didn't hear him go out all morning, so she assumed he was still in the flat. As it got towards lunchtime she heard him making phone calls. She felt reassured, which was damned annoying, but how could you help what you felt?

He reappeared at one o'clock. 'Let's go out, get some lunch,' he said.

'Can't. Busy,' said Gracie, tapping away at the keyboard.

'Okay, *I'm* going to lunch. It's Christmas Eve. Why don't you, in the spirit of the season, join me, you stubborn cow? I'm extending an olive branch here or some fucking thing.'

'No, you go,' said Gracie, not looking round.

'You'll be okay here on your own?' he asked.

'I'm a big girl, Lorcan.'

'Fine. Give me a spare key, you got one?'

Gracie stretched over to her bag, which was on the bed. Rummaged in there, and came up with a set of spares. Handed it to Lorcan. 'Round one's the outer door, square one's the inner.'

'Thanks,' he said, not entirely without sarcasm.

She heard him go down the hall and out. She sat there staring at the screen as the silence of the flat settled around her. Finally, she switched off. Went through to the lounge. Wondered if she'd get any replies. Thought that there was every possibility that the clever bastard was right and that no one was going to risk getting dragged into something messy by saying a damned thing. She could only hope he'd be proved wrong. For a change.

So what now?

She couldn't just stay in here stagnating.

A flashback of last night came into her brain. The bone-chilling cold of the snow, Lorcan picking her up, thawing her out. She felt a shudder go right through her. *Anything* could have happened to her. He was right. But she couldn't just hide away in here. She refused to.

She snatched up her coat and bag and headed out the door. She'd pick up a taxi in the high street, go join the throng and do some late Christmas shopping. It was a novelty to say the least. She didn't do Christmas shopping, as a rule, but she could buy something for Suze, maybe cheer her up just a little. It was broad daylight and she was getting restless. She couldn't come to any harm.

Outside, the air was chilly. The snow was piling like icing on a cake up on the verges. Underfoot, there was grit and some slush, but it was okay so she started walking along the road, but then she realized that there was a man sitting in a parked car across the street, watching her.

When he saw her head turn in his direction he slumped down and lifted a paper and appeared to be examining it intensely. Gracie felt her heart start to stampede in her chest like a bolting horse. It was a hideous feeling. If he got out and ran at her, what the hell would she do?

She walked on a few paces, and whipped her head round quick, and sure enough he was watching her, he *was*. It could be the same one who'd hit her last night, the one who'd been trying to drag her away and do God knows what to her . . .

'Gracie!'

She halted and gave a small shriek, nearly quivering with terror. Lorcan was getting out of the black BMW up ahead.

Gracie clutched her chest and hurried up to him.

'That man,' she said, teeth chattering with cold and fear.

'What man?' Lorcan was looking around.

'In the fucking *car*, Lorcan. He's watching me.' Gracie nodded towards the car and its skulking occupant.

'Him?' Lorcan shrugged. 'Don't get your pants up your crack, Gracie. He's one of ours.'

'He's . . .' Gracie's mouth had dropped open. She tried to get the words out, but couldn't.

'One of ours,' repeated Lorcan. 'One of the mob boys, anyway. I made a few calls this morning. Got some muscle on George's hospital door, and your auntie Vera's, and yours. Where are you going?'

'You didn't listen to a damned word I said in there, did you? I told you I didn't want this.'

'Want it or not, Gracie, you got it.'

She stared at him in consternation. She wasn't sure whether

to laugh, kiss him or smack him hard upside the head. 'I thought you'd be long gone.'

'Nah, I was waiting for you. Knew you'd push it, Gracie. I *knew* you'd come out. So where shall we go for lunch?'

'So tell me what you learned this morning,' said Lorcan as they sat in a densely crowded restaurant.

They'd ordered the set menu of the day – Christmas lunch and all the trimmings.

'It'll be fucking horrible, it always is,' predicted Lorcan cheerfully when the waiter had taken their order and hurried off. 'Have you ever had a decent Christmas lunch in a restaurant?'

'No,' said Gracie, and thought of the Christmas Eves they'd spent together in the past. Out to lunch – and he was right, every one of them had been indigestible – then home to bed.

Mustn't think about that now.

'We always used to go out to lunch, then home to bed,' he went on, pouring out the wine.

Fuck it. 'Well we won't be doing that today,' said Gracie icily.

'You know what?'

'What?'

'I think that's a shame.'

Gracie nearly choked on her house white. 'You *what?*'

Lorcan shrugged. 'Well, as we're getting so close to the divorce courts, it'd be nice to end things on a bang, don't you think? Instead of a whimper.'

Gracie was shaking her head. 'No. That's *not* a good idea. I don't want to start muddying the waters. You've made your intentions plain. You want rid. Fair enough. *Rid* you shall have.'

'Actually I'm not entirely certain about that.'

Now Gracie really *did* choke.

'Steady,' he said.

'Look, can we drop this?' wheezed Gracie.

'Water?'

Gracie nodded and he poured from the jug.

'So, dropping it. Fine. What did you find out this morning?'

'Nothing much.' Gracie's eyes were watering. What the hell was he *playing* at? She had to wrench her mind away from what he'd just said, and from the images that had started dancing in her brain as a result of it. 'Sandy Cole's a bit of a curiosity, though,' she managed.

'Sandy? The girl at the hospital, the one who's engaged to George?'

'That's the one. She sent George a lot of emails, saying what a great time she'd had with him.'

'Well . . . so what? Obviously they've got closer than a client/worker relationship calls for, which happens, and now they're engaged.'

'Yeah, only . . .' Gracie hesitated, thinking. '. . . The thing is, Mum didn't have a clue about their engagement.'

'Maybe they wanted to keep it secret until they were absolutely sure?'

'What, George keep a secret? George could blab for England.'

'He can't blab now.'

They looked at each other. That much was true. Chillingly so.

'And maybe he just didn't get a chance to tell Suze about it before the accident.'

'I dunno.'

Their starters came – chicken liver pâté and Melba toast.

203

Gracie started eating, thinking that life was exceedingly strange. A week ago, the last thing she expected to be doing on Christmas Eve was eating lunch with her estranged husband. But actually . . . and this was the disturbing thing . . . she realized that being with Lorcan felt okay. She hadn't expected that.

'I'm going in to see George tonight, and I hope Sandy'll be there,' said Gracie. 'I'd like to talk to her, find out exactly what the deal is with her and George.'

'The deal is, they met through the escort work and now they're engaged and George never got a chance to tell Suze.'

'I dunno.'

'Will you stop saying that?'

'She just doesn't seem like George's type, that's all.'

'Gracie, you don't have a clue what George's type is. You don't even *know* George now.'

'Yeah, but I *did* know him,' retorted Gracie.

'People change.'

'Do they? Really?' She looked at his face intently. Wondered if that was possible. If what had once been unworkable could possibly ever work out any differently. She thought of Harry, little Harry, who had always been such a delight, and now it hit her how much she had missed him – *and* George, come to that. Now George was so ill. And Harry, gentle, handsome Harry, was in trouble up to his neck – that much was obvious.

'So what is George's type?' Lorcan asked her.

Gracie shrugged. 'I don't think the George I knew could ever be a one-to-one "great romance" sort of person. Even as a kid he was everybody's pal and nobody's best friend. He never had any little girlfriends back then. He had *friends*, male and female. Harry, on the other hand, had proper dates when he was nine, ten years old, hardly out of short trousers.

It was hysterical. The girls were practically storming the door to get hold of him. It was a big family joke.'

'But you haven't clapped eyes on either of them for nearly fifteen years,' he pointed out.

'I know. Maybe you're right. Maybe George has changed.'

'Maybe *Sandy* has changed him.'

'Yeah, and maybe not.'

Lorcan prodded the pâté with his knife. 'I was right, wasn't I? Is this crap or what?'

Gracie had to raise a thin smile at that. 'It's crap,' she agreed. And she didn't have much of an appetite any more, anyway.

35

Christmas Eve

'See? Result,' said Gracie as she viewed George's bulging inbox that afternoon.

It was half past three and nearly dark outside. After their mediocre restaurant lunch, she had insisted on coming back to the flat so that she could see if George had mail. Lorcan had insisted he was coming with her, and to be honest she wasn't sorry about that. The heavy was still outside, sitting in his car. She was protected on all sides, and that was – much against her better judgement – a nice feeling.

'You know, you're not supposed to open random emails. Might admit a virus and fuck up the system,' said Lorcan casually, standing behind her as she sat in front of the screen.

'So bloody what?' flung back Gracie, clicking on the first. 'In the overall scale of things, one fucked-up computer isn't that important. What *is* important is finding out what's been going on with George.'

'Yeah, but if you balls it up you won't get any more emails

coming through, and if you think you'll get an IT fixer out on Christmas Eve, you got another think coming.'

'Shut up, Lorcan.' He was right of course. But desperate times called for desperate measures.

Lorcan sat down on George's bed. 'Anything?' he asked.

'Messages of sympathy,' Gracie frowned, deleting those.

'Most won't answer at all,' said Lorcan, lying back on the bed, arms folded behind his head. 'I told you.'

'Shut the fuck *up*, Lorcan.'

'I've missed this, all the cheery banter. All your sweet little ways. Telling me to shut the fuck up every five minutes. All that marital bliss bollocks.'

Gracie ignored him and kept opening emails.

So sorry to hear about George, they said.

Give him my love, they said, with a smiley face.

Get well soon, they said, with many kisses.

Then she opened another and it was all in huge capital letters, screaming at her from the screen:

WHERE IS HARRY? HE WAS COMING FOR DINNER NEARLY A WEEK AGO, BUT NEVER SHOWED UP. YOU'RE HIS SISTER? IS THAT TRUE? HE NEVER MENTIONED YOU. WHERE ARE YOU? CAN WE MEET UP? OR CAN YOU GIVE ME YOUR TELEPHONE NUMBER? I'M SORRY TO HEAR ABOUT HARRY'S BROTHER. CAN YOU PLEASE GET IN TOUCH SOONEST? I'M VERY WORRIED ABOUT HARRY.
JACKIE SULLIVAN.

'Look at this,' said Gracie excitedly, and Lorcan hauled himself off the bed and peered at the screen.

'Looks like a result.'

Gracie clicked on 'Reply' and typed quickly. Then she pressed 'Send'. She scrolled through the other emails, clicking on and deleting them as she went. Then she went to 'Old' and scrolled through those. 'Sandy sent George a lot of emails.'

'Well, you'd expect that.'

Gracie opened a few and read them. 'She's hellishly keen by the look of these.'

'You'd expect that too.'

'Look at this one. *Hope you liked the flowers*. She sent *George* flowers?'

'Well, why not? Equality.'

'Yeah, but George? He was never in touch with his feminine side. Hey.' Gracie smacked her forehead. 'I think I saw those damned flowers. Roses. They were dead by the time I got here.'

Gracie scrolled through a few more new emails and then exited the programme. She pushed away from the desk and stood up.

'What now?' asked Lorcan.

'We wait, and we hope Jackie Sullivan checks her emails more often than I do.'

Lorcan looked at the bed. He looked at Gracie. 'What we were discussing over lunch,' he said, and caught her wrist in his hand. 'We could—'

'No, I don't think we could,' said Gracie, trying to pull away.

'*I* think we could,' said Lorcan, and gave a tug.

Gracie was jerked forward, her knees striking the edge of the bed and throwing her off-balance. She landed half on the bed and half on Lorcan.

'This is a very bad idea,' said Gracie as his arms went round her.

He shrugged and held on tighter. 'Think of it as a farewell bonk,' he said.

'How romantic,' sneered Gracie, feeling more than a bit breathless at this close contact. He was very warm, and it felt sort of *nice* snuggled up against him.

'You want romantic? I can do that.' Now his mouth was dangerously close to her own.

'Wait!' said Gracie. Lorcan paused. 'What's the point of this?' she demanded. 'We'll get together again, and then we'll just tear each other to bits . . .'

'We could try not to,' he suggested, kissing her cheek.

'We'd fail,' she sighed.

'Defeatist.'

'*Realist*, actually.'

'We could do a deal. Make it a rule to play nice. To compromise, meet each other halfway. Do you think we could do that?'

'I dunno. Could *you*?'

'Maybe,' he said, and kissed her very lightly on the lips.

Oh God I'm in trouble here, she thought.

'Maybe we should talk about it,' said Gracie, almost mesmerized by the brilliant blue of his eyes.

'Maybe.'

'Right.' With a conscious effort, Gracie hauled herself up and away from him. This time, he let her go. She stood up, smoothed down her clothes. She stared down at him sternly, despite her legs feeling as if they were just about to dissolve with sheer lust. 'But talk first, sex after, okay?'

'Okay,' sighed Lorcan, sitting up.

'I'll make us some tea,' said Gracie, and swept out of the room and down the hall.

* * *

Jackie Sullivan replied three-quarters of an hour later, while Gracie and Lorcan were sitting in the lounge watching *Santa Claus the Movie* on the telly and eating fried egg sandwiches. 'Could do with some decorations in here,' said Lorcan. 'Lights. Maybe a tree.'

'I hate all that stuff.'

'I know. You and the Grinch, separated at birth.'

It had always been Lorcan who bought the tree, decorated their apartment over the casino with tasteless swags of tinsel and bunches of mistletoe. Lorcan's family delighted in Christmas, whereas Gracie's much smaller clan – her mother and dad in particular – had only ever used the occasion to get pissed and start fighting. She remembered so strongly, even after all this time, sitting on the stairs with George and Harry and listening to the traditional pre-Christmas shrieking row going on downstairs.

Those two should never have been together in the first place, she thought.

She looked across at Lorcan, slumped there on the sofa, and thought that maybe she'd been repeating patterns of behaviour learned in her youth, in her own marriage. Like her mother and father, she and Lorcan had always fought tooth and nail.

She shuddered. No, they were better apart. They ought to divorce now, wipe the slate clean, start again. She had the papers right here in her bag. She could sign them, hand them to him right now, say take it to the courts, it's finished. Only . . . she kept thinking about what he'd said. That they could try, they could talk.

'Whoever invented Christmas needs shagging,' said Gracie, and phoned the garage to ask when her car was going to be ready. The phone rang and rang. No one picked up.

'For fuck's sake,' she said loudly.

'Problem?'

'I'm calling the garage. No answer.'

Lorcan looked at her wide-eyed. 'Gracie. Are you completely mad? It's Christmas Eve. No one is working, and no one gives a shit about your tyres; they're all headed home to be with their families. Give it a few days, maybe there'll be someone about.'

Gracie gave up. Hearing the ping of an email arriving in George's inbox, she hopped to her feet and went through to George's bedroom to check it out. Gracie's excitement rose as she saw it was from Jackie. She read the email, and quickly replied, then logged off and went back into the lounge.

'Anything?' asked Lorcan, yawning broadly.

'Maybe,' said Gracie. 'Jackie Sullivan and her daughter are calling over at ten. I'm hoping they can shed some light on what's going on with Harry.' *Please God*, she thought.

She sat down and looked distractedly at the movie for a while.

'There are mince pies in the fridge,' she offered after a few minutes.

Lorcan gave her a wide-eyed look. 'You bought mince pies? Gracie, what next? Stollen? Christmas cake? Turkey and all the trimmings? Chestnuts roasting on an open fire?'

'I'll roast *your* chestnuts in a minute.'

'What *are* you doing for lunch tomorrow, anyway?'

'Same as always,' said Gracie. 'Chicken salad.'

'That's my girl.' He stood up and held out a hand. 'Come on. Let's go roll the dice.'

'Pardon?' Gracie stared up at him in puzzlement. Was he trying to get her back into bed again? And did she *want* that? Oh, she did. Shameful to admit it, but she did. Sod the talking. She really, really wanted to sleep with Lorcan again, even if it *was* for the very last time.

'You got a dress with you? Something presentable?' He looked down at her. 'You used to have that black wrap dress you took with you when you were travelling on business.'

'I have it.' The crepe jersey dress, a great old workhorse of a garment, was in her bag in George's room.

'I can't go out,' said Gracie. 'I told you. Jackie Sullivan's coming.'

'I know that. We'll be back in plenty of time. Go put your dress on, Gracie. I'm going to show you my casino.'

George and Harry

DECEMBER

36

George was getting very used to the escort biz now. Harry and George had worked their way through a vast array of women since George first had his business brainwave in front of the telly one drink-and-pizza-fuelled evening. George prided himself that they were doing a good job, researching their clients' interests, studying the etiquette book they'd got from the grunge shop, dressing well, being polite, making the ladies feel good about themselves.

He knew damned well there was *something* going on with Harry and the cougar – he couldn't think what, she was old enough to be Harry's mother, after all – but hey, so long as Harry continued to pull his weight with their many other clients, that was entirely Harry's business.

This evening Harry was with the cougar again, and George was in an Italian restaurant awaiting the arrival of Ms Sandy Cole, who had once again requested his services. She had also requested that they meet here, as usual; she specifically asked not to be collected from her home in Maida Vale, which was good – it saved George the bother of schlepping all the way over there. And also made him think that someone was at home, someone she didn't want to have to explain him to.

Maybe her parents.

Maybe her husband.

Whatever, it was her business, not his. His business was to charm, to entertain, and, if requested, to bonk. No more, no less. That was the deal.

Sandy arrived right on time. She was a pretty young thing – around twenty-two, he guessed – and skinny, with long ash-blonde hair, intense brown eyes and a closed-off, defeated, almost childish air about her.

'Hi George,' she said, coming up to the table. They'd seated him near the bogs tonight, and he'd protested, but the place was packed, there was nowhere else. It wasn't the sort of place he'd have chosen for a romantic night out, but the choice had been hers so he had to make the best of it.

He stood up. 'Hi Sandy,' he asked.

She nodded and they air-kissed and sat down, Sandy beaming happily, George wondering not for the first time what a young, pretty girl like this needed with an escort.

'What would you like to drink?' asked George, as the waiter came over with the menus.

'White wine,' said Sandy. 'Please.'

'Bottle of white,' said George, and the waiter rushed off.

'This is a nice place,' lied George, and started giving her the patter he did so well. Soon she was laughing and chatting to him, relaxing. 'What do you fancy?' he asked, opening the menu and perusing the goods on offer.

'The penne,' said Sandy.

'Good choice, I'll have that too,' said George, and gave the waiter their order when he came back with the wine.

'I meant to tell you last time we met,' said Sandy.

'Tell me what?'

'That you're better looking than your photo on the website,' said Sandy.

'Thanks,' said George, surprised. He wasn't used to being complimented on his looks. Harry fielded all of those, as a rule.

'I like photos but they are so one-dimensional,' said Sandy. She pulled a tiny digital camera out of her bag and placed it on the table. 'Brought mine tonight, thought we could have one taken together if that's all right . . .?'

'Sure it is.'

'Photos don't show the life-force, do they? You've got a lot of life-force.'

'Well, there's a lot of me to *have* a lot of life-force,' said George with a smile.

'Don't put yourself down. You're gorgeous.'

'Well, so are you.'

'Nah, I'm not. I'm a dull little office mouse; nothing exciting ever happens to me.'

'What did you say your job was?' asked George, thinking that he was in for a long evening. And he really should have made a note of her job last time they met, even if she had bored him stiff; women loved it when you remembered stuff about them.

'I'm an administrative assistant in dental supplies.' She smiled then. 'Told you I was dull.'

'So what does an administrative assistant do all day?'

'I take telephone orders from dentists. Drills. Mouthwash. Bibs. Sterilizers. Been there for five years now.'

Yep, that was dull all right. George looked at her and decided it was time to pile on the old charm. 'You know what I thought when we first met?'

'No. What?'

'That you were too young and pretty to need an escort's services. That you must have guys queuing at the door.'

'Ha! I wish.' She sipped her wine and gave him a little sideways look. 'But thanks for saying that.'

'I mean it.'

'Sure you do.'

Silence fell between them. Dean Martin was giving it some '*Amore*' in the background, and there was the happy buzz of conversation all around them. Waiters were shooting back and forth from kitchen to tables, people were coming and going to the loos; they were right on the flight path here and that was pretty damned annoying. George got his mind off his annoyance and concentrated instead of giving this – yes, all right, she *was* dull – girl another scintillating evening.

'So tell me some more about yourself,' he said, leaning forward, giving her the 'come on, I'm keen' body language.

'Oh, there's nothing much to tell. I'm single. Live at home with my parents. Go to work, come home, you know how it is.'

'And you just fancied a few nights out?'

'It's my birthday,' she said, and blushed, and buried her nose in her glass again.

Fuck, how sad is that? thought George.

Their food arrived. The waiter brandished a large pepper mill at them, then hurried off.

'Well, let's celebrate that,' said George with a wink. He lifted his glass and clinked it against hers. 'Happy birthday, Sandy Cole.'

When Sandy got home, Noel was waiting for her and he was in a bad mood, just as she'd known he would be. He didn't like her going out. The minute Sandy put her key in the door she was full of apprehension. She went into the shabby little lounge where he was sprawled out on the cheap moquette sofa. Dumped her bag and coat on a chair. The air was thick with the scent of cold pizza, beer and weed. He had a spliff in his mouth and the telly was roaring away. He looked up at her expectantly.

'Where you been then?' asked Noel.

Sandy was staring at the telly, acting casual. 'Molly's,' she said. 'I told you.'

'It's late.'

'We got talking, you know what she's like.' Sandy knew that Molly would cover for her; Molly was a good friend. She knew he'd check, because he was bloody paranoid. He'd text Molly and say: Was Sandy with you tonight? And Molly would text back: Sure she was.

But he seemed satisfied. He turned his attention back to the telly, some moronic game show or other. Sandy stifled a sigh and looked at him. He was tall and well built, running to fat around the middle, but that was because he never did a fucking thing from one day to the next. He had thick brown hair, a long thin face, brows that almost joined in the middle, giving him a bad-tempered look at all times. Which sort of summed him up, didn't it? Because he *was* bad-tempered all the time. And useless. And . . . sometimes, not often . . . he'd shove her, or tell her she couldn't go out, or he'd check her phone and accuse her of having men in, which was an utter bloody *joke*, because he was always hanging around this place they rented together like a bad smell.

Rented together. That was *also* a laugh. She paid the rent. He just bought ciggies and beer and a few takeaways when she wasn't here to cook, because he couldn't be arsed to do it himself. He had to be the laziest, scruffiest man she had ever met, and she felt that she'd been had, done over, made a fucking fool of, because he hadn't been like this at first.

Her mum, with her excellent radar for losers, had warned her about him at the start. But back then of course Sandy had thought he was good-looking; she'd been in love with him; she had dreamed of them living together, maybe even getting married, having children.

Now, she was very careful to take her pill, the pills she had to hide away from him because he wanted them to 'start a family', when what he *really* meant was that he wanted to keep her tied up indoors with a baby, didn't want her going down the shops or even outside the frigging *door*. This house, which once had fuelled all her girlish dreams, was now her prison. And he hadn't bought her a birthday card. Not even a *card*.

'I'm going on up,' she said, and picked up her coat and bag and went upstairs.

She took a shower, soaping herself, thinking about the evening she'd spent with George, and how wonderful it was to be treated like a lady for a change. They'd eaten a lovely meal, chatted. There hadn't been any sex . . . but there *could* have been. Feeling so resentful, so hemmed in as she did these days, she wished she *had* booked George for sex too. But it would have made her very late, and she was a bit afraid to go that far. Then she would really be what Noel kept accusing her of, she would really *be* a slapper, and he would have justification then in pushing her around, watching her when she was on the computer, checking her phone, even checking her *body* to make sure she hadn't been with another man.

Chance would be a fine thing, she thought as she dried herself and slipped on her robe.

But she'd had the chance, right there, tonight.

It was her birthday, and he hadn't, the mean bastard, even bought her a card.

Next time, she was going to make the leap. Go the extra mile. She thought of George, big, charming, smelling sweetly of some woody cologne, smartly dressed, making her laugh out loud. To have a man like that . . . and then she heard Noel laugh at something on the telly downstairs. It was a coarse, ugly sound. She went into the bedroom and crawled between the sheets. He wouldn't come up for hours – all those spliffs and lying around all day meant he never slept well, and that meant she didn't either. When he did come upstairs, she'd pretend – as she always did – to be asleep.

She closed her eyes and thought of George. She dreamed of leaving Noel, but she was too afraid of him to do it. His sudden outbursts of temper scared her. So she fantasized of another life, away from this one. Being George's girl, strolling hand in hand with him down the high street, laughing, chatting. Looking at engagement rings in jeweller's shop windows. Planning on getting married, setting up house together somewhere nice. Having a little boy who was dark-haired and chunky, like George. She fell asleep, half smiling, thinking about that.

37

After a hard night at the coalface keeping Sandy Cole entertained, George arrived home feeling worn out. He let himself in quietly, and passed along the hall. The lounge door was shut, and he couldn't hear the telly going or see light spilling out from a crack under the door. Alfie must have turned in for the night. George went into the bathroom, took a piss, brushed his teeth. Then he went into his bedroom, closing the door behind him. Undressed, and fell into bed, and was out for the count in seconds.

He woke up in darkness, thinking that it was morning already. He sat up in bed. Switched on the light. Looked at the clock on the bedside table. Three forty-five. Something had woken him up. Usually he was a very sound sleeper. Maybe a motorbike passing outside on the road. An ambulance. A police car. Something.

He clicked off the light and lay back down again. And then he heard it. A faint noise . . . like someone crying.

Alfie?

He sat up and put the light back on, pulled on his robe. Alfie was having nightmares again. Poor kid.

George went through to the hall, opened the lounge door. The heart-wrenching sobs shot up in volume. Quickly, thinking that Harry must be in bed by now and asleep, and not wanting to wake the whole household, George went into the lounge and closed the door behind him. He fumbled over to the little lamp beside the telly and switched it on. Instantly the room was lit with a warm orange glow. Alfie was curled up on the sofa bed, thrashing, turning . . .

'Hey, kid,' said George.

Alfie was asleep, dreaming about god-knew-what horrors.

George sat down on the edge of the sofa bed and put a hand on Alfie's shoulder.

'Alfie! Mate. Wake up, you're dreaming. *Wake up.*'

Suddenly the blue eyes were open. They stared up at the ceiling, their expression one of fixed, stark dread. Then Alfie blinked, turned his head. Looked full at George. Realized where he was.

'Oh *shit*,' moaned Alfie. He put his arm over his eyes.

'Bad dream, uh?' said George, patting Alfie's shoulder awkwardly.

'I keep on getting them,' muttered Alfie.

'What are they about? Do you ever remember?'

'Jesus, remember them? I wish I could *forget* them.' Alfie dropped his arm and gave George a weak smile. His brow was damp with sweat, his cheeks wet with tears.

'Is it always the same dream?' asked George, feeling more than awkward now. He didn't know *shit* about bad dreams or good ones. Personally, he rarely dreamed; he was hardly the person to play amateur psychologist, now was he?

'Always the same one,' sighed Alfie, sitting up. He was naked to the waist, his skin fine and shining in the soft light. To George he looked like a painting, something ethereal and beautiful. George caught himself thinking that, and thought *what the fuck . . .?*

'It's always Deano. That bastard.'

'Who's Deano?'

'Trust me, you don't want to know.'

'I do. Or I wouldn't ask.' Maybe Alfie would tell him – at last – what had gone on before George met up with him. He'd never probed, knowing that Alfie must have been traumatized by whatever shit had gone down before the night in the alley.

And so, for the first time, Alfie told George all about Deano, and about himself. How he had been living with his dad in Surrey – his parents were divorced; mum had taken off when he was eight.

'That's rough,' said George, who could understand Alfie's distress, he really could.

'Worst of it was my stepmum. She hated me. Thought I was getting in between her and dad. I wasn't. I always tried to keep out of the damned way. Short of becoming invisible, there was nothing more I could do.'

'So what happened?' George enquired, thinking he already knew the answer.

'I left. Came up to London. Slept rough for a bit. Then I met this bloke, Lefty, and he said he could fix me up with a job . . .'

Uh-oh, thought George. 'And did he?'

'Yeah, he did. Just cleaning and washing up in a club in Soho, one of those weirdo places with orgy rooms and dungeons, where everyone wears chains and rubber, fetish stuff, you know the type of thing?'

George did, and it made his blood run ice-cold to think of sweet, angel-faced Alfie in a place like that. *Dungeons*, he thought. *The ones he dreams of.*

'Deano owns the club. And he . . . he was nice to me at first. Really nice. Then he started . . . you know.'

George stared at Alfie. 'What, you mean he was bullying you?'

'No.' Alfie squirmed. 'Coming on to me.'

George felt rage take hold of him. Poor little Alfie. What the fuck had been going on with this bastard Deano? He swallowed hard, feeling sick and furious. 'Did he do anything to you, Alfie? Anything he shouldn't?'

Alfie looked down. 'Yeah. He did. He treated me like . . . like a pet, sort of. Drugged me.' A tear slipped down Alfie's cheek. 'Shagged me.' He looked up and his eyes were wet.

George was struck dumb with horror.

'Lefty . . . the guy in the alley? Lefty kept giving me pills, I felt out of it most of the time. When I ran away, I felt . . . it was like I was drunk, I couldn't focus on anything, couldn't make out where I was. I couldn't get far. I stole Lefty's Oyster card and I got down the tube and I just *ran*. But he was following me. I couldn't shake him off. It was like one of those dreams where you're trying to run but your legs won't move. So Lefty caught up with me and he was going to take me back to Deano. And then *you* showed up.'

'Thank Christ,' said George with feeling. To think of what Alfie had been through made him feel sick to his stomach. If he hadn't . . . well, he couldn't stand to think what would have happened to Alfie if he hadn't got there at that time. God bless drunken Laura Dixon, because if she hadn't got so off her face, he'd have taken that cab with her and he'd never have seen Alfie being accosted in the alley by that bastard. Now he was *glad* he'd whacked the cunt with that scaffolding pole. He was only sorry he hadn't walloped him harder.

'Listen,' said George. He put a reassuring hand on Alfie's shoulder. 'You got nothing to worry about and nothing to be scared of, not any more. You're safe here. And you can stay as long as you like, you know that. We both like having you around. We'll fix you up with something, some little job if you want, maybe down the casino where I work, how about that?'

'Don't your brother-in-law own the place?'

'That's the one. I'll just say the word, he'll fix you up,' said George; but he wasn't too sure about that, not really, because Lorcan was looking ready to rip someone's head off these days and beat them with the soggy end. He didn't like all these sickies George had been taking, but what could George do? Most of the escort work was evenings, and most of the *casino* work was evenings too. He'd give up the casino work soon, they were earning enough not to bother, but meanwhile he didn't want to twist Lorcan's tail too much.

'You've been so damned good to me, George,' said Alfie. 'Thanks.'

'Hey, what are friends for? Come in to work with me tomorrow night, we'll see if there's anything going.' George smiled and stood up. 'Now get back to sleep, okay? And no more bad dreams.'

38

Jackie had cancelled her last booking with Harry in a terse email.

'You've pissed off the cougar,' George said, making tut-tut noises with his tongue.

Harry knew he had. And finally he caved in. He phoned her. She sounded cold, distant. Harry hated that. The truth was, he hated being at odds with Jackie; he loved seeing her, and what the hell, it wouldn't hurt him just this once to meet up with her daughter like she wanted, bend the truth a little (okay – a lot) and have a pleasant evening with the pair of them.

How could that hurt anyone?

All right, he'd have to lie through his teeth – and Harry had always been relentlessly truthful, ever since he could crawl; he was *nothing* like George with his well-meaning but shockingly flexible half-truths and tall tales – but what the hell? And she was so pleased he relented. They were friends again.

'You'll love Emma,' she promised.

'Yeah, yeah,' smiled Harry.

'And she'll love you.'

And she might have done, if fate hadn't stuck two fingers up at the whole arrangement and cocked it up for good.

He was at her Notting Hill address, as promised, at eight o'clock that Friday. For tonight he was going to be the Harry all her friends and associates had heard about – Harry the architect who passed clients on to Jackie the interior designer, Harry who dressed a bit arty-farty because that's what architects did, right? He'd read up on architecture over the course of the last month or so, determined to get the tone just right. He felt by now he could almost *design* a fucking building if called upon to do so. He'd dressed nicely, appropriately: a good-quality blue shirt under a tweedy jacket, black cords and Converse trainers. He'd slung a blue-knitted scarf around his neck. He looked the part. And he could see from Jackie's expression when she opened the door to him that she was pleased he'd made a real effort to complete the deception.

'Don't you look great,' he said truthfully. She was dressed up in a shell-pink dress that flattered her pale colouring. Big silver bangles decorated each well-toned arm.

'Come in,' she smiled, and suddenly Harry felt nerves take hold. He still felt uncomfortable with this. Blurring the lines between work and play. But she took his scarf and jacket, and led the way into her big, beautiful drawing room with its roaring open fire and huge Knoll sofas placed on either side of it.

There was a dark-haired girl with a heart-shaped face sitting on one of the couches, a half-full wineglass in her hand. When she saw her mother come in with Harry, she stood up, smiling.

He felt his heart physically *lurch* in his chest.

'This is Emma,' said Jackie proudly. 'Emma, this is Harry.'

'Hi,' said Emma. She had a friendly, open expression.

She extended a hand. Harry shook it. He wanted to *kiss* it, stupidly enough, but that would have been just too naff for words. His heart was running around, doing cartwheels. His stomach was clenched hard, as if he'd just suffered a near-terminal blow. Jesus, she was lovely. *Stunning.*

'Hi,' he said, finding his voice with an effort. Her eyes were pale denim-blue, like her mother's. They were kind too, like Jackie's. 'How are you?'

'Fine. Jet-lagged.'

'Hong Kong,' he said. 'Wow.'

'It's great. *So* beautiful.'

Like you, he thought.

'Must be. Never been.' Never been *anywhere,* Harry added silently to himself, and after the crashing sensation of instant-aneous love came a devastating realization: she was out of his league. It was impossible.

They all sat down. Jackie poured him a glass of wine and he swigged it quickly, trying to steady himself.

Don't be stupid, he warned himself. *Love at first sight? What a joke.*

And yet, he felt it.

He knew it was ridiculous, but there it was.

They chatted. She told him all about her life in Hong Kong, working in the PR department of a big banking conglomerate in the Jardin, and enquired about his and Jackie's work connections. Hating to lie, Harry was still pretty good at it. He expanded at length about the projects they'd undertaken together. He was feeling worse and worse about the true story of his life. A dole-drawing loser, on the make. Taking advantage of lonely women. That was the *real* Harry Doyle.

'I've booked a table at Nobu,' said Jackie, glancing at her watch. 'We'll go out and get a cab, shall we?'

They were in the hall putting on their coats when the doorbell rang. Jackie wondered: 'Now who could that be . . .?' as she opened the door.

The woman called Camilla from Covent Garden was standing there, hard-eyed and dark-haired. She had a clutch of fabrics in her hand.

'Jack darling, I was passing so I thought I'd drop in these samples for the bedrooms . . . oh, hello Emma! I had no idea you were home.'

'Just got back,' said Emma.

'Oh, and Harry's here. Hello again, dear.'

'Hi,' said Harry, feeling something coming, some stirring of trouble deep in his gut.

'Jack tells me you and Harry were at uni together,' said Camilla.

There was a thick, resounding silence. You could almost *cut* it, it was so profound. Harry saw Emma look with a frown of puzzlement at her mother, then her eyes skipped to Harry. Camilla was looking at all three of them expectantly.

Then Emma, bless her, said: 'Yes, that's right. We were, weren't we, Harry?'

She was smiling into his eyes, but he knew he was caught out. There was a glimmer of amusement in her expression, but there was also a heavy, irritated dash of *what the fuck is going on?*

'Yeah, just catching up,' he mumbled, feeling bad.

'Well . . . I can see you're going out, so I won't hold you up,' said Camilla. 'Night, all.'

She handed Jackie the samples and turned and went off down the steps. Jackie closed the door slowly, her smile fading.

Silence fell in the hall again.

'Right,' said Emma, and she looked angry now. 'Who's going to tell me what the *hell*'s happening here?'

Jackie and Harry exchanged a glance.

'Well?' demanded Emma.

It was Jackie who bit the bullet and told her.

'You hired a male *escort*?' raged Emma. 'You *hired* a man half your age?'

They were back in the drawing room. The fire had died down and the room was growing cold – like the atmosphere. They were sitting there, still wearing their coats. Emma was sitting on one side like judge and jury, Harry and Jackie were sitting opposite her like the accused.

Jesus, what a temper, thought Harry, impressed. Slow to anger himself, he admired anyone who could so easily kick off and let rip. Emma, it seemed, could do both quite easily. He could see her fiery nature might cause a problem or two when she became Mrs Doyle, but . . . what was he thinking? She was never going to be Mrs Doyle. He'd been exposed for what he truly was, and she looked pretty damned disgusted about it.

'It wasn't *like* that, Emma darling,' Jackie was protesting.

'Oh then, what was it like?' said Emma, breathing hard with fury.

God, she was gorgeous.

'I was lonely. I . . . I'd lost my confidence after your

father died. Couldn't seem to get it back. I turned down every invitation, terrified of going out alone. And then I stumbled across Harry's website, and I thought, there's the answer. I'll just hire an escort, and it'll all work out well. And it *did*. Harry's become a very dear friend of mine.'

Emma was looking from Jackie to Harry and back again. Suddenly her mouth dropped open and her nose wrinkled like she'd smelled something nasty. 'Oh. My. God.'

'What?' asked Jackie.

'You didn't. You two, you didn't . . .'

'Have sex' hung in the air, unspoken.

'Of *course* we didn't,' said Jackie forcefully. 'How can you even *think* that?'

Nicely caught, thought Harry.

'And you're not an architect at all,' said Emma.

'No. Sorry.' Harry looked at Jackie. *Told you this wouldn't work out*, said his accusing gaze.

'You just do this . . . escorting,' she said, her delectable mouth now pursed in disapproval.

'That's it,' said Harry. He felt better now it had all come out. Cleaner.

'It's just . . . disgusting,' she said with a shudder.

'Hardly that, dear,' protested Jackie, hurt on Harry's behalf.

'Yes it is,' said Emma. She got to her feet and eyed them both coldly. 'Look, I'm going up to bed, I'm too tired for dinner. You two go on ahead. Okay?'

And she left the room.

Harry and Jackie sat there and looked at each other.

'Dinner?' he suggested.

She shrugged. 'May as well.'

They stood up.

'Do you think she'll get over it? I mean, you can see it would be a bit of a shock.'

'I don't know.' Jackie looked at him. 'Harry?'

'Yeah?' He was rewrapping his scarf round his neck and wondering if it was too soon to tell Jackie that he had just fallen in love with her daughter. It was, he judged. *Way* too soon. And anyway it was hopeless. He was so far beneath her on the social scale, he could never even think of getting close.

'Um . . . Emma. She must never know that you and I . . .' 'Had sex' hung in the air again, unspoken.

'Got it,' said Harry. 'She'll never hear about it from me.'

'Or me,' said Jackie, and linked her hand through his arm. 'Come on, let's go and have dinner.'

39

'Ah, shit, shit, *shit,*' moaned Lefty, and took another hard snort of the butane.

They were standing out on the cold street again. Mona wished she was somewhere, *anywhere* else rather than here with this crazy junkie.

More and more, he seemed to be losing it.

More and more, she was scared shitless.

He'd killed that cab driver. And she had been party to it; she'd seen it *happen.* And God, she still felt sick about it. When Lefty had approached her again in the club days later, she had shaken her head at him. She'd been up on her podium, jigging away in her thong and a leather mask. Looking down on the revellers, it looked like a scene straight from hell in here. People tied up in chains. Fat guys in skintight rubber suits, *not* very attractive. The big heavy curtains over the archway that led into the orgy room were pulled back a little, and she could see heaving naked bodies in there. But she was used to that; it didn't bother her. What *did* bother her was this fucking lowlife Lefty who had grabbed her leg and was holding on.

'No. Uhn-huh. Whatever you got to say to me, I don't want to know. You just piss off, Lefty. I've had enough,' she'd yelled down at him.

Lefty's grip on her leg had tightened, the nails digging into her flesh.

'Ow! For fuck's *sake*.'

'You can't back out now, girl,' said Lefty, having to shout too, to make himself heard over the crashing, grinding noise of the club's huge sound system. 'You are in *way* too deep.'

And she was; she knew it. She'd witnessed a murder. She looked into his crazed eyes and wondered if she ought to go to the police, tell them what was going on. But she couldn't. The Bill would laugh in her face. She had a record. She didn't want to get herself in more trouble than she could handle. She couldn't handle *this*; how would she take the Bill coming on hot and heavy, looking into her background, checking up on the facts? What frightened her most was the prospect of social services steaming in and taking Josie away from her.

No – no police.

Lefty was right. She couldn't back out. But every time she thought of that night, the cab driver squealing like a pig while Lefty hacked at his throat, and then the cab twirling down into the black depths of the Thames, she was filled with sick horror. What if the damned thing popped up again? She'd heard that could happen, gases and stuff from dead bodies, would that be enough to propel a car from the riverbed up to the surface? If it was and if it did, she knew she would be in deep, deep shit.

'What now?' she asked him, thinking, *Oh God please get me out of here.*

'We'll keep checking the cabs and the night buses. Do the underground again. Anything. Whatever it takes.'

And so they did. It was a long, long night; but hey, there was a bonus. This time, Lefty managed not to kill anyone – although several times he *did* come close.

40

George was just about to start work. He'd got all togged up in his purple dealer's waistcoat in the locker-lined staff room. He was dealing *vingt-et-un* tonight, good old twenty-ones. He had Alfie with him. There was a whiff of faint disapproval among some of George's work colleagues as he joined them in the staff room, Alfie dogging his heels.

'Jesus, it's George. Where you been, Georgie boy?' asked Ned, one of the mouthier lads who was half in and half out of his work clothes.

'Caught a damned virus or something,' said George. He knew he'd been taking far too many sickies, bunking off on far more lucrative escort work. People were noticing. People were getting resentful. He was sure Lorcan would have noticed too, big style. And would probably kick his arse from here to New Year, but he *also* hoped that being Lorcan's brother-in-law would extend him some small privileges, allow him just a little wiggle room.

All dressed up for work, he left the utilitarian bleakness of the staff section and took Alfie with him out on to the plush, carpeted and brightly gleaming casino floor. They went through into the back where the manager's office was situated, beside the count room. Maybe he wouldn't bother Lorcan with this. Maybe he'd just chat it over with the manager, Thomas, who was a slightly easier touch. But he didn't get the chance to go for the soft option. Lorcan was passing by outside the count room, and he snagged George then and there.

'Oh! Lorcan. Hi, mate,' said George chattily.

'Fuck me! It's not George is it?' quipped Lorcan.

'Sorry. Been down with a virus, it was really nasty.'

'Next time you go down with something, a doctor's note would be good.'

'Will do,' George assured him earnestly, pulling Alfie forward. 'Can I just introduce Alfie, a friend of mine? He's looking for work.'

'Does he catch many viruses?'

'That's funny,' said George with a hectic laugh.

'It's not *that* funny.' Lorcan looked Alfie up and down. 'Go see Thomas, I think there's a couple of trainee floor-walkers needed.'

'Great!' George hurried away.

Lorcan stopped him with a hand on his arm. 'George.'

'Yeah, Lorcan?'

'You take the piss with me any more, you're out. First and last warning, okay?'

George's smile vanished. He gulped. 'Sure, pal.'

'And I ain't your pal, I'm your employer. Don't take fucking liberties.'

George nodded. Lorcan went off into the count room.

'Jesus. He's a bit heavy,' said Alfie.

'Yeah,' said George, and went and knocked on Thomas's door. He was going to have to jack this in and concentrate on the escort work. Lorcan was right, he *was* taking the piss, and Lorcan had been fair to him in the past. He deserved better. But first, George was going to get Alfie fixed up with a job.

'So, what'd he say?' asked George when Alfie emerged from the manager's officer and came over to the table where George was busy dealing out cards to a punter.

'Looks good. I filled out an application form. Put your address on it, that okay?'

'No problem.'

'I really appreciate this, George.'

'Look, hang around, go and have a go on the slots or something, get yourself a drink. I'll be off in a couple of hours, okay?'

They went home to the flat together. Harry was out on an escort job. It was a cold, crisp night, so they heated up some pizza, drank some coffee, and then George made up the sofa bed for Alfie. They said goodnight, and George pushed off to bed, thinking that once New Year was out of the way, he was resigning from Lorcan's pay roll and expanding the escort biz. Not *too* much though; he didn't want the taxman getting wind of it. That would never do.

He fell asleep dreaming of the piles of money he already had in his bedside table. The women, he could take or leave. Shameful to say, maybe, but the truth. He never had been pussy-mad like Harry. And once or twice – oh, and this was even more shameful, wasn't it? – he had felt a hot tug of attraction to a boy he'd met in passing. Not often . . . not often enough to worry him, maybe, but it had happened, it was there. So the women? Not too bothered.

But after years of being flat stony broke, he just *loved* the money.

When George awoke in the dead of night, he just knew it was Alfie again with the dreams. Like a mother who could detect a feverish infant through a brick wall, George could now sense Alfie in distress even when he was in the next room. He was so close to Alfie now that he thought he would know about it even if Alf was in the next *county*.

Groaning, he crawled from the bed, wrapped his robe around him, and padded off down the hall. He slipped inside the lounge, closed the door behind him. It was a regular routine now. Don't wake Harry. Wake up Alfie, reassure him everything was fine.

'Alfie! Alfie my son, wake up!' he hissed, crossing the room in the dark, flicking on the table lamp so that a cosy glow lit up the room, chasing back the shadows.

George sat down on the sofa bed and looked at Alfie, his angelic blond curls plastered around his thrashing head.

'No, no . . .' Alfie was moaning.

'Come on Alf.' George shook his shoulder gently. Alfie's skin was damp, hot and smooth to the touch.

Suddenly Alfie's eyes were open. He stared at the ceiling, then his head turned and he was looking straight at George.

'All right, Alf? The dreams again, yeah?'

Alfie drew a shuddering breath. A tear snaked down from one eye and fell on to the pillow.

'It's all okay, Alfie. No problems. No worries.'

'I know. It's stupid.' Alfie put an arm over his eyes. 'Oh *shit*,' he said softly.

'Get you a drink or something?' offered George.

Alfie dropped his arm. 'No. Just . . . stay with me a bit, will you, George?'

'Can do.' George dragged a spare pillow across, put his legs up on the sofa, made himself comfortable. 'Bet you'll get that job at the casino,' he said, to distract Alfie from his woes.

'You really think so?' Alfie's expression was unsure.

He looked young in the soft light, and very vulnerable. George thought that he would like to get hold of that twisted git Deano Drax and beat seven kinds of shit out of him. Now he was beginning to understand Alfie better, and to appreciate why he'd said no police. It was for the same reason that so few female rapes were reported. The victims felt too humiliated, too soiled and embarrassed to have to relive it all over again under questioning. He could see now that Alfie felt *exactly* like that. And at the same time . . . it was horrible but it was true . . . he could see how Alfie, so stunning, so *beautiful*, could appeal to a sick perv like Drax. Or to *anyone*, come to that.

'Sure I think so. You'd be great in the job.'

'Your brother-in-law didn't seem very happy with you.'

'Lorcan's like a bear with a sore head most of the time,' sniffed George. 'You don't want to take any notice of that.'

'You don't talk about your sister much?'

'No. I don't.' George thought about it. It was a sadness for him, not seeing Gracie. He'd loved his big sis, back in the day. But she hadn't contacted them, Dad hadn't contacted them, and Suze had bad-mouthed the pair of them until George thought that if he *did* try to get in touch it would cause all sorts of shit to start flying. Then Mum would be upset, and what if she was right and they really didn't want

241

to know him after all this time . . .? And so the years had gone by, and there had been this *void*. But it didn't seem now that there was a damned thing he or anyone else could do about it.

'It'd be good to have a sister,' said Alfie, an only child.

'Good? What, all those hormones and giggles and knickers hanging up in the bathroom, all that stuff?'

'Someone to boss around,' Alfie said, and raised a smile.

'Jesus, you never met Gracie!' George had to laugh at that. 'Boss her around and she'd kick you straight up the bollocks.'

'Did she kick *Lorcan* up the bollocks?'

'I think she came damn close.'

'So they couldn't live with each other?'

'Have a day off will you? She's in Manchester, he's in London,' said George. 'Read the signs, Alfie. Read the signs.'

'That's a shame.'

'Yeah, it is. Lorcan always seemed like the only one who could handle Gracie. If *he* can't, no one can.'

'Funny, what draws people together,' said Alfie.

'Yeah. Funny.' George propped himself up on one elbow and smiled down at Alfie. 'You feeling better now mate?'

'Yeah, but . . . stay, will you?'

'Sure.' George felt a shiver of unease. He was sleepy, he could nod off at a moment's notice, and what would Harry think if he strolled in here in the morning and found him lying on the sofa bed with Alfie?

He'd think we're a couple of queers, thought George, and he remembered the cab driver who'd picked them up on the night they met, the way he'd looked at them in the rear-view mirror, that knowing, faintly sneering look . . .

'I'd better be getting back to bed,' he said, drawing back, feeling confused all of a sudden, almost disorientated.

'No, don't!' Alfie's eyes were wide and pleading. 'Stay with me George. Please.'

'Alfie . . .'

'*Please.*'

'Okay,' said George, giving in. What could it hurt, after all? They were pals; he was just reassuring a pal who'd had a hard time of it. That was all.

He switched the light off and lay down, still securely wrapped up in his robe. Alfie flipped the duvet back and George nearly said *whoa, what's going on here?* But he didn't. Alfie needed him. He got under the duvet and snuggled down – no part of him touching Alfie's body, he made very sure of that. Pretty soon, he was asleep.

In the dim half-light of morning George came awake to the unexpected warmth of another body pressed against his own. He lay there for a moment, thinking *what the . . .?* And then he remembered Alfie's nightmares and that Alfie had asked him to stay; and he had. He'd fallen asleep . . . and now Alfie was cuddled up close in the crook of George's arm, his blond head tucked in beneath George's chin, his arm flung across George's chest. Alfie was hugging him like he was a favourite teddy bear or some damned thing, and it felt . . .

George lay there, feeling like he had just entered another country, another *world*.

It felt *wonderful*.

What the hell was happening?

He stirred slightly and Alfie felt the movement. Alfie was awake too. His head raised and George could see Alfie's eyes were open. And then Alfie stretched up just a little and kissed him right on the lips. Alfie's mouth was soft, pliant. His breath smelled like strawberries and lavender, sweet as the sweetest nectar. Relaxed and full of sleep, George responded. Kissed him back. It was the strangest sensation; like coming home after a long, arduous journey.

Alfie's mouth opened and George's tongue explored it. George had never kissed anyone quite like this, so whole-heartedly; and he had never felt this huge surge of compassion along with an entirely healthy dose of lust.

He had done women by the score, but that had been almost mechanical. *This* was something else. His erection was sudden and enormous. He felt Alfie's hand sliding inside his robe, scudding over the hairs on his chest, leaving a tingling trail of want – and then dropping down. Alfie sighed as his hand went where it wanted to be, cupping George's naked balls and then travelling slowly, sinuously up the length of his penis to the dampening tip.

Suddenly George came fully awake. He shot off the sofa bed, yanking his robe around him to hide the full shameful extent of his arousal. Jesus, what was he thinking?

'No! George, don't . . .' said Alfie, but George was already out of the door and heading for the shower, feeling disgusted with himself, his treacherous body still thrumming with need. He jerked himself off in the shower, his mind full of images of Alfie, and then he stood there for a long time under the warm flow of water, leaning his head against the cold tiles, panting, gasping, and wondering what the fuck was happening to him.

Bender, whispered a voice in his head.

But he wasn't that at all.

Was he?

41

Harry was surprised when Emma phoned him on his mobile.

'Where'd you get this number?' he asked, delighted but wary, thinking that he was going to get another ear-bashing off this adorable creature. He didn't want to fight with her, he just wanted to hug her and look at her and keep her close to him, that was all.

'My mother, of course. Should escorts hand out their personal numbers to clients like that?'

'Your mother's not a client, she's a friend.'

'She started out as a client,' said Emma.

'I know. But only because she was lonely and unhappy, and missed your dad.'

There was a brief silence while she digested this. Then she said: 'I want to meet up with you. Is that okay? Do I have to pay for your time?'

Harry took a breath, stifling an angry reply. After all, how would *he* feel if *his* mother had hired an escort? Bad enough the procession of no-hoper boyfriends Suze had shuffled through the house over the years since Dad left. But hiring in a pro? He wouldn't be pleased at all. He could see where Emma was coming from.

'No, you don't have to pay for my time. I'll meet you. Where's good?'

They met up at Jackie's Notting Hill house.

Harry looked around when Emma let him in the door, wondering if Jackie was here too.

'Mum's out on business,' said Emma.

'Right.' Harry unravelled his scarf and unbuttoned his jacket and looked at her.

Jesus, she was so lovely. And so far out of his league. Her dark hair was curling softly on to her shoulders. She was wearing a primrose-yellow pullover with a woven tan belt and a denim skirt over long tan boots. Her movements were quick, jerkier than Jackie's. Her hands were delicate, pale-veined and well cared for. Her eyes when they met his were the same tremulous, heartbreaking blue as her mother's.

She led the way into the drawing room where the fire was burning brightly. They sat down, her on one couch, him on the other. Opposites in every way. Him from the rough end of the tracks; her from the posh end. They looked at each other and it was like staring across a huge gulf.

'I was surprised to get your call,' said Harry. 'I didn't think you'd want to speak to me. I thought you were *disgusted* by the very idea of me.'

Emma's mouth twisted. 'She's my mother. How would you feel . . .?'

'Yeah. I know.'

Emma was silent, staring at him.

'What?' he asked.

'I just wonder what drives a person to do that. Sell their bodies for money, I mean.'

Harry shrugged. 'You just said it. The money.'

'I think that's terrible.'

'I know.'

'How much?'

'What?'

'How much do you charge? Like, per date? Or per hour? Mum wouldn't say.'

'Oh.' Harry felt horribly uncomfortable with this line of questioning. 'A hundred pounds. Plus—'

'What? Extras?' Emma made a grimace of disapproval.

'If they want them, yes.'

Emma stared at him, her mouth working. 'You know, my mother appears to be very fond of you. She obviously sees you as a friend, not as a—'

'What?' Now Harry felt a twinge of annoyance with her. 'A male whore?'

'Your words, not mine.'

'Hey, you got something to say, just say it.'

Emma shrugged and dragged a hand over her face. She eyed him beadily.

'What?' he demanded.

'Just *swear* to me,' she said through clenched teeth, 'that you never had sex with my mother.'

'I swear to you,' said Harry, hating the lie but knowing he had to tell it. 'I never had sex with your mother. She's a lovely lady. We're friends. That's it.'

'Oh, thank God for that,' groaned Emma, and stood up.

What the hell now? wondered Harry. She certainly was a mercurial girl. He liked that. She came over to where he was sitting and stood there in front of him, reached into her skirt pocket, pulled out a wad of money and counted out ten £10 notes. She threw them down on to the couch beside him. Harry looked at it, bemused.

'I want to book your services,' she said, and then she sat down on his lap, and kissed him.

It was hopeless to try to say that he didn't want it to be like this, that he adored her, that this escorting crap wasn't him, the *real* him, it was just some mad idea of George's that had blossomed and expanded until it had overtaken them completely. He was sorry he'd agreed to it now, even if it did pay. It seemed to be intruding on life in ways that he didn't like.

'Em . . . stop,' he managed, but he was thinking *oh shut up you fool, ain't this what you wanted from the first moment you laid eyes on her?*

But he didn't want her thinking of him this way. As a chancer, as a little crook on the make. He didn't want her to think he'd take her money and lay on the charm because he'd been paid to do it. He wanted to do this as an equal. But he wasn't her equal. He knew he wasn't, and would never be. So . . . he gave in, gave himself up to the sheer pleasure of having her close.

'What do you mean, stop?' she asked, nibbling at his throat, sending shivers down his spine. Christ, she was lovely. 'I've *paid* for this.'

Harry was trying to push her away while she was – yes, she really was – trying to get his hands on to her breasts.

'It's upstairs outside only on a first date,' he joked lamely.

Her eyes stared into his. 'This isn't a *date*, Harry Doyle,' she said softly. 'This is me paying you, and you putting out.'

Harry stared right back at her.

Never look a gift horse in the mouth, George would say. Emma wanted him. And by God he certainly wanted her. Her eyes were darkened, smoky with desire. 'All right, Harry,' she said softly. 'Anything. Anything you want. Because you know what, Harry Doyle? You're the most exquisite-looking man I've ever met.'

'Thanks,' said Harry, still trying to push her off his lap. This wasn't right. No *way* was this right. 'Em . . .'

'No one's ever called me Em before,' she said.

'Sorry.'

'No, I like it.'

'Em . . .'

'Shut up, Harry.'

They lay in her bed an hour later, arms and legs wrapped around each other, sated.

'I can't believe you just did that,' said Harry sleepily.

He was having to do rapid re-evaluations about Em. She might *look* like Jackie, but she was totally different from her mother, that much was clear. Em was impulsive; Jackie was not. Emma was deliciously sexual; Jackie was a nice middle-class lady who would never succumb unless she was desperate or deranged, as she had been on that night . . . but no. He mustn't think about that. He and Jackie had *never* slept together. That was the deal. That was the way it had to stay.

'I can't believe I did it either,' said Em, snuggling in against him with a sigh and a smile. 'Wicked, right?'

'Wicked in every way,' agreed Harry.

'Your skin's so pale. Like ivory,' she murmured, smoothing a hand over his smoothly sculpted chest.

'Yours is tanned,' said Harry, turning over so that he could stare down at her. 'All over.'

He couldn't see enough of her. Her breasts were gorgeous, small and pert. Her waist was tiny. Her hips were very slight. The V between her legs was dusted with a pale cloud of blonde hair. He felt powerful beside her, masculine in a way he had never quite felt before.

'Rooftop sunbathing,' she yawned.

'In Hong Kong.'

'Mm.'

'So exotic.'

'It's the most beautiful city on earth. There are all these elevated walkways, and at night it's just magical, all lit up, and there are mountains, little islands, lovely beaches . . . it's great.'

This girl is in love with a city on the other side of the world, thought Harry. *Fuck it.*

'Em,' he said.

'Hm?'

'Will you marry me?'

Emma gave a hoot of laughter. 'Don't be silly, Harry,' she laughed, and hugged him.

42

George was having all sorts of trouble. He didn't know whether he was punched or bored. When he opened the door and there was a girl standing there with a big bunch of roses for him, he took the damned things in a daze.

Someone was sending *him* roses?

'Aren't they gorgeous?' asked the girl, and George agreed that they were, although what the fuck did he know about flowers except that they grew in dirt?

He closed the door and stood in the hallway reading the card. It said: *All my love, George. Sandy.*

George sighed deeply. Oh terrific. He'd already had words with Sandy Cole about this sort of thing. Granted, she'd started out as a fantastic client. Before and after her birthday night out, she'd hired him regularly, a couple of times a week. He suspected she was nearly bankrupting herself to do it. And then the gifts had started. First, expensive cologne. And now roses. Who the hell sent a *man* roses?

He'd talked to her after the cologne incident. He hadn't wanted to hurt her feelings, and of *course* he hadn't wanted to offend a client, but she had to be told. This was business. She was a lovely girl, and he enjoyed their times together, but it was *strictly* a professional thing, and the gifts were . . . well, a bit inappropriate, couldn't she see that?

Sandy had seemed to be mortified. She'd said yes, she completely understood, she'd overstepped the boundaries and she promised she wouldn't do that any more.

And now – the roses.

She hadn't taken any notice of what he'd said.

None at all.

'They're nice,' said Alfie, coming out from the lounge to find George standing there holding the cellophane-wrapped bunch of red roses.

'Well I don't want the fucking things,' said George, and walked through to the kitchen and threw them straight in the bin.

'You can't do that,' said Alfie, retrieving them.

George glared at him. 'Yes I can, Alf. I just did. Okay?'

And George went off to his bedroom, slamming the door behind him.

Jesus, now he had his very own stalker. And now he'd yelled at Alfie. He shouldn't have done that. But he felt so damned *awkward* around Alfie now, ever since that . . . well, he couldn't bear to think about it, but when he did, *if* he did, he thought of it as that *incident*.

All right, so Alfie was obviously gay. So what? They couldn't shoot you for it. The fact that Alfie had come on to him was another issue entirely, and it kept nudging at his brain, even though he tried to block it out. He was straight. He had *always* been straight. Hadn't he?

Hey George, are you absolutely sure about that? kept flitting around the edges of his mind, like Muhammad Ali dancing like quicksilver around a sluggish opponent before delivering the knock-out punch.

I'm straight, he told himself, over and over.

But there had been incidents, hadn't there? All the friends he'd had who'd been girls. Friends, yes – but not girlfriends in the proper sense of the word. There had been the occasional bit of necking and fumbling with one or two of them; it seemed almost obligatory because all his male mates were at that stage. And certainly as he grew into adulthood he had always been able to get it up for women when that was required. But how much had he actually wanted that? Had he been doing it because it was sort of expected?

And once, at secondary school, there had been Jeff. A bit girly, keen on art and fashion, and he and George had been great friends, *close* friends, until some of the other boys had started saying that Jeff was arse, and someone had actually said, laughing, joking, was *George* arse too, because he seemed to like hanging around with Jeff so much?

George had felt a spasm of horror at that. He had decried that theory, loudly.

'Who you calling bent, you *cunt*?' he'd roared, and he'd given the boy who'd said it the pasting of his life.

After that he had avoided Jeff. Mud would stick, and he couldn't have that. He had a reputation as a hard nut to protect. He was *straight*. And so he ignored the hurt in Jeff's eyes, and went off with the other boys, the really macho ones like himself, and laughed in his turn at gay boys like Jeff, even though – deep down – he felt like shit about it.

Now, he did a bit on the computer, answering emails and taking a few more bookings – and there was Sandy again popping into his inbox. He was going to have another word, this was getting tedious – couldn't the silly cow take a hint?

He shut down after about an hour and went out into the lounge.

Alfie had placed the roses, neatly trimmed and arranged, in a vase of water, and stood it on the table. Alfie himself was slumped on the closed-up sofa bed opening a letter. He looked up at George, his eyes wary and hurt. George remembered that look, that same look, in Jeff's eyes. He'd wimped out then, left Jeff to the wolves. The poor little git had suffered several beatings after George abandoned him to the rougher elements at school. George had tried to ignore all that, but at bottom he had felt bad about it, really bad: ashamed.

'Post's been.' Alfie waved the open letter he held at George and risked a small, tentative smile. 'Look, George. I got the job.'

Hadn't the poor little sod been through enough, without him coming over all moody on him? George forced a smile in return. Poor cunt couldn't *help* being a shirt-lifter, could he? He was still Alfie, still a friend, still a great laugh.

'Well, done Alf,' he said. 'Come on, let's get down the caff and celebrate.'

43

Sandy turned off the computer the minute she was aware of Noel standing behind her in the doorway of their little 'office'. Some bloody office – it was a box room really, eight feet by five.

'Who you talking to on that?' he asked, puffing on a spliff.

Sandy half turned in her chair, keeping her face blank and her voice casual, even though he'd given her a bit of a scare, creeping about the place like that. 'Just some mates,' she said, her nose wrinkling as a warm waft of Noel's unwashed socks and sickly sweet skunk drifted over her. Damn, how could he have come up the stairs so quietly? He'd obviously *crept* up them, determined to catch her out.

She was resenting him more and more. Couldn't he see that if he kept *spying* on her like he did, then she was more likely to cheat? And anyway, she hadn't cheated at all, not really. Not *technically*. She hadn't slept with gorgeous George; they'd just dated. Sandy lived for her dates with George. All right, she paid him, but she knew he just took her cash because he was hard up and needed it. She knew he was in

255

love with her, just as she was in love with him, and one day they were going to be together properly, live in the country maybe, keep chickens and grow veggies – it would be so wonderful.

Only for the moment she was here, with Noel.

Suddenly he spun her chair around and crouched over her, holding on to the armrests, breathing skunk and suspicion all over her from inches away. She could see all the black-heads over his nose, could smell his foul breath – and Jesus, couldn't he ever take a bath?

'You been talking to men on that?' asked Noel, his ciggie still between his lips, one eye squinting and watering as smoke drifted up from the spliff.

'Nah,' said Sandy with a half-laugh. 'You want to stop smoking that stuff, Noel. It's making you paranoid.'

'I ain't paranoid. I know you're talking to other men on that fucking thing.'

'Don't be daft.'

'Don't call me daft!' yelled Noel.

Sandy literally jumped in her seat, startled by the loudness of his tone. Her heart started beating very hard, and she felt her stomach coil into tight, sick-making knots. He never used the computer, never showed any interest in it. She knew whatever secrets it contained of hers were safe.

She stared at him, and wondered how on earth she had ever found him attractive. He was crass and ugly. She hated him. She wanted out. And one day, she'd get that. All she needed was to talk to George, make sure of their plans, then she would be *out* of here.

'You're a crafty, cheating little mare,' snapped Noel, and he slapped her, hard.

Sandy was knocked sideways, but his arm and the arm of

the chair stopped her from falling to the floor. She cried out in pain and surprise and raised a hand to her face. He'd never really hit her before, although he'd raged and shouted and sometimes he'd pushed her, more times than she could count. She was used to all that. But *this* . . .

He drew back his hand and slapped her again, and again.

Her cheeks stung. She could taste blood in her mouth; she'd bitten her tongue. Tears of pain and panic sprang from her eyes.

'I'm not cheating, Noel,' she managed to sob out. 'I *swear*.'

'No? How do I know what you get up to in that bloody office of yours? You could be having it away over the desk in your lunch hour for all I know.'

'I wouldn't do that.'

'Yeah you would, given half a chance. You keep saying your boss is an ugly little bugger, but how do I know that's true?'

It *was* true. Her boss looked about ninety: what the hell would she want to screw him for? Noel was getting worse and worse with all this shit he smoked. He was already paranoid. Soon he'd be hearing voices. She wanted to get out of here, get away with George, before it got to that stage, so she was glad she'd made another date with him just now. George would be her salvation.

'You cheat on me, you cunt, and I'll kill you,' roared Noel.

Sandy said nothing. It seemed safest. Nothing got through to him, anyway. She just nodded her head, which was starting to hurt with tension. She listened to him going back down the stairs, and swivelled her chair back towards the computer.

She wiped at her eyes. Her face was a hot, painful mass. She looked longingly at the blank screen. She wanted to go back online, talk to George, tell him what was happening, be reassured he loved her as much as she loved him. She knew he did, deep down, although he never said so. But she didn't dare, not tonight. She was going to meet up with George on Thursday. She was just going to have to wait until then.

44

Harry was sitting in Jackie's kitchen. It was morning and they were having breakfast together, just like they often had before Em came back from Hong Kong. Emma had just gone out to the hairdresser's. She'd met Harry just as he was arriving and she was leaving, and Jackie had come out into the hall to find them kissing. Now Jackie was placing the cafetière on the table, smiling so widely she could hardly contain herself.

'No need to look so smug,' said Harry, but he was smiling too.

'There's *every* need,' said Jackie, sitting down at the other side of the table and beaming across at him. She pushed the croissants towards him and he took one.

'Did you set us up?' wondered Harry aloud.

'I just knew you'd be good together. I *knew* it,' crowed Jackie happily.

Harry was breaking up the croissant, scattering buttery crumbs. His smile faded.

'Jackie,' he said seriously, 'that's all very well, but come on – what's the point? Her life's out in Hong Kong. And for God's sake, get real. She's so far out of my league we're nearly on different bloody planets.'

Jackie poured out the coffee into two mugs.

'Look, when I met Donald, my husband, he wasn't from a well-to-do family. I was. My parents were furious when we fell in love. But it worked for us, despite all their opposition. We were blissfully happy for thirty-two years.'

'Jackie, I don't even have a proper job. I'm a flaming *escort*. What wife would want her husband doing that sort of thing for a living? How would *I* feel if she did it? Well, I'll tell you. I'd be gutted.'

'Wife?' asked Jackie, bright-eyed. She paused with her mug halfway to her lips. 'Harry . . . oh darling Harry, are you saying you want to marry my daughter?'

Harry held his hands up. 'Now don't go getting excited. I'm not going to. I wouldn't have the fucking nerve.'

'But you want to?'

'I've wanted to ever since I first laid eyes on her.'

Jackie let out a scream of delighted laughter.

'But I told you,' said Harry sternly. 'Hold it down to a dull roar. I'm not proposing. I'm going to let Emma go back to Hong Kong and get on with the life she *should* have. She could marry anybody. Someone who'll give her the lifestyle she deserves. She don't want to get tucked up with a loser like me.'

'Harry, you're not a loser. You're the most charming, gorgeous, *fabulous* man.'

'It's not going to happen, Jackie. I mean it. You can scheme and rub your hands all you like, it *ain't going to happen*.'

'And you can pass in any company,' Jackie was going on, as if he hadn't even spoken. 'You're a very fast learner.'

'No, Jackie.'

Jackie picked up a croissant, her cheeks pinkening. 'And you're a fantastic lover.'

'*Jackie*.' It embarrassed him to be reminded of that night he'd spent with her. He could see that it embarrassed her too, so why couldn't she just let it drop?

'Well you are. It's nothing more than the truth.' Jackie kept her eyes down as she tore off a bit of croissant and slathered it with conserve. 'That night with you . . . well, it was a revelation. I didn't think I'd ever want . . . sex . . . again, not after Donald. But you made me realize that I was still a fully functioning woman, Harry. You were so kind, and so gentle, and, let's face it, so very sexy too.'

'*Jackie*.' Now he was beyond embarrassed. 'We said we weren't going to mention it, remember?'

'I'm just *saying*,' said Jackie. 'You were marvellous in bed. And . . . I'd like Emma to know that sort of joy, Harry. I really would.'

Then the kitchen door swung open and Emma was standing there. Her face told the full story. She'd heard every word. She had her bag slung over her shoulder and in one hand she was holding her mobile phone. She looked down at it, then at the two of them, frozen at the kitchen table.

'I forgot my phone,' she said numbly. 'I came back for it.' Emma's stricken eyes fastened on Harry's face. 'You swore to me,' she said. 'You *swore* that you didn't . . .'

Harry couldn't stand it. She looked devastated. He jumped to his feet, rushed over to her. 'Em, it isn't—'

'Oh, are you going to say it isn't what it seems?' Emma took a step back, away from him. She was shaking her head, not wanting to believe it, but she'd just *heard* it. 'You're joking, aren't you? It's *exactly* what it seems, Harry. You've slept with my mother and then you slept with me, and that's damned *disgusting*.'

'Em, it wasn't like that,' said Harry, reaching out for her, desperate to explain.

'*Don't you dare touch me!*' she screamed, and lunged forward and slapped him, hard.

Harry fell back, his face white with the shock of it.

'And as for you,' Emma turned on her mother, 'I can't believe how you lied to me.'

'Emma darling, no . . .' started Jackie. 'It shouldn't have happened. It *wouldn't* have, if I hadn't been so much still in mourning for your father.'

'Don't drag Dad into this,' said Emma, trembling with fury. 'I can't believe this of either of you. You're like *dogs* in the street.'

'For God's sake, Emma,' said Jackie.

'Well you are. How could you do this to me, do *that*, and then lie about it?'

'We had to lie about it, you silly mare,' said Harry softly. 'Jackie's right. It shouldn't have happened. But it did. And we knew how you'd react, that it would hurt you. So we agreed that you must never know.'

Emma's mouth was quivering with emotion, bitterness in every line. Tears spilled over and made tracks down her cheeks. 'Well, at least I know now what you're really like, Harry Doyle,' she snapped, her voice breaking. 'What was it, a joke to you? Something to brag to your mates about? Do the mother and the daughter too? Is that it?'

Harry stood silent for a moment. He'd always known it was going nowhere, anyway. He'd have liked some time with her, at least, but that wasn't to be. Maybe it was better – kinder and less painful – to end it quickly, like this. The love of his life, and she was going to bugger off back to Hong Kong and take his heart with her. But he'd live. He'd have to.

'Yeah, now you know what I'm really like,' he echoed. His cheek was throbbing, painful, where she'd struck him. He looked at Jackie, sitting there in pieces, tears starting to drip down her face, her eyes wild with distress. Not fifteen minutes ago she'd been so happy, so elated. 'I'd better go,' he said.

'Yeah,' said Emma furiously. 'Go on. Fuck off, Harry. You lying bastard.'

45

Noel had been slipping in a few cheeky computer lessons with a friend. He was determined to find out what Sandy was up to online, so when she went out to work he went upstairs and logged on. He got the shock of his life.

There was *his* woman, parading herself in a photo on Facebook with a big fat bastard with darkish hair. Looked like they were in a restaurant or some such shit. A red candle dripping wax down over one of those raffia bottle things.

He'd found Sandy's notebook in which the silly mare kept all her various passwords. You weren't supposed to write the sodding things down, didn't she know that? Was she a complete fool?

Well, yeah, obviously she was. Because he had easily found her Facebook password and now he was sitting here at her computer and he could see the evidence of her betrayal with his own eyes. She'd been making a fucking fool out of him. She'd listed her status as 'Single'.

Noel sat there and stared, enraged. He looked at the guy in the picture and thought, *Man, you are so dead.* He was going to have it out with her the minute she put her lying face through that door tonight. He stared and stared at the screen, at the man's face. Not handsome, not really. The short-cut hair looked sort of dark red. There was a big shit-eating grin on the idiot's face. What had that mare been up to? But she would pay. And so would that fat fuck in the photo. Him, most of all. He would pay in blood.

46

Serendipity was a word that Lefty Umbabwe had never heard of, but his pal Gordon had. Serendipity was happenstance, good things just falling into your lap for no good reason. Like Felice, Gordon's new lady. His *old* lady, who had divorced him two years ago, saying that he was stifling her, had departed his life with his three kids. He'd been down after that, depressed; she'd been awkward over access and hadn't mellowed much until she found a new bloke, then it had all ironed out nicely. And then – *serendipitously* – he had met Felice, who was a stripper at the club opposite where he worked the door at Deano Drax's dive in Soho.

Mindful that his first marriage had foundered, Gordon was careful to keep the magic alive in this, his second. Felice was high maintenance, and sometimes that was a pain, but she was a looker, and he was proud to be seen about with her on his well-muscled arm, so he treated her good. Took her out to dinner, out to clubs, and – as Christmas was looming and he was feeling flush – the casino.

They played a little blackjack, then had a go on the roulette tables, Felice getting all excited and leaning over the table until he was frightened her tits were going to fall right out of the high-priced dress she was wearing. Gordon had been in casinos on the Continent and in the United States where they played double zero, but he liked the English system of having only one zero. It increased the punters' chances, raising the odds to a pretty good thirty-five to one. However, Felice soon started losing and looking put out. Determined to lift her spirits, he booked in to the adjoining restaurant to ply her with food and maybe even some of the cheap house champagne.

They were crossing the casino boulevard, heading out to the lobby to enter the restaurant – Gordon was promising himself a quick peek at the prices before they went in. Tormenting himself really, because they were for certain-sure *going* in – Felice was expecting a meal, bubbly, the works, after her little disappointment on the tables. What Felice wanted, Felice got – or there was hell to pay.

And that was when *serendipity* took a hand. Because there was Deano's boy Alfie, crossing the boulevard, wearing the purple livery that all the staff here wore. He wasn't a punter, so no need to make a fuss by trying to detain him. No, the little bastard *worked* here, and so Gordon could pass on the good news to Lefty, making sure of course that Lefty coughed up a hefty wedge first, for the information. Thus covering the cost of the evening's entertainments.

So, everyone was happy. Felice, Gordon, and Lefty.

Not Alfie, of course, and that was a shame. Alfie had a world of hurt coming to him. Deano Drax was going to ream his arsehole good after this. But so what? That was not Gordon's problem.

* * *

When Gordon crawled from his pit after a very satisfactory night with the well-pleased Felice next morning, he called Lefty straight away.

'Got some news for you,' he told Lefty, as he stood in the kitchen in his vest and boxers making a cup of tea. 'Come on round, my son.'

Lefty was there within half an hour. Gordon had been careful to take Felice up a brew and to tell her he had company coming over and to stay upstairs for a bit.

'Okay, lover,' she said sweetly, and rolled over and went back to sleep. She was a lazy mare anyway – he'd found that most strippers were; they rarely rose before one o'clock – but that suited him because he liked having the mornings to himself.

If she knew it was Lefty coming, she'd only kick off anyway; she hated Lefty and wouldn't want him through the door. Everyone knew that Lefty was on the butane and was as stable as warmed-up Semtex as a result of it. He made women nervous.

Gordon thought that Lefty looked like shit, but that was pretty much the norm. He'd had his stitches out, so he looked a little less like Frankenstein now and a little more like normal. Gordon felt a bit sad looking at the wreckage of his old friend as he ushered him into the kitchen. Once, Lefty had been fit, clear-eyed and athletic; then some tosser – Gordon suspected that twisted article Deano – had got him onto Es and grass, and it was a short hop then to the crack pipe. The butane was cheaper and so much easier to source; so it had quickly become Lefty's preferred drug of choice.

And now look.

Lefty was bog-eyed, wheezy, sniffy and unwashed – shot away half the time. No wonder Felice wouldn't want him indoors, Gordon was starting to get that way himself. He looked at his old friend and felt the sadness give way to disgust. What the fuck had he done to himself, the bloody fool?

'Christ, you look a mess,' said Gordon, as Lefty came in and slumped against the worktop.

Lefty shrugged. He didn't care. He was already hyped, fresh from his latest fix.

Gordon decided there and then that their friendship was at an end. After this little transaction, that was *it*. No more cosy chats, no nothing. He was done with this whole bloody scene.

'What news?' asked Lefty.

'About Deano's little passion. His little runaway.'

'Alfie?' Lefty straightened; a flare of hope lit his bloodshot eyes. 'What, you seen him?'

Gordon shrugged, deliberately casual. 'Might have.'

Suddenly Lefty's eyes were flat and murderous. 'What the fuck you mean, *might* have? Either you have or you haven't – you foolin' with my mind, boy?'

'I ain't foolin', Lefty,' said Gordon with a half-smile. *And you ain't got much of a mind left, dope-head.* He knew he had Lefty by the short and curlies on this. Lefty needed the info, and after last night's blowout with Felice he needed some wedge. This was all going to work out fine. 'I seen him.'

'Where?'

'Ah, now. That would be telling. Fact is, I've been making a big effort, trying to help you out with this.' *Like fuck.* The kid had fallen right into his lap. But Lefty wasn't to know that.

Lefty paced about. He clutched his head in agitation.

'Man, come on. Spit it out. You seen him *where?*'

'Let's talk a deal first.'

'A *deal?*' Lefty stopped walking. 'You're supposed to be in tight with me. What you mean, a deal?'

'I want paying for my efforts, Lefty. Wouldn't you say that was fair?'

Lefty started pacing, faster now, shooting anxious looks at Gordon. Lefty had had the motherfucker of all times these past few weeks. Walking around the city at night with that tart Mona, and then there had been something with a taxi guy, some disagreement, something . . . he couldn't quite remember what . . . but he knew there'd been trouble. But he'd persevered, his old mum told him you should always persevere, and he *had*. He'd been so worried about his mum, after what Deano had said. All the time, he'd been getting more and more anxious, taking heavier hits of the can; sometimes he could barely even *think*, he was so spaced out and so *freaked* out by this whole situation.

And now Gordon had found the boy, and wanted paying?

All right.

Lefty took a grip of himself. What he felt was a killing rage. He wanted to take Gordon's smug head and batter it against the corner of that kitchen cabinet, see the blood fly, let rip; but he wouldn't, he couldn't afford to. He *owed* Gordon, the fat fuck was right; and he needed that information.

'How much?' asked Lefty.

'For this sort of info? Couple of ton ought to do it.'

'You got it,' said Lefty. Couple of *ton?* 'Now come on. Spill.'

'Cash first,' said Gordon.

'Don't get paid 'til tomorrow.'

'Can I trust you, Lefty?' Gordon was looking at his ex-friend speculatively.

'Man, we're brothers, we're *pals*. I wouldn't cross a pal, Gordy. Never.'

My arse, thought Gordon. *Lying little git would cross his own grandma for a fix*. But he knew where Lefty lived. And if Lefty defaulted, he was going to come down on the fucker like a sack of shit.

'Right then,' said Gordon. 'We're agreed.'

'Right, man. Right.'

Now Lefty was looking at him hopefully. 'Come *on*, man,' he whined.

So Gordon told him where he had seen Alfie.

Lefty grinned happily. All would be well. Then he had a thought: 'You don't tell Deano about this, okay? You got me? That's *my* shit, man. My good news. Understood?'

Gordon nodded. He didn't want to get involved with it in any way, shape or form; he was a doorman, and that was all. Fuck Deano and his young boys.

'Understood,' he said.

47

Alfie was as happy as a pig in shit. He was loving the job, he was living with George and Harry; everything that had been so awful and so frightening about his world had somehow resolved itself into this arrangement that worked so well for all of them.

Well, he *hoped* that was the case.

He knew he had freaked George a little with the cuddles and kisses, but he couldn't help that, he really couldn't because he *loved* George, he adored him, and he had been stifling an impulse to get closer ever since he'd met him. It had been killing him having to suppress how he truly felt.

Now, George knew.

And at first – granted – George had been shocked.

That had hurt Alfie so much.

But now, George had mellowed. He had never mentioned that night again, but he was acting normally around Alfie, laughing, joking, having breakfast down the caff, still dating the women and – Alfie supposed, and felt a bit unhappy about it – still shagging them too, and taking their money for it. Harry had even suggested that Alfie go on the pay roll when he hit his eighteenth birthday. Well, why not? Harry said he was a good-looking boy; there was mega money to be earned. Why slog his guts out down the casino when the escorting biz paid so much better?

It had been George who had clamped down on *that* idea. And that had pleased Alfie immensely, because it gave him just a little hope that George might love him too, and might not *want* him getting involved with women. Whatever, Alfie knew that he could never get it up for a woman, anyway. He knew that horrible nonce Deano and his lapdog Lefty had spotted that in him early on. It made him shudder to think about it – all that had been done to him and how it could have ended.

It hurt Alfie that George could actually *go* with women. Maybe George was bi- and just didn't know it yet. Certainly he had responded when Alfie had fondled him, kissed him. Or maybe he really was gay and was trying very, very hard not to face it, not to come out. Alfie hoped it was that. Because if it *was*, then one day George could be his and his alone.

One day.

Alfie dreamed of that.

And while Alfie dreamed, and Lefty Umbabwe was hearing about Alfie's whereabouts from his ex-friend Gordon, the tides near the bridge rose and fell. Lefty hadn't considered tidal movements or heights when he'd pushed the cab containing its dead driver into the river. He hadn't considered *squat*. He'd been too jazzed for that.

But him and Mona had pushed it in at high tide, into water that was seven metres deep. Now, the tide was low, barely a metre of water there. The movements of the water and the traffic on the river had jolted and bumped the car along the muddy bottom and now it was lying on its roof just under London Bridge.

Someone was bound to see it there.

And eventually – of course – someone did.

Sally Paige was hurrying among the hordes of commuters, office workers just like herself, over the bridge. It was nearly nine o'clock in the morning, and she was trying not to breathe in, because the river was low. It looked like a narrow oily grey slug down there, and where the mud of the river bottom was exposed there were trolleys, bikes, flotsam and jetsam. The mud stank to high heaven and she hated that smell.

Sally hated a lot about her world. She hated her go-nowhere job, and the bossy cow who sat opposite her in the accounts department of Turbell and Whey, a small and extremely dull engineering firm; and most of all she hated her husband, who bored her witless. She'd been married to Simon for twelve years and the habits that had once endeared her to him now made her want to shriek with rage. The sniffing – *why* wouldn't he use a handkerchief like any normal person? The bum-scratching. The insistence on a brisk morning hump, despite Sally's often-stated preference for evenings. She *hated* morning humps. It was nearly Christmas, and Christmas was always crunch time for Sally. Every year she said to herself: this is it; this year I'm going to do it. I'm going to leave him.

Every year, she stayed.

But *this* year . . .

She came to a halt. People stepped around her, glaring, but she walked over to the edge of the bridge and looked down at the river, thinking of that fountain in Rome, what was it called, yeah, that was it, the Trevi Fountain, where you threw in a coin and made a wish. Her breath pluming out in front of her in the cold, dank, tainted air, she ignored the roaring traffic and the steady flow of pedestrians and thought to herself: *This time I'm going to do it.*

She looked down at the grey oozing river, and a glint of metal caught her eye. Some junk or other down there. Yeah, she'd leave him, make a fresh start in a bright, hopeful New Year. Maybe even get another job. She felt her heart lift at the very idea of it. That glint again.

She craned over the parapet a little, curious. The smell rose up to her, making her gag. Mud and water. But there was definitely something down there, just under the bridge. Round things, like car tyres. And oh yes, the big, boxy rectangular shape of a car, but . . . yes, it was upside-down. Somebody must have just dumped it in there. She could see the windows on one side, dulled by silt and weed, but something . . . something was lolling against the window, something that looked like . . .

'Oh *shit!*' she burst out, clutching a hand to her chest.

Then she started to scream.

48

It was chocolates this time. *Plain* chocolates, because he'd expressed an innocent preference for them once in the course of conversation. There had also been the cologne, the black leather wallet engraved with his initial 'G'; there had even been – for God's sake – *Gucci underpants*. And the roses. Now that had been downright embarrassing. A woman, sending him roses!

'Look,' said George as he sat with Sandy in the Italian restaurant she favoured, the one she always wanted to go to. She'd given him the red-ribboned box of chocolates at the start of the meal, and he had thanked her but held back on telling her to slow down until they were on their pudding, in case she kicked off. He didn't want a whole evening of histrionics. Cheese board for George. Tiramisu for Sandy. 'We really have to talk.'

'Oh!' Sandy gave a little laugh and put down her spoon. 'That sounds ominous.'

'It's just . . . these presents. Come on. You can't afford them . . .'

'Yes I can. My gran died six months ago. She left me some cash.'

It was a lie. Granny Cole was alive and well and living in Holywell. Sandy had bought all George's gifts on the plastic, paying off the minimum on her card each month. Her debt was mounting, but she ignored that, pushing it to one side. He was worth it, she told herself. And she had even . . . well, this was a big secret, one she hugged to herself with great glee, but she had even bought herself a ring, an engagement ring. She kept it well hidden from Noel and from George, but at work she wore it, told everyone that George had whisked her off to Paris and proposed to her there; it had been *so* romantic, and all the girls at work were pea-green with envy.

The sad truth was that on her last break what she'd really done was sit indoors watching telly while Noel got doped off his head. There had been no trips on the Seine, no Paris-by-night. In fact, no fuck-all.

'Yeah, but look . . .' George was struggling with this. To get expensive gifts from women made his skin crawl, made him feel demeaned, made him feel like a fucking oily *gigolo*. He had gone into the escort biz for the money. He had expected that sex with women would be a part of that equation, and that was okay. Not that Sandy had ever indicated she wanted *that*. All she ever seemed to want was to sit here, in this same restaurant, boring the arse off him with tales of her deadly dull little life.

'I like buying you things,' said Sandy, giving him a flirtatious look.

'I know you do. And I appreciate it, but I would really rather you didn't, okay?'

Sandy sat back and looked at him. 'I've read about male

escorts up West being given apartments. Sports cars. Exotic holidays,' she said.

'Yeah, I know, and I'd *hate* that,' said George emphatically. He didn't want the silly tart getting herself deep in debt and then blaming it on him.

Now there was a glint of tears in her eyes. She looked down at her half-eaten tiramisu then back up at George.

Shit, now I've upset her, thought George. Well, maybe that was a good thing. Sandy was beginning, ever so slightly, to give him the dry heaves. He decided that the next time she sent one of her emails with the cute smiley faces and the hugs and kisses, he was going to press the delete button.

'I'm sorry,' she said in her small, childish voice.

'It's okay,' said George, smiling reassuringly. Get this evening over, and he'd be *gone*. Enough of Sandy and her creepy, insidious little ways. He had plenty of other clients – straightforward, successful businesswomen with plenty of cash to splash and lonely evenings to fill. He'd stick with those. Sometimes there was a little problem with the sex, which he wouldn't admit to a living soul, but he could do it. He told himself that, over and over. He could do it. 'Look, I'm sorry, but I had to say it, okay?'

'Okay,' said Sandy weakly, prodding the tiramisu with her spoon.

'You're a lovely girl, Sandy,' said George.

She brightened then, raised a small smile.

'I hope I haven't offended you,' said George. He really did hope that he hadn't. He wanted a nice clear line drawn under this. No hassles. No comebacks.

'No. You haven't,' she said, and Sandy started eating again.

* * *

'Good night?' asked Alfie, looking up from the sofa as George came into the lounge, shucking off his coat. The telly was on; the flat was warm and cosy. Harry was out on a job.

George tossed the box of chocolates down beside Alfie. 'Here,' he said.

'What, did the client give you these?' asked Alfie, pulling off the ribbon greedily.

George made a face. 'She did.' He looked at the roses that Alfie had put in a vase. 'And I wish you'd flung those bloody things.'

'I couldn't just *bin* them: they're nice,' said Alfie, diving into the chocolates headfirst.

George watched Alfie chomping away and had to smile.

'You'll get gut-ache, eating this late in the day,' said George, yawning. 'I'm all in, I'm off to bed. G'night, mate.'

'Night, George,' said Alfie, past a mouthful of caramel and chocolate.

George was awoken in the small hours of the night by Alfie crying from the lounge.

Oh fuck, he thought, his heart breaking into a fast canter. He lay there in the dark, remembering the last time he'd gone in to see Alfie. Remembering Alfie kissing him, and remembering that he, George Doyle, had responded, and would have gone further – much, much further – if he hadn't come to his senses in time.

No, no. He wasn't going down *that* blind alley again.

He turned over, pulled the pillow over his head, blotting out the sound. Let Harry go in and see to him – if he was back yet, which George sort of doubted; he usually heard Harry's key in the door, and he hadn't.

No. He wasn't going in there. Alfie would probably wake

himself up in a moment with all the noise he was making. And then he'd go back to sleep. It would all be okay.

George lay there. He could still hear Alfie's cries, and they made George feel sick and anxious for him. It felt like hours, lying there, tense and tormented, wanting to go to him, but frightened to. Finally – it seemed to take forever – Alfie was quiet, and slowly, inch by inch, George relaxed, and was starting to drift off to sleep when he heard his bedroom door click open, then shut.

Oh no.

'George?' It was Alfie, coming to the bed, slipping under the covers, snuggling up against him. At the contact, George felt as if someone had plugged his entire body into the mains and fried him alive. His whole skin was suddenly, intensely, sensitized. He always slept naked, couldn't bear to wear boxers or pyjamas or anything on him at night – although he kept a spare pair in his bottom drawer, in case of emergencies. And . . . oh fuck it, Alfie was nude too. He could feel Alfie's smooth, lightly muscled nakedness pressing against him, could feel Alfie's arm reaching across his chest, burning a trail of fire in its wake.

Oh God.

'I had the dreams, George,' said Alfie, burrowing his head in under George's chin, the warm brush of that thick corn-gold hair and the sweet salty scent of Alfie's skin sending George's senses into a whirling nosedive. 'Why didn't you come? I had the fucking *dreams* . . .' Alfie half sobbed.

George swallowed hard. He felt like he was way up on the top board at the swimming pool, getting ready to dive in . . . or fall off. *This* was what he'd been afraid of. Finding out the thing about himself that for years he had been trying so hard to ignore.

'It's okay, Alf,' he managed to get out. 'It's okay, I'm here.'

He hugged Alfie hard against him, squeezed him tight.

Oh, such a feeling. George closed his eyes and gave himself up to it.

Alfie. Oh Alfie, I love you so much, he thought, and then his eyes opened, startled. He wondered if he'd said it aloud because he had *felt* it, had felt it and heard it and knew it was the truth.

'It's okay, Alf,' he said to the shivering boy, and kissed his hair, and then Alfie lifted his head and George could see the faint wetness of tears on his pale moonlit face.

'Please kiss me, George. *Please*,' moaned Alfie.

George kissed him; he kissed Alfie as he had never kissed any woman – with his heart, his body and his soul. He felt close to tears himself, he loved Alfie so much.

'I love you, I love you,' he found himself murmuring ecstatically against the boy's soft, silken skin.

'I know, George. Oh, you bloody fool, don't you think I know that?' Alfie was half laughing and crying all at once. 'I love you too, George. I love you.'

They made love, and George was gentle and slow and easy, the way he'd never been with any woman. This was right, this was *so* right. And when finally, at last, his orgasm came like a warm, shuddering, exquisite jolt of lightning, and Alfie's came too, there was only peace and contentment and complete, utter joy afterwards. The way it had never been with any woman he'd ever been with.

They lay together afterwards, warm and happy, murmuring their love for each other, kissing each other's tears away, laughing, snuggling down together, and finally sleeping like spoons, George behind Alfie, his arms wrapped securely around him as if he would never, ever let him go.

49

Across town, Harry was still working. The evening had gone well; he'd escorted top corporate lawyer Becca Stanway to dinner at Langan's; they'd had a great meal and then they'd got into a taxi to go back to her place.

She'd paid him not the usual hundred, but five hundred pounds. She'd handed it to him in a discreet white envelope over their starter of scallops, samphire and black pudding. He'd gone to the Gents mid-evening, counted out the cash, and been both amazed and a bit doleful. Extras were expected, and he was up for it, he was *always* up for it, like an Ever Ready battery, that was Harry.

Only . . . he felt numb at heart. After Emma had found out about him and her mother, ever since then, he'd felt like someone had deep-frozen his internal organs; he would perform because he *had* to, but it meant nothing. Less than nothing.

But now it was put-out time. The minute they got inside her flat, Becca – who was gorgeous, with straight long blonde hair, a perma-tanned body and beautifully French-manicured nails – led him into her bedroom, which was tricked out all in neutrals, with flowing curtains of white star-marked voile at the windows and surrounding the four-poster bed, and dense, deep cream carpet underfoot.

'Hurry up,' said Becca, striding off into the en suite in her strappy five-inch heels. 'Get naked, Harry.'

Harry stood there. Now he not only *was* a tart, he truly *felt* like one. He hated this. Oh, granted, it had started out as a light-hearted jape. George in the lead, saying hey Harry, how about you and me doing this, couldn't we use the readies? And oh, there had been readies all right. *Bags* of cash. But they'd both ignored the core message of that cheesy old Richard Gere film, hadn't they? And the message was: Richard Gere had landed up to his neck in the shit.

And hadn't they done that too?

Well, maybe not George. But Harry? Oh yes. Perhaps not as *badly* in the shit as the character in the film. But Harry looked at the facts and they weren't cheering.

The *fact* was, if he hadn't got involved in yet another of George's mad schemes, he would never have met Jackie. And if he hadn't met Jackie, he wouldn't have met Emma, either. If he hadn't done *that*, he wouldn't be standing here now feeling like someone had scooped out his innards and left him feeling empty and bereft.

What was that stupid old saying? Better to have loved and lost than never to have loved at all? Well, that was crap. He'd been happy before all this had started. Now, he was miserable. And now . . . oh shit, here came Becca in nothing but a pair of sheer royal-blue Agent Provocateur panties, still teetering along on her five-inch heels, ready for action and holding an open jar of chocolate body paint.

Harry stared at her. Her body was gym-toned, her breasts

obviously surgically enhanced; she looked truly fabulous. Yet he felt like stone. He felt *nothing*.

Becca sent Harry a come-hither smile and headed for the bed. She sat down, dipped a finger into the paint in what she clearly thought was a sexy manner, and smeared a touch of the paint on to each of her erect nipples. Then she put the pot aside and leaned back on her hands and smiled at him.

'Come and lick me, Harry,' she said.

Well, he could do that. Maybe this was what he needed. A hot session with this gorgeous-looking woman might just shake him out of the morose mood he was in.

He took off his jacket, dropping it on to the floor, and went over to the bed. He gripped Becca's exquisitely sculpted thighs and eased them apart. He knelt between them. Her smile widened. Then he leaned forward and kissed her. Her lips parted voraciously, her tongue shooting into his mouth so suddenly that he had to stop himself from pulling back in surprise.

It wasn't like kissing Emma.

It was *nothing* like that.

He moved away from her mouth, annoyed with himself, thinking, *What the hell is the matter with me?* He trailed a line of light kisses down her throat, over her collarbone. Becca moaned and pushed her pneumatic breasts at him.

Well, here goes nothing, thought Harry, and started licking at the chocolate paint. It was sickly sweet. Becca moaned louder. The paint was so sweet it was making him feel a bit nauseous, in fact. He drew back.

'Becca . . .' he said, about to suggest something else, *anything* else, the stuff was foul.

'No, keep doing that,' she said, and yanked his head back

towards her breast. He hesitated. Their eyes met and she must have read the reluctance in his because hers were suddenly harder, more demanding. 'Come *on*, Harry, it's what I'm paying you for.'

She was right. Harry got back to the task, hating it. Hating *her*. The paint tasted disgusting, and it set a tingling at the back of his throat, a rush of strange sensations right up to the top of his head. Weird feelings stabbed downwards, hitting his groin, making his cock stir. *This* time, Harry drew back so suddenly and so forcefully that he fell back on his arse on the shag pile.

'What the *fuck*?' he demanded, his head spinning.

He looked up at Becca, smiling there as she bent and slipped off her panties.

'Yeah, come on Harry. Let's do it,' she said, leaning back invitingly.

Harry scrambled to his feet. His head felt strange, all rushing sounds and kaleidoscopic lights. He looked at the innocent pot of body paint on the bedside table, then at Becca.

'You put something in that,' he said.

Becca lay back and nodded slowly. 'Got it in one,' she said.

'What?'

She shrugged. 'Just a little coke,' she said.

Harry stared at her. Harry was the mildest-mannered, sweetest of men, but suddenly it all crashed in on him, the enormity of it all. Losing Em. Knowing he wasn't good enough for her. Knowing he was now just a piece of meat, a cheap hooker, being paid for and pawed over by women with more money than sense.

'Wait a minute,' he said, breathing hard. 'All right, you're paying for my body. I get that. But now you think that gives you the right to *dope* me?'

Becca looked up at him with a tinge of irritation. 'Look, Harry,' she said, 'It's just a couple of lines of coke I mixed in there, just a little something to mellow us out. Jesus, you certainly seem to *need* it. You've had a face like thunder for half the night, and is that what I pay for? I don't think so. I just thought a little relaxation would do us both good, okay?'

'No, actually it's *not* okay,' said Harry, enraged. 'What the fuck next, Rohypnol? What sort of sad bitch are you, that you've got to drug a man before he'll hump you?'

Becca's face flooded with angry colour. She sprang up on the bed and glared at him. 'If *that's* how you feel, you'd better just piss off,' she yelled.

'Yeah. That is how I feel.' His head whirling, he crossed the room unsteadily and picked up his jacket. He fumbled inside, found the envelope full of cash. He flung it on to the floor. 'And here's your full refund.' Notes spilled out on the carpet but he didn't give a shit. He shrugged on his jacket.

'You useless bastard,' shouted Becca. 'I bet you couldn't have got it up anyway.'

Harry strode to the door. He looked back at her, with her chocolate-smeared breasts and her face distorted and ugly with temper. 'Night, Becca,' he said, and left.

'Fuck *you!*' she screamed after him.

Lefty phoned Deano. He said: 'I found out who took Alfie, Deano.'

'Tell me.'

'George Doyle.' And Lefty gave Deano all George's details.

* * *

It was very late when he got back to the flat, but Harry was so buzzed that he knew he'd never settle down to sleep. He wanted to talk to George, just a chat, just to talk things through.

Ah, who am I kidding? he thought.

What he wanted to say to George was that he'd had enough of the escort business. That he never wanted to have to do any of these women for cash, ever again. Even the bloody dole office and the boredom of just kicking his heels all day was better than this. He felt hurt, near tears, desperately sad over losing Emma. And more than that. Meeting Jackie and then Emma had forced him to confront things about himself that he had always shied away from. He *was* shiftless. He *was* lazy. He had no ambition. He had been wasting his life, letting it drift by – his one precious, unrepeatable life.

Why the fuck had George done this to him? He'd changed Harry from an easy-going young man about town – lazy and shiftless, true, but *happy*.

Now, he couldn't even remember what happiness was. He was disgusted with himself. It was *good* that Emma had dumped him, because she deserved so much better than a useless waste of space like him. He would only have made her miserable. They could *never* have made a go of things, and now he could see that, could admit it to himself, even if it pained him.

He knew it was terribly late, but he had to talk to George about it all, or go off his head. He walked along the hall, still wearing his coat, and gently opened George's door.

All right, if George was deeply asleep he wouldn't wake him. But he *needed* to talk. The coke he'd ingested was still buzzing around his head, making him feel hyper. 'George?' he whispered, looking towards the bed.

And there, in the white cool moonlight spilling in from the window, was George, his arm flung around the slumbering Alfie. The musky scent of sex hung in the air.

Harry stepped back, recoiling with shock from the evidence of his own eyes.

George . . . and *Alfie*?

Harry stepped back, gently closing the door on the sleeping couple. He padded off down the hall, went into his own room, and sat on the bed for a long, long time.

50

At breakfast next day, when Alfie nipped off to the corner shop to fetch milk, Harry took the opportunity to lay it on the line for George. He couldn't just ignore what he'd seen. He wanted to, but he couldn't.

'I wanted to talk to you last night,' he said, as George buttered toast.

'Yeah? What about?' George was smiling, in a good mood. In a *great* mood.

'About the fact I'm not doing the escorting any more,' said Harry.

George stopped buttering. 'What? Why?'

'Because I hate it, George. Because I feel like shit when I do it. Because I'm a fucking *whore*, and I don't like it.'

George laid down the knife. 'So what will you do?'

Harry shrugged unhappily. 'God knows. Go back on the dole. Get a job. Something. I just know I can't go on doing it, okay?'

'Well if that's how you feel . . .' said George.

'It is.'

'Well then it's fine.' George started scooping marmalade on to the toast. 'You've got to do your own thing, that's okay with me.'

'George.'

'Un-huh?'

'There's something else.'

'Shoot.'

'I came in your room to talk to you last night.'

George paused with the toast halfway to his lips. His eyes met Harry's. 'Ah,' he said.

'"Ah"? Is that all you can say?' Harry looked outraged. 'Jesus H Christ in a sidecar, George, I didn't have a clue. I mean . . . you . . . and Alfie.'

George put the toast down, his smile fading to nothing. 'You're pig-sick, right? You think it's the most disgusting thing you ever saw.'

'*No*,' said Harry hastily. 'Well yes. *No*. Fuck it, George, you might have given me a bit of warning. I just . . . couldn't believe it, that's all. You and Alfie. I always thought you were *straight*.'

George gazed at Harry sadly. 'I always thought I was straight too. You think I'm not just as shocked as you are? Think again. I tried hard enough to be that. But now I can see it was just that – trying to be something, trying so hard; and finally, I just failed.'

'Jesus, it's not a *failure*, George,' said Harry, desperately praying that the right words were going to come out of his mouth somehow. He felt like his whole world was spinning out of control. George was somehow not George at all; George was . . . well, they'd laughed light-heartedly and yes, a bit cruelly, about homosexuals together in the past. Called them shirt-lifters. Benders. And all the time, George must have been just *pretending*. George wasn't the George he'd always known, not at all.

'I just . . .' Harry hesitated. 'Well, *Alfie*. You and him. And he looks so bloody young.'

'He's seventeen,' said George.

'He looks a lot younger.'

'I know that. But he isn't. I'm not a fucking paedo, Harry. I would *never* do a thing like that – bed anyone underage. You know that.'

'Yeah. I do.' Harry ran his hands over his face, up into his hair. 'Jesus, George, it's just such a *shock*.'

'I know.'

'I'm gonna have to get used to it,' said Harry. He looked at the tablecloth for long moments. 'Anyway, I've decided I'm going to quit the escort stuff, and I'm going to move out, give you and Alfie a bit of space.'

'*Shit*, Harry,' groaned George. 'You're disgusted. I was right, wasn't I? You can't stand to be around two raging faggots like me and Alf.'

Harry shook his head. 'Don't be stupid. I love you man, you know I do. And Alfie, I got no problem with him, he's great. You and Alfie? Well, it's a shock but . . . it's cool. Although Mum's gonna go completely apeshit, no grandkids, she is gonna *flip*, you do realize that?'

George sat back in the chair. He *hadn't* thought of that. But he knew Harry was right.

'I'm going to have to tell her,' said George. 'Get it out in the open. Sooner the better.'

Harry tilted his head and looked at George. 'You think it's serious then, you and Alf? Not just a fling?'

'I love him to bits, Harry. I really do.'

'Oh shit,' said Harry with a wry smile. 'Not you too.'

George's attention sharpened. 'What, you mean you've got someone?'

Harry shook his head. 'I haven't got her. Not at all. But I'm in love with her, that's for sure.'

'She feel the same?'

'She hates my guts. I slept with her mother. The cougar.'

'And she found out.' George stared at Harry's face in concern. He had never seen his younger brother looking so downcast, and he felt bad for him.

'Got it in one,' said Harry, trying to smile but not succeeding.

'That would be sort of hard to take.'

'I know. But since the thing with Em . . . well, I don't think I care whether I boff another woman as long as I live right now.'

'Hey, boy, boffing's what you *do*,' said George, trying to inject a little lightness.

Harry had to smile at that. 'Well, *sensei*, I am just gonna have to do something else, okay? Something different.'

'I'm sorry,' said George, meaning it, his eyes on Harry's miserable face. 'I'm *really* sorry it didn't work out for you. What will you do, then?'

'Get a proper job?'

'That could be on the cards.' Harry stood up. A proper job doing what? He had no qualifications. He'd never cared about that before, but he did now. He looked down at George and his face was very serious. 'I'm going out,' he said. 'Got a booking at lunchtime, I'll go straight on to that. But it's the last one, okay George? The very last.'

Alfie came back in, bringing a gust of cold winter air and a litre plastic bottle of semi-skimmed. Harry was already at the door, shrugging on his jacket. Alfie beamed at him. Harry nodded, straight-faced, and passed on by.

Alfie came to the table where George was sitting, looking morose. Alfie put the milk down. 'You told him? Already?' he asked.

George looked up. 'Didn't have to. He came into my room to talk during the night. Saw us.'

'Ah.' Alfie sat down and looked across at George. There was a brief silence. 'So . . . how'd he take it?'

George blew out his cheeks and sat back. 'Pretty good, really. Harry's a diamond.'

'It must have been a shock for him.'

'Yeah. But it'll be cool. And anyway, Harry's got troubles of his own without worrying about mine.'

Alfie didn't ask what Harry's troubles were. He was aware that they were all treading on new and dangerous ground; he didn't want to upset anyone by intruding where he shouldn't.

'So . . . what's happening today?' he asked George. He felt anxious now. Maybe George had decided last night was a mistake, who knew?

George looked at Alf. He said as gently as he could: 'Look, Alfie, give me a break, will you? All this . . . it's a lot to take in. A hell of a lot.'

'No it isn't,' said Alfie, feeling a spasm of fear. George was regretting last night. 'I love you, you love me . . .'

'Alf!' snapped George, standing up. 'For fuck's sake, can't you see? This is *huge* for me. I need some space, okay?'

And he snatched up his coat and followed Harry out the door. The silence of the flat settled around Alfie. He stared at the closed door and hoped that everything was going to work out. Right now, he doubted it.

George went round to see Suze later in the day. He often popped in on her – being careful to avoid the times when he knew that creep Claude was going to be there – and today he had something really important to tell her, and he also really wanted to get out of the flat, give himself a little space in which to think.

He'd spent the night with Alfie.

The night just gone kept replaying in his mind. He still couldn't quite believe it. But it had been the most thrillingly exquisite night of his entire life. Waking up to see Alfie's corn-gold head lying beside his on the pillow had seemed entirely natural and right.

And wasn't that ironic? He had gone into the escort biz as a wide boy on the make, determined to screw a good wedge out of a legion of grateful women – and had stumbled across Alfie, who meant more to him than any woman ever had.

He thought about Harry, who was planning to move out. George didn't want that. He didn't want Harry made to feel awkward – it was his home, after all. And Suze was going to go ballistic. Harry was dead right about that.

London buzzed all around him as the dark afternoon faded into black night. Lights twinkled on and he ambled along the Embankment; the river police had divers down under London Bridge. They were hoisting something big – it looked like a cab – out of the water with a crane.

He was in love. It wasn't a cause for concern, a reason to be fucking miserable. It was the best thing that had ever happened to him. It was going to be the best Christmas *ever*. When at last he reached Suze's gate, someone called his name. It was the last thing he remembered.

Two hours later, Suze came to put out the bins in the dark and saw something on the pavement outside the gate.

Probably a wino. She stepped a little closer, not really wanting to get involved, and found that the wino looked sort of bulky and . . . oh *shit*, there was George sprawled face-down on the pavement and people – the *fuckers!* – were stepping around him, thinking he was just a drunk, just a waster.

'George!' she shrieked, and that brought Claude haring out of the half-open front door to stare down at Suze's eldest son, her beloved boy, lying there on the cold ground with the side of his head a bloody mess. It was Claude who called for the ambulance.

Once Harry was out in the street he walked and walked, trying to take in all that was happening before his date with Rosie May, his latest – and his last – client.

She'd only booked this morning, it was a bit of a rush job, but Harry was okay with that. Sick as he was of the escorting now, he wasn't about to let the poor woman down. He took the tube over to Soho where she had asked that they meet, at a club there. She'd said she'd meet him at the bar inside, and that she had long dark curly hair and olive skin. She'd know *him* straight away, anyway, she'd said in her email, from the gorgeous pics on the website, it wasn't a problem.

Harry was a bit surprised to find himself pitching up outside the door of a fetish club. All right, live and let live, but she hadn't said in her emails that it was one of those. She was celebrating the opening of her new Soho sex shop and she wanted a nice-looking escort to show off to her staff and her friends, earn herself a bit of kudos.

What the hell, he thought, and went in. The bouncers on the door frisked him, and then he walked on in to the club where the volume of the sound system nearly peeled the skin from inside his ears. It was hot in here, and there were even lunchtime punters in the place, jigging around on the dance floor.

Harry crossed to the long spotlit bar area and looked around. Jeez, the freak show in here. Plastic everywhere – chains, whips, thongs . . . and there was a pretty woman sitting alone at the bar, a woman with dark curly hair and *café-au-lait* skin. He made his way over to her.

'Rosie May?' He glanced at his watch. He wasn't early, so where were her staff, her friends?

She smiled, but it had an edge of unease to it. Well, that was the norm. *Lots* of ladies felt apprehensive when they'd hired an escort. He smiled too, held out a hand.

'Hi, I'm Harry Doyle,' he said. 'Can I get you a drink?' He noted she didn't have one in front of her.

Rosie shook her head and jumped down off her stool. Her movements were quick, lithe, nervous. 'No thanks. The guys are all downstairs waiting, come on.'

Harry followed her across the room. It tickled him to think that regular people, *respectable* people, executives and bankers and stuff, would come here in their lunch hour, pull on the old plastic suit, fasten the nipple clamps and zip up the bondage boots, and rave it up. Well, who was he to judge?

Rosie was going down a flight of steep stairs, Harry close at her heels. They came out into a room that looked . . . well, there were red-painted walls, and there were chains and manacles on two of them. There were two men there, big bruisers like the ones on the door. Harry had a momentary stab of unease and he took a step back, towards the stairs.

The two men eyed him like they were about to *eat* him and spit out the bits.

Harry looked at Rosie. 'What is this?' he asked, half

smiling, wondering if it was a prank, some sort of a set-up; maybe George was playing a practical joke. But . . . this one didn't look very funny.

Rosie didn't answer. She was stepping back, flattening herself against the wall where the chains dangled. Her gaze was downcast; she was looking anywhere but at Harry's face.

'Rosie?' he asked faintly.

There was someone else coming down the stairs with a heavy tread. A big man emerged and stood there smiling at Harry. He was bulky, almost spherical. He had a bald, highly polished head, cold black beads for eyes and a neat little goatee beard. He was wearing a camel-hair coat with a brown velvet collar. He looked at Rosie.

'You done good, girl,' he said. 'I seen you here, ain't I? In the club? What's your name?'

To Harry it looked as if Rosie was going to sink back into the wall until it opened and swallowed her up. She glanced up at the huge man and instantly looked away. 'Mona,' she whispered.

Mona?

Now Harry *knew* this was a set-up. Another man came down the stairs; a tall skinny black man with a greyish pallor, wearing a long black leather coat. He was breathing hard, like an asthmatic. He looked at Harry and started to grin. All these people, smiling at him. Harry knew this was not good news.

'I won't forget this, girl,' said the big man and, with one last glance at Harry, 'Rosie' scuttled away up the stairs.

'This is his brother, Deano,' the black man was saying to the big one. 'This is Harry Doyle.'

Shit, George, what you been up to now? Were these money-lenders? Fences? Drug dealers? What?

'I don't know what this is all about,' said Harry, feeling

his whole body tense, his heart speeding up. 'But I'm sure we can discuss it.'

'Oh, you're *sure*, are you?' Deano gave a laugh, and the three men with him snickered like the well-trained dummies they were. Then Deano's smile dropped from his face like a mask. He looked at the two heavies. 'Hold him,' he said, and he came at Harry with both fists swinging.

Harry felt himself being grabbed. He struggled, but couldn't move an inch before Deano ploughed into him. He felt a horrific pain in his jaw, felt a hideous series of sharp jabs to his stomach as Deano's fists pummelled him. He sagged between the two men, groaning, retching, while Deano came in again and again, kicking, hitting, shouting obscenities at him – that he was scum, that he'd pay, they'd *all* pay, all the Doyle bastards.

It seemed to go on forever, but it was minutes, just minutes. They let him fall to the floor where he lay, vomiting weakly, his body a heaving sea of agony.

'Let's get him out to the car,' said Deano, and he was lifted, dragged up the stairs and out through a door into an alley.

They let him fall on to the freezing, snow-covered cobbles, his blood dripping down and staining the white snow to crimson. At that point, mercifully, Harry passed out.

51

Hours later, Harry was in hell. Lefty was in the bar in the rocketing heat and noise of the club. He finished his drink, pleased with himself. Deano had a Doyle scum to take his temper out on, and that was good. Not *the* Doyle, not *George* Doyle, but close enough for jazz. Deano had George's address now; it was just a matter of time.

He sat there and watched the rubber-suited freaks and chained-up sex slaves. He gave a nod to Mona, who quickly looked away, trying to pretend she hadn't seen him. One of the boys gave him the nod that Deano was back and wanted to see him, so he went over to the door of the back office. He gave the knock, and then Deano was there, filling the doorway.

'Lefty my boy,' he said. He glanced behind him, seemed to come to some sort of decision, and ushered Lefty inside.

Then Deano shut the door. The office was quiet, the noise from the club muted. It was cooler, too, but Lefty was aware that he was sweating with nerves. He always did when he was around Deano. Deano was a maniac. You never knew *what* this fucker was going to do.

There was a boy, the same dark-haired boy Lefty had seen in here last time he called, lying with his eyes closed on the couch. The boy's face was as smooth and unlined as an alabaster sculpture, his eyelids tinged with a delicate tracery of blue veins. The long sweep of his dark lashes was almost heart-rendingly beautiful. Did Deano want to discuss business in front of his latest pash? Lefty looked uncertainly between the sleeping boy and his employer.

'Don't worry about that,' said Deano with a dismissive wave of a hand. He went over to the desk and went round behind it, sat down heavily. He looked up at Lefty with expectation. 'So. You got my boy?'

Lefty gulped and gave Deano his full attention. 'Yeah. I found him, Deano.'

Deano nodded his huge head and looked around with theatrical care. 'Then where *is* he, Lefty?'

'Don't you worry, I got him in my sights. I'll get him tonight.'

'So where is he? Right now?'

'He's got a job in the casino. When he comes off his shift, I'll get him.'

'You sure about that?' Deano eyed Lefty dubiously.

'Yeah, Deano. It's as good as done.'

'No, it ain't as good as done. Because it ain't *done*. Suppose Alfie gets wind of it and takes off before you can get too near?'

'He can't do that, Deano. He don't know a thing.'

'Well, let's hope so.'

Lefty thought he was doing good. He thought a little praise for all his efforts wouldn't have gone amiss right now, but he didn't say so.

'The boys picked up George Doyle, right?' Lefty asked,

subtly reminding his employer that *he*, Lefty, had nailed George's arse through his contacts.

'Sadly no,' said Deano. He spread his hands wide. 'They couldn't find him at the flat. Went to his old lady's. And there he was, being loaded into the back of an ambulance.'

'What the fuck?'

'That's what I said. Seems like that bastard's upset someone else too. But no matter.' Deano gave a chilling little smile. 'I'll catch up with him later. *If* he's around to catch up with, which the boys said looks kind of doubtful. You're *sure* you've got Alfie staked out?'

Lefty nodded, but he wasn't sure at all now. If George had been hospitalized – shit, what had happened there? – and Harry was off the scene, would Alfie now be hanging around to find out what was going on?

'It's in the bag, Deano. I swear.' Now Lefty was *really* sweating. He was telling Deano it was all fine, all okay, but Deano was doubting him, he could *see* Deano was doubting him big time.

'Only, it was all in the bag once before, you remember that?' Deano mused, smiling all the while at Lefty. 'I left you in charge of Alfie, and what happened? I think you remember, Lefty. You fucked up. *That*'s what happened. You lost my boy, and I've been deprived of his company. I've missed my boy, you know. Missed him bad.'

'I know you have, Deano, and I'm sorry for that. But now I'm going to put it right for you, okay? I'll put it right tonight. No worries.' The sweat was cascading down Lefty's face.

Shit, he wanted out of here.

Deano straightened suddenly and struck the desk with both shovel-like hands, palms down. He nodded and beamed at Lefty; but it wasn't a friendly smile. It was a smile the crocodile gives to the wildebeest a split-second before it traps its head and crunches down with killing force.

'I *know* you're going to put it right for me, Lefty. You know how I know?'

Lefty shook his head dumbly. His eyes skittered sideways and landed on the boy like a meat fly finding flesh. *Why didn't the noise wake him?* shot through Lefty's butane-addled brain. The noise of Deano's hands hitting the desk had made *him* half shit himself with fright, but the slumbering boy hadn't moved a muscle.

Now Lefty's attention was divided between Deano, who was getting to his feet, and the boy. Sleeping too *soundly*. Lefty was suddenly very worried about that.

Deano's eyes followed Lefty's darting glance as he came around the desk.

'Oh yeah,' he said, looking at the sleeping boy with a sigh. 'That. It's unfortunate, Lefty, but what can I say? Sometimes I don't get the pure stuff; sometimes some cocksucker adulterates it and, I'm afraid, well, a person gets a hot dose and then . . .' Deano put his fingers to his head and made a loud noise, like a pistol shot.

Lefty jumped.

Oh shit, I want out of here, he thought in terror.

The boy. His eyes went to the boy again, and yes the boy was pale, *very* pale, why hadn't he seen that before? The unblemished skin of his face had a blue tinge to it. 'You see, Lefty, accidents can happen,' Deano went on, approaching him. Lefty stepped back, but there was nowhere to go, nowhere to run.

'Oh my *fuck* . . .' he murmured under his breath, and he understood now, he knew what he had walked in on. He was sharing the room with a psychopath and, yes, he had always known that when he was in Deano's company, but he was also sharing the room with a *corpse*.

'Yeah, I can see you understand, Lefty, and that's good, because I've got a little job for you.' Now Deano was right in front of him: huge, threatening, terrifying. Deano reached out one massive hand and clapped Lefty companionably on the shoulder. 'Now, what I want you to do Lefty—' he indicated the dead boy with a nod – 'is get rid of that. Okay?'

'Oh hell . . . Deano . . .' Lefty was shaking his head. He knew he'd done something bad to that taxi driver, but he'd been on a bender and he hadn't been too sure of what was happening; but he was sure *now* – he wasn't too jazzed to know that he didn't want to handle a corpse tonight, not if he could avoid it.

'Now come *on*, Lefty my boy,' said Deano reassuringly, as if talking to some dumb animal. He squeezed Lefty's shoulder, drew him in against the huge heat and bulk of him. Lefty shut his eyes and prayed for deliverance. 'You tidy up that little mess for me – and make sure you do it right, you got that? – then you get Alfie and you bring Alfie back to his papa, okay?'

'Yeah,' Lefty gasped out. He opened his eyes and Deano's big bowling-ball of a head was inches from his own, the shark-black eyes staring at him. He could see every pore on Deano's huge fat cheeks, was drowning in Deano's distinctive and downright repulsive smell, a noxious mixture of strong cologne and old, stale sweat. 'Sure, Deano. I'll go get the car, bring it round the side.'

'Yeah. That's fine, Lefty.' Deano just stood there, still clasping Lefty's shoulder, staring into his frightened eyes. 'Only before you do, I want to show you something.'

Oh no, just let me get out of here, thought Lefty, panicking now. He had decided that he was just going to take off, just run as far and as fast as his legs would take him; he didn't want to be handling any more dead people. And as for returning Alfie to his proper owner, well fuck *that*. Gordon could tell this fat motherfucker if he wanted to, but Lefty promised himself that he was *out* of here.

'Show me what?' asked Lefty, gulping, sweating, feeling sick and craving a fix and wanting out so badly he was dangerously near to just wrenching himself out of this bastard's hot grasp and running until he could run no more.

'Just a little something,' said Deano, and he was leading Lefty across the room with an arm around his shoulder. Lefty couldn't do anything but go where he was bid. Deano stopped at a door behind and to the left of the desk. He opened it and pushed Lefty into the doorway.

Lefty heard a cry. But he was staring into darkness, and could see nothing.

Deano reached around the frame and found the switch. The light came on strong, vivid, almost blinding after the darkness. Lefty blinked. It was a storeroom, painted white, no more than six feet by eight. There was nothing in it but a chair, and

Oh Jesus oh God oh no

tied to the chair, sitting there gagged and bound and with tears of fear and dread springing from her eyes, was Lefty's mother.

'Holy *shit*!' sprang from Lefty's lips. He surged forward. 'Ma . . . oh Jesus, don't . . . Ma . . .'

Deano grabbed Lefty and flung him back against the wall of the storeroom. Lefty's mother let loose a strangled half-scream. Lefty found himself staring straight into Deano's eyes from inches away. Deano wasn't smiling any more.

'Now see, Lefty? I took out a little insurance. You were taking *so* long to find my boy that I started to think, you know what? That Lefty's a junkie and he's a screw-up, so I'm going to set a little something aside just in case he thinks he can walk away and not deliver what he's promised.'

Lefty was shaking his head frantically. 'No, Deano!' he shrieked. 'I wasn't going to walk away, I swear.'

'Good. That's what I like to hear. Now.' Deano yanked Lefty away from the wall and flung him back through into the office. Ignoring Lefty's mother, he switched off the light in the storeroom and closed the door on her.

'Ma . . .' Lefty moaned, and started back towards the door. Deano caught him and cuffed him hard across the face. Lefty fell back.

'You'll *get* your ma when you've done the cleaning-up here and when I've got Alfie safe back with me. You got that, boy? That all clear enough for you?'

Lefty nodded, half crying with terror and anxiety now. His ma was a good woman; she didn't deserve this. He had to do what Deano said. Get rid of the dead boy. Bring Alfie in. Then he'd get her out of here, and he'd make it up to her, it would all be cool. He would *make* it cool.

'*Clear?*' roared Deano.

Lefty jumped. 'Yeah, Deano. I swear it. It's clear.'

'Good.' Deano flung Lefty from him in disgust. 'Now go get your car.'

52

Lefty felt like he had taken a wrong turning somewhere, and now everything was chaos. It was as if he was trapped in one of those crazy computer games where you had to overcome this obstacle to face another one, then another, then another; and if you didn't triumph every time then you lost the game and you were fucked, the dragon would eat you, you would be dead.

He went to fetch his car, a beaten-up old BMW, thinking that this was not good, that DNA evidence would be all over *him*, and not Deano. Deano had killed the boy, overdosed him, so why the hell should Lefty have to incriminate himself to save Deano's stinking rotten skin?

But he had to. Lefty was crying and shaking and gasping, knowing he had to do what Deano said or the consequences would be beyond bad.

That was when he saw Mona, who had just finished her shift, getting into *her* car. He took a pull from the butane can in his hand and went over there, reached in through the open window and turned off the ignition, grabbing the keys.

'Hey!' shouted Mona, looking up at him with wild eyes. Then she saw who it was. 'Oh *fuck*,' she groaned.

'Take it up the alley there,' said Lefty, slapping the keys back into her hand.

'You *what?*'

Lefty reached in and grabbed her chin. He shook her head like a marionette's. 'Take the fucking *car* up the fucking *alley*, you got that, bitch? Then get the damned boot open and get back behind the wheel.'

'Sure,' said Mona hurriedly. She could see he was tanked and when he was like that he could do anything. As long as she lived, she would never forget the young cab driver's face as Lefty slaughtered him. Lefty let her go and, trembling, she pulled in up the alley at the side of the club like he said. Then she got out and opened the boot and quickly got back behind the wheel.

Lefty had walked up alongside her car, and now in the headlights Mona could see him at the open side door of the club. For one crazy moment she thought of just locking her door, closing the window, throwing the car into reverse and getting out of that alley faster than a bat out of hell. But she was afraid. She knew what Lefty was capable of. She was *paralysed* with fear of what he'd do if she disobeyed him.

Now he was carrying something wrapped up in a tarpaulin. Maybe a roll of carpet, something bulky like that. He went round to the back of the car and Mona heard the solid *thump* of the thing being decanted into the boot, felt the suspension judder beneath the sudden impact, and she thought, *That ain't no carpet, that's too heavy.*

Into her mind sprang a vision of the cab driver, screaming his head off while Lefty killed him.

No she didn't want to think about it. Whatever was in

that tarp, she wasn't going to concern herself with it, not at all. She closed her mind to all possibilities. It was just some . . . *thing*, that was all. Deano wanted something shifted, and they were going to shift it, right?

Right.

Again, she saw the cab driver. So young. Shrieking as his life splattered in dark red liquid gouts out of him, and all over the inside of his cab.

Stop it.

The side door of the club closed and now Lefty was coming round to the passenger side of the car. Again Mona felt it, that sudden urge to bolt, to flee. But too late. Now he was in there beside her. She glanced round at him. She could see sweat glistening on his skin. He looked sick, almost demented, his eyes dancing madly in his head.

'Start this fucker up,' he snapped at her. 'Come *on*. Hurry it up.'

Mona started the car. All she wanted was to get home, bathe Josie, read her little girl a story. But she backed the car down the alley and then followed his directions until they drew up in a busy street lined with houses. Lefty got out, pulling the keys out of the ignition again. Then he slammed the passenger door shut and walked off up the drive of one of the houses, leaving Mona sitting there with her skin crawling with terror. Her ears were sharply attuned to the thing in the back. It was silent. It was

Dead

Oh shit, she wouldn't think about it. She switched on the CD player; it was Sade singing a bluesy track. Anything to stop her hearing if that thing started to move.

And now Lefty was back, and he was carrying something. He opened the passenger door, threw a *shovel* in the back, and then said: 'Come on then, let's get the fuck on the road, what's up with you?' And he drew a deep breath of butane from the can.

Oh my God, thought Mona in a paroxysm of fear and dread.

It really was a body in there. And Lefty was going to bury it.

Following Lefty's directions, Mona drove them out to Epping Forest and they found a deserted spot. She parked up, dry-mouthed with terror, and sat there in the sudden silence with her heart racketing around in her chest. She felt like she might die at any second, that her heart was just going to *stop* with the horror of it all.

Lefty was reaching back, grasping the shovel. He got out.

'Come on then, I need a hand here,' he said and, like someone walking in a dream, Mona got out, and locked the car door – although she had no idea why she did that, just habit; no one was out here in the arse end of nowhere, no one was going to want to pinch her ratty old car, who was she kidding?

She went round to the boot, opened it. In the faint moonlit darkness the tarp looked dark blue. It looked body-shaped, too. Mona couldn't believe she was standing here getting ready to do this with this maniac. She had planned a deep bath, a pizza, something on the TV; what she had *not* planned was digging a grave.

Lefty, weighted down by the shovel, was awkwardly grabbing one end of the tarp.

'Come *on*,' he spat at her, wheezing hard. 'Get a hold.'

Mona, shuddering with revulsion, did as she was told. She grabbed a hold of the other end of the *body*

thing and between them they started crab-walking their burden into the woods. The thing was surprisingly heavy. Mona started wondering whether she had the feet here, or the shoulders. Felt – *oh fuck* – like the shoulders. God help her.

A surge of sickness swept up into her throat but she swallowed it. Just kept walking, carrying the thing, following Lefty's directions, thinking, this is murder, isn't it?

But no, she hadn't murdered anyone. She *wouldn't*. She was just doing what she was told. Hadn't she read somewhere that that was what the SS said, the Nazis when they were gassing the Jews? *It wasn't our fault; we were just doing what we were told.*

The thing was heavy. Her arms were aching, drooping under the weight of it when finally Lefty said: 'Okay, this'll do.'

He dropped his end and Mona, thinking *oh fuck, the head, that's the head I got here*, put down her end more gently. Lefty found a spot, threw off his long leather coat and started to dig. Well, at least he didn't expect her to help with *that*.

'Fucking ground's frozen. Like iron,' he complained, sweating despite the cold, and cursing.

Mona looked around with a shiver. The breeze lifted, whispering through the denuded trees and probing her shuddering body. Lefty was digging like a man possessed, stabbing at the cold earth with extreme determination. Slowly the hole he was digging grew bigger and deeper. There were trees all around them, forming a thick intricate tracery of finger-like black outlines against the dark blue night sky. A person could easily get spooked in a place like this. An owl hooted in the distance. Somewhere, something shrieked. Probably a fox or some damned thing. She was shivering in earnest now.

The hole was getting pretty big. Lefty was down there, throwing out shovel-loads of dry black dirt. And then she heard it. Every hair on her body seemed to stand on end. Her stomach shrivelled into a hard, painful knot.

The thing inside the tarp had groaned.

Lefty heard it too.

He stopped digging and looked up at her.

They stood there in total silence.

Again, the thing in the tarp groaned.

'Holy *shit*,' said Lefty, and leapt up out of the hole. Before Mona could draw breath to protest, Lefty hit Mona's end of the thing with the shovel.

Mona shrieked.

The thing inside the tarp shrieked too.

'Sonofabitch . . .' muttered Lefty. Wild-eyed and sweating and gasping, he swung the shovel again, again, again, until the thing made no more sound.

Mona was backing away, terrified, revolted, clutching at her mouth, oh shit, she was going to be sick, she couldn't take any more of this . . .

Whatever was in there, it was dead. She hoped.

Because now Lefty grabbed the other end, the *feet* end, and was easing the thing into the hole, snatching up the shovel again, starting to pile the dirt back in and the sound, oh Jesus the *sound* it made hitting that tarp, the cold hard slither of the dirt as it fell back into the hole. She hoped, she *prayed* that Lefty had killed whoever was in the tarp, killed him good, because otherwise the poor thing was going to die a slow, lingering death, suffocating beneath the cold earth.

Mona was crying, shattered. She crept forward, not wanting to but unable to help herself. She peered into the hole and now, with Lefty forking the soil into it with almost manic drive, she could barely see the tarp at all. A few more shovels full of dirt, and the job was done. Lefty hit the top of the soil, leaving a bit of a mound because he knew it would sink, and he didn't want that happening, didn't want some fucking dog walker or some rambling bastard to find it and start shouting. Carefully he piled the leaves he had displaced all over the grave, and then he snatched up his coat, put it on. Drew a wheezing, painful breath. Reached inside his coat and took a long, blissful pull of butane.

Mona stood there, shivering, shuddering, staring at him with disgust and fear.

'Job done,' said Lefty with a wild white grin. He surged past her, hefting the shovel over his shoulder. 'Come on. That's part one done. Now for part two.'

Oh shit, thought Mona, and trailed after him, afraid to be with him, but even more afraid to be left standing here alone, in the woods, with that thing buried just feet away from her.

53

'The weather outside . . . oh come on, Harry. You know the song. How does it go?'

Harry Doyle didn't know how the song went. He knew he was going to hate those few lyrics forever, he knew *that*. Apart from that, his only thought was: *I'm going to die, and it's all my own stupid fault*. His body was stone cold, every muscle clenched and trembling with terror. And this big rotten *bastard* was singing a flat rumbling line or two from a cheery Christmas song, and asking him if he knew how it went.

He didn't know how it went. But he knew how *this* went. *This* was him sitting in an icy-chilly garage, naked to the waist, barefooted and tied to a chair with duct tape. His skin was shrivelling with the cold and damp – the place had an old asbestos roof, and the beams supporting it were dark with the sleety rain that had seeped in.

There were rows of old paint tins up on some rickety-looking shelves. A rusting tool box on the floor, alongside a line of blue gas bottles. A pile of wood under an old workbench that he knew – because he had been in here all last

313

night – served as a des res for a rampaging horde of mice. He'd felt them scurrying over his feet during the hours of darkness. At least it wasn't rats, thanks be to Christ. A chest freezer was chugging away over in the corner. Food in there. Better not think about that, because he was beyond hungry. Starving. Water dripped on to his freshly shorn head now and then and, sometimes – when the fat git wasn't here and when the need for a drink consumed Harry like a man marooned in the desert – he turned his head, caught a few sour droplets in his mouth. He was shivering. His hand was agony but he thought that the bleeding had stopped. Too fucking *cold* in here to bleed for long.

'*You better watch out* . . . you know that one, Harry?' And he was off again, the evil bastard, prancing around Harry's chair in his camel-coloured coat, mocking Harry's powerlessness; oh yeah, *he* was toasty warm, nice and cosy, while Harry was freezing his arse off. '*Santa Claus* . . . what's up, Harry? Don't you know it? Don't you like that song?'

There was nothing about this that Harry liked. It was nearly Christmas. He thought of his mum and his brother George, and Em.

His mind was wandering. He snapped it back, paid attention. While the great big horrible bastard was talking, or singing, or both, then at least he wasn't pulling out any more of Harry's fingernails, and he wasn't laughing about cutting Harry's bollocks out either. Both very good indeed.

'I . . . like the modern stuff more,' Harry managed to get out through chattering teeth.

Oh God, how had he got into this? he wondered in despair.

But he knew the answer to that. By being a stupid, greedy little cunt, and by being too easily led by George. George had always been a gobshite, always getting them both into trouble; Harry should have known better.

The talking was good; he had to keep doing that. 'Mariah Carey,' he got out. 'I like her stuff. And George Michael.'

As soon as he'd said *that*, he knew he shouldn't have.

'Oh yeah.'

Now the big man had stopped dodging around. The man's head was huge, like the rest of him. He had a little goatee beard, dark but with a stripe of grey down the centre. He was very still. He leaned in close to Harry's face. Harry smelled cologne, sweat and coffee breath. Not nice. Bushy black eyebrows. Dark eyes beneath them, hard as polished pebbles as they stared into Harry's. 'You like all that, don't you, Harry boy? Like the gay scene, yeah? But some things you don't arse about with, Harry. A pun there, you get that? Eh?'

He nudged Harry's shoulder, hard.

Harry nodded.

'*Arse*, see?'

Harry nodded again. He felt exhausted, near tears, desperate. Had to talk to the bastard, but right now he couldn't find the right words, and he was scared of stumbling across the wrong ones. He glanced at the open door behind the man, and thought he saw movement there. He thought – oh and this was crazy, this was proof that his mind was close to gone – he *thought* for one mad moment that he saw his sister Gracie's face staring back at him.

Crazy.

Gracie was in Manchester. Gracie didn't care about him, or George, or Mum.

'You a giver or a taker, Harry? Uh? You know what I mean, right?' The man was smiling at him.

He's crazy, thought Harry. *He's crazy and I'm fucked.*

'Yeah. I know what you mean,' he said, and coughed. His throat was dry, so painfully dry. He'd been in this hellhole since yesterday afternoon, without drink – except for those precious droplets of rank water falling from the roof – and without food. He wondered how long he could go on, could *survive*, like this.

'Thought you would. Only some things, Harry – *some* things you don't take. Some things get people upset, would you agree with that?'

Harry nodded, his head slumping forward on his chest. He couldn't do this any more. He was done for. He was never going to get out of here.

'That's good.' The man drew back. 'You just think about that, Harry. And . . . I'll see you tomorrow.'

The big man walked away, opened the door, and was gone.

Harry heard the key turn in the lock.

Silent tears fell from his eyes. He was too weak, too tired, too frightened to cry out loud.

Gracie

DECEMBER

54

Christmas Eve

Lorcan's casino was really something to see. There were seven American roulette tables, three tables given over to three-card poker, four for blackjack or *vingt-et-un*, and two for *punto banco*. The boulevard and the setting were nothing like hers. Gracie's place was modern and had banks of slots lining the foyer before you got into the casino boulevard proper, to lure in the downmarket gamblers; but everything about Lorcan's casino said classy Edwardian plush.

There were no slots, for a start. There was red and gold everywhere, lush *fin-de-siècle* paintings with gold-leaf frames, huge crimson drapes and gold-tasselled fastenings, deep blue tables, each with a mahogany surround polished and burnished to a dense, glossy dark red. The carpet under the punters' feet was hand-woven, a swirling canvas of reds, golds and warm royal blues.

The place was packed.

'Christmas Eve,' said Lorcan, leading her down the

319

boulevard, snaffling two glasses of champagne from a passing purple-waistcoated employee and handing one to Gracie.

'Cheers,' he said, clinking his glass against hers. 'What shall we drink to, Gracie?'

'George's recovery,' said Gracie, who was suddenly over-whelmed to be here among all these talking and laughing people, listening to the clatter of the ball ricocheting around the glittering roulette wheel. No wonder he'd wanted to show it off to her: it was magnificent.

'Five black,' said the croupier, and someone shouted excitedly as the winnings were scooped their way.

'It's fabulous,' Gracie admitted, feeling sick with envy. Her place was a wreck right now, and it was up in the air whether or not she was going to be able to reopen anytime soon.

'*You* look fabulous, Gracie,' said Lorcan.

So do you.

She didn't say it aloud. She felt weird and displaced. It was so strange, to be with him again. So strange, but it felt so *right*. Even when they were bickering, she enjoyed it.

'Want to spin the wheel, Gracie? Take a chance?' asked Lorcan.

Gracie's eyes came up and met Lorcan's blue gaze.

'What, on the roulette table?' she asked him.

'No, I don't mean that,' said Lorcan. 'You know I don't. Let's go up to the flat.'

The flat was modern, large, and very male. It was a bachelor pad, minimalist and pared to the bone. There was a big TV in the living room, a bank of huge chocolate-brown leather sofas, a table, a fireplace. Lorcan switched on the lights so that they were low and seductive, and flicked the remote at the fire. Gas-fired flames leapt up and Gracie laughed. There was a large fake Christmas tree beside the fireplace.

'Look up,' said Lorcan as he closed the door behind them, the remote still in his hand.

And of course there was a dense sprig of white-berried mistletoe hanging down from the ceiling.

'I suppose you bring all your girlfriends up here and get them under the mistletoe?'

'Girlfriends?' Lorcan half smiled and slipped his arms around Gracie's waist. 'Gracie, I'm a married man, or had you forgotten that?'

'A married man who now wants to become a *divorced* man,' she pointed out. He was very close – close enough to be extremely disturbing. If he kissed her now . . . how would she react? She didn't want to find out . . . did she?

'Yeah, and how do you feel about that, Gracie?' He pulled her in closer; the fronts of their bodies were touching, all the way down to their toes.

Well, how did she feel? She remembered opening the letter with the divorce papers inside. How deflated she'd felt, how sad all of a sudden. And then, when she'd first seen him again at the flat, that sense of undeniable excitement. Followed of course by irritation and anger, because he wanted rid of her.

Well come on, Gracie, don't you want rid of him too?

And therein lay the trouble. She wasn't sure she did.

'I don't know yet,' said Gracie, twining her arms around his neck and arching her brows at him. 'Maybe I need convincing . . .?'

'What you need is your arse smacking,' said Lorcan, his mouth moving down towards hers.

'Ha! And you think you're going to do it, do you?' she teased.

321

'I think you want me to.' Now his mouth was so close to hers she could feel his warm breath, could smell the peppermint sweetness of it. She felt more than saw him aim the remote toward a discreetly placed sound system on the far wall, and music started to play. Soft, seductive music. Music she hadn't listened to for five years, ever since they'd split for what had seemed to be the last time, because if she *had*, she would have broken down and cried. Michael McDonald was oozing his seductive gravelly voice through 'Stop, Look, Listen (To Your Heart)'. It was their song.

'Oh for God's sake,' said Gracie, half laughing but also more than a little inclined to sob like a child. 'What a smooth bastard you are.'

'Stop talking, Gracie, and start kissing.'

'No. I can't think straight when you kiss me.'

'Good.'

Their lips met.

This was a memory, twining around her brain like the song. A memory of happy times, of laughter, of a passion that could rock her world – and frequently did, before the arguments, before the huge clash of wills that had eventually ripped their marriage wide open.

His tongue was in her mouth, teasing hers, taking her over.

She jerked her head back, looked into his eyes. He looked at her and smiled. 'Go on, Gracie. Take the risk. Spin the wheel.'

It was frightening. She had no idea where this was going. It had taken her a long, long time to regain her equilibrium after the split. She'd been a wreck for months – crying, staying in bed all day, hitting the bottle more than she should; but now all bets were off. She'd loved him forever. She *would* love him forever, she realized that now. It was deeply, deeply scary.

But she wanted it.

She wanted *him*.

She pulled his head back down to hers and kissed him, really kissed him, and it was as if all those years of hurt had fallen away. All that mattered right now was that they were here, together.

'Better,' he murmured against her mouth.

'Oh shut *up*, Lorcan,' she mumbled. 'Just shut up and take me to bed, will you?'

Lorcan bent and picked her up into his arms; they were still kissing as he crossed the room, kicked open a door, and laid her down on a huge bed. He drew back then, pulled at the waist tie on the black wrap dress she wore, spread it open. She was wearing nothing underneath.

Lorcan stared at her, then reached out, skimming one big hand over the hot white curve of her hip, tracing the indentation of her waist, then gliding on up to cup one full, magnificent breast.

'You know, I'd forgotten how pale your skin was,' he murmured, and then his lips were at her breast too, teasing the nipple into hardness.

Gracie leaned back, ecstatic, giving herself up to the moment, moaning softly, but then he was gone, moving away from her.

'Oh Jesus, Lorcan,' she groaned.

He was throwing off his clothes. A minute, and he was back with her, pushing the dress off her shoulders and scooping up her naked body so that it lay across his.

'Fuck, I should have done this the minute we met again,' he muttered against her neck, his teeth nibbling at her throat, his body so familiar and yet so deliciously strange. She remembered him now, remembered all of him, how gorgeous he was, how incredibly handsome. And how big . . .

A groan escaped her as he moved on top of her and parted her thighs, driving into her, unable to wait a moment longer.

Lorcan paused, panting, staring down at her with concern. 'All right?' he asked.

'Fine,' she managed, wrapping her legs around his waist, smoothing her hands into the hair on his chest, wondering what was happening, how she had stumbled back into this, and where it would take her.

But all that mattered was the here and now, and as he started to move inside her, the heat and heaviness and hardness of him seduced her completely.

It was bliss. It was so wonderful that she wondered now how she had stayed sane all these years without him. She held on to him. She knew his rhythm just as he knew hers. It was so right, so perfect. She could feel his skin growing damp and slick with the extremity of his passion, she could hear her own breath coming in urgent little gasps. Then he was hard, so very hard that she could barely stand it. Her head went back with abandon and she arched up against him. He was coming. He was coming inside her.

Gracie stiffened. Wasn't this what they'd argued over so many times in the past? He wanted children; she wanted her career. She wasn't on the pill – the damned thing made her feel sick. She'd become so carried away by the moment that she'd failed to even *think* about contraception.

She thought about it now. Thought about the possibility of having Lorcan's child, and what that would mean. A fresh start together? Or more arguments, more heartache?

Lorcan was withdrawing from her, flopping back on to the bed, his breathing unsteady.

Gracie lay there, horrified at herself. What the hell could she have been thinking of?

Nothing. Only satisfying her lust; that was all. She thought of all those awful, painful rows they'd had. She couldn't go there again. She just *couldn't*.

Now he was turning back towards her, his hands reaching for her, starting to attend to her pleasure now that he had attended to his own.

'No – don't,' said Gracie, and sat up, reaching for her dress. Her body, her treacherous body, was still humming with desire, wanting to continue. 'Why not?' asked Lorcan.

'Because I . . .' Gracie groped for the words and simply couldn't find them. Instead she said: 'I've got to get back to the flat. That's why. I'm expecting someone.'

And before he could protest any further, she stood up, rewrapped her dress firmly around her, and said: 'I'd better get a taxi.'

Lorcan gave her one long, exasperated look. Then he swung his legs over the side of the bed and sat up. 'No need. I'll drive you. But trust me Gracie – one day soon we're going to do this properly, and we *are* going to talk.'

An hour later they were back at the flat when the doorbell rang.

Gracie went to the intercom and told the woman who answered her to come on up.

A few minutes later, Gracie opened the door to two small pale women, one blonde and in her fifties, the other a brunette in her twenties with a lovely, heart-shaped face.

Mother and daughter, she thought instantly.

The heavy was standing right behind them. 'You expecting these people?' he asked Gracie in a flat Essex monotone.

'Yeah. Thanks.'

He nodded and went back off down the stairs. The two women watched him go, their expressions nervous.

'Jackie?' asked Gracie, looking from one to the other of them.

'I'm Jackie Sullivan,' said the older woman, holding out a hand. 'You're Gracie, yes? Harry's sister? Oh goodness . . . of course you are. You look so much like him.'

Gracie shook Jackie's thin, cold hand.

'This is Emma, my daughter.' Gracie shook Emma's hand too; her grip was stronger, warmer. 'We're both extremely worried about Harry,' said Jackie, and her eyes filled with tears. Emma's did too. They clung to each other like a couple of waifs and looked pleadingly at Gracie. 'Do you know what's happened to him?' asked Jackie.

I wish, thought Gracie, and her mobile started ringing. She ushered Jackie and Emma into the flat as she picked up. 'Hello?'

It was Suze, babbling and crying and making no sense at all.

'Mum, slow down. What are you saying?' urged Gracie, watching Lorcan introduce himself to their visitors as 'Gracie's husband'. Cheeky git. Then an image of what they had been doing, naked and locked together just a couple of hours ago, shot into her brain. She actually felt herself blush.

'The hospital phoned,' Suze managed to get out.

Gracie clutched at the phone. Oh fuck. She thought of that horrible moment when George's heart had stopped. This was it. George was dead. George had gone and *died* on them.

'Oh God,' she managed to get out. '*No*. Oh Mum, I'm so sorry . . .'

Suze's voice caught on a sobbing laugh. '*No*, you silly cow. He ain't *dead*. They're saying George is showing signs of coming round.'

55

Jackie and Emma decided to go with Gracie and Lorcan to the hospital.

'We won't come up to intensive care with you,' said Jackie. 'We'll wait downstairs in the café. But we have to talk to you about Harry. You do understand?'

Gracie said she did.

'And I hope your brother's getting better, I really do,' said Jackie.

Lorcan drove them to the hospital. Halfway there, Emma said: 'I don't want to worry anyone, but that man, the one who came upstairs to the flat, I think he's following us . . .'

'He's a friend,' said Lorcan.

Gracie shot him a sour look. But inside the hospital, when they parted company with Emma and her mother, she was glad of his company. The place was thronging with people – as always – and Gracie found the crush of bodies, the bright lights and the sheer heat inside the building daunting, given her state of mind. She was afraid of what they were going to find waiting for them up in intensive care. Was

328

George going to come out of this whole and well, or as a brain-damaged stranger?

Suze was waiting in the small room outside the intensive care unit. There was a crying young couple there, too, and a stocky middle-aged man who was reading a paper but who glanced up at Lorcan as he came in. Lorcan nodded to him, he nodded back.

The muscle on George's door, thought Gracie, and felt even more overwhelmed as she thought of how George might emerge from this, and where Harry might be, and that someone was busy blitzing their way through the Doyle family like a howling shit-storm. Someone had tried to abduct her. Someone had tried to axe Suze's front door with a chainsaw. Someone had attacked George. Did that same someone now have Harry in their clutches? *Someone* had sent those bags of hair. And what could they be doing to him? Maybe by now they had killed him, disposed of handsome, kind, laid-back Harry like a piece of rubbish? She wasn't religious but now she found herself praying hard, praying to God or whoever might be listening to save Harry, to keep him safe.

'You okay?' asked Lorcan, grasping her arm as she lurched slightly at the door of the waiting room.

'Fine,' said Gracie, and went over to Suze.

Suze stood up and stared at Gracie. Gracie could see her own turbulent thoughts reflected in Suze's eyes. The near-hysterical joy of Suze's phone call was a dim memory. She, like Gracie, was frightened of what lay in wait for them all now. Gracie could see Suze's fear; Suze's hands were shaking and she was pale as milk.

'I thought Vera'd come with you,' said Gracie.

'She dropped me off outside,' said Suze. 'Come on, we'd better get in there.'

Suze gave Gracie a trembling smile and reached out and grabbed her hand. Surprised and pleased, Gracie squeezed her mum's hand reassuringly.

'We'll do it together, okay?' said Gracie.

'Yeah,' said Suze, but although she still smiled, her eyes were full of fear.

They wouldn't allow more than two people at a time, so Lorcan waited outside while Gracie and Suze went in.

They approached George's bed. He was moving. Gracie felt her heart start to beat very fast. He was moving! But then they drew nearer. The nurse met them there.

'It's something they all have to go through,' she said firmly. 'We're bringing him round very slowly, and I know it looks bad, but it isn't. Trust me. He isn't in any pain.'

Gracie and Suze drew closer to George's bed as the nurse went hurrying off.

'Oh fuck,' moaned Suze, and Gracie put an arm around her mother's shaking shoulders and hugged her tight.

'It's going to be all right,' she said.

But oh God, she doubted that. Because George, big bruiser George, was still attached to a bank of monitors and beeping machines. His legs were moving rhythmically, straining at the tucked-in bedclothes. His arms were moving too. Every few minutes the nurse came dashing back to check that nothing had come loose. Gracie and Suze stood there staring in horror at George's face. His eyes were still closed, but he was frowning hard and his face was twisted as if in anguish; his mouth was wide open. It looked as if George was screaming, but no sound was coming out.

'Oh no, oh George, my poor little Georgie,' said Suze, starting to cry.

'You heard what the nurse said,' said Gracie, although she

felt sick and distressed just looking at George. 'He's not in pain. It looks bad, but it's not.'

'He's screaming! He's screaming but he can't make a sound because of that thing in his throat. Oh my poor George,' sobbed Suze.

'Come on Mum. He's coming round. It's something he has to go through, you heard her. But he's coming round, and that's got to be good.'

'Is it?' Now Suze was shouting, glaring at Gracie with pain-filled eyes. 'Is it? What if he's mental, Gracie? What if there's too much damage, and he's not George any more?'

'You'll have to keep it down please,' said the nurse, coming over looking irritated. 'We can't have the patients upset.'

'How long will he be like this?' Gracie asked the nurse as Suze started to sob uncontrollably.

'It takes as long as it takes,' said the nurse. 'Sit her down outside, all right?'

Gracie was pleased to. It hurt her horribly to see George like that. Suze was right. It *did* look as if he was screaming, and it was awful to think of him trapped within his own body, unable to make a sound. How could the nurse really know what was going on inside George's brain? Was he in pain? Was he frightened? Who the hell knew?

Oh Jesus, I've got to stop thinking about it.

She took Suze out into the waiting room.

Lorcan was gone, but the muscle was still there in the corner and Sandy was sitting there too. She saw Gracie and Suze come out and stood up expectantly.

'How is he?' she asked.

'Coming round, but it's not pretty,' said Gracie, guiding Suze into a chair.

'I'll go in,' said Sandy. 'That boy was just here.'

'Which boy?' asked Gracie, feeling shattered. She found herself wishing that Lorcan hadn't pissed off somewhere – he was probably in the ground-floor café exerting that famous Irish charm on Jackie and Emma Sullivan.

'The blond boy who tried to pass himself off as George's brother,' said Sandy.

The muscle looked up.

'That right?' Gracie asked him.

He nodded.

'Who *is* that man?' asked Sandy, staring at the muscle with suspicion.

Gracie ignored the question. 'How long ago was he here? A couple of minutes?'

'He was literally *just* here. Seconds ago. He saw me here – he must have recognized me from before – and then this man stood up and asked who he was waiting to see, and he just left.'

Seconds ago.

'Get Mum a coffee, will you? Look after her,' said Gracie to the muscle and, pulling Sandy after her, she went out into the corridor. People wheeling trolleys, people pushing invalids in wheelchairs. No blond boy.

'When you spot him, tell me, okay?' she said quickly to Sandy.

Dragging Sandy along behind her, Gracie hurried off towards the lifts. There was a bank of them, each big enough to take a hospital bed; all three doors on one side stood open, and there was no blond boy in any of them waiting for the lift to descend.

Gracie hurried over to the opposite side. One had the doors closed and was going down. The other two had people bustling around it, visitors, nurses, patients . . . no blond boy.

'Come on,' said Gracie, and hared off to the stairs, pushing through the swing doors at a run, Sandy puffing along behind her.

They went down to the next floor, pushed out through the doors, looked at the lift – it was still going down. Gracie dragged Sandy back into the stairwell and started down again. At the next level they came out and looked hopefully at the lift again. The doors opened. There were four people inside: an elderly couple, a porter pushing a bed with a stick-thin woman in it. No blond boy.

'*Shit!*' snapped Gracie.

Where had he gone?

'Maybe he took the stairs,' said Sandy with a shrug.

'No, we'd have heard him.' Everything echoed like crazy in the stairwells. Theirs had been the only footfalls; Gracie was certain of that.

Still clutching Sandy's hand, she dived back into the stairwell and hurtled up the two flights to the intensive care level once again. Looked up and down the corridors. No blond boy. Then she spotted what she was after and dived through the door marked with a tiny stick-figure man.

'Oh for God's sake,' complained Sandy on finding herself in the Gents toilet.

The toilets were empty, but one of the cubicle doors was shut.

Gracie put a finger to her lips. They stood silent, just inside the door. The toilet flushed. Then a strikingly good-looking blond teenager came out and crossed to the sinks and washed his hands. He glanced up at himself in the mirror, and then he saw the two women standing there watching him. He stiffened in alarm, splashing water down the front of his jeans.

'What the . . .?' he said faintly.

'That's him,' said Sandy.

'Who the hell are you?' he asked.

'I'm Gracie, George's sister,' said Gracie. 'And this is Sandy, his fiancée.'

The boy's mouth dropped open. 'His *what?*'

'Now can I ask who you are? You've been passing yourself off as George's brother, but you're not.'

The boy was shaking his head. He started towards them. 'I'm *out* of here,' he said, and tried to push past them.

Gracie grabbed his arm, trying to keep him there. He yanked hard, nearly dragging her with him out through the door.

'No, stop,' shouted Gracie. 'Who are you? Come on. What would it hurt to tell me?'

Suddenly there was a blade in the boy's hand. Gracie stepped back, her chest fizzing with sudden alarm. Sandy let out a small shriek. The boy's eyes were wild with fear. He waved the knife in their faces.

Fuck, thought Gracie, freezing. *Didn't see that coming.*

'Okay,' she gasped out. 'Okay.'

The boy stepped past them to the door. Then the door pushed inward and Lorcan stood there. He looked at the blade in the boy's hand, at Gracie and Sandy. He lunged forward and grabbed the boy's wrist and squeezed, hard. The boy let out a scream of pain, and the knife fell to the floor. Lorcan pushed in further, sending the boy stumbling back against the row of sinks.

'What's going on here?' demanded Lorcan, looking like he was about to take the boy's head off. He shook him, hard. Alfie's head collided with rock-hard porcelain and he let out a yell.

'You little fucker, what do you think you're doing?' spat out Lorcan in a rage.

'Don't!' shouted Gracie; she could see that Lorcan was about to give the boy a pounding. 'Lorcan, don't. He's terrified.'

'He fucking-well *will* be in a minute . . .' Then Lorcan stopped. He held the boy in front of the long slab of mirror and stared at him. 'Hold on a second. Don't I know you? Aren't you . . . Alfie? George's pal?'

56

Christmas Eve

'What do you *mean*, engaged?' Alfie was asking Sandy, looking at her like she was an escapee from a lunatic asylum. 'George ain't engaged, not to *anyone*.'

They were sitting in the hospital canteen, all of them. Lorcan, Gracie, Suze, Jackie and Emma, Alfie and Sandy Cole. The heavy was still upstairs, outside intensive care.

'Maybe you don't know him very well,' said Sandy, staring sniffily at this impossibly beautiful boy.

'No, I *do*. I think *you're* the one mistaken here.'

'What are you to George anyway?' demanded Sandy.

'*Look*,' said Gracie pointedly. 'Can we all calm down?' She looked at Alfie. 'Do you know anything about George's injury? How it happened? *When* it happened?'

Alfie shook his head dolefully. 'No. I don't. I wish I did.'

'George got you the job at Lorcan's place, is that right?' asked Gracie, glancing towards Lorcan for confirmation.

Alfie nodded. He stirred his coffee and sighed.

336

'You're a friend of George's,' said Gracie.

'I was staying with him. Him and Harry.'

'So where *is* Harry?' said Jackie quickly, leaning forward. 'Do you know?'

Alfie shrugged and reddened. 'No. I know he was going to move out. But he just went out and didn't come back.'

'Why was he going to move out?' Now it was Suze's turn to speak. She looked raddled, wrung out in the harsh fluorescent lighting in the café. Seeing George like that had shaken her badly. 'George and Harry have always got on. They've never argued.'

'They didn't *argue*,' said Alfie, looking awkward.'I think . . . well, Harry just wanted to move on, that was all.'

'But no forwarding address?' queried Lorcan. 'That don't make sense, if the split was amicable.'

'Look, I don't know why Harry left or where he went. And after this happened to George, I felt spooked in the flat on my own. So I moved out too. I had wages, so I checked into a B & B.'

'And came visiting George claiming to be his brother,' said Gracie.

'I had to do that. They wouldn't have let me see him otherwise, and I *had* to see him. He's been so good to me. Him and Harry. I had some trouble . . .'

'What sort of trouble?' asked Lorcan.

Alfie shrugged. 'I left home last year. Came to London. Met a guy called Lefty and he said he could get me a job. Turns out he was working for Deano Drax.'

'Deano *Drax*?' said Lorcan.

Gracie looked at him sharply. 'You know him?'

Lorcan nodded. 'I know *of* him. He runs a fetish club in Soho. Likes young boys, so the rumour goes. Nasty bastard.'

Gracie looked across at Alfie. 'What, you mean this "Deano" wanted to—'

Alfie twisted his lips in a grimace. 'Lefty drugged me up for him. Christ, you'd have to be doped to go with a twisted minger like that. But I managed to get away. Then Lefty cornered me . . . and George was just passing by. George saved me. Gave me a roof over my head. Him and Harry were just great to me.' Alfie was looking at Sandy again. 'I can't understand you saying what you did, though. George, engaged? No. That's not possible.'

'It *is* possible,' said Sandy hotly. 'He's engaged to me. Look.' She flourished the ring at him.

Alfie sat back, folded his arms. 'Crap,' he said.

'Now look—'

'Shall we not fight among ourselves?' suggested Lorcan. 'The main thing is, George is on the mend.'

'We don't know that yet,' said Suze dejectedly. 'God, he just looks so ill. It looks like he's screaming his head off and can't make a sound. And how do we know what he's going to be like when he *does* come round? He could be paralysed. He could be brain damaged.'

'We have to try and be positive,' said Gracie, squeezing Sandy's hand because she looked so distraught at what Suze was saying. Then she looked at Lorcan. 'Do you think the "scorched-earth" policy would be Deano Drax's sort of thing?'

'The *what?*' asked Suze and Jackie at the same time.

'Like Saddam Hussein did after the Iraq war,' said Gracie. 'Burning things. Destroying things. Trashing *everything* left behind.'

Lorcan was staring at the table, looking thoughtful. He looked up at Gracie. 'That twisted git's capable of anything, from what I hear,' he said.

'Setting the fire? Doing Mum's door with a chainsaw? Slashing my car tyres? Sending us Harry's hair?'

'*What?*' demanded Emma, going deathly white.

'We each got a packet of Harry's hair,' said Suze with a shudder.

'Then Harry didn't *leave*,' said Jackie forcefully. 'Someone must have snatched him. Oh my God.' She put her hands to her mouth, horrified. 'We must tell the police.'

'The notes with the hair said no police,' said Gracie quickly. 'We can't risk it. We might be putting Harry in terrible danger if we did that.'

Jackie sank back in her seat, her face a mask of terror and confusion.

'And nobody knows even now where Harry is,' said Emma, close to tears. Jackie hugged her. Gracie felt so sorry for them. It was obvious that they both cared hugely for Harry.

Gracie looked at Lorcan. 'Everything's pointing towards Deano Drax,' she said to him. 'Wouldn't you say? Drax must have bashed George's head in when he found out – somehow – that Alfie was with him. That bastard.'

'Looks that way,' said Lorcan.

'So what do we do now?' asked Gracie, her voice betraying her desperation. She thought of Harry, in the clutches of an evil man like that. Thought of the bags of Harry's hair. And shuddered with dread for him.

Lorcan was looking very angry. 'That bastard needs his arse kicking,' he said.

Emma was looking at him with stricken eyes. 'What do you think's happened to Harry?'

Lorcan shook his head. 'I wish I could answer that.'

'Will you try to find him?'

339

Lorcan looked at her. Read the desperation and the love in her eyes. 'Yeah. Of course I will.'

'Hold on . . .' said Gracie, alarmed.

'Then . . . if you see him, *when* you see him, tell him I didn't mean it.' Her voice caught on a choked sob. 'Tell him I'm sorry. Tell him Em sends her love.'

Alfie stood up. 'Getting another drink,' he mumbled, and went off to join the queue.

'Look, we mustn't do anything stupid,' said Gracie, looking at Lorcan. She knew how impetuous he could be.

'What, we got to sit around while that *gobshite* runs rings around us?' he challenged her.

'No, but—'

'No,' snapped Lorcan. 'Fuck *that* for a plan. If Drax had that fire started—'

'What fire?' butted in Suze.

'There was a fire at Gracie's casino,' he told her. 'She could have been killed.'

'Yeah, but I *wasn't*,' said Gracie firmly, not wanting Lorcan to go off on one and put himself at risk. 'Jesus, will you calm down? I wasn't even there. Drax knew I wasn't. He had someone watching me, he *knew* I lived elsewhere.'

Lorcan looked unconvinced. 'So he set light to your property instead,' he said angrily. 'Look, we know he hurt George. He nearly killed him. We're near as dammit sure he's got Harry somewhere. He's attacked you. He's tried to attack Suze. That bastard wants *stopping*.'

Sandy was looking round with disparaging eyes. 'Where's that cheeky little sod gone?' she asked of no one in particular.

Gracie tore her eyes away from Lorcan. 'What?'

'You don't think he knows more than he's saying?' said Suze.

'Who, Alfie? Like what?' queried Gracie. Lorcan's hot words had unsettled and distracted her. She had to drag her attention back to Suze.

'Like . . . oh, I don't know. I just think he's hiding something, that's all. I could be totally wrong.' Suze was staring at the queue now. 'He's not in the queue,' she said. 'Where *is* he . . .?'

Now they were all looking at the queue of customers at the kiosk. Alfie wasn't among them.

Lorcan stood up. 'Shit. I'll go look for him.'

Gracie watched him go anxiously. Within five minutes, he was back.

'He's not in the loos or anywhere,' said Lorcan. 'Looks like he's taken off.'

'Huh! Didn't like the company, I suppose,' said Sandy acidly.

Alfie couldn't stand another moment in the hospital. His mind was in a whirl. He'd been knocked sideways by the sight of George reviving; hopeful and horrified and just wishing the George he loved would come back to him again. But what *would* come back? A shell? His stomach was churning with the worry of it all. And that girl, Sandy what's-her-face, saying she and George were engaged – what sort of shit was that? Had George been lying to him, was George in fact *cheating* on him with that dumb bitch?

No, he had to get out of there. Had to take his mind off it all or start screaming and be unable to stop. He caught the tube and then walked through the dark icy streets, all strung with Christmas lights and full of last-minute shoppers, to the casino. He went to the back entrance, where all the staff clocked in every day, hoping for a sight of one of his many workmates to chat to, and it was then, right then, that he was grabbed from behind. Something noxious was slapped over his nose and mouth. There was a strong chemical scent and a feeling of falling, tumbling end over end into darkness. And then – nothing.

57

'For fuck's sake, what you done to him?' Mona wailed, shivering and shuddering behind the wheel of her little car, which was now a vehicle involved in criminal activities, in *murder*, in moving bodies to their grave. And the nightmare wasn't over yet. After he'd buried the *body*, he'd had her drive across town. They'd parked up. Lefty got out and she thought, *Drive away, I'll just drive away*, but she couldn't, she didn't have the nerve.

When Lefty came back to the car with something slung over his shoulder, she thought: *No, please God no, not again, not another body.*

'I ain't done *nothing* to him,' said Lefty, grunting with effort as he dropped Alfie into the passenger seat. 'Shit, how can anyone as small as that weigh so much?' he complained, grimacing and straightening. He'd pulled a muscle in his back or something, it was painful. He took a quick toke of the butane and felt better, anaesthetized. Anaesthetized, just like Alfie.

Mona was looking with fear-filled eyes at the blond teenager slumped beside her in the car. His head was down on his chest;

he was out of it. Was he dead? She didn't trust Lefty not to have killed again. Killing was what this sick bastard *did*. And how the hell had she got herself involved in this? She was up to her neck in it now and, oh sweet Jesus, she wanted *out*.

She peered at the boy while Lefty walked around outside the car, massaging his back and swearing constantly. The boy was breathing. She could see that, and it steadied her, made her feel just a fraction better. But only a fraction.

The boy was alive.

But with Lefty involved, how long before he wound up dead like the others?

Lefty, lit by the headlights, was strolling around in front of the car. Cursing. Pulling the can out, taking another whiff. Rubbing his back. And while he was doing that, she could . . . she could slam the passenger door shut and lock the doors, close the electric window on her side because she'd driven with it open, it was freezing, her whole body was cold, but the fresh air was better than the Lefty-induced fug inside the car.

But now the moment when she could have acted, could have stopped this, had passed. Lefty was coming back to the car, pushing in beside the boy, Christ, she could hardly reach the gear stick or the handbrake. Now she wondered what she could have been thinking. Give the mad bastard half a reason to, and he'd do her too.

But you'd be saving the boy's life, whispered in her brain.

Oh yeah. And what about hers? Were there any medals being dished out here for heroes? She didn't think so.

'Drive,' said Lefty, tense and fidgety with blind purpose. 'Go on. Back to the club.'

So she drove.

* * *

And now here they were, back in the alley beside the club, where it still thrummed with music like the heartbeat of an animal. Mona stopped the car at the side door and Lefty got out. The boy was still unconscious, his head slumped forward. She tried not to look at him. Tried not to think about what was going to happen to him.

The door into the back of the club was opening. Caught in the bright glare of Mona's headlights, Lefty walked around the front of the car again. A big figure loomed in the club doorway.

Deano, she thought, and shuddered.

Lefty was talking to him, his movements both placatory and entreating.

Horrible little worm.

She saw Deano's big bowling-ball head turn and felt his dark cold eyes resting on the car. Mona shrank down in her seat, feeling her guts shrivel with disgust and fear. She knew he must see Alfie in there; the interior light was on because the passenger door was open, and Alfie was completely exposed – and so was she.

How the fuck did I get into any of this? Mona wondered again, and cursed the day she'd been roped into Lefty's twisted little world.

But she could get out of it.

She could get the *boy* out of it too.

Again that little voice was whispering in her mind, telling her she could do it, she could do it.

Crazy.

It was a mad idea, and she had to forget it. Just let them take the boy inside and she'd go home, home to her baby and her mother, home to normality and goodness, or at least to the *illusion* of it, because she knew this was going

345

to haunt her. She would see forever this young blond boy in her mind, being dragged and dumped and brought back to Deano to do with as he would. She would look out from her cosy little world and know that there was sickness out there, and madness, and she wouldn't be able to rest easy if . . .

If she didn't do something right now.

Deano was stepping out into the alley beside Lefty. All Deano's attention was focused on the car. Mona looked at Deano, at the sheer size and bulk of him, at the high-toned way he was dressed – his camel-hair coat expensive, his suit Savile Row, his shoes shone to a high gloss – but inside, *inside*, she knew he was filthy, stinking, corrupt.

She closed her eyes, breathed deep, suppressed the urge to act. Thought of her baby Josie, sweet little child . . . oh, but what if this ever happened to Josie? What if some sick bastard wanted her, the way Deano wanted this boy here? And what if someone stood by and did nothing when Josie needed help? What would she think of that person? That person would be *scum*, as bad as any nonce.

The decision was instant, crazy, manic.

Mona reached across the unconscious boy and slammed the door shut. The interior light went out. She saw out of the corner of her eye that Deano and Lefty had stopped moving, startled. Her heart was beating very fast: was she going to have a heart attack? She felt sick, enervated, jumpy. She was going to do it.

Lefty was hurrying forward now. So was Deano.

Holy shit.

Mona scrabbled at the keys in the ignition. Her fingers felt clumsy all of a sudden, they didn't feel like her own nimble hands at all. She fumbled and gripped the key and turned it. The engine fired straight away. She threw the car into reverse.

But Deano was already there at the passenger door. Mona fumbled again, found the central locking. The lock on the passenger door and on her own clonked down. *Thunk*.

Then Lefty reached in through the open window beside her and grabbed her by the throat.

Mona let out a half-strangled yell as he shook her. His other hand came in and fastened over the front of her face. He was cursing, spraying her with saliva, shouting, calling her bitch and cunt.

Gotta get this car moving, she thought, but she couldn't see and he was throttling her. Spots danced in front of her eyes. This was all going horribly wrong. She heard the glass shatter on the passenger window and now she could see to her horror that Deano's big meaty hands were coming inside the car, knocking in shards of glass that fell in a glittering cascade to the floor, reaching in to pull Alfie out.

Mona felt Lefty's hand over her mouth. She opened her mouth wide and bit down as hard as she could, tasting blood and feeling the gristly *crunch* as her teeth almost met in the middle. Lefty shrieked. His hands were suddenly gone.

Whimpering to herself in a paroxysm of fear, Mona found herself staring into the shark eyes of Deano, who was leaning in to get Alfie. Moving automatically now, her throat hurting, crying with terror, Mona slipped off the handbrake and the car shot backwards down the alley.

Deano fell away, his roar of rage coming after her, but he had Alfie half out of the car and the impetus of its movement took Alfie all the way out.

Shit.

She'd wanted so much to save the kid, but it was not

to be. She saw Lefty floundering in the headlights, clutching his hand, but he was a junkie, he wasn't *really* feeling it, and now he was coming, he was running after her. She hadn't saved the boy and if she wasn't damned careful she wasn't going to save *herself* either; they would *both* be fucked.

Oh Christ oh shit oh help.

The car careered back down the alley and hurtled out into the main road. Mona felt a teeth-jarring crash and glanced in the rear-view mirror and saw that she'd struck another car side-on. Lefty was still coming, running around to her side of the car. He was leaning in again. There were horns blaring, people shouting, Lefty right there with her, his curses raining down on her; it was all crazy, she felt that *she* was crazy, and oh shit she had to get that window shut.

She threw the car into first. Lefty was craning right in now, slapping and punching at her with his bloody hands, trying to get the keys out of the ignition. Mona, screaming and crying in fright and rage, pressed the electric window switch and it slid up.

Lefty was still leaning in as Mona shot forwards along the main road, honking crazily at the other cars to get out of the way. She saw a red light, there was traffic stopping, there was a stationary car right in front of her. She couldn't stop; she couldn't ease up for a moment because, if she did, Lefty would get her. She threw the wheel over and smashed down the side of the stationary car.

Metal screamed. So did Mona.

She bounced off that car and hit a bollard.

Then she was hurling the car around a right turn, more red lights, fuck, there were cars shrieking toward her, horns blaring, drivers swerving, the scream of tyres as they tried to avoid her, Lefty still clinging on to the side of her car, his head inside, his arms out, and she saw a huge truck coming toward her, she was too close, she was going to hit it.

Almost in slow motion she saw the huge shape of the thing coming at her. She wrestled with the wheel but it was too late. She hit the truck on one side, felt the crunch and the grind of metal, felt the shuddering, jarring impact of it all through the car.

Jesus, that was close.

She'd nearly killed them both. Shivering and crying with terror, she drove on. Lefty was quiet now, but still hanging on, his head trapped there by the electric window. And now Mona decided what she was going to have to do. She was going to confess, tell them what Lefty had done, burying the body, killing the cab driver, *everything*, and that Deano had the boy. Frightened as she was of the police, these awful people frightened her even more.

She drove until she found a police station, then she pulled up outside and clambered over and out the hole where the passenger door window used to be. She fell to the hard pavement, jolting every bone in her body. She crouched there a moment, beyond terror, beyond all sense.

She had to get help.

Her head spinning, feeling close to passing out, she stepped out in front of the car and looked at Lefty. She put a hand over her mouth. Then she turned away and, slowly at first, almost drunkenly, staggering and sobbing but then speeding up, driven by panic, Mona started to run away from the police station, towards home, towards safety.

The two PCs were just coming off duty when they saw the battered remains of the car parked haphazardly outside the station. They looked closer.

'Fuck *me*,' said one of them.

Trapped by its neck, by the electric window mechanism on the driver's side, was a human head. There was blood spattered all down the outside of the car. There was no body; only Lefty's head remained there, ripped off at the neck, his eyes open and staring blankly at nothing.

58

Lorcan took Gracie back to the apartment over the casino, after they'd dropped Suze back at Vera's.

'There's nothing to be gained by staying here,' he said at the hospital. 'They'll phone us if there are any developments.'

And there he was again, taking charge, dominating everyone around him. Including her. She didn't like it, she had *never* liked it, but right now it gave her a feeling of safety – and that she was grudgingly willing to accept.

They were inside the apartment, the lights low, music playing. A Christmas tree was lit beside the fire. Gracie looked up at the mistletoe as they came in, and she caught Lorcan's slight smile.

'No,' she said firmly, moving away. 'When you kiss me, you know I can't think straight.'

'Damn, and I thought that was a *good* thing,' said Lorcan, pulling her into his arms anyway.

'It's not a good thing at all,' said Gracie, aware of her whole body melting, *yielding*, in the most irritating way when

351

it came into contact with his. 'It is in fact a very *bad* thing. Because look where it led us.'

'Back into bed?' Lorcan queried, his eyes playing with hers. 'Sorry, but I still think that's pretty good.'

'Yeah, but it doesn't stop there. It'd be fine if it did. But sooner or later we have to get out of bed, and then we start to fight, and then we get upset, and it's just not on.'

'That was five years ago, Gracie,' said Lorcan.

'We're still the same people.'

'Are we though? We're both five years older. You've had your dream of running your own place in Manchester, I've had mine here. Back then, we couldn't reconcile the two. Now, maybe we can.'

'Oh yeah?' Gracie looked at him sceptically. 'How?'

'You could let your manager run the damned place, check in with him a couple of times a month, move back in with me here.'

'Lorcan . . .'

'*Or* we could find another place. We could actually start a family together. Your biological clock has *got* to start ticking soon.'

It hadn't. And if it *had*, Gracie would have ignored it, stuck her fingers in her ears and sung 'la-la-la' very loudly until it stopped. She loved running the business. But . . . here she was, back in Lorcan's arms, and it felt so right. Were they just a hopeless pair of fools that they couldn't make this thing work? Maybe they were both as bad as each other, both wanting to be the boss, the one in charge?

But now Lorcan had thrown something else into the mix. *Divorce.* So horrible. So final. And it had jolted Gracie, she had to admit that, if only to herself. It would be a clean break, an opportunity for both of them to start again.

Just because the old attraction was still there, that didn't mean they could live together now any better than they had five years ago. They'd tear lumps out of each other, she was sure of that – just as they always had. She wondered if Lorcan had *deliberately* played the divorce card, to shock her into reviewing the situation.

She sighed wearily. She was so worried about George and Harry, so concerned for Suze, that anything else was just too much. Now, being back here, being involved all over again, she felt the strong reconnection of that family tie that once had been severed. True, she still felt off-balance, and sometimes the longing to just turn her back and return to her own sparse, yet cosseted way of life, so free of complications, so bereft of hassle, was almost overwhelming.

'I ought to go back to George and Harry's flat,' she said.

'Not a good idea. You're safer here.' He glanced at his watch. 'Look, I have to go out. Something I have to do.'

'Right.' *Where?* she wanted to ask, but stopped herself.

'Stay here, make yourself comfortable. I won't be long.'

But he was gone so long that Gracie started to feel anxious. She kept herself busy by watching TV until late, then she turned out the lights and wandered into the bedroom. She felt tired, but was too hyped-up for sleep.

Something I have to do, he'd said.

She sat on the bed in the dim light cast by the bedside table lamp and looked at her watch. Nearly one o'clock in the morning, what the hell was he doing at that hour? She looked at the bed, but she knew she wouldn't sleep until he returned.

Her mind started playing the age-old tricks on her, the ones known and dreaded by every female since the world began.

Had something happened to him? If you'd asked her if she gave a stuff either way a month ago, she'd have sworn she didn't; but she did, and she hated the fact and the gnawing sense of worry it brought with it.

Suppose he'd had an accident? Or suppose – oh God, and wasn't this the more likely answer? – suppose he'd gone to confront this bastard Deano Drax that Alfie had been telling them about? She felt a cold chill of fear crawl up her spine at the thought of that.

Something I have to do.

Like what? That scene at the hospital flashed into her brain: Lorcan getting madder and madder about Deano Drax.

Oh no.

He wouldn't.

Would he?

Yes. He would. She *knew* he would. Lorcan was hot-headed, full of fire. He'd been brooding about Drax's misdemeanours and now he'd gone to confront him. Gracie picked up her mobile to call him. His phone was switched off.

For God's *sake*.

She looked around, wondering what to do. Was she just supposed to sit here like patient long-suffering little wifey, when Lorcan might be in trouble, in danger? Lorcan was still married to her, still connected to the Doyles. And Deano Drax was wreaking havoc among them. Would he draw the line at Lorcan? She didn't think so. She thought of Brynn, staggering half-alive from the burnt-out flat above the casino in Manchester. Brynn had never hurt a soul.

Deano Drax might have Lorcan right now.

Fear stirring her into agitated movement, Gracie stood up and left the bedroom. She crossed to the apartment's main door and looked outside. The heavy was sitting there. He looked up at her expectantly.

'Do you know where Lorcan's gone?' she asked.

He shook his head.

Gracie paused for a beat, thinking. 'Do you know Deano Drax's club in Soho?'

He nodded.

'You got a car?'

Another nod.

Gracie nodded too. 'Okay, get the damned thing revved up, let's get over there.'

The club was shut by the time they got there. Gracie and the heavy trudged against the thickening sleet and the biting north wind down the alley beside the club. The heavy dutifully tried the metal side door. Locked. He looked above it to the armed and blinking security alarm. He turned and looked at Gracie.

'What now?' he asked.

What indeed. Gracie stood there, hugging herself against the cold, looking up and down the snow-clad alley as if searching for inspiration. There were two big dumpster-style rubbish bins beyond the door, blocking the front of what was clearly a disused garage.

What to do, what to do?

Lorcan could be locked inside the club for all she knew. He could be unconscious. He could be hurt. She looked at the side door. It was a solid door, burglar-proof. And they daren't try to breach it anyway. Even an attempt could trigger the alarm. The alarm could be connected to the local cop shop and if they started the Bill swarming around, that would take some explaining. And they couldn't risk explanations.

Start talking to the police about this, and Harry – and now Lorcan – could be toast.

Then they heard it. A whimpering, like an injured dog.

Gracie looked at the heavy. He looked blankly back at her.

'You hear that?' he said.

Gracie nodded. It was a chilling sound. Suddenly she was glad she wasn't standing here in this freezing cold alley on her own. 'Where is it . . .?' she asked, turning, trying to nail the direction.

'There,' said the heavy, and nodded towards the bins.

Lorcan?

Gracie felt her stomach knot, felt the heavy lurch of incipient sickness. Oh God – was that Lorcan in there? What had Drax done to him?

She felt herself starting to shiver with dread. The heavy was striding towards the bins. The shadows were deeper back here, the whole atmosphere frozen and ominous. Gracie forced her legs to move, forced herself to follow him.

The heavy was throwing back the cover on the closest one. An aroma of rotting vegetation arose and swirled around their heads. Gracie was afraid that she was going to vomit, right here and now.

The heavy looked into the depths of the bin.

'Can't see nothing in here,' he said, and slapped the cover back down.

Which left the other one.

Oh shit, please don't let it be Lorcan.

The heavy was striding to it, pulling open the lid. Again, the sweet aroma of degradation filled their nostrils, and there were new things in here too. Oh joy. Cooking oil and sweat.

Sweat? thought Gracie.

'Something in here,' said the heavy, and reached in.

The whimpering got louder. The thing in the bin was trying to shout out.

That's not Lorcan, thought Gracie. *That's a woman.*

Feeling faint with relief, she moved forward and peered inside. It was so hard to see a damned thing back here in the shadows, but there was someone in there. Terrified eyes stared up at them. There was a gag covering the mouth.

'Come on, help me,' said the heavy. 'Let's get the poor bitch out of there.'

Gracie helped. It was awkward; the middle-aged black woman was heavy and stiff with cold. They somehow got her out of the bin and she collapsed in a heap on to the hard cobbles. Her hands were tied behind her back. Gracie knelt and fumbled with the gag until she got it free. She threw it aside.

'My boy, he's gonna hurt my boy,' the woman whined loudly, her face a sheen of sweat and tears.

Gracie looked up at the heavy. He shrugged.

'Who's your boy?' Gracie asked the shaking woman.

'Lefty!'

Now where had she heard that name before?

'You're talking about Drax?'

The woman was nodding frantically. 'He locked me up in the back room. He locked me up, tied me to a chair, that man is *crazy*. Then Lefty came and the man threatened him, said he wanted his boy Alfie back or he'd do things to me.'

'Alfie?' Gracie yelped. And now she remembered where she'd heard the name Lefty. Alfie had mentioned him as they all sat together in the hospital cafeteria. Lefty had procured Alfie for that nonce Deano.

She looked down at the woman. Grabbed her plump shoulders. The heavy was trying to untie her hands, but they were securely bound. The woman's desperate eyes stared wildly into Gracie's.

'Where's Lefty now?' asked Gracie urgently.

'I don't know,' the woman wept. 'But he came back, that *monster* came back, and he had a blond boy in there, in the office. He was asleep, drugged, something. I don't know. That bastard Drax took me past him, gagged me, put me in that filthy thing with all the rubbish, said he'd see to me later.'

Shit, thought Gracie. *That's Alfie. He's got Alfie.*

The heavy at last got the woman free of her bonds and she brought her arms round and rubbed gingerly at her bruised wrists.

'Where's Deano now?' asked Gracie. 'Is he still inside? Is he still in there with the boy?'

If he *was*, then Gracie was calling the police right now, to hell with it. It was *way* past time that bastard was locked up.

The woman shook her head. 'No, he left. Drove off with the boy in his car, a big black car.'

'Where would he go? Do you know where he'd go?'

The woman was shrugging, looking around her with dazed, unfocused eyes.

Gracie grabbed her shoulders again and shook her, hard.

'Come *on*. Lefty. Your boy. Did he see Deano just here, always here? Did he go to Deano's home sometimes?'

'No . . .' The woman was near breaking point, Gracie could see that. Exhausted. Terrified. Beyond all sensible thought.

'Lefty could be with him at his home,' said Gracie, knowing that Lefty was all the woman was capable of focusing on right now. 'If Lefty's with him there now, we can help. Do you know where Deano Drax lives? Then we can find Lefty.'

It was a lie, but it was a necessary one. All Gracie would want to do for a lowlife kiddie pimp like Lefty was kick him straight in the nuts, but she needed this woman to come up with something. She thought of Alfie, little blond Alfie. Thought of Lorcan. Drax could have them both. She *had* to get something out of this woman.

'Come the fuck *on*,' snapped Gracie. 'Think.'

'Steady,' said the heavy, watching her.

'*You* be steady,' said Gracie hotly. 'We've got to get to that fucker. I'll call the police if I have to, right now, *they'll* know where he . . .' She fumbled in her coat pocket. Her mobile wasn't there. *Shit.* She'd left it at Lorcan's.

'I got it,' said the woman.

'What?'

'Deano Drax's address,' she said. 'Lefty went there sometimes. He told me all about it. A big place. A big country house with a thatched roof and lions on the gate.'

'Tell me,' said Gracie.

59

Lorcan got back to the casino very late, much later than he'd expected. They'd been working overtime to get the thing just right, and he'd paid through the nose for the damned thing, but now he had it, and she was going to be so pleased. Delighted. It could be his last Christmas present to her – or the first to cement their new relationship.

He went up to the flat. The first thing he noticed was that the man he'd left guarding the door was gone. Off to take a piss or something, fair enough. He let himself into the flat. All was normal, quiet, warm and cosy.

'Gracie?' he said quietly, switching on the low, ambient lighting in the sitting room.

He crossed the room, slipping off his coat. She was probably in bed by now, asleep. He thought of her curled up there, her brilliant mane of hair spread out across the pillows, and smiled. He walked into the bedroom, moving quietly so as not to wake her.

From the light spilling into the bedroom from the sitting room, he could see that the bed was empty.

He felt his guts tighten in alarm.

He put on the light. 'Gracie?'

Lorcan crossed quickly to the en suite, pushed the door open. It was empty.

He got out his mobile. It was switched off. He often did that; he hated the damned thing. He switched it on, checked his messages. Nothing from Gracie. He didn't have Paul – the heavy's – number. He phoned hers instead. It rang and rang. He could *hear* it ringing. He drew closer to the bed. Gracie's mobile was on the bedside table, flashing, vibrating and ringing. She didn't even have it with her.

He went back outside the door. Looked again at the empty chair there in the hall. Wherever she'd gone, it looked like she'd taken some backup with her. He hoped so, he really did. He went to the bedside table, grabbed a pen and paper, scrawled a note. *Gracie, if you come back and read this, STAY HERE.* He tucked it under her phone. Then he switched on his own mobile, praying for her to contact him any way she could and say she was okay. He snatched up his coat, and went out again.

60

The first thing the police did was call the pathologist and SOCOs to establish a crime scene right outside their own front door. The next was contact the DVLA and place the wrecked car's registration number. It gave them Mona Thomson's name and address. They got straight over there, and found Mona just coming out of her front door with her grizzling daughter clutched in her arms and her mother following on with bags and a suitcase.

'Mona Thomson?' asked the police. There were two of them, a man and a woman. Luminous jackets. Scary.

'No,' said Mona, gulping, eyes wide and frantic. 'She used to live here, she moved out.'

The police stood there and looked at Mona, at her daughter still in a thin nightdress, at the bags, the suitcase, her mother's anxious face.

'Only there's been an incident with a car, and its owner is Miss Mona Thomson, listed at this address,' said the male police officer.

'She ain't here,' said Mona, raising her chin, lips trembling.

'Are you Mona Thomson?' asked the female police officer.

'*Shit*,' wailed Mona, and crumpled. The little girl caught her mother's distress and started crying too.

'She ain't Mona Thomson, she don't even *know* that girl,' piped up the mother, quivering with indignation.

Mona sent her a look. 'It's all right Mum. It's okay.'

'No,' said her mother, and now she was on the verge of tears too. 'It's *Christmas*,' she said desperately.

And I'm Santa Claus, thought the male policeman. He'd heard it all before. The denials, the threats, the pleas and the weasel words.

'Miss Mona Thomson?' asked the female police officer.

Mona nodded slowly. 'Yeah. That's me,' she said.

'If you could accompany us to the station . . .'

And so it began.

Her mum took Josie back to her house and Mona sat in the interview room at the station late into the night. She'd seen the furore at the front of the station, the tent, the police tape all around it; inside was her car, with Lefty's head jammed in the window. She wasn't sorry about *that*, anyway. She told the police that in no uncertain terms.

'Lefty Umbabwe was a bastard,' she said, clutching her hands around the Styrofoam cup of coffee they'd provided for her.

'Tell us about it,' said the hard-eyed detective. He had straight mud-blond hair, a long, lugubrious face and narrow, deep-set conker-brown eyes. He looked tired and fed up as he sat opposite her. His female assistant, a skinny, hawk-nosed and spotty brunette, watched Mona with a stony face.

Mona scarcely knew where to start, but eventually she did. She told them about Lefty being a heavy butane user and about him being a procurer of young male meat for Deano Drax.

The female plain-clothes officer was writing it all down. She asked Mona for Deano Drax's details, and Mona said she worked in Deano's club and that was how she had become embroiled in Lefty's concerns.

'He had to find the boy, Alfie,' she said, cupping her hands around the cup to keep warm, to stop the shivering that was part cold, part fear. 'Deano was frantic to get him back after Alfie managed to give Lefty the slip. Lefty knew that Deano would rip him an extra arsehole if he failed. He was hopping mad about it, so Lefty was desperate. He said I had to help him, make it look like I was Alfie's mum or some fucking thing, out on the streets searching for him. We looked and looked. Couldn't find him. I didn't *want* to help, but he forced me to. I was glad the boy got away. I've seen others hanging around with Deano, and it's horrible.'

'What then?' asked the weary-looking cop when Mona halted, drank a little.

Mona shuddered.

'It got worse and worse. He got more desperate. He was shit-scared of Deano, he *had* to get a result. Then one night . . .' Mona's voice tailed away. Her eyes were suddenly blank, lost in memory.

'Go on.'

'There was a cab driver. He was young.' Mona swallowed hard. 'Lefty was talking to him, asking if he'd seen this boy, this teenage blond, pretty as an angel, you couldn't mistake Alfie for anyone else, he's so beautiful. He was talking to the driver, and . . . all of a sudden, I don't know how it happened, but Lefty just lost it. Completely lost it. I was just standing there beside him and suddenly he starts stabbing this poor guy in the throat, and then . . .'

Mona stopped again. A tear slipped down her cheek. They said nothing, but sat there watching her, allowing her time to gather herself together. Eventually, Mona took a shuddering breath and went on.

'He forced me to help him. I didn't want to. He told me to get in the cab. Then he pushed the dead man to one side and drove over to some old docks, near London Bridge. He pushed the cab into the river. I helped him; I had to. But I didn't want to. You got to believe that. I was sick and I was afraid of him. He'd just killed a man in cold blood; I couldn't believe it. I was *afraid*.'

More tears poured down Mona's face. The police sat there, watched her.

Mona swiped at her face with a shaking hand and ploughed on.

'Then, a while after that, he wanted me to go out with him again. I tried to refuse, but he wouldn't let me. He told me we'd use my car. We were at the club, Deano's club, and . . . oh fuck . . .'

'Take your time,' said the female police officer.

Mona ran a trembling hand through her hair. 'It was horrible. *Horrible*. He brought this thing out to the alley where I'd parked the car. It was wrapped in a sheet, tarpaulin, that stuff, you know?'

They nodded. The female officer was taking brisk notes.

'And I thought, what the hell is that? I didn't have a clue.

But Lefty told me to drive, so I did. We went out to the forest and . . . he dug a hole. He dug a *grave*.'

Mona gave a sob. 'There was a body in there, but it was light, I knew it was light because Lefty lifted it so easily, and he wasn't Rambo. And I started to think . . . *shit*, I've been thinking about it ever since, I haven't been able to sleep for thinking . . . I started to think that it was one of Deano's boys, that they'd overdosed a kid and Lefty was disposing of the evidence for him.'

'What happened then?' asked the male officer.

'He dug the grave . . .'

'Can you remember where it was?'

Mona shook her head tiredly. 'No. Well, maybe. It was dark, I was scared, I wasn't thinking about anything except the fact that he was burying a body and I was involved, I knew about it, so would he kill me too, tip me in there with it? I didn't know *what* he was going to do.'

'Go on.'

Mona stopped, plucking at a hangnail.

'Mona?' prompted the female officer.

'It was awful,' said Mona, looking up at them both with tears in her eyes. 'This . . . *body* . . . it started moaning. It *wasn't dead*. And it was like when he knifed the driver, it was just like that. He just acted really quickly. Really . . . quick. You know?'

They nodded.

'He hit it with a shovel. It . . . the kid in there, I could tell it was a kid because of the voice, the sound, the scream . . .'

'It's all right, Mona, take your time.'

'The kid screamed,' said Mona, and now she was sobbing brokenly, trying to get the words out in between gasping breaths.

'The kid screamed, but he just went on hitting him until he didn't scream any more. I can't forget it. Every night I go to sleep, and I see it over and over again . . .'

'Go on.'

'And then he found Alfie. He found the poor little cunt.' Mona looked up at them. 'I prayed to God he wouldn't find him, but he did. And I tried . . . I had Alfie in the car, and I thought, I can't do this, I thought about the taxi driver and the murdered boy and I thought, enough, I can't do this any more, if he kills me then he kills me, I just can't go on with this. I'm a *mother*,' she cried in anguish. 'That boy he hit with a shovel, *he* had a mother too. That woman's never going to see her son again because of Deano and what Lefty did. I couldn't go on with it, do you see that?'

They nodded.

Mona wiped at her eyes and gave a tired sigh. She paused, collecting herself.

'So I thought, what the hell. I tried to get Alfie out of there, but Deano smashed in my car window and pulled him out. Then Lefty tried to grab me and I wound up the window, but he wouldn't let go, he wouldn't. I didn't know what to do. If he'd got hold of me then he'd have killed me, I knew it. So I drove. I was terrified. I drove until I saw the police station, then I stopped, and it was then that I realized . . .'

'That Lefty was dead,' said the male police officer.

Mona nodded.

'I just panicked. I ran for home, and we were going to go up North, hole up somewhere, I don't know. We just knew we had to get out.'

The officer stood up. 'Take a breather, Mona,' he said, and beckoned his fellow officer to follow him out of the room.

Once they were outside in the corridor, he said: 'Get her another coffee and get back in there and talk to her, get any more info you can. I'm going to get Deano Drax pulled in, see if we can't get that boy back before . . .'

He didn't finish the sentence. The female officer nodded. She didn't want to *hear* that sentence finished, either. She understood. She went off to the coffee machine, thinking about the dross that was wandering around on the streets and wishing she knew a lot less about life than she did.

Christmas Day

61

Harry was feeling very tired, and very cold. He was also in a lot of pain. And now the man was back, leering over him with his big head and his cruel eyes. And this time, as if it mattered, *this* time the man had a gun in his hand.

Oh just shoot me then you fucker and be done with it, thought Harry.

Harry had heard about old people actually *wanting* to die, and he had never understood it. To Harry, life had always been sweet, to be savoured. But now, he understood those old people: infirm, filled with pain, just downright bloody *tired*. Life got thin, he could see that now. Life became too much. And then . . . well, was death so terrible, really?

An end to the pain.

An end to the torment and the fear.

No, not so terrible.

And now the git thought he could frighten Harry by pointing a gun at his head? What a laugh.

'You ever played Russian roulette, Harry?' the man was asking him.

It was an old gun, Harry could see that. This was no fancy Russian piece, no RK whatever. This was an old thing with a blued barrel and a six-cylinder. A revolver, his weary brain supplied. That was it.

Harry shook his head tiredly. *No.*

The man had a box of bullets on top of the big chest freezer. He flicked open the six-cylinder chamber on the gun and he held up one gleaming bullet for Harry to look at. The man smiled broadly, and inserted the bullet into the gun. He snapped the chamber closed and pointed the gun at Harry's head.

Em, thought Harry.

He looked down the barrel of the gun.

But Em didn't want him; she despised him. Em was lost to him forever. He was weary, filthy, beyond hungry, beyond anything but this tiny, cramped, crippling world of pain. He'd had enough. So what if this bastard shot him now. So *what?*

'It's Christmas Day, Harry, and this is my gift to you. A little excitement to brighten your dull days. What do you think of that? You put one bullet in the chamber,' the man was saying. 'And then – guess what, Harry? – you just pull the trigger and you hope, Harry, that the bullet isn't in that *particular* chamber, because it'll blow your brains to fuck. That's Russian roulette, Harry. What do you think of *that?*'

Harry shrugged. *Like I care.*

The man's smile faded. He liked his victims terrified, babbling, begging for mercy. He didn't like them like this – beaten, beyond hope. This was no fun. No challenge. Angrily he placed the muzzle of the gun against Harry's forehead, grinding the cold metal against Harry's shrinking flesh.

'Say goodbye, Harry,' said Deano.

He pulled the trigger.

Harry flinched.

Nothing happened. Just a *click*. The chamber rotated. Was this new chamber empty or full? Harry slumped there, uncaring.

'You're a brave man, Harry Doyle,' said Deano, almost admiringly. He put the gun aside on top of the freezer. 'That's the first, though, Harry, and there are five more spins of the wheel. You like this game?'

Harry nodded tiredly. Love it, hate it. Who gave a shit?

'Back soon,' said Deano, and left the garage.

Harry sat there, listening to the whir of the freezer motor, not even thinking any more about the food that must be in there. He was beyond hunger. Beyond thirst. Beyond the need for anything except for this to end. And end it would. Five more chances. One of them would be lethal. He didn't care.

Not any more.

Em was lost to him anyway.

62

The snow was coming down thicker and faster as the heavy drove himself and Gracie toward Deano Drax's place. The car was struggling, the back wheels spinning sideways as they went off the main drag and on to the country lanes that would lead them to Drax's hideaway.

'We're never going to make this,' said the heavy, wrestling with the wheel as the car spun wildly on another sharp turn. The wipers were whooshing across the screen, the snow coming down so hard and fast now that they were barely coping.

Gracie looked at him. He had a big bald head, a sharp pecker of a nose, fleshy cheeks pockmarked with teenage acne scars, and hazel eyes. He didn't look as if he was enjoying this any more than she was.

'You got a mobile on you?' she asked.

He patted his pocket. 'Yeah, but I'm not sure how much battery I have.'

Shit, thought Gracie. *If that's flat, we're out here in the middle of nowhere with no means of communication.*

'What's your name?' she asked.

'Paul.'

'Shouldn't you be at home with your family, Paul?'

He gave her an exasperated look. 'Yeah. Should be. But here I am, babysitting you.'

Paul took a hard curve and the wheels spun sideways again.

'Steady,' said Gracie.

'You want to drive? It's a fucking nightmare.'

'No I don't.'

'Then shut up will you?' He was silent. 'This is a stupid fucking idea,' he said after a few beats.

'Look, I told you. I think this Drax arsehole might have done Lorcan some damage.' Gracie drew a calming breath and tried to keep the explanation succinct. 'Lorcan's gone out, I don't know where, and he hasn't come back. It looks like Drax put my brother George in hospital. And it looks as if he's already nabbed my *other* brother Harry. Now Drax has snatched Alfie – we *think* it's Alfie – so it's perfectly feasible that he could have nabbed Lorcan too. Lorcan was all stoked up, ready to do Drax some serious damage. And I think . . . I think he's gone to do it.'

'You tried his mobile?'

'That's the very first thing I did. It wasn't turned on.'

'Get the police involved,' advised Paul, wrenching the wheel hard round as the car lost its grip yet again.

Gracie let out a *huff* of breath. 'Look. Back there at the club, I would have. But I don't have my mobile.'

'Well, let's try mine. If this Drax is as bad as you say, let's try taking the sensible option.'

He thought she was crazy. Hell, *she* thought she was too. She had no idea what she could do up against a bastard like

Drax. But she knew she had to do *something*. 'Give it here then.'

He tossed her his mobile. She flipped it open, fiddled with it in the dim light it cast, trying to familiarize herself with it. She stared hard at the screen, saw the amber warning light.

'Shit,' she said.

'What?'

'You're right. The battery's pretty low.'

'How about the signal?'

Gracie tilted the phone in various directions. 'Patchy.'

'Try it anyway.'

Gracie tapped in 999, but the signal was too bad. She heard no ring tone. She halted the call, if only to preserve what was left of the battery's life. She sat there, staring at the snow hurtling towards them, then being shoved to one side by the steady, almost hypnotic *whumph whumph whumph* of the wipers.

'I read somewhere that the phone company can track a person down to a few feet using the signal from their mobile phone,' she said, and then they were rounding a hard curve in the road and suddenly, too suddenly, there was something ahead in the road, a fucking *tree* was lying across it, and the car was going too fast.

Gracie let out a yell and automatically put her hands up in front of her face. Paul stamped on the brake. The wheels lost their grip. The car careered almost gracefully off the road, rotating like a spinning top. Then it shot down a steep bank, the engine roaring, then rolled end over end and came to rest on its roof. The wheels spun on thin, cold air. The engine coughed once, then died. All was silent beneath the falling snow.

63

Sandy and Suze were back at the hospital, sitting with George. It was Christmas Day, the day when families should be together, at home, safe and secure. But here was poor George, confined to intensive care, surrounded not by laughter and love but by beeping monitors and briskly efficient nurses.

'At least it don't look like he's screaming any more,' said Sandy, who was on George's left side, holding his hand.

'No,' said Suze bleakly, who was on George's right, holding his other hand.

George was lying still now, and it was as if he was asleep, just asleep and likely to wake at any moment and start with the cheery George-type banter. He wasn't puffy any more, and the frightening movements had stopped. Suze focused on the steady rise and fall of George's chest.

Sandy's eyes followed hers. 'It's good he's breathing on his own now,' she said to Suze.

George was indeed breathing for himself. That was progress. But Suze felt consumed with dread for him. What if he woke up demented, brain-damaged? What on earth would they do then? What if he wasn't right in the head, her poor clever lovely George?

She knew you were supposed to think positive, be calm, but she couldn't. She was this boy's *mother*, and all she could think was the worst. She always had. An ambulance passing in the night, sirens blaring? It was George or Harry they were going to collect, broken into pieces, from some road accident, some fire, something *awful*.

It was a woman thing, she supposed. Other families had come in here today, to be near their loved ones on Christmas. A special day, a happy day for most; but for Suze and Sandy, and for all these other poor souls in the intensive care ward, a day of torment.

Suze thought of her childhood Christmases, spent with her mother. Her parents had separated when she was seven and she'd been an only child. Christmas hadn't been that much fun. Dad had left and didn't show any signs of ever coming back, or of making the slightest effort to keep in touch with his daughter. They'd been poor, her and her mother, although Mum had tried her best to make the day good for Suze.

Then, marriage to Paddy Doyle. She had created her own happy Christmas tableau then, and added three kids to the mix. But she and Paddy had followed a pattern set by her own parents. Arguments. Clashes. She'd sought refuge in the arms of other men and Paddy had found out. Then Paddy had left and taken Gracie with him up to Manchester, cutting the family into two halves.

Suze thought of Gracie, and her daughter's fractured marriage. There were patterns there, and she hoped that Gracie would be the one to break the cycle; but she doubted it. Some things went too deep to alter.

Gloomily, Suze sat there and sighed. And now look at the mess they were all in. Someone coming at her door, the door to her *home*, with a chainsaw. Getting bags of Harry's hair sent to them. Anything could be happening to him, and what could they do about it? Whichever way you looked at it, they were fucked, the whole damned lot of them. Suze sat there looking at the steady rise and fall of George's chest, and thought miserably about all the hurts and injustices that an unkindly nature had inflicted on her over the years. It would take a fucking Christmas *miracle* to make this situation any better.

'Suze,' said Sandy.

'Hm?' Suze looked across at Sandy, whose eyes were round with wonder.

'Suze, *look*.'

Sandy was staring at George's face.

George's dark brown eyes were open. Slowly, they blinked. They moved around the room almost vaguely. Then they moved down, and settled on Suze's face. Then they moved to the left, and alighted on Sandy's. Some spasm flittered across George's face. He opened his mouth, but no sound came out, just a gasping wheeze.

Suze was on her feet in an instant, leaning over George. 'Don't worry lovey, you're all right,' she said quickly, the words tumbling over each other. 'You can't speak, they've had to put a thing in your throat, but you're all right, don't worry, it's all okay,' said Suze. She let out a sudden laugh, and now her tears of joy were splashing down on George's face. He looked up at her.

Oh Jesus please let him be okay now, thought Suze. If this was their Christmas miracle, then a Christmas prayer wouldn't go amiss, surely?

George's eyes slipped to the left again, to Sandy. He opened his mouth, but again there was no sound.

Sandy leaned in with a smile. Their eyes met. She kissed his cheek.

'Nurse!' called Suze, and George's nurse came hurrying over to welcome him back to the land of the living.

64

The whole world was upside-down, and full of eerie silence.

'Paul?' gasped out Gracie. She felt a deep sense of unreality. It was still snowing, but the wipers had stopped working. Through the windscreen she could see nothing but a solid film of snow, tinted pale primrose by the glare of the headlights. The seat belt was cutting into her flesh, holding her suspended, upside-down, in her seat. Her breath plumed out into the rapidly chilling air inside the car. She was aware that she was shivering with shock as well as cold. The window on Paul's side was gone, shattered into fragments. That side of his face and his right-hand shoulder looked bloody.

'Fuck it, *Paul*,' said Gracie, louder.

No reply. His eyes were closed. Gracie was scrabbling for the seat belt release, her shaking hands failing to find it half a dozen times before finally, cursing, shivering, she had it and pressed it. She fell free of the belt's restraint, her head and shoulders hitting the car roof, her legs sprawling. How to get out? She still had Paul's phone in her hand. She stuffed it into her coat pocket and crawled, crab-legged, awkward, disorientated, over the unconscious Paul. She grabbed the jagged window opening and hauled herself through and out. Branches caught at her, dragged into her hair and dug into her stomach.

She fell, panting, whimpering, into a snow-filled ditch. She sat there for a moment, too stunned to move. Slowly, half afraid to find out, she checked herself over for injuries. But she was okay, not a mark on her. She looked back at the car. It was sloping down, bonnet-first, into the ditch, resting on the driver's side against an old, twisted oak tree. Now she could see what had happened when the car spun out of control and turned over. The car had struck the oak on Paul's side, shattering the window.

Gracie dragged herself to her feet, staggered up to the car where Paul still sat pinned by his seat belt, upside-down, unconscious.

'Paul!' she yelled at him.

No answer. Just the moaning of the hard chilling northern wind through the branches of the trees.

Gracie looked all around her, wondering what the hell to do now. She could see faint lights in the distance up ahead. A farmhouse, hopefully, where she could summon help. She'd have to go on foot, alone, from here. Not a cheering prospect. And what about Paul? She couldn't just leave him like this: he'd freeze to death. She flipped open the phone.

Shit.

Now the battery was dead.

She left the damned thing switched on and tucked it into Paul's jacket. Wondered whether she ought to at least get him upright, but she'd heard you could make matters worse by moving crash victims, exacerbating injuries. No, she was going to have to push on, reach that house up there, get some assistance. There was nothing else she could do.

With a last desperate look at Paul hanging there, Gracie struggled up the bank of the ditch and back on to the grass verge. The snow was relentless now, slicing towards her almost horizontally, stealing her breath away and tinting the whole night-time world pale blue. Ahead, there was light, warmth, help. She had to go for it; there was nothing else she could do. She scrambled over the fallen tree that had been Paul's undoing, then slowly, stumbling a bit but then gaining pace, Gracie started walking.

The lights of the house seemed to recede as Gracie trudged through the snow, twisting her ankles a dozen times on unseen obstacles. Every step she took seemed to take the damned things further away, not closer. She could have howled aloud with the frustration of it. She was so worried about Lorcan, and Harry, and Alfie – and now there was Paul back there in the car, probably freezing to death, if not mortally injured already. She *had* to get help for them all. When she reached the farmhouse – *if* she ever did – she was through playing silly buggers. She was going to call the police, call out the whole fucking army if necessary. She was done with pussyfooting around. Deano Drax had to be stopped, right now. Eventually, she rounded a corner, and at last she could see the outline of a big thatched house.

There were lots of lights on in there. It looked cosy, welcoming. Gracie started forward, walking past two big pillars on which hung large, dark-painted wrought-iron gates. The gates stood open. She paused there. Then slowly, she looked up. On each one of the pillars was a huge stone lion, pawing the frigid air, wearing a collar of snow and roaring up at the cold night sky.

It was Drax's place.

Gracie froze, her heart hammering, her mind in a flat spin. What to do, what to do? She looked to the left and to the right, but there were no more comforting lights, no *nothing*. This was the only place out here. She thought again of Paul, lying injured back along the road. He could die, and if he *did*, then she was responsible. She'd wanted to come out here, not him. She thought of Lorcan. He was a big hard bastard but he wasn't twisted like Drax. Anything could have happened to him. As for Harry, he could already be dead for all she knew. And Alfie. What about him? He could be here, inside this house, kept prisoner, abused, hurt.

She looked up at the lions. They seemed threatening, warning her to back off. But she couldn't. Whatever it cost her, she knew she had to go on.

65

'Oh you better watch out, you better . . . come on, Harry. Join in.'

Deano Drax's tuneless horrible nasal whine was going to be the last sound he heard on this earth, Harry knew that now. The man couldn't sing. Drax was prancing around Harry's chair, saying *join in, join in*, wailing out these *fucking* Christmas tunes until Harry felt he was going to just flip and scream the place down.

How long had he been in this hellhole now? He'd lost all track of time. Days, he thought. Although it could be over a week. He just didn't know. He knew he was filthy, sweaty, bloody. The thought of a hot shower, of being clean and warm, was too painful even to contemplate.

Harry didn't join in. Deano Drax stopped his merry little jig and stood stock-still in front of Harry. He bent forward and stared into Harry's face.

'I *said*, join in,' he growled.

Harry said nothing. He wished the fucker would just shoot him. It'd be a merciful release right now.

As if Deano had heard Harry's thoughts, he was reaching out, taking the gun off the top of the chest freezer.

Ah shit, thought Harry. *What the hell?*

Deano pointed the muzzle of the gun at Harry's head and gave a grin.

'It's Christmas Day, Harry. You probably didn't realize that, right?'

Christmas Day. Harry thought of what he should be doing. He could be at Mum's with George, getting the full Christmas works, turkey and stuffing and . . . oh *shit*, all that food, what did he have to go and think about food for? . . . and probably with Alfie too. Instead, he was about to get killed. No more pain, though – that was a bonus.

'Of course you didn't,' went on Drax. 'Otherwise you'd have joined in with my songs, wouldn't you Harry? It's traditional, isn't it. Carols at Christmas, and party games. Do you like party games, Harry?'

Harry didn't like party games. Wearily, he shook his head.

'That's a shame, because I do. And we still haven't finished the game we were playing before.'

Now Drax was shoving the cold, hurtful metal muzzle of the gun up against Harry's cheekbone. Harry gasped at the pain, but was too weak, too beaten, to utter a protest.

Get on with it then.

'Russian roulette,' breathed Deano, looking into Harry's eyes.

Harry stared right back at him. The evil bastard was getting off on this, he could see it. He loved to hurt people.

'Here we go then, Harry. Let's see what the game nets us, shall we?'

Oh shut up and shoot me.

Deano squeezed the trigger. Harry shut his eyes, screwed

them up tight. There was a dull, solid *click*. Despite himself, Harry flinched.

Deano drew back, smiling broadly, stroking a spade-like hand through his neat little goatee beard. 'Lucky that time, Harry. *Very* lucky.' And then the smile dropped from his face and he rammed the black muzzle back against Harry's flesh, grinding it hard into his cheekbone. And he fired the gun again.

Click!

Deano started to laugh.

Harry let out his breath. He felt the warm trickle of blood on his face where the gun had cut in. Well, he was still alive. Three bullets down, three to go. One of those would kill him, for sure.

'The game's getting exciting now, Harry,' said Deano, drawing back with a smile and a shake of his massive head. He placed the gun carefully on the freezer lid again. He looked at Harry almost tenderly. 'Wonder when your luck's going to run out?'

Think it already has, thought Harry, as Deano fiddled in his tool box and came up with the pliers once again.

66

Lorcan was going clean off his head. He was trying to think as Gracie would think, trying to work out what had been going on in her febrile little brain while he'd been out. All right, he'd been out for longer than he'd expected. Had she started to worry, thinking something had happened to him? Had she got a call from the hospital – maybe George had taken a turn for the worse? Had she got restless – this was always a possibility with the Gracie he'd known – and gone over to Auntie Vera's to see her mother for something?

For what?

Gracie and her mother had never got on. He didn't *think* Gracie would actively seek out her mother's company, except in an emergency – but he could be wrong. So, the hospital then. He called them, bypassed all the usual tedious questions about whether he was a relative or not.

'I'm his brother-in-law,' he explained to a distracted-sounding nurse. 'I'm trying to reach his sister, my wife. Gracie. There's been a family emergency. Tall, red-haired woman. Is she there with him?'

The nurse went off to check. *Come on Gracie, be there*, thought Lorcan.

It seemed to take forever, but at last the nurse came back. No woman matching that description was visiting intensive care at that time, she said.

'Yeah, but Gracie could have popped out to go to the loo or grab a coffee. Is anyone else there visiting George Doyle?'

'No, I'm sorry.'

Lorcan hung up, and phoned Suze's mobile.

'Is Gracie there with you?' he asked when she picked up.

'No she's not,' said Suze. 'I thought she was with you.'

'Any idea where she'd be? I left her right here at the casino, now she's gone.'

'Listen, I gave up trying to understand Gracie *years* ago,' said Suze with a sniff.

'You've no idea where Gracie could have gone?'

'Nope. None at all.'

Great.

Which left him with two thoughts, neither of them very comforting. Had Drax grabbed her? He'd tried it once before. Or *someone* had, anyway. Had he been so long delayed that she'd thought something had happened to him? Did she think that Drax had him? Was she even now on the way over to Drax's club to see if he was there? Or had she gone back to the boys' flat for something?

'Fuck it,' said Lorcan, and picked up his coat and hurried out the door.

67

Gracie had no idea what to do next. She was shivering with cold and sweating with nerves at one and the same time as she crept closer to the huge bulk of the house, which seemed to crouch in blackness against a star-studded sky.

There were lights on downstairs – no doubt these were the lights she had seen from the lane where she and Paul had come to grief. Stepping warily, Gracie moved closer until she could see in one of the windows. The window was decorated with a leaded lattice and she could see that the glass was so old that in some of the diamond-patterned sections it had bulged out, giving a curiously distorted effect as she peered inside.

She found herself looking into a sitting room, replete with low dark beams, red-themed cosy couches, and an old brick inglenook fireplace in which a big fire was roaring away. Alfie was sitting on one of the couches, his head thrown back, his eyes closed.

Gracie froze. What, was he asleep? Drugged?

Alfie wouldn't be relaxed enough to sleep if Drax had

grabbed him. She had seen how much Alfie hated Drax when he'd talked about him at the hospital. If he was in Drax's clutches, Alfie would be in a state of fear. He *had* to be drugged.

She moved on. It was no use trying to alert Alfie that she was there. Drax could be right there in the room, just out of her field of vision, and she would be alerting him too. Her bowels felt almost liquid with terror as she thought of coming face to face with Drax. And where was Lorcan? Was he here too, held prisoner somewhere? It was a big house and the entire upper storey was in darkness.

This is impossible, she thought.

She walked on, cautiously, padding through the snow, thinking that at any moment a security light was going to come on, that in some way Drax was going to be alerted to her presence. The snow muffled her footfalls but she couldn't see where she was treading. Flowerbeds, solid obstacles, all were shrouded in a concealing blanket of white. She could so easily trip and fall, twist her ankle, and then where would she be? Up shit creek, that's where.

The snow was continuing to fall steadily, deadening sound. She felt totally alone here outside the house; she could see no lights anywhere in the surrounding countryside. She rounded the corner of the house, skimming a hand lightly along its walls to steady herself in the blue-tinted semi-darkness of the snow-filled night.

Now she was around the back of the house, and she could see light spilling out from another window up ahead. She slowed, all her senses alert to danger. Maybe Drax was in this room, having left Alfie at the front of the building.

She drew closer and saw that there was a half-stable door near the window – and the door was standing ajar. She swallowed hard and wondered if she was actually going to throw up, she felt so sick with apprehension. Her legs didn't seem to want to move any more. Or at least not in *this* direction. Everything in her was saying, *Don't do this. Run.*

But Drax had Alfie. He might have Lorcan too. *And* Harry. She drew closer and risked a peep in at the window.

It was a kitchen. An honest, homely, practically laid-out farmhouse kitchen, with a big refectory table in the middle of the floor, more beams on the ceiling, an Aga, and an old-fashioned butler's sink just below the window through which she was looking.

The room seemed to be empty. And the door was open. Why was the door open, letting out all the heat into the frozen December night?

Because Drax was outside.

The thought popped into her brain and her breathing stopped dead.

She looked behind her. Saw nothing. No one was rushing towards her through the snow, ready to maim or kill. Her heart was thudding sickly in her chest now. Was Drax out here, stalking her? She drew back from the window, blinking, all her night vision gone. She sagged against the wall of the house, blinded, waiting for someone to attack her.

Nobody did.

After a few beats, her vision came back again. Now she could see that there was another building further along, and the door there was half-open, a fainter light spilling out on to the snow. Was it a garage, a storeroom? She heard movement coming from that direction.

Maybe Drax was out there, fetching something. People kept freezers, washing machines, tumble dryers in the garage sometimes, didn't they? Maybe Drax did too.

What to do, what to do?

In turmoil, wanting to just flee, Gracie wrestled with herself. She knew she'd never get another chance like this. There would be a phone in there; maybe she'd be able to summon help. Before she could bottle it, she forced her legs to move forward. She stepped over the doormat, careful not to make a sound, and she was in; she was standing inside Drax's kitchen.

68

Lorcan rang the bell of George and Harry's flat until his finger was numb. He stepped back, looked anxiously up at the first-floor windows. Everything was in darkness up there. He went back to his car and drove carefully over – slipping and sliding all the way – to Drax's club. The roads were quiet, not much moving on them except the odd gritting lorry. On the weather reports they'd been telling people not to go out if they could avoid it. To stay home, in the warm bosom of their families. There was another ten centimetres of snow predicted to fall overnight, and Gracie was out here somewhere, wandering the streets, doing what?

Looking for him?

Or maybe she'd heard something from Harry?

He didn't know.

All he *did* know was that he was frantic. When he got to the club, all was in darkness there. He went up to the main door, then went around the alley at the side, looked at the side door, thumped on it a couple of times. No one answered. All was quiet and calm under the soft torpid quilt of the snow.

Lorcan looked around desperately, wondering what to do. He was terrified for Gracie now, certain she'd gone after Drax with only Paul for protection, and he didn't think Paul would be enough. He got out his mobile, and made a quick call. Then he waited. Within minutes, his phone rang with the information he needed. He went back to his car, got in, and started to drive.

69

Gracie looked around the kitchen, her heart in her throat, her eyes wide with fear. She decided that what she needed was a weapon. She had no intention of actually *using* it, but it would just make her feel better. She looked along the glistening black granite worktops. A breadmaker. A container stuffed full of cooking utensils. Kettle. Toaster. Knife block.

Her breath caught. *Knife block.*

Christ, she couldn't stab anyone. She just couldn't. Her eyes skimmed on past the obvious, on to the more everyday. Microwave. Mugs. A dresser, stuffed full of blue and white china. Oh, this was homely. Not what she'd pictured in the home of an animal like Drax, but she supposed even perverts had to eat.

She went back to the container of utensils. There had to be something. Then she spotted the ice pick. She grabbed it. Hefted it in her hand. Looked at the sharp end, the twin picks to chop at ice. She reversed it in her hand. If she had to hit him at all, it would be with the blunt end.

A bubble of hysterical laughter almost escaped her then.

Shit, she was losing it. She went to the inner kitchen door, trying to orientate herself. She opened it, went through, careful to close it very quietly behind her so that Drax wouldn't come back in, see it standing open when he knew he'd closed it, and smell a rat.

What the hell am I doing? she wondered, but she was crossing a big beamed hall now, past a big long-case clock ticking away in the corner, maybe counting down the seconds that were left of her life.

Stop that.

How the hell was she going to get out of here? She was in, and that was fine, that was great, but she had to find Alfie, and she had to get them both out, and how exactly was she going to do that before Drax came and found her?

Terror slithered down her spine, making her shiver hard and stop in her tracks outside what she believed must be the door to the sitting room she'd seen Alfie in. Only, what if it wasn't? What if she opened the door and it wasn't Alfie in there but some of Drax's pervy mates?

She put her ear to the door and listened hard. She couldn't hear a damned thing. There were no other doors on this side of the hall; this *had* to be the sitting-room door, didn't it? She felt trembly, her legs unsteady, her hands awkward, fearing at any moment that Drax was going to come roaring up behind her, demanding to know what the *fuck* she was doing.

Gently, she turned the handle and pushed the door open, just a crack.

There was a loud *pop*. Gracie nearly hit the ceiling she jumped so violently. Then she heard crackling . . . the fire. It was only the fire, maybe a bit of resin dribbling from a log had made that noise.

She had to go in. She pushed the door open, edged her head inside just a little. The room was just as she'd seen it from outside: lavish with Oriental rugs and vast red brocade sofas, the lighting low and cosy, the fire crackling warmly in the hearth. Gracie had to shake herself a little, because this felt so unreal. The whole house was like an ad in *Homes & Gardens*, and *Drax* lived here. It was clear that, even though he was a detestable creature, Drax had an eye for beauty – in furnishings, surroundings – and in young boys too.

She moved inside, pushing the door closed behind her. She could see Alfie's tousled blond head against the back of the sofa. Grasping the pick securely, she went around the sofa and bent down and looked at Alfie.

The smell that surrounded him was the first thing that hit her. It was bitter, chemical. And overlaying that was the sickly-sweet scent of dope. His eyes were closed. He looked fine, as if he was just dozing there.

'Alfie,' hissed Gracie.

His eyes opened and Gracie's heart plummeted. His pupils were enormous. He was doped to the eyeballs. He looked at her and his face tried to form a smile. One hand rose, then flopped back down on to the red brocade.

'Gracie, Gracie, Gracie,' he slurred.

Shit, he was really stoned.

Drax hadn't lost any time in softening Alfie up again for the kill, and how exactly was she going to get him out of here in this state? She didn't have a clue. She went over to the window she'd looked through before. It was locked, and there was no key visible anywhere. She turned back to Alfie. All right, she was going to have to get Alfie out through the front or back doors. Meanwhile, there had to be a phone in here; she would ring for help, ring for Lorcan, for the police.

'Alfie.' She went back to him, shook his shoulder hard. 'Can you walk; do you think you can stand up? Come on Alfie. Try and fight it, will you? We've got to get out of here.'

Alfie let out a giggle. His head waggled on his shoulders like it was too heavy for them. His eyes were unfocused. 'Mickey, look. Look, Gracie.'

He was trying to point to a side table. Gracie went over. There was a vintage Mickey Mouse telephone there. Mickey grinned up at her in his red shorts, holding out the canary-yellow receiver in his big white-gloved hand, inviting her to make a call.

Mickey's grin looked somehow threatening under these circumstances. She thought of all the boys Deano had entertained in this very room, maybe amusing them with this novelty phone before he pounced. She gulped down some air and gingerly picked up the phone. It had one of those old-fashioned dials on it, and her finger was shaking so badly she could hardly use the thing. She stood there and realized that she didn't know Lorcan's mobile number. It was stored on *her* mobile, and she didn't have the damned thing with her.

Police then.

Nothing else for it.

She dialled 999. Waited. Cringing, almost whimpering in terror because she knew they were both as good as trapped here and that Deano Drax was going to walk in soon, find her here, do her damage. She clutched at the ice pick so hard that it dug into her skin.

'Police, fire or ambulance?' said a female operator in her ear.

'Police,' said Gracie, even her voice trembling now. 'Hurry,' she added. 'And ambulance too – the man who came with me is out on the road, the car's upside down, he's unconscious.'

'Where are you? What's happening?'

Gracie stopped dead. She didn't have a clue where she was, what road this was, what the name of the house was, nothing. She felt panicky tears starting in her eyes.

'Deano Drax's house in Essex,' she said, and dredged from her frozen mind every other tiny detail she could muster before she hung up the phone.

It was then that she heard the screams coming from the garage.

70

It was no weather to be out in. All the reports on the news said so. Don't go out unless you absolutely have to. It was, so far as Lorcan could see, sound advice. It was freezing cold, and once you got off the main roads there were no gritters, so what you were driving on was basically a skid pan, which meant that he didn't dare put his foot down or he'd just spin straight off the road, get stuck, and then he'd *really* be up shit creek.

He wasn't even sure this was where Gracie had headed. He didn't know *what* went on in her mind. But it was a hunch, a strong one. And the hunch told him she was still in love with him and she believed he was in trouble.

'Ah, *fuck*,' said Lorcan as the wheels lost traction again. The car drifted sideways and Lorcan stifled the impulse to wrench at the wheel or brake hard. He went with the skid, and presently the wheels gripped again, and he was able to proceed – driving at a snail's pace, but there was no other way. Now the roads had become unlit country lanes, twisting and turning through pitch-black fields. His headlights speared ahead into the darkness. An owl swooped in front of the car, and he braked in surprise, nearly skidded; held it, thinking, *Come on baby, steady.*

Every slight bend was a potential crash site now. Lorcan drove with grim care, concentrating only on the endgame – finding Gracie. If Deano caused her any grief, he was going to rip his sorry arse out of his body. He steered carefully around each bend, fearing a skid at each and every turn, knowing that if the car was forfeited then he was bollocksed and would just have to go on foot.

He stared at the road, and nursed the car along. The headlights probed ahead. Another damned turn, sharper this time, *much* sharper. And it was then, easing the car oh so gently into the turn, that he saw the car upside-down in the ditch and thought, *Oh fuck. Gracie.*

It wasn't Gracie, it was Paul. He was sitting on the snow-covered bank beside the car, nursing his head in both hands. Lorcan stopped the car, leaving the engine running, and got out. Paul turned his head, winced, and got back to the head-hugging again.

'Paul? You okay?'

'Fucking wonderful,' groaned Paul.

Now Lorcan was looking in the car, fearing the worst. Shit, what if she was in there, dead? He was half afraid to look, but he *had* to. The car was empty. He stood up, looked at Paul.

'Where's Gracie?' he asked.

'Dunno. Don't remember anything apart from the car spinning off the damned road,' said Paul.

Lorcan forced himself to calm down, because right now he felt that he was about to pick Paul up by his ears and spin him round until he hollered. 'What do you mean, you don't know where she is? She was with you, right?'

'Yeah. She was. So I guess she went on alone.'

Alone to Drax's place? Acute anxiety was twisting Lorcan's gut into knots now. He couldn't believe she'd be so fucking foolhardy as to do that – but then, this was Gracie. Sometimes you didn't know *what* she was going to do.

Or maybe she'd been injured in the crash, and crawled away, and was even now lying nearby in the snow, dying?

Lorcan hurried back to his car and brought a torch. He looked at the passenger side interior of Paul's car, but there was no blood, no sign of any trauma. He flashed the torch around the ditch, back up the lane, then further on down. He couldn't see her. He stood there, his breath pluming out in the frozen air, and looked at the lights away up in the distance. He flicked off the torch, went to Paul.

'Can you walk?' he asked.

Paul nodded, wincing. He stood up shakily. Lorcan got an arm around him and helped him round to the passenger side of Lorcan's car. He closed the door carefully on Paul, then ran round to the driver's side and, cursing the conditions that stopped him from driving like Lewis Hamilton on the track, he drove on, very slowly, very cautiously, heading for the lights up ahead.

71

Gracie clapped a hand over her own mouth to stifle a small shriek of shock. Someone had screamed. Literally *screamed*, so loudly that she had heard it in here, and she was pretty sure that it had come from the garage.

What the hell was going on out there?

She looked at Alfie. He'd heard it too, even in his drug-befuddled state. She could see that his silly, smiling expression had faded to be replaced by bewilderment. She bent down to him again. Looked him in the eye. 'Alfie?' she tried.

No good. He was out of it.

And meanwhile, in the garage, Deano was doing something dreadful to someone, and she thought that someone must be Lorcan, and she *had* to do something, she couldn't just stand here waiting for the police, they might not even be able to get through on these treacherous roads. She might be condemning Lorcan to death if she did nothing. 'Alfie, I'm going outside,' she said to him. 'I think Lorcan's in trouble out there. I'm going out to help. Okay?'

He just stared at her, dazed and confused.

For God's sake, I could really use a hand here, thought Gracie.

But there was no one to help.

Whatever was going to be done, *she* would have to do it.

Urgency gripped her now. If Drax was hurting Lorcan, she just couldn't let that happen. She might *already* be too late. Leaving Alfie reclining there in his drug-hazed stupor, she went quickly to the door leading into the hall and with a hesitant look out there she slipped through.

Shaking, feeling so frightened she could have vomited on the spot, Gracie went back to the interior kitchen door and opened it just a crack. She peeked through. She thought Drax was going to come shouting and cursing at her, but no, the kitchen was still empty, the outer door still slightly ajar.

She felt at any moment that her legs were just going to give way beneath her. She wanted to run, far and fast in the opposite direction, but Lorcan was out there, he was in danger, and she loved him too much to let any harm befall him. And what about Harry? He could be out there too. Hurt. Needing help.

She crossed the kitchen quickly, not allowing herself time to think. If she did, she knew that she would simply lose her nerve and flee. She opened the door and slipped outside.

Instantly she could see nothing. It was very dark. Slowly her eyes adjusted after the glare inside the building. She could see faint light still spilling out from the garage. And now she could hear someone sobbing.

Sobbing.

And – oh fuck, oh help – it sounded like a man.

What the hell was he doing in there?

A cold, compelling rage gripped her as she thought of what could be happening. She got her legs moving, *forced* herself to head in the direction of the garage. She had no idea what she would find in there, but it wasn't going to be pretty. She crept along the side of the house, using a hand against the wall to steady herself. In her other hand, she clutched the pick so hard it hurt.

Now, having heard that blood-curdling scream, she wished she'd had the nerve to pick up one of the knives instead. But she wasn't a killer.

Yeah, but you might be dealing with one here, said a quiet voice in her head. *You fight fire with fire, don't you?*

The ice pick was going to have to do. She crept closer, closer, until now she was outside the garage door, she was right there, and she could hear tortured breathing and then . . . oh fuck, someone laughed. Someone actually *laughed*.

It was Drax. It had to be.

She edged closer, wanting to turn tail but unable to. She had to see this through.

'So now come on, join in,' said a hard, harsh male voice. *Drax*.

Gracie braced herself and took a peek around the edge of the doorframe. She could see . . . the back of a huge man, bald-headed, bulky, wearing a camel overcoat, hopping from one foot to the other, *dancing* around someone sitting in a chair.

'You like the modern stuff? Okay, we'll sing them then, shall we? What would you like? That Chris Rea, I like that one. "Driving Home for Christmas". You like that, Harry?'

Harry. It was Harry he had there. So where the hell was Lorcan? Was he here somewhere too?

'Yeah,' she heard Harry say tiredly, his breath ragged. 'Yeah, why the fuck not? I like that one. Get it over, will you? I'm tired of this. Just fucking-well *shoot* me, Drax, will you?'

'Not until we've sung a couple of Christmas songs together, Harry my son,' said Drax, and his voice sounded reproachful, almost hurt.

It was Harry who'd screamed. Harry he was hurting. And . . . did he really have a gun?

Gracie's rage was icy now. That twisted, horrible *bastard*. She didn't know *anyone* gentler than Harry. And he was tied there, imprisoned, being hurt by this *arsehole*.

Gracie risked another peek around the door. Drax was facing her.

Shit!

She drew back, her heart seizing up in her chest. Had he seen her? She didn't know. At any moment she thought he was going to emerge from the garage, grab her too. For a moment it was quiet inside there. She held her breath, not daring to move an inch.

He did, thought Gracie in cold horror. *He saw me.*

'So what game shall we play now then, Harry? Hm?'

'What the fuck do I care?' mumbled Harry. He sounded tired, frightened, finished.

Gracie was standing there, frozen, still not daring to move. He hadn't seen her. If he had, he'd be out here by now, grabbing her, hurting her too. Slowly, she exhaled. Drew in a deep, shuddering breath.

'Now that's not nice, is it Harry?' chortled Drax. 'I know. We'll play Russian roulette again, how's that?'

Oh my God, thought Gracie. *He* has *got a gun.*

Lorcan stopped the car outside the open gates of Deano Drax's place. Just as well they didn't have to go any further because up ahead looked pretty much impassable anyway. It had been a struggle, just getting this far. He switched off the engine and the lights and darkness fell around him and Paul. He glanced across at his companion. Paul looked done for. He was slouched back in the seat, eyes closed, and he looked deathly pale.

'You okay?' asked Lorcan.

Paul's eyes flickered open. A wry grimace touched his mouth. 'This wasn't how I'd planned to spend Christmas,' he said.

'Nor me,' said Lorcan.

'I feel weak as a kitten.'

'Just the after-effects of shock,' said Lorcan. 'You'd better stay here, in the car. I don't want to take it any closer, announce my arrival.'

'Think if I try to stand up I'll just fall down anyway.'

Lorcan nodded. He looked up at the lions rampant on each high brick-built post, rearing up against the buffeting snow.

'Here goes nothing,' he said, and got out of the car and started walking up Deano Drax's long, winding driveway.

72

Sandy had spent Christmas Day evening holding George's hand as he lay in intensive care. She had slipped out of the house, saying she was going over to her Mum's place, and Noel was zonked out, stoned as usual, he didn't give a fuck. George was awake now, conscious, eyes wide open, apparently doing well. He still couldn't *speak*, he still had this weird thing in his throat, but he had indicated by clumsy sign language that he wanted a pencil and a notepad to write something down on. Finally, after several more sessions of desperate writing movements, the nurse brought him what he wanted. When he saw Sandy coming into the room, he hid the pad and the pencil under the bedclothes.

Sandy had been there for over two hours, wittering on to him about how crap her Christmas had been, and how wonderful it was to see him getting better, and that when he was out of here they would just take off somewhere together, have a lovely holiday.

George lay there and wondered where Alfie was. And where was Mum when you needed her? All he could do was lie there and listen to Sandy droning on and on while he kept an anxious eye on the nurse, hoping she wouldn't go too far away. She didn't. He was only just out of the woods, so she was still watching him closely. Sooner or later, Sandy was going to have to go home, wasn't she?

At last, she did. She kissed him on the lips and – thank God, at last – she left.

The minute she was out the door, George got out the notepad and pencil and started writing. He felt weak and his writing was odd, like a very old man's, but he wrote what he needed and waited until the nurse was passing close. He beckoned her over. Showed her the pad.

'What is it, George?' she asked. She seemed like a nice girl, a small blonde with concerned blue eyes and a robust country glow about her.

George pushed the pad up in front of her face.

The nurse read what he'd written there.

She looked at him.

'I'll do that,' she said. 'Right away. If you're sure?'

George nodded emphatically. Then he thought of something else and wrote some more. Showed this to the nurse. She read it, and said: 'No of course I won't let her in here again. Not if you're sure . . .' She knew the anaesthetic drugs could be affecting him, even now. Making him imagine things.

George pointed urgently to what he'd written first.

The nurse read it again. *Sandy Cole who was just here is claiming to be my fiancée. She's not. She's a crazy cow and she's been stalking me. She hit me over the head with a brick outside my mother's house after I told her to fuck off.*

The nurse hurried off to phone his mother, and the police.

73

There was no more time to think. Let herself *think*, and she'd talk herself right out of it. Gracie grasped the ice pick firmly in her right hand and peeked around the doorframe. Drax's back was to her.

It was now or never.

Gracie threw herself forward, swinging her arm back as she moved. Drax never even saw her coming. She was right upon him. Gracie, suddenly high on adrenalin, saw a flash of recognition in Harry's eyes, saw Drax's huge head start to turn in the direction he was looking. In that instant of clear realization, in the sure knowledge that she would never get another chance and if she failed now there would be no going back, Gracie hit Drax as hard as she could across the head with the blunt end of the ice pick.

There was a hollow, sickening *thunk*.

Drax pitched forward across Harry's legs and rolled off them. He hit the floor on his back, one knee raised; then the foot slid away and he was flat out. His eyes were closed, his mouth open. Gracie stood there, gasping, thinking that she'd hit so hard she'd probably killed him.

'*Gracie?*' Harry was staring at her as if he was hallucinating. 'What the fuck . . .?'

Gracie was staring down at Drax. She couldn't believe she'd done that, actually hit someone with the sincere wish that they'd die. Blood was seeping out on to the concrete of the garage floor from Drax's head. She suddenly felt that she might throw up. She swallowed hard, and looked at Harry instead.

Oh fuck. *Harry*. Only this wasn't the handsome, carefree, mild-mannered Harry she'd known when he was just a boy. Drax had hacked his hair off; what little remained was sticking up in all directions. His face was pale, gaunt, streaked with tears, lined with anguish. His hands were tied, and three of his fingers ended in bloody messes where the nails had been ripped out. One of them was bleeding steadily even now, dripping on to the concrete floor. She thought of that horrible, heart-wrenching scream she'd heard while she was trying to rouse Alfie, and felt sicker still.

The bastard had been *torturing* Harry, just because he was a Doyle, just because he was George's brother and George had had the temerity to rescue Alfie from his clutches. She suddenly felt like she wanted to kick Drax's prone body until she had no strength left to kick any more. Now she understood a killing rage. She turned away from the sight of Drax with a bone-deep shudder, and concentrated instead on Harry.

She moved around him, started untying the ropes that held him there. He stank like a polecat. The poor little bastard had been tethered here so long that he'd soiled himself where he sat. Fury enveloped her at the thought. Her hands were shaking so badly she could hardly get the ropes unfastened.

'We haven't got time for talking, Harry,' she said, aware that her teeth were chattering now – was she in shock? She thought she probably was. 'Got to get you out of here. Alfie's inside.'

'Alfie? Is he . . .?'

Gracie nodded, knowing what he wanted to say, knowing he couldn't bring himself to say it. Had Drax sexually abused Alfie, or physically hurt him too? 'He's fine,' she said quickly, her hands working now, untying, unravelling. 'He's stoned, but he seems okay.'

Harry's hands were free. Now Gracie had to get closer to Drax's fallen body. She didn't want to, but she had to, to reach Harry's feet. She shut her mind to Drax's closeness, refused to dwell on images of him springing up, grabbing her, killing them both.

He's probably dead anyway, she told herself, and got to work on Harry's bindings.

Her hands were working better now. All she had to do was be cool, be Gracie, be herself. Forget the horror of their situation, forget all of it. Focus. Block out everything else. Get Harry free.

The last of the ropes fell away. Gracie stood up. She looked around for the ice pick but it was small, the light was bad, she couldn't see it. No matter.

'Can you . . .?' she asked, as Harry sat there. He didn't leap up. She realized he'd been sitting there for so long the movement had gone from his legs. He probably could barely stand, let alone run.

Shit, she thought in desperation. They had to get *out* of here.

'I don't think I can walk,' said Harry, and there was a ghost of a smile on his lips.

'I'll help you,' said Gracie, and suddenly she was Big Sis again, helping Harry out of trouble. She bent and put her arm around his shoulders. 'Come on. One Two. *Three*.'

On the count of three she heaved and Harry pushed upward. He stood there on his feet, weaving around like a drunk.

'Okay?' she asked.

Clearly he wasn't. Harry was wincing, shivering, obviously in a lot of pain. But he nodded.

'Come on. You can do this,' she said firmly.

She started to move back towards the door. Harry came with her, shuffling, trembling like an old man.

How long had he been tied up there?

'Can't feel my bloody legs,' said Harry through gritted teeth.

'The feeling'll come back.'

Maybe he had frostbite, out here in the cold for Christ knew how long. He was moving so slowly, so painfully. Gracie supported him as best she could, but he was nearly done for, she could see that. He was within a whisker of just giving up, giving in.

She couldn't let that happen.

'Em sends her love,' she told him suddenly.

She saw a flare of something in his eyes then.

'Em? You've met Em?'

'Yeah, and she's worried about you.' Gracie dredged her fuddled brain for more. 'She says to tell you she didn't mean it. That she's sorry.'

A weak tear trickled from the corner of Harry's eye at her words.

'Come on. We've got to keep moving,' Gracie urged.

They moved. Oh so slowly. Gracie could have shrieked with impatience and fear, but she kept herself in check, kept helping Harry on, on. He was trying harder now. What she'd told him had helped.

And then she heard Deano Drax stirring behind them.

74

Alfie felt exceedingly strange. He was staggering along beside the wall towards the garage. He thought that Gracie was there and that Gracie needed him. At least, that was what he *thought*. He could be wrong. She had been floating in front of him just a while ago. Maybe a day ago. Maybe an hour, or a second. Somewhen, anyway. He was . . . he was pretty stoned. Drax had given him some stuff, injected him. He had fought, he thought he had fought, but Drax was huge and powerful, too powerful for Alfie to fight off.

George came into his mind then, and the girl, Sandy . . . engaged? What was that? And then he could see angels floating down through the black lacy outlines of the trees around the house, but the angels weren't good, they were evil, with fangs . . . they would kill him.

Oho, *bad* trip.

This was a trip, right? He hoped it was. Angels drifting down and becoming . . . snow. Just snow, falling on his face, melting on his eyes, his lips. Cool, cool water.

But Gracie needed him . . . didn't she?

He could be wrong.

He could be heading for Deano, not Gracie.

He could be heading straight for hell.

Where was Lefty? Usually Lefty gave him the hits, not Deano.

Lefty could be waiting for him up ahead.

Or Gracie.

Or both of them. Who knew?

He was outside the open garage door now, looking in. It was like twilight in there, lit by one of those things you fix on the wall. He could see floating things, ghosts maybe, tins of paint sprouting arms and legs, and Gracie was there, Gracie with a halo of luminous green all around her – and that was Harry, he was *sure* that was Harry, although he looked so different. And that . . . that was Deano, with his head all bloody, moving towards Gracie and Harry. Gracie was holding Harry up. There was a big coffin, freezer, *something*, against the wall, and oh, this was really appropriate, he thought: look at what's on top of this thing.

Alfie lurched forward, pushing, *stumbling* past Gracie and Harry, and picked up the gun.

It was all a dream, anyway. Not real. He wasn't *really* holding a gun. Harry wasn't really there with his hands bleeding and his head looking like a mad barber had been trimming it up. Gracie wasn't really there either, with her green glow and her face twisted in desperation and anguish.

All a dream.

So it was okay to shoot Deano.

Perfectly okay.

Alfie didn't even take aim properly. He pointed the gun at Drax's big torso, and pulled the trigger.

75

Nothing happened. There was a sharp *click,* but the gun didn't fire. Deano didn't fall, Deano didn't stop coming.

Was this a dream?

Alfie couldn't be sure, but if it was a dream then it was a bad one. Deano turned on him like a raging bull, snatching the gun out of his hand. Harry and Gracie stood there, a perfect little tableau. Brother and sister, watching everything happen around them, powerless. Because now Deano had the gun.

Gracie watched Deano and thought: *But didn't I just bash his fucking brains out?* He was weaving slightly, grimacing; she'd hurt him, but not badly enough. He was on his feet and he had the gun. She should have whacked him again while he was down, she could see that now. Too late. Harry was leaning against her; she knew that if she took her arm away he would simply fall to the floor. There was nothing she could do. Alfie was swaying on his feet, staring blearily around at them all as if unsure whether this was reality or nightmare.

'You been keeping count, Harry?' Deano said, screwing up his face. Blood was dribbling down from his head, splashing on to the immaculate camel-hair coat. He touched a hand to his scalp, then looked surprised at the blood on his hand. He stared with pure venom at Gracie, then at Harry. He pushed forward, pulling Alfie off-balance into the middle of the garage. 'Get *in* here,' he said roughly, as Alfie stumbled and almost fell. He pushed the three of them together and then he thrust the gun up underneath Harry's chin. 'You been keeping count, you little tosser? Because *I* have. There're two shots left, and only one of them's got firepower. You understand? So out of you two Doyle cunts, just *one* of you's going to die tonight. So who's it gonna be?'

He was aiming the gun at Harry, but now he drew back a pace, back towards the doorway, and had Gracie in his sights.

'You hurt me,' he said with a grimace. 'You bashed my fucking head. Ruined my good coat.'

'I wish I'd finished you off when I had the chance,' said Gracie, looking death in the eye.

'Well now you ain't *got* the chance, bitch,' he said, and pulled the trigger.

Both Gracie and Harry let out a shout. But again there was just the *click* of the empty chamber.

Now Drax was grinning through his pain, enjoying playing with them.

'That's it then,' he said. 'The last one's got the bullet in it. So say goodnight, sweetheart.' He levelled the gun at Gracie's head.

Lorcan appeared behind Drax in the doorway just as he pulled the trigger. Lorcan lunged forward, shoving Drax off-balance. The gunshot made a huge noise, and the bullet whizzed by within inches of Gracie's head. Lorcan followed Drax forward, knocking Gracie and Harry and Alfie aside. He grabbed Drax's huge head in both hands and smacked it hard up against the garage wall, once, twice, three times.

Drax wavered on his feet. Fresh blood spurted out, spattering the garage wall. Lorcan smacked him up against the wall again. Again. All the while he was swearing, calling Drax a bastard, a fucker, he'd completely lost it.

'Lorcan,' said Gracie urgently, trying to grab his arm. 'Enough.'

Drax was half-dead on his feet now, weaving about like a punch-drunk boxer. Lorcan kept whacking his head against the garage wall.

'Enough!' shouted Gracie again. Fuck, she didn't want him getting landed with a murder charge. Drax was finished, she could see that. But Lorcan just kept on hitting him.

Lorcan butted the huge bowling-ball of Drax's head once more up against the garage wall. There was a lot of blood now, and Drax was out of it. And *still* Lorcan was smacking him up against the wall, hammering that huge head into a pulp.

Gracie grabbed Lorcan's arm and held on. His head swung round and he was looking at her with murderous rage in his eyes. Then his expression cleared. He was still. Finally, he straightened. Let Drax fall in a heap to the concrete floor. He stared down at Drax, then looked at Gracie, who slumped against the freezer, and Harry, who had sunk down on to the chair where he'd been held prisoner, and Alfie. Lorcan took a deep, calming breath, let the anger go.

'Everyone all right?' he asked them.

Gracie nodded shakily. She had never been so glad to see

anyone in her entire life. 'We're fine. What the fuck are you doing here?'

'Right back at you,' said Lorcan; and it was then that they heard the sirens approaching.

76

Eventually the police arrived. They had a lot of trouble just getting through. And then – and Gracie had seen this coming, wasn't she the pure cool brains of the outfit after all? – they were *all* arrested. Lorcan protested, heatedly, but Gracie didn't. Alfie was too zonked out to care, and Harry too weak. As for Deano, he was as good as dead as far as she could tell.

The cops took one look at Deano spark out on the garage floor covered in blood, saw more blood on Lorcan's hands and all up his arms, and drew rapid conclusions. The air ambulance was called, but it was debatable as to whether or not it could fly in these conditions. Certainly they'd never get an ambulance up these roads, but if push came to shove, they'd try. Lorcan told them quickly about Deano imprisoning Harry here, and that Deano mustn't be allowed to get anywhere near Harry again because he would try and do him damage.

To the police, Deano didn't look in a fit state to hurt a fly, much less a person. Lorcan however was a big bastard and a discernible threat. They put the handcuffs on Lorcan.

After what felt like a lifetime, the air ambulance arrived,

along with the medics. Deano Drax was strapped into a stretcher with big foam head supports, and Harry was too. They were all taken to hospital, and there was a lot of form-filling, more questions, *endless* questions, and Gracie sat into the small hours of the morning in a bleak little waiting room, a policewoman at her side, while Lorcan, Alfie, Harry and Drax were all checked over.

Lorcan came into the room at about three a.m., still in the cuffs, with a bandaged hand and a policeman in tow.

'They're keeping Harry in,' he told her.

'Can I see him?'

'Not right now. He's badly dehydrated, they've got him on a drip.'

Gracie slumped, exhausted. All the adrenalin of the past few nightmare hours had surged in upon her and now she felt like someone had simply pulled her plug out. 'When can we get out of here?' she asked the policewoman.

'Now,' said the woman, standing up with a glance at her colleague. 'We'd like you to come to the station.'

Gracie groaned and, leaning on Lorcan, followed the two officers out of the building into the snowy night. Outside the main hospital door, a weary-looking man with a head of mud-blond hair and a long, sober face came towards the two officers, accompanied by a skinny, hard-eyed female.

'Take a seat just there, will you please?' said the male policeman, and Lorcan and Gracie sat down just inside the door with the policewoman watching over them.

The male uniformed policeman was in a huddle just outside the door with the weary-looking man and woman. They were talking intently. They kept glancing over at Lorcan and Gracie. Finally, all three stepped inside the building and approached.

'Good evening, sir. Miss,' said the tired-looking man.

He had that 'I've-seen-it-all' expression that both dodgers and enforcers of the law invariably wear. He showed them his ID. 'I'm DI Sanderson. My colleagues tell me you've had a run-in with Deano Drax.'

'You could say that,' said Lorcan.

Sanderson nodded to the policeman. He uncuffed Lorcan. 'Let's talk about this down at the station, shall we?'

They climbed wearily into the back of an unmarked police car and the two plain-clothes officers got in the front and drove them to the station. They were escorted into a comfortable interview room, given hot drinks and sandwiches. Then the questions began, and continued for several hours while notes were assiduously taken.

Christmas Day was gone; now it was Boxing Day morning. Families were relaxing at home with their loved ones, while Gracie and Lorcan sat there and answered questions. Finally, when it seemed as if they were stuck in some weird twilight world where normality was a thing of the past, the weary-eyed male detective said: 'I think that's all for now.'

'I'm worried about Drax being near Harry,' said Gracie.

'There's an officer keeping watch on both of them. And Drax, as I understand it, isn't going to be a danger to anyone for quite a while.'

He stared at Lorcan. Lorcan stared right back.

They all stood up.

'We'll get someone to take you both home,' said the detective, and leaned across, offering his hand to Lorcan.

Lorcan hesitated, then took it.

'Well done, sir,' said the detective. He looked straight into Lorcan's eyes. 'And if anyone ever asks, I didn't say that. All right?'

77

Without a word to each other, Gracie and Lorcan fell into bed back at the flat over the casino, in a state beyond exhaustion; and they slept until late in the afternoon. Gracie awoke to find herself wrapped around Lorcan's body like a vine around a tree.

'Oh,' she said, surprised to find herself alive, and in bed with him. She pulled away.

'Don't,' he said, and leaned in and kissed her.

Gracie pulled back.

'What?' asked Lorcan, enveloping her in his strength.

'Why did you go out?' she demanded as it all came flooding back over her like a cold, breath-snatching tide.

Lorcan stared at her. 'Why did *you*?'

'Because you'd fucking-well vanished and I thought Drax had you. That man's *insane*. Answer the question. Why the *hell* did you go out like that? He put George in hospital. Attacked Mum's front door with a chainsaw and tried to *abduct* me. You didn't tell me where you were going. You had your phone switched off. You were ranting like a crazy man about Drax at the hospital. I panicked. What the hell was I supposed to think?'

'That I'm a big boy and I don't need a nursemaid?' suggested Lorcan.

She thumped his chest. '*Don't* take the piss. Why did you go out? Just tell me.'

'Why did you?'

Gracie sat up. Lorcan yanked her back down.

'You know what?' she said. 'You're fucking infuriating.'

'I'll tell you why,' he promised. 'Later.'

'No. Now.'

'*Later*, Gracie.'

He was pulling her in closer, kissing her again, robbing her of all sense. Gracie didn't fight too hard. It was so blissful, being in bed with him. She had forgotten how good it was. She relaxed and let it happen. He made love to her, and she reciprocated. Later, when they lay spent together, Gracie looked at his bandaged hand and thought back to him hammering Deano Drax's big bald head against the garage wall. She shuddered. If a solidly made six-foot-four-inch man like Lorcan wanted to do you damage, exactly how much damage were you talking? She thought of the detective's words, that Deano Drax was going to be out of it for some time.

Forever would be better, she thought.

Deano Drax was worse than an animal. He was demented. He'd taken a grudge against one member of a family and worked it up into a deadly vendetta against them all. She thought of what he had done to Alfie, and felt a wave of bile come up into her throat.

'Let it go, Gracie,' said Lorcan, lying back with his eyes shut. 'We're all okay. That's what counts.'

No use asking how he'd known where her thoughts had strayed. They'd always had that facility, to pick up on each other's concerns, even before they were put into words.

'Drax will recover,' she said in a small voice, cuddling in closer against him. 'He'll come back at us.'

'That detective said he was going to be doing a lot of time,' said Lorcan.

'How long? Ten years? That's eight with good behaviour, then he'll be out again. Do you really think he's going to forget this? Forget we crossed him?'

'Leave it for now, Gracie. No good fretting about the future. Let's handle the present first, okay?'

'Tell me why you went out.'

'Later,' he said, and yawned, and pulled her in tight against him.

Lorcan slept; Gracie couldn't.

They ate dinner in the casino restaurant, then Lorcan took her hand and led her out to the well-lit car park at the back of the building.

'I don't want to go out,' she said, hanging back. She felt safe up in the flat with him; right now she didn't want outside company, she just craved recovery time – and him.

'I know. We're not,' he said, and walked on, taking her with him.

Gracie gave up and followed.

'Just got something to show you,' he said.

'Can't you just *tell* me?' complained Gracie, shivering out here in the frosty air without a coat.

'Nope. Got to show you. Look.'

And there was her Mercedes, sitting there on the cobbles with a big red bow strung across its bonnet, sporting a new set of tyres and with its silver surface gleaming in the over-head sodium lights.

'Oh my God,' gasped Gracie.

'They valeted the inside too,' said Lorcan. 'Worked on Christmas, to get it done. *This* is why I went out, and I couldn't tell you where I was going because it would have spoiled the surprise. I was going to present you with it when I got back. The garage was running behind with it, I had to wait around. So I was very late. And when I got back, you were gone.'

Gracie opened her mouth to speak and felt tears well up instead.

'Hey,' said Lorcan in surprise, pulling her close. 'Gracie? Don't cry.'

'It's just all so stupid,' Gracie managed to get out. 'I didn't care about the bloody *car*, Lorcan.'

'You were so upset when the tyres were slashed.'

'Yeah, but that was before . . .' Gracie's voice tailed away. She was so confused. She felt like the past few years had been a strange, exotic dream. *Things* had become so important to her in that life. The glitzy apartment. The shiny, top-end, luxury car. Spa holidays. Five-star, all the way.

But now . . .

Oh *now* she was beginning to see that there were other things that mattered so much more. Her family, for instance. The family she had lost touch with and now she could get to know again, if she wanted to. Sweet, gentle Harry, and big-mouthed, lovable George, and even her mother, even Suze, who in Gracie's opinion had shit for brains but she was *still* Gracie's mother, there was still some feeling there.

'You like it then?' Lorcan was looking at her.

An icy swirl of snowflakes hit them. Lorcan pulled her in closer.

'Yeah,' said Gracie, half laughing and half sobbing too. 'I like it.'

Lorcan stared at her. '*Now* why are you crying, you silly bitch?' he asked, and Gracie laughed and cried all the harder.

After Christmas

78

Sandy went into intensive care after Christmas to see George. She hoped that he would understand, that what she had done had been done in a moment of anger; it hadn't been intentional. It certainly hadn't been premeditated. She was fully intending to explain all that, to lay it all out and hope that he would forgive her for it, so that they could take up where they'd left off, get married. Noel was the past. *George* was the future.

George was sitting up now, starting to get some colour back in his cheeks. He'd lost weight. He still couldn't speak because of the tracheotomy, but he had a notepad and pencil near at hand.

Sandy came in, and kissed him on the cheek, and clasped his hands tight in hers.

'I'm so pleased you've come round, George. So pleased. And so *relieved*. I know I hurt you, but I didn't mean to do it.' Sandy was sitting there staring at him earnestly. 'I just . . . you hurt me so much when you sent me that text, George. I couldn't believe you said that, that we were finished . . .'

George grabbed the notepad and wrote: 'What do you mean, finished? We never even started.'

Sandy looked at it. A twinge of irritation made her face pinch up.

'Look, George. It was just a mistake. We were getting on so well, weren't we?'

George scribbled: 'No we weren't.'

Sandy looked at the words, bit her lip as if trying to hold in anger.

'George, now you know we were. I just got so *mad* when you said that. If you were joking, it wasn't very kind of you.'

George wrote: 'I wasn't joking.'

Sandy snatched the pad and pencil out of his hands and threw both to the floor.

'Now George you're being very naughty,' she told him with a trembling voice. She stared hopefully at his face. 'We can start again, George. I'll leave Noel. I hate him anyway. We'll go somewhere together. It'll all be fine.'

The nurse came forward and touched Sandy on the shoulder.

'Um, Miss Sandy Cole?' she asked.

'Yes. Why?'

'These people want a word with you,' said the nurse. She bent and picked up the pad and handed it to one of the men who stood there.

Sandy looked back, beyond the nurse. Two security guards were standing right there, watching her.

'If you could come with us . . .' said the one who held the notepad.

'A word about what?' Sandy was asking as they led her away.

The nurse exchanged a long look with George.

'A restraining order would be a good idea,' said the nurse.

George nodded. A padded cell would be better for *that* mad bitch. *Fuck* the escorting. He was through with all that shit, as of now.

They met for afternoon tea at the New Covent Garden Hotel in the dog days between Christmas and New Year. Emma and Jackie were waiting for him, and they both rose nervously to their feet when he arrived.

'Oh my God,' said Em, tears starting in her eyes.

'Darling Harry, are you all right?' asked Jackie.

What had he done to deserve these two? Harry hugged them both. Three of his fingers were heavily bandaged but no longer painful. Doing anything, even buttoning his fly, was awkward; but he'd live. His hair had been a problem. The first time he saw his reflection in a mirror, he'd laughed out loud. Deano Drax would never make a barber. In some places, he was nearly bald; in others he had six or twelve or two inches of auburn hair remaining. *Not* a good look. One of his first jobs once he'd been out of the hospital's clutches had been to get his arse over to a good hairdresser, tout suite.

'Oh my *God,* what *happened*?' asked the male stylist.

A nutter happened, that's what.

'Student prank,' said Harry.

'Well my dear you should *sue*,' said the stylist, and proceeded to trim off anything that remained of Harry's previously long and lustrous locks.

'Fuck me,' he'd said when he looked in the mirror at the finished job.

He looked very unlike himself. With a uniform inch of hair over most of his scalp, and the worst of the bald bits concealed, added to his weight loss courtesy of the Deano Drax starvation diet, he looked harder, meaner.

'You look so different,' Em told him now. 'That *hair*. You are going to grow it back, aren't you?'

'If you like,' said Harry. He rather liked the lean-fighting-machine look, but he could see that Em wasn't impressed. She preferred the louche cavalier Harry, and what Em wanted, she got, as far as he was concerned.

'We were so worried about you,' said Jackie, when they all sat down and tea and cakes were ordered.

So was I. 'Hey, I'm fine. It's over.'

'That man . . .' said Emma.

'Deano Drax.'

'Why did he do this to you, Harry? What did you *do*?'

'I didn't do a thing. It was George.'

'Your brother?'

Harry nodded. 'George rescued Alfie from Deano Drax. After that, Deano was after all the Doyles with a vengeance.'

Jackie's face was clouded with concern. 'But . . . he's locked up now, isn't he? He won't do anything like this again . . .?'

'My brother-in-law talked to the police yesterday. Drax is still in hospital, in a coma. They think he'll come out of it. And after that, it'll be prison for a long stretch.'

'But what if they eventually let him out?' asked Emma, with a shiver.

'They won't,' said Harry, trying to convince himself as much as her. He was afraid they would.

'We were so scared,' she said, her blue eyes locked with his. 'We thought we'd lost you.'

'Me? Nah.' Harry grinned reassuringly, although he didn't feel like it.

Harry knew they were right to be concerned for the future. No one could predict what would happen with Drax. And now he was feeling better, he had to face the fact that he was going to lose Em very soon. She was due to go back to Hong Kong next week, after New Year. She would go on with her life, a high-flying, exciting life of opportunity, and he . . . well, what the fuck was *he* going to do? He'd already decided that escorting wasn't for him, although taking part in it had been a revelation to him. He'd met Jackie, and Em, after all. So there was no way he could say it had been all bad. But . . . what now?

Their tea and cakes arrived. Harry fell upon the cakes like a starving man which, up until a few days ago, was precisely what he had been. His two girls watched him indulgently. He felt so at home with them, so happy. But it would all end soon.

And then . . . what?

He just didn't know.

79

Gracie, Suze and Lorcan called in to see George just before New Year. He was out on a normal ward now, and he could speak. His head was still a bandaged mess, but that would heal. He was returning, oh so slowly, to normal.

When they arrived, Alfie was there. They stood at the door to the ward. There were six beds in there, all occupied; George's was at the far end on the left, beside a big window. Weak winter sunlight was filtering through the grime and alighting on Alfie's blond hair, lending him a halo of gold.

Alfie and George were holding hands and looking into each other's eyes. As they stood there at the door, George said something and Alfie laughed, then raised George's hand to his lips and kissed it.

'Oh,' said Suze, startled.

Gracie looked at Lorcan, then back over to her brother and the boy sitting with him. She refocused. Realized that what she was looking at was a pair of lovers, totally absorbed in each other. Everything clicked into place. Alfie's outrage at Sandy's claims that she and George were engaged. George's behaviour in his early years, the way he had always seemed to keep girls at a distance. Suddenly, a lot of things made sense.

'Jesus,' said Suze, and Gracie could see that she was really shocked.

'Why don't you take a moment outside?' Gracie suggested.

Suze looked at her daughter. 'Did you *know* about this?' she hissed.

'No. I didn't. But this is still George, we still love him.'

'I don't know . . .' Suze shook her head.

'Come on. Just take a minute, okay? Lorcan, stay with Mum outside, will you? Just for a while. I'll go see George.'

Lorcan and Suze went back outside and Gracie went over to the bed. She noticed that Alfie slid his hand away from George's as she approached, but George snatched it back again.

'Hiya George,' she said.

'Gracie,' said George hoarsely. 'After all this time. What brought you back down here?'

'*You* did,' said Gracie with a smile. 'And a fire at my casino, and a bag of Harry's hair. Hi, Alfie.'

'Hi Gracie.' Alfie beamed at her.

'Did you actually know I was standing there talking to you, back in Drax's sitting room?'

'I thought you were an angel. But what you were saying sort of got through, so I followed you out.'

'Alfie's been telling me what happened out at that bastard Drax's place,' said George.

'It was pretty scary,' said Gracie.

'But Drax is out of it, right?'

'Yeah, he is.' She hoped Drax was going to be put away for a long, long time, but there was a niggling doubt at the back of her mind, a feeling that this might not be over. She turned her thoughts away from that, back to George – and Alfie.

'Has this been going on long?' she asked.

'This? This what?' asked George.

Gracie nodded to Alfie, then to George. 'Come *on*, George. What do you think I am, blind?'

'Ah,' said George.

'We're in love,' said Alfie, sticking out his chin, daring her to make trouble.

Gracie smiled. 'Alfie, I'm on your side.' She glanced between them. 'God, George, you might have given us a clue though. And I think Mum's in shock; she's outside but she just saw you and Alfie holding hands.'

'Fuck,' said George, his face falling with dismay.

'She'll come round,' said Gracie. 'Although I don't think your fiancée Sandy's going to be very pleased.'

'She's mental,' said George.

'That *bitch*,' said Alfie vehemently.

Gracie looked a question at them both.

'She was a client I escorted,' said George. 'But she started getting funny ideas. That we were dating, that we were engaged. Crazy ideas. Finally I snapped and texted her to fuck off, and she stalked me as far as Mum's then hit me with a fucking house brick. The police are dealing with her now.'

'We were starting to think that Drax must have done it,' said Gracie. 'Actually she maybe did you a favour. With you in intensive care, Drax couldn't easily get to you. And he would have, that's for sure. He got Harry, and he damned near got me. He even tried for Mum.'

George looked unhappily at Gracie. 'Mum's gonna hit the roof over this. Me and Alf.'

Gracie shook her head. 'Shouldn't think so. You've got her at a point of weakness. She's just so damned glad to see you alive and well, she'll get over the surprise.'

'You don't disapprove then?' asked George, looking awkward.

'What, of you being happy? Why should I?'

'Well, that's good news.' George stared at his sister for long moments. 'It's really good to see you, Gracie. After all this time.'

'You too, George. Thought we'd lost you.'

'Me? Nah.' George leaned over and grabbed his deck of cards from the side table. 'Let me show you this new trick I've been teaching Alf. Come on, Gracie. Pick a card. Any card . . .'

She selected a card.

'Seven of spades, right?'

Gracie showed George her card. It was the seven of spades.

'I don't know how he does that,' said Alfie.

'Tricks of the trade, m'boy, tricks of the trade,' winked George. He looked at Gracie and his smile faded. 'How's Dad then, Gracie?' he asked awkwardly.

Gracie stared at George for a long moment. It must have hurt him so much – and Harry – when their dad apparently just turned his back on them. But she knew that Paddy Doyle had phoned Suze time and again, asking to see them, but she wouldn't allow it. He'd sent cards and presents for them, but Suze, so consumed with anger at Paddy, wanting to hurt him, had intercepted them.

Suze had ducked out of this, but Gracie wasn't going to. She braced herself. She sat down and took George's hand in hers. And then she told him about Dad.

New Year's Eve

80

They celebrated New Year's Eve at Suze's place. The front door, so badly scarred by Deano's boys and their chainsaw, had been replaced with a new reinforced-steel one. In Suze's living room, they all gathered together to bring the old year to a close and to celebrate the birth of the new – Gracie and Lorcan; a thinner, slightly frailer George with Alfie; Harry with Em. Suze looked around at them, her kids all together again, and felt a surge of maternal pride as she doled out the drinks for the midnight toast.

She was going to start the New Year without a partner. Fucking Claude, what a drip he'd turned out to be. But there were singles bars and there was online dating; there was lots out there for a single woman in her fifties these days. It was no big deal. She looked over to where Alfie was sitting with George. Now *that* had been one hell of a shock – but, well, George was okay and that was what counted. She didn't much *like* the idea that her eldest son was a bender, but really, when you got right down to it, did it matter?

Suze looked over to where Harry and Emma were standing, gazing deep into each other's eyes. Actually, even though she was a posh bird with a cut-glass accent, Suze quite liked Emma. But then, Emma was going back to Hong Kong tomorrow, so it was just ships passing in the night. A shame.

Suze looked over at Gracie. Their eyes met. Suze gave a little smile and a wink. Gracie raised her glass. She mouthed 'Happy New Year, Mum.'

'You too,' Suze mouthed back. All right, they were worlds apart, but Suze was so glad Gracie had come back at last. And – she glanced at Lorcan, who was standing near Gracie – she knew she wasn't the only one who felt that way.

Time to let the past go, she thought.

Gracie came over. 'You okay then?' she asked her mum and, after a moment's hesitation, she dropped a kiss on to Suze's cheek.

Gracie thought it felt strange, doing that. But sort of nice, too.

'Fine,' said Suze, giving her daughter a quick hug. 'I meant to tell you – Claude sent me a card.'

'He what?'

'Yeah, he did.' Suze pulled a face. 'He wants to try again.'

Gracie didn't want to say straight out that Claude was an arsehole and Suze was a million times better off without him, even if it was true. The peace between them was still too fragile; she didn't want to risk it.

'And . . . what do you think about that?' she asked carefully.

Suze looked at Gracie and suddenly they were both laughing.

'Oh God,' said Suze when she could get her breath. 'Your face! No, Gracie, I'm not going *there* again. And look, I'm sorry I believed him over you. I really am.'

'It's okay,' said Gracie.

'I loved your father,' said Suze. 'I know we argued, but I loved him.' She looked at Gracie. 'You're so like him. Wedded to the job, aren't you, just like he was. He worked too hard, and I was stupid, shouting at him, and then stopping him having contact with the boys. I just wanted *more* of him and, when he wouldn't give me that, I went off and found someone else. It didn't mean a damned thing, Gracie; it was Paddy I wanted.'

Now there were tears in Suze's eyes.

'Hey, don't,' said Gracie, feeling tearful too at what Suze had said.

Suze sniffed and blinked. Fixed a smile on her face again. 'No you're right,' she said. 'It's New Year. Fresh start.'

Suze looked at the clock. 'Hey, everyone! Two minutes to go!' she shouted, and they turned the radio up to listen to the chimes of Big Ben.

'Harry,' Em was saying, her face grave as all around them the excitement grew. 'I've got something to tell you.'

'Oh?' Harry looked worried. He knew what she was going to say. She was going to say, so long, it's been fun, but I'm going back to my real life tomorrow, so this is goodbye. He was feeling a bit down tonight. He was still shocked – reeling, in fact – from what Gracie had told him about Dad being dead and gone for over a year. Now there would never be a chance of reconciliation between him and George and their father: that ship had sailed. And now, Em was going too.

'Just that I've been thinking really hard about everything.'

'Oh?'

'Yes. Harry, I—'

'You don't have to say it,' butted in Harry. 'I understand perfectly, Em. You've got your life, I've got mine . . .'

445

Em's face froze. 'Is that how you feel?'

Jesus, the new year's going to be horrible without Em, thought Harry.

'No, I don't,' he said. He had nothing to lose by speaking his mind now anyway. 'I'd like you to stay here with me, but that's stupid.'

'Is it?'

'Of course it is. You want to go back to Hong Kong . . .'

'No I bloody don't,' said Em. 'At least, not without you.'

Harry's mouth fell open. 'You mean you want me to go out there with you?'

'Why not?' Now Em's eyes sparkled with enthusiasm. 'You'll love it out there, Harry. Why don't you come?'

He could. He really could. He had dosh from the escort work. Harry thought about it for all of five seconds. Then he nodded.

Emma gave a shriek of excited laughter and threw her arms around his neck. 'I love you, Harry Doyle,' she said, and kissed him. What the hell, he thought. Take a chance. Roll the dice. He kissed her back. Somehow, he was going to make this work.

Gracie was standing next to Lorcan. She gave him a stern look.

'Don't kiss me at midnight,' she said firmly. 'You know I can't think straight when you do that.'

The countdown began

'Five!' everyone yelled.

'Four!'

'Three!'

'Two!'

'One!'

'Happy New Year!'

Lorcan kissed Gracie hard and long.

'This don't change anything,' said Gracie when she finally came up for air. She felt like the room was spinning around her. Party poppers were being let off and multicoloured streamers were festooning them. She clutched at Lorcan, steadied herself.

'I know that,' he said. 'We never did get around to the talking, did we? You going to sign those divorce papers?'

'Guess so,' said Gracie.

Lorcan gave a slow, sad smile. 'Then this is it, Gracie. This is goodbye.'

'Yeah,' said Gracie, and then everyone launched into 'Auld Lang Syne' and she had to fight against the urge – *so* un-Gracie-like – to break down and cry.

A couple of days after New Year, Gracie kissed Suze and her brothers goodbye with firm promises to speak very soon and *never* to lose touch again. She drove back to Manchester, parked her car in the secure underground park and went up to her flat. Once, she'd loved it so much, but now it felt cold and alien to her; not like home at all. She put her bag down in the little kitchen area and stood there, thinking.

She took out the divorce papers and looked at them. She'd had them with her all the time she was in London; she could have signed them, could have *handed* them to Lorcan or posted them straight back to the courts, easy. Yet she hadn't.

'Fuck it, what am I *doing*?' she asked herself.

Following her heart? Or her head?

She'd always been the calculating one, the clever one. The cold one? Was she really that too? Maybe she was. She sat down at the kitchen table and coldly, calculatingly, she thought it all through.

*   *   *

Lorcan was in the casino. It was heaving with high-rolling clients – Saudi princes, footballers, Russian oligarchs. He moved among them smoothly, greeting, smiling, exchanging cheery words with the staff and the punters, while inside his chest his heart felt like a lump of lead.

She was gone.

It was over.

He'd gambled, and lost.

Fuck it, he'd thought he was getting somewhere with her. Five years of missing her, and finally he'd had enough. The thing with George had happened and he'd thought: now is the time. He'd decided to force her hand. Not knowing which way she'd jump. And of course, being Gracie, she'd jumped the wrong way. Called his bluff. Now, the courts would finish up what was left of their marriage and it would all be done and dusted.

God, what a waste.

Then he saw her. She was weaving through the punters down the casino boulevard, a stunningly striking six-feet-tall woman with a thick dark-red hank of hair twisted into a plait that hung down over her shoulder. She was wearing her plain black wrap dress, and her cool grey eyes were searching for him . . . and finding him.

He held his breath as she came closer.

She wasn't smiling.

She came right up to him and now he could see that she was holding some papers in her hand.

The divorce papers.

Oh shit.

'I had these with me all the time I was down here,' she said, her eyes locked with his.

Lorcan swallowed hard. 'Then why didn't you sign them

and give them to me, or post them back to the courts?' he asked.

'Oh now, let's think about that . . .' And Gracie carefully, deliberately, ripped the papers up into tiny pieces. They fluttered to the casino floor.

Lorcan stared into Gracie's eyes. 'Meaning . . .?' he asked.

'What do you *think*?' asked Gracie in exasperation.

She stepped forward, put her arms around his neck, and kissed him. 'We'll try, okay? We'll compromise. We'll talk. Yes?'

People around them were staring and smiling.

Then Gracie drew back a little. 'I decided to take a chance,' she said with a smile. 'Roll the dice.'

'Oh, Gracie,' said Lorcan with a grin, 'thank fuck for that,' and kissed her back.

81

They decided to reaffirm their wedding vows in a small ceremony at the newly refurbished Savoy in June. George and Alfie were blissfully happy, living together in their little flat, and Suze was cruising the net for a new love. Harry and Em were out in Hong Kong, doing a lot of rooftop sunbathing, but they would be coming back to attend the ceremony. Em's mother Jackie was going to get an invitation too.

Meanwhile, April was turning into May; all the trees were budding, the sun was shining and there was a biting north-easterly breeze blowing as Lorcan parked the BMW and walked alone into the reception area of the large unit. The weary-looking DI Sanderson, whom he'd encountered back in December of last year, was there waiting for him. They shook hands.

'Thought you'd want to see this,' said the detective.

'Thanks, but I'm not sure I do,' said Lorcan.

'Come on.'

Sanderson led the way. Lorcan followed. There were locked

gates, entry systems and buzzers. Security guards thinly disguised in white jackets to look like nurses, padding by in white coats and crêpe-soled shoes. Finally they came to a room at the end of a long hallway and were met by a bulky dark-haired man wearing a short-sleeved white tunic, like a dentist's. The male nurse/guard unlocked the door, pushed it open, walked inside. He smiled at the man who was sitting in the chair, gazing out of the securely barred window into the small courtyard garden beyond. There were apple trees out there, blossoming in a froth of pink and white; and camellias, their blooms turned brown by frost.

The man in the chair wore a pale blue dressing gown and pyjamas. He looked up as the three men came in and Lorcan felt his guts shrivel with a tremor of dread. Deano Drax was staring up at him. Lorcan felt every muscle in his body tense. The last time he had seen this man he had been raging, threatening; a huge, blundering force of evil.

'This is Detective Sanderson, and this is Mr Connolly,' said the nurse, moving forward to pull the blinds back a little further. 'Pretty out there, ain't it, Deano? You like the garden, don't you?'

Lorcan forced himself to return Deano Drax's stare. Deano's head bore heavy scars and a deep indentation.

I did that, thought Lorcan and, although it was a sickening sight, he couldn't bring himself to regret it.

Extensive brain damage had been the diagnosis on Deano. Transportation to a secure mental unit had been the inevitable solution.

Lorcan felt a tremor of unease run through him at the sight of Deano. He'd inflicted the damage, but given those circumstances he knew he would do the same again if he had to.

Deano was still looking up at him. And . . . now Lorcan

could see that a change had been wrought in him, a *radical* change. Deano's eyes, once demonic, threatening, full of hatred and bile, now had the peaceful and untroubled expression of a child. They looked at Lorcan as a five-year-old might – curiously, expecting treats, toys, good things.

'Connolly,' said Deano, repeating what the nurse had said.

Lorcan shivered slightly as Deano spoke. Even his voice was different. But was it an act? Was it all pretence?

Lorcan swallowed hard, cleared his throat. 'I'm married to Gracie Doyle,' he said. 'Her brothers are George and Harry Doyle.'

The ones you were determined to hound to the point of death and beyond, he thought.

But Deano's eyes were clear, without recognition.

He looked at his nurse, as if searching for reassurance. Then he looked again at the detective, and finally at Lorcan. 'Will they come and see me?' he asked, and his face held nothing but childish hope. New playmates might be on offer.

Lorcan glanced at Detective Sanderson. 'I don't think so,' he said.

Deano's smile drooped a little. 'Oh.'

'Never mind, Deano. We'll play roulette after lunch,' said the nurse.

Lorcan felt his guts clench hard. 'Roulette?' he echoed.

'We got a little mini-roulette wheel out in the day room,' explained the nurse with a smile at Lorcan. 'Deano loves to play that thing, don't you Deano?'

Deano nodded.

Finally, Lorcan began to relax a little. The Deano he'd encountered was gone. It was true. There was nothing left of the killing machine that had once existed.

Deano was looking at him. 'Will you come back and see me?' he asked.

Lorcan took a long breath. 'Maybe,' he said, although he knew he never would.

'Will you bring Alfie?'

Lorcan felt all the hairs on the back of his neck stand up when Deano said that. Holy *shit*. A thrill of deep unease crawled its way up his spine. But he looked into Deano's eyes and saw only innocent enquiry, not malice.

Drax still remembered Alfie.

Such had been the extreme nature of his obsession with the boy, Alfie's name – and maybe also Alfie's image – had become lodged in the shattered remnants of Drax's brain. Lorcan felt a stirring of pity for the man then. Somehow, in his twisted way, perhaps Drax had *loved* Alfie. But, being so damaged himself, he had blundered through life damaging others, perhaps unwilling to change the pattern, perhaps unable to.

Lorcan cleared his throat, shook his head. 'No,' he said. 'I won't be bringing Alfie.'

Sanderson stirred at his side. 'Right,' he said. 'Bye then, Deano,' and they were ushered from the room, led back along the long hallway and out to reception.

'Happier now?' the detective asked him.

'Yeah,' said Lorcan, feeling like someone had just lifted a huge weight from his shoulders. The old Deano would have kept coming forever. But that Deano was dead.

'We won't meet again,' said the detective. 'Goodbye, Mr Connolly.'

'Bye. And thanks.'

They shook hands. Lorcan went outside, and got into the BMW. Gracie was there in the passenger seat, staring at him anxiously.

She could have gone in there, seen Deano, if she'd wanted. But the very idea had made the flesh creep off her bones. She was relieved that – apart from the remaining nightmare that was Deano Drax – everything was starting to settle down at last and make sense. The insurance was going to pay up on the fire damage, now that it was clear that Drax's people had started the fire at Doyles and not her. The frontage had been rebuilt, and Gracie had met with Brynn to let him know that she wasn't coming back to work there.

The news had saddened Brynn, but it meant that her marriage was back on track, so he was pleased for her and happy to take over as general manager. She'd been standing at the door of Doyles, just before she'd been off to the estate agent's to put her flat on the market, saying goodbye to Brynn, when she had a thought about something Lorcan had said.

'Brynn, there's something I want to ask you,' she said.

'Go ahead.'

'Lorcan pays some boys a skim, for protection.'

'Right.'

'We don't do that. Do we?'

Brynn was silent. Staring at the ground.

'*Do* we?'

Brynn's eyes lifted and met hers.

'Shit,' said Gracie. 'We do.'

'Paddy let them take the skim right up until he died,' said Brynn. 'Kept it out of your way 'cos he thought you might disapprove. Then I just took over. They come to the count room, take their wedge and leave. No problems. They still do. Sorry, Gracie.'

So Lorcan was right. She *was* like a babe in the woods. She hadn't had a *clue*.

'They didn't protect us very damned well, did they? We had the fire,' she pointed out.

'Yeah, but I thought about that. Probably they had business connections with Drax. Couldn't step on his toes too hard.'

Gracie sat in the car now with Lorcan, thinking about Drax's filthy tentacles reaching out across the country to touch her, hurt her. It was a gorgeous day, but just being here and knowing Drax was near blighted it.

She shivered, reached out, grabbed Lorcan's hand.

'Come on, tell me,' she said anxiously. 'What's he like?'

Lorcan looked her straight in the eye.

'It's over, Gracie. He won't be a danger to anyone any more.'

'You're sure?'

'Yeah.' *But he remembered Alfie.*

What else might Drax one day remember?

'Thank God,' said Gracie, and leaned over and kissed him.

Lorcan kissed her back, running his hand lovingly over the small, perfect bump of her pregnancy. Whatever happened in the future, he was here for her and for their child, to protect them and love them.

'Come on then,' she said against his lips with a warm smile. 'Let's go home.'

[END]